The Mad Girls of New York

The Mad Girls of New York

A NELLIE BLY NOVEL

MAYA RODALE

BERKLEY
New York

BERKLEY
An imprint of Penguin Random House LLC
penguinrandomhouse.com

Library of Congress Cataloging-in-Publication Data

Names: Rodale, Maya, author.
Title: The mad girls of New York / Maya Rodale.
Description: First edition. | New York: Berkley, 2022. | Series: A Nellie Bly novel
Identifiers: LCCN 2021044371 (print) | LCCN 2021044372 (ebook) |
ISBN 9780593436752 (trade paperback) | ISBN 9780593436769 (ebook)
Subjects: LCSH: Bly, Nellie, 1864-1922—Fiction. | LCGFT: Biographical fiction. |
Historical fiction. | Novels.
Classification: LCC PS3618.O3547 M33 2022 (print) | LCC PS3618.O3547 (ebook) |
DDC 813/.6—dc23
LC record available at https://lccn.loc.gov/2021044371
LC ebook record available at https://lccn.loc.gov/2021044372

First Edition: April 2022

Printed in the United States of America
1st Printing

Book design by Nancy Resnick

For women who help other women

Courage in women is often mistaken for insanity.

—Psychiatrist of suffragist Alice Paul

CHAPTER ONE

Welcome to New York

I'm off for New York. Look out for me.

—Nellie Bly

NEWSPAPER ROW
NEW YORK CITY, 1887

Nellie did not take New York by storm. Not at first, not as she had planned. She had arrived in spring, when the city was bursting into bloom and the air full of promise, with a hundred dollars in her purse along with her clips from her days at the *Pittsburgh Dispatch* and ambition to burn. Of course she would get a job as a reporter for one of the big city papers (even though it was hardly done for a woman). Of course she would become a sensation (even though it was widely agreed that a woman should do no such thing).

Nellie was good at two things: asking questions and believing in herself.

But even Nellie was starting to lose her spark and swagger as spring, with its blossoms and joyous air, turned into a hot, stinking New York City summer and no one on Newspaper Row had the time of day for a girl reporter. Not the *Herald,* not the *Sun,* not the *Mail and Express,* not the *Times* and not the *World.* She really had her heart set on the *World,* but at this point, she would take anything.

For months now, she had been walking up and down Newspaper Row, going from one newspaper office to the next, inquiring about available positions, only to be turned away, sometimes to uproarious laughter from some red-faced older gentleman, or with a smirk from some young man with less experience than she. A girl! In the newsroom!

And that was if she could even get past the intimidating men hired to guard the gates and protect the reporters and editors inside from dangerous creatures like outraged readers, or people who believed themselves slandered in the pages—or young, female aspiring journalists. Was she dangerous? She didn't feel dangerous.

Nellie had started out young, fresh-faced, smartly dressed, wildly optimistic and cheerful. Too cheerful, perhaps. But as the days wore on, the heat and the rejections were starting to crawl under her skin. No one wanted to hear of her qualifications or her ideas for stories about immigrants and women and interviews with notable women of the day. No one wanted to see her clips from the *Dispatch,* like her series about factory girls or her reports from Mexico. All those precious clips were now softly frayed at the edges from so much time in her purse.

The heat was taking the curl out of her hair.

It was now September and she had one—*one*—soul-crushing assignment from good old Erasmus, back in Pittsburgh. A pity assignment, a way to throw her some money so she could carry on struggling in the big city. But it was, if she did say so herself, a smartly conceived way to get herself in front of all those big, important and powerful newspapermen who refused to give her the time of day. Nellie's idea was to interview all the top newspaper editors in the city about women's role in journalism. She had dreamed it up as a ruse to get past the guards at the front door of all the offices and into the newsrooms—a way to demonstrate a female reporter at work, right before their eyes. Her hunch was correct: Editors were more than willing to talk to her if it meant she had to smile and take notes while they shared their (absurd) opinions on lady journalists.

Women can't get the story

To Dr. Hepworth at the *Herald,* Nellie posed the question: "Do you object to women entering newspaper life?"

Dr. Hepworth, who had served in the war as a preacher, gave her a kindly smile, the sort one gave to small children before attempting to explain a complicated concept. She smiled blandly back at him and prepared herself for his answer.

"I personally may not object," he said, stroking his mustache as he spoke thoughtfully, "but the fact is a girl just isn't going to get the news."

"Please do explain."

"Well, I cannot send her to a crime scene; the police will only give her as little information as possible to get rid of her. The criminal courts will be no different. Crime scenes and courts are no place for ladies; therefore a female reporter would be worse than useless."

"And that is a fact?"

"Yes."

"What about crime scenes involving women? Or women who are taken to the criminal courts? You're not suggesting that if we went down to the courts right now, we'd find only men."

"Well, the sort of women that you'd find there aren't *ladies*." Hepworth's cheeks colored slightly. A gentleman didn't discuss these sorts of women with someone like Nellie, who seemed respectable enough. Or was she? She caught his gaze lingering, as he tried to decide. Nellie knew she looked quite respectable, thank you very much, but her mere presence in his office suggested otherwise. He was most likely struggling with the conundrum. Nellie pressed on with her questions. "Could those women become journalists?"

"Of course not." He chuckled. "They are disreputable and uneducated."

Nellie frowned slightly. "So, a woman must be respectable to be a reporter, yet she cannot be a reporter because she is too respectable to go to the places a reporter must go." Hepworth blinked at her. Nellie met his gaze. "I just want to make sure that I understand you. To confirm that you see no opportunity for a woman in journalism."

"No," Hepworth said with a huff. And after some thought he added, "Though the ladies' pages would be an option."

God save Nellie from the ladies' pages. If a woman was lucky enough to get a job working for a paper—which spared her from working in a factory, or as a domestic or a wife (shudder)—she would have to spend her days writing about household hints and recipes, garden shows and charity luncheons. It was mind-numbingly tedious and she wanted to avoid it at all costs. It was one reason why she had left Pittsburgh.

Hence her arrival in New York City.

Hence her attempts to get hired to cover the news. Actual, breaking news.

Nellie wrote down *women can't get the news,* then she thanked Dr. Hepworth for his time and service in the war and went on her way.

Women are not as accurate as men

From there, Nellie went next door to the *Sun,* where she met with the esteemed Charles Dana. When she arrived, he slipped on a pair of gold-rimmed glasses and gazed at her curiously, as if he had never quite seen a woman involved with journalism before. She was seated in a comfortable chair in his office, which was quite homey with all its books and papers. There was a lovely view of city hall and the leafy park surrounding it. She was ready with her notebook open and her pencil poised.

Nellie was ready for the worst but hoping for the best.

"Women are not regarded with editorial favor in New York," Dana told her with the confidence of a man of a certain age who had thousands of daily readers of his paper, paying to consume his opinions along with their morning coffee. Still, it rankled. Especially when he said things like: "Women are simply not as accurate as men."

Nellie wrote this down, verbatim.

"A journalist must be accurate," he told her, as if she was unaware of that fact.

Here Nellie groaned mentally for the fate of the interview.

Women are too emotional

"Women are too emotional," Robert Morris at the *Telegram* informed her with great authority. "We can't have a girl reporter swooning at a murder scene or fainting at a fire."

Nellie had to bite the inside of her cheek to keep from scoffing. She'd seen danger and violence aplenty at home (her mother had *not* remarried well). She'd seen deadly fires so close that the heat of the flames had singed her skirts. At fourteen, she'd testified at a trial, solemnly taking the stand and telling the whole truth and nothing but the truth. Her story on factory girls wasn't for the faint of heart—those machines could and did mangle a hand or scalp—and Nellie recorded all their stories, sparing no detail.

All of which was to say that Mr. Morris, like most men, had a precious idea of a woman's constitution that did not seem to be based in the facts of women's lives.

"Women are fundamentally unequipped for the rigors of reporting," he told her in no uncertain terms. She wrote this down calmly and *unemotionally*, even though she wanted to throw a dictionary at his head. "All the sensations and scandals in the press are inappropriate for ladies' eyes. We could never task a female reporter with that class of news."

Nellie pasted a polite smile on her face. One always had to be polite when challenging a man in a position of authority; they didn't take kindly to it. In fact, one could say it even made them *emotional*.

"Women read the newspapers, just as men do. What is the difference between reading and writing that class of news?"

He gave a hearty chuckle. "That's why we have the ladies' pages, my dear. So the ladies have something suitable to read."

"And do you really think that's the *only* section of the newspaper that they read?"

The flicker of shock in his eyes told her he hadn't ever thought about it.

Women don't need the money

At his desk in the corner of the bustling newsroom, Foster Coates at the *Mail and Express* shared the opinion that there was probably nothing wrong with a woman writing for a newspaper. He continued to say, in so many words, that men were the ones who, in addition to being more constitutionally suited to the rigors of the job by being emotionally dead both inside and out, were thus the better to report the facts.

"Furthermore," he said, with a dramatic pause. "Men have families to support. They have wives, children and other helpless dependents."

"What about women without a father, husband or brother to support them?" Nellie inquired coolly. *Asking for a friend. Asking for me.* Asking for her mother, back home in Pittsburgh, waiting for Nellie to establish herself in New York so she could support them here. Asking for all the women like her mother, with dead or drunk or deadbeat husbands. Asking for the smart spinsters who had known better than to marry but who still needed to eat.

"Well, a woman ought to find one! Any man should do." Mr. Foster chuckled. Nellie couldn't bring herself to laugh along with him, even politely, because she knew that not any man would do. Some men were definitely worse than no man at all.

A woman's experience isn't enough

At the *Times*, Nellie pretended to be an applicant. *Pretended.* She had to laugh at that, since in truth she would gladly accept almost any job at this point, if it would only get her in a newsroom. Or in proximity to a newsroom. She had no doubt that once she was in, she could conquer everything.

"And what might you do?" The editor, a balding man by the name of Charles Ransom Miller, inquired. Her heart skipped a beat. This was . . . promising?

"Anything," Nellie replied. "Literally anything. There's nothing I can't do, given the chance."

Nothing she wouldn't do. Probably. She didn't want to seem too eager, but also, she was very eager. Her funds were dwindling. Her pride wanted encouragement. Her brain wanted something to take on.

Mr. Miller regarded her thoughtfully for a moment. A long moment in which she felt hope. But then a man—one younger than her, with a pimpled complexion and wearing a wrinkled suit—approached, also to apply. And just like that Nellie was shuffled out of the way, out the door and back onto the street.

We already have one woman—isn't that enough?

When Nellie got to the building that housed the offices of the *World,* she paused reverentially outside while busy men and working-women swarmed around her. The *World* was a paper for the rest of them—not the wealthy, or snobby or elites, but the immigrants, the poor, the masses, the workingmen and -women. It was a paper for sensation, crusade and scandal. It was her first choice of a paper to write for, if she had a choice.

At the *World,* Nellie walked slowly through the lobby in awe. After confirming with the guard on duty that she did indeed have an interview, she rode the elevator to the top floor and managed to catch a moment with the editor, Colonel John Cockerill, who seemed annoyed to be interrupted from a profanity-laden tirade at a young male assistant ("Damn it to hell, Hearst, if I've told you once . . . !"). Nellie dared to intrude.

"Women in journalism?" He repeated her question with a bark. He pushed his hair out of his eyes. Like he had to think about it because he had honestly never considered it before. Hope, it fell in her chest. "A man is of far greater service," he said. And then: "Anyway, we have a woman on staff already. So, it's not a personal objection."

Nellie bit back a sharp hiss of *Who is she?* Who was this lucky woman who had the constitution to withstand crime and sensation, who could write down facts and report them, who could get intelligence from the police and the criminal courts? *Who was she?*

She was probably just writing for the ladies' pages, Nellie thought meanly. She was probably just writing about who wore what to which party while people starved in the streets. She probably wrote about high fashion and swishy silk dresses, salacious gossip and elegant charity luncheons. There was nothing to be jealous of.

She was still jealous.

And now she was increasingly desperate. And, damn it, Robert Morris at the *Telegram,* she was feeling emotional.

And then her purse was stolen on the train back uptown.

Her purse with her clips, her notebook full of quotes and every last penny to her name.

CHAPTER TWO

The Girl Puzzle

MRS. PARKHILL'S BOARDINGHOUSE
NEW YORK CITY

The next morning, Nellie awoke on her narrow bed and looked out the window. Or tried to. As befitting most rooms that she could afford in the city, her view was of a neighboring building's brick wall. But if she turned her head just so, and contorted her body in a certain way that rumpled the blanket and pinched her neck, she could catch a glimpse of sky, all bright and clear blue. It promised to be a beautiful day.

Except for the fact that she had no money, no friends, no job, and no real prospects.

Nellie couldn't even get back to Pittsburgh, if she were that desperate. Which she was not. Yet. Even though Nellie was on the verge of becoming a cautionary tale to other aspiring young women.

Her grip tightened around the pair of scissors she had borrowed from Penny, the housekeeper here. The blades were hard and sharp in her palm. *Should she do it?*

It wasn't in Nellie's nature to lie abed and feel sorry for herself. Not when she had her mother, Mary Jane, in her head with one of her sayings: *Energy rightly applied will accomplish anything.* Which was not exactly working out for Nellie at the moment. But soon . . . Something good had to happen soon.

She couldn't languish, anyway, with this restless energy pulsing through her. The city was happening out there—not here, in room 2R (rear) at Mrs. Elizabeth Parkhill's Boardinghouse—and Nellie wanted more than anything to be a part of it. She had burned her bridges to be here.

But something had to be done.

Something had to *change.* She had been wearing the same dress, the same hat, the same boots, and knocking on the same editors' doors with the same result. She knew just the thing. Hence, the scissors, sharp and pointed in her hand.

Nellie sat up, then stood up, then positioned herself in front of the small mirror that hung on the otherwise spartan walls of her room. She lifted the scissors to her face, past her mouth, past her slightly upturned nose, past her gray-blue eyes, past her nicely arched eyebrows. *Was she really going to do this?*

Desperate times called for desperate measures.

She reached for her comb next and pulled a length of her brown hair out of her bun and forward, over her face. She lifted the scissors. Ready. Nellie paused.

There was no going back after this.

Whenever the world had seemed *stuck,* Nellie's mother would move the furniture around, sew a ruffle on a dress or redecorate an old bonnet. There was no way for Nellie to move the furniture in her rented room; the space was so small one had to wonder how the bed, dresser and chair fit in the first place. She didn't have the patience to sew a ruffle on her dress or fix the hem. But Nellie could make a little difference that she hoped would make all the difference.

Snip.

A strand of her hair fell to the floor. Maybe if she looked a little different, her life would be a little different.

Snip.

There was no going back now.

Snip. Snip. Snip.

There was a knock at the door.

Most likely her landlady, inquiring about the rent.

Nellie set down her scissors, her bangs half-trimmed, and opened the door.

It was Mrs. Parkhill, her landlady. Nellie smiled. Mrs. Parkhill smiled. They both knew what this was about.

It wasn't uncommon for women and families to rent out spare rooms in their homes to make ends meet. Some even ran fully established houses full of lodgers. These days, Elizabeth Parkhill had a veritable empire of lodging houses that she owned and ran throughout the city. An impressive feat for any woman, and all the more so for Elizabeth because of the plain fact that the world did no favors for Black women like her.

A woman named Penny ran the house here—providing meals, taking care of laundry and the like—and was easy to evade when it came to paying rent. But Mrs. Parkhill, the owner, saw to the business of collecting rents and managing boarders. Over tea one afternoon, Nellie had peppered her with questions and learned that she'd come to New York after the war, took over one boardinghouse and then systematically expanded her business until she'd managed the impressive feat of owning real estate and running her own businesses. She was no fool.

"Good morning, Miss Bly. I'm here to see about the rent."

"This month's or last month's?" Nellie quipped.

If Mrs. Parkhill was amused, she did not show it. Though was that a hint of sparkle in her eyes? Surely she had to remember what it was like to be ambitious and newly arrived to the city. "Yes. Both."

Nellie opened her mouth to speak, but Mrs. Parkhill raised her hand and waved her off. "And yes, I am aware that your purse was stolen."

It had been such a foolish, amateur mistake. She'd been on a crowded elevated train, lost in thought, and some little street child slithered through the crowd and snuck off with her bag—containing the last of her money and all of her clips—before she even realized what had happened. By then the doors had closed and her cry of anguish had alarmed more than a few passengers. She'd almost had a fit of hysterics—even though she was made of stern stuff and prided herself on staying calm. But indulging in a public display of hysterics was to chance being sent to the insane asylum at Blackwell's Island, and if there was anything she had learned so far in the city, it was to (1) hold on to your purse with your life and (2) don't get sent to Blackwell's Island.

"I have a promising lead," Nellie said confidently. Mary Jane had always instilled in her the practice of declaring things confidently, as if that alone could make them true. But Mrs. Parkhill was not falling for it.

Mrs. Parkhill tilted her head. "Miss Bly, do you still not have a position?"

"I just haven't found the right one."

"Shopgirl or factory girl not good enough for you?" This was punctuated with a raised eyebrow.

"I didn't come to New York to be a shopgirl or factory girl."

Mrs. Parkhill heaved a sigh and lifted her eyes toward the heavens. "Lord save me from young women with big dreams coming to the city."

"Like yourself?" Nellie dared an impish grin. Her landlady gave a short huff. "At any rate, I'm on my way downtown this morning," Nellie continued. She had just decided. But also, what choice did she have, really? Lie in bed in despair or get herself downtown and try, try again?

Mrs. Parkhill gave Nellie one of those looks that would have made a lesser man or woman shrink or spill all her secrets and promise anything. But Nellie didn't lie. She might have just decided, that very instant, to go back down to Newspaper Row, but now she was firm in her plans. Her future depended upon it.

"Whatever you're doing to your hair is not going to help your prospects." In addition to a room and board, Mrs. Parkhill also provided free, unsolicited advice.

"It's called bangs. It's the new style."

"You look like a woman in the throes of a nervous episode. How is that supposed to convince anyone to hire you?" Nellie didn't have an answer to that. "Well, I suppose if you can't find work you can always cut off the rest of your hair and sell it. You should fetch a pretty penny for it."

"Always an option," Nellie replied. For a split second she considered it: She could crop her hair and sell it for just enough money to return to her mother in Pittsburgh, and then beg for her old job back after leaving that cocksure note on Erasmus's desk (*I'm off for New York. Look out for me.*) How mortifying. Not an option at all.

Mrs. Parkhill turned to go, but Nellie, who now had renewed determination to convince someone on Newspaper Row to hire her, caught her before she left. Nellie flashed her best smile, the one that always got her out of trouble, and spoke in her most cajoling voice. "Mrs. Parkhill, can I also borrow cab fare? I need to get downtown. It's a matter of some importance and urgency."

SOMEWHERE ON BROADWAY

In a cab on her way downtown, Nellie fluffed her newly shorn bangs with her gloved fingers. They were straight, mostly, and a little too short. At a certain angle, they looked fetching. Or so she told herself. That's what she got for her impulsiveness.

Thanks to Mrs. Parkhill lending her cab fare—very explicitly a loan and not a gift, and which was to be repaid with rent immediately—Nellie made it downtown in record time, until the carriage hit traffic on Broadway. Thanks to the ride, she was spared from being a sweaty, wrinkled mess after an hour on the train and battling crowds. She looked good. She looked respectable and professional.

But now Nellie was anxious, with a restless energy she needed to dispel before she presented herself once more. A few blocks' walking should do the trick to calm her nerves. She had no plan other than to be near the action and seize any and every opportunity to get in the door or get an interview.

Admittedly, it was not much of a plan.

"I'll get out here, thanks."

Here was on Broadway, near the Bowery. The busy road was lined with impressive cast-iron buildings reaching five or six stories high. They all possessed huge, soaring windows to let in natural light, the better for men and women to work inside at long, seemingly endless shifts sewing garments or assembling hatboxes or other menial tasks.

The sidewalks were crowded with all kinds of people going about their lives with a glorious indifference for one another. It had to be admitted that when she'd first arrived, she had been taken aback by the way people from so many different backgrounds mixed so freely, especially in this neighborhood. It was such a sight to behold that fancy folks from uptown often came slumming through the neighborhood in their fine carriages to watch. Blacks rubbed up against Irish and German immigrants, who mingled with the Chinese. At night, men dressed as ladies and drank next to laborers, and women mingled freely with all of them. Everyone was *of* here and no one was *from* here, and they were all just trying to make it or at least get by.

This morning, one woman in particular caught Nellie's eye. Or rather, her hair did—a glorious auburn verging on fiery red. The shade caught your eye and the rest of her held your attention. She was tall, clear-skinned, plainly if respectably dressed in a dark blue dress that fit well though was free of embellishments. By all appearances, she seemed to be a nice and respectable middle-class wife.

And she was drunk. Stumbling-around drunk.

At this hour of the morning! On Broadway!

Or was she?

Nellie slowed from her brisk *I have places to be thank you very much* pace to observe as this woman wavered on her feet, precariously close to the road, where horses and carriages thundered past. She was in front of a grocer's, where crates of fruit and vegetables were stacked high on the sidewalk. Next door was an apothecary and next to that, a dance hall. Maybe it was the reporter in Nellie that made her slow down and look twice. Maybe it was her sense of sisterhood that gave her pause to see if this woman was all right. Whatever the reason, she took a moment to watch.

A delicate hand to the forehead. The classic preamble to a swoon.

A wild-eyed glance all around her.

No one seemed to care that she was in a state of distress. A man in a disheveled suit, with traces of last night's antics still on his face, ambled past her without a second look. Another woman ushered her three small children out of the way and gave the swooning redhead a sharp, reproving look.

In the blink of an eye she was down. The redhead, not Nellie. Just there on the street corner, crashing into the pile of crates and sending apples rolling into the road, where they were promptly trampled under hooves and carriage wheels.

Nellie could no longer stand idly by—she pushed through the crowd of curious onlookers (oh, now they were interested!) to the pile of skirts sprawled across the apple crates.

A Chinese woman was making an attempt to rouse her. Nellie sank down beside her. They shared a look of concern and camaraderie before turning their attentions to the redhead. "Ma'am! Are you all right?" When there was no response, Nellie shouted for someone to call for an ambulance.

A thickset man in the crowd scoffed. "She just needs a cup of cold water."

"Yeah, in her face! That oughta wake her!"

A buxom woman, overdressed for daytime, smirked. "Oh, she just needs to sleep it off!" Then, with a dangerous smile: "I have a room she can use."

And a buttoned-up matron huffed what a disgrace it was for a lady to conduct herself thusly, prompting an eye roll from more than one of the other women who had gathered.

Probably all true. But still, Nellie pleaded. "Please, just call for an ambulance!"

Finally, someone shuffled off to flag down more help. Nellie did not have time for this, but she couldn't just leave the woman on the sidewalk. Not with the way these people were milling around, waiting for the opportunity to look for her purse or spare change in her pockets. If they were even waiting at all; many people just walked past and one even stepped over her to get on their way.

Ah, New York.

Finally, a horse-drawn ambulance clattered up and slowed to a stop nearby, and an attendant launched himself onto the sidewalk, his boots landing near the woman, who was slowly stirring awake.

"She fainted," Nellie told him. They both watched as the woman came to, slowly, with a low moan and a dazed expression. The ambulance driver was a youngish man, with stubble across his jaw and his brown hair slicked back. His uniform had stains that Nellie didn't want to know about.

"She with you?" he asked.

"I don't know her," Nellie said.

"All right then, I can take it from here."

"Oh . . ." the redhead moaned. "What happened?"

"You fainted, ma'am," Nellie said. "Are you all right?"

"Oh . . ." She swooned away again.

"All right, I'll take her," the ambulance driver said reluctantly.

"Where will you take her?" Nellie asked. She'd read unconfirmed reports in the paper of Blackwell's Island and its abuses. The reputation of the dispensaries and hospitals was only slightly better. And the cost could bankrupt a workingwoman. But she very clearly needed medical help.

"Bellevue Hospital," the driver answered. Nellie was hesitant to leave this woman in the care of a strange man, but she had her own business to attend to. And it was not as if she had any medical training that would help the woman recover from whatever had knocked her over on Broadway. Still, she had some notion of care and sisterhood. "I'll go with you," Nellie said.

"No. Take me to the doctor. Alone." The redheaded woman was barely conscious but adamant all the same. Some debate ensued, and in the end, the woman very much wanted to be taken to a hospital, swooned again to prove it was necessary, and both she and the ambulance attendant went on their way to Bellevue. Nellie set off downtown. Alone.

The *World* beckoned.

But something caused her to look back. Just a feeling, like a whisper of wind on the back of her neck. So she stopped and looked over her shoulder.

She saw the woman standing now, swaying, with strands of that red hair falling loose around her face. The ambulance attendant had his arms around her, fingers splayed around her waist, the better to help her stand (or so one hoped). The redhead happened to glance after Nellie. Their gazes locked. And then . . . the redheaded woman *winked.*

CHAPTER THREE

Gather Up the Real Smart Girls

THE OFFICE OF THE *NEW YORK WORLD*
NEWSPAPER ROW

Nellie arrived perplexed, still distracted. That wink! What could it possibly mean? When Nellie stood on the sidewalk and looked up and up and up at the *World* building—it towered over the other newspaper offices on Newspaper Row both literally and figuratively—she forgot about the wink and remembered her purpose.

Get in. Get an assignment. Get a job.

A daunting prospect. She stared up to the very top, where a golden dome gleamed against a blue sky and towered over the whole of New York. The bottom floors were leased to other businesses and offices so it was easy enough to enter the lobby and stroll about. But the guards in front of the elevators, standing protectively over the upper floors, where the newspaper offices were located, gave her no end of trouble.

They always wanted to know who she wished to see, if they were expecting her, the nature of her business. The editor she wished to see, Colonel John Cockerill, had once had an angry reader storm into his newsroom back in St. Louis wielding a loaded pistol, outraged over something that had been printed in the previous day's paper. Gunshots had been fired. Cockerill was later acquitted of the murder but had to leave town. Rumor had it that was how he ended up running Pulitzer's New York paper. She supposed she could understand the need for security.

But just look at her!

A young woman of three and twenty, pretty, neatly dressed and by all accounts respectable. There was nothing dangerous or threatening about her appearance. With her steps full of purpose, and her blue-gray eyes blazing with determination, Nellie strode through the doors, across the marble lobby floor and straight toward the elevators. She walked like she had a meeting, like Mr. Pulitzer himself was expecting her, like she was on the way to fulfilling her life's purpose and destiny.

But at the elevators, a guard awaited.

There, Nellie was stopped.

"Whoa there, little lady." He gave her a friendly smile. This particular guard was the large, lumbering sort who was probably more adept at intimidating people than moving nimbly to catch them should they, say, dart past. Something to consider. He gave her a lopsided smile and a nod, like, *You poor thing. You must be lost. The ladies' department stores are twenty blocks uptown! Silly dear.*

She greeted him with a firm "Good morning, sir."

"Are you lost, ma'am?"

"I am not. Actually, I—"

"Well, you can't just waltz in here, little lady. This is a place of business."

He was all smiles when he thought she was a lost soul, and he could not fathom that she might have business of her own.

"I *am* here for a business matter."

He looked at her suspiciously. "What sort of business?"

She could practically see the wheels turning in his head, considering that perhaps she wasn't a lost lamb, but a woman of vice intent on plying her wicked trade in the middle of the day in a place of work. Honestly. Men had such imaginations.

"I'm here for an appointment at the *World*."

"Are you now?"

"Mr. Pulitzer himself is expecting me."

Nellie was not fond of lying, for a variety of reasons—honor, morals, journalistic integrity and such. And also this one: the slow slide of a smile on this man's face as he caught her in a lie and was *delighted* by the catch and terribly excited to tell her so.

"Mr. Pulitzer is on his yacht."

Nellie smiled, even as she thought a dozen different swear words at once. Nellie smiled, even as she was annoyed that she had cut her bangs for no reason and now this guard would warn all the others about the "girl with the crazy bangs." Any hope she had of getting in was officially, totally and utterly shot to shit.

For her next attempt, Nellie tried to slink inside with a group of men, but a woman in a hat stood out among all the suits. She tried to link arms with another unsuspecting man and pretended to be his guest, chattering all the while to keep him engaged. She considered getting some street urchin to cause a commotion that would be a distraction, but she was fresh out of coin and they didn't work for free. The lunch hour was approaching—maybe there would be an opportunity then? If not, she would have a few more hours in the afternoon to try her luck at other papers.

The heat was getting to her.

To her bangs, making them frizz.

To her dress, making it damp with perspiration.

Soon she would start to smell like August in New York, which would do her no favors.

Nellie beat a retreat and lingered near the newsagent shop in the lobby, pretending to look at the day's headlines while really keeping a watchful eye on the elevators as she debated what to do next. It wasn't long before a woman emerged—a rare sight. Not just any woman, either. She appeared crisp, cool, collected, like the late summer heat wasn't happening all around her. Everything about her—from her darling little feathered hat perched on her silvery white hair, to the fitted jacket with grosgrain trim, to shiny leather boots pointing out from under a skirt that only just grazed her ankles—was fitted and styled to perfection. Nothing about her apologized—she moved with a purpose.

Who was she? Whoever she was, she carried herself like she had conquered the city already; years ago, darling.

On her way out, the guard tipped his hat to her.

Curiosity and envy and burning ambition rose in Nellie all at once. How could this woman come and go as she pleased from the *World*? What were her secrets? How could Nellie meet her?

Fact: Nellie needed to know her.

So Nellie didn't think twice—she followed.

THE LADIES' ORDINARY

The saloon around the corner was the regular haunt of the male reporters in the neighborhood. They could be found there for lunch at midday and drinks at all hours. Nellie caught a glimpse of all the men inside, sprawled in chairs or hunched over plates and pints and laughing loudly. The door was open, and the sound of all those men carousing spilled out into the street to mix with the clatter of horses and carriages and construction sounds and other noises of the city.

Nellie followed the woman past all that, noticing that she

didn't spare such a pedestrian scene a glance, even though the gaze of more than a few men lingered over her, very much intrigued.

The woman turned the corner and soon approached a plain, unmarked door at the back of the saloon, pulled it open and disappeared inside. When Nellie caught up, she almost missed it—it was the kind of door one walked past without noticing, or definitely didn't look twice at if for some reason one's attentions happened on it. A door. Unmarked. It wasn't so nefarious-looking that one feared rape, murder and other terrible fates behind it.

But Nellie being Nellie, she would open the door anyway, just to see. She did so now.

At first, the sound of female voices at full volume hit her. Women talking, laughing, even shouting at one another. Their voices were mixed with the sounds of cutlery clinking on plates, pints being drained and set down with a thud on the long wooden tables. Chairs being pushed out or in. Women coming, going. Most of them, though, were having lunch.

The woman she had followed stood up at the carved wooden bar, smoothed over by time, and waited patiently for the bartender's attention. Up close, Nellie could see that she was at least fifty, maybe older, but she looked as bright and fashionable as any pretty young thing. Her hair was a pretty, silvery gray. There were fine lines around her eyes and mouth, suggesting she smiled often and spoke freely. Her complexion was luminous, and Nellie felt a moment of envy.

The bartender turned to give her attention. She was a broad-shouldered woman with her hair severely pulled back in a tight bun, as if she didn't have the time to be bothered with styling it. Her expression warned that she did not suffer fools, nonsense or drunken antics.

"A pint and trimmings, please, Pauline," the beautiful silver-haired woman said. Pauline nodded and said it would be right out in a moment. Then her gaze shifted to Nellie, next in line. Her brow lifted, wordlessly asking for Nellie's order.

"The same. A pint and trimmings, please."

"That'll be five cents."

That would be five cents that Nellie did not have. All at once she remembered the stolen purse, the late rent, the borrowed cab fare. That burn-her-bridges note she'd left for her editor in Pittsburgh and the bridges she'd actually burned. If only the floorboards would swallow her up. If only.

Worse, the silver-haired woman had her cool blue eyes trained on Nellie, like she was taking the measurements of Nellie's bust, waist and soul. Did she know?

"Oh!" Nellie pretended to have remembered something suddenly. "It turns out I have forgotten an appointment." She smiled sheepishly, as if it were just a misunderstanding and she was not, in fact, about to expire from embarrassment on the spot. "If you'll excuse me."

Nellie turned to go; the sooner she got out of here, the sooner she could get on with the business of being rejected for jobs. Her skin was hot with mortification and sweaty from the heat. The only thought in her head was to escape. But the silver-haired woman's voice rang out, "Add it to my tab, Pauline."

Nellie turned suddenly, cheeks pinked. The silver-haired woman had come to the rescue, like a fashionable fairy godmother, with an invitation to lunch.

Her name was Harriet Ayer, she told Nellie, after Nellie thanked her profusely. She walked them to a table in the middle of the room, through the crowd of women as they ate a hearty lunch, drank and chattered away.

"Hello, Dorothy, I brought a friend today. This is—"

"Nellie. Nellie Bly."

"Hi, I'm Dorothy." Nellie didn't think twice about taking a seat at the table, even as her mind was buzzing with questions about what alternative universe she had discovered and who all these women were.

Nellie, being Nellie, started to ask questions. Where was she? The Ladies' Ordinary, behind Devlin's Saloon, a space where women could eat, drink and socialize without being bothered by men. Who were all these women? Workingwomen from the neighborhood—proofreaders, typesetters, bookkeepers, clerks, shopgirls, and a few reporters.

They all wore the same working-girl uniform: a plain dark skirt paired with a crisp white shirtwaist. But Nellie noticed that they all added their own embellishments. Jackets had grosgrain ribbon trim or little epaulets at the shoulders. Shirts had decorative buttons and hats were all uniquely decorated. *Something* had to distinguish them from the others so they didn't get swallowed up and forgotten in some great mass of working females. They were working girls not just by their clothes, but by the way they got down to the business of lunch and conversation with an urgency and intensity because they had other important things to do.

Did they come here regularly? Every day. The hot meal ("trimmings") and pint was the best deal in the neighborhood. Besides, it was nice to relax in a space where there were no men leering or asking who they had abandoned at home.

The polite getting-to-know-you chatter between Harriet, Dorothy and Nellie had barely begun when a woman practically crashed into their table. In truth she did no such thing, but she had an energy about her that felt like it.

"What a *day*," this woman said dramatically.

Dorothy laughed. "It's only half past noon, Marian."

Marian was looking at Nellie and Nellie was looking at Marian. They were looking at each other in that way of *I know you but can't place you . . .*

"Well, do tell, Marian." Harriet waved her to sit down. They were all friends here, apparently.

Marian gave a dramatic sigh. "I had a little encounter with the public ambulance services. I do not recommend it."

All at once it clicked for Nellie. "Oh! You're the woman who fainted!"

Marian's eyes narrowed at her. "You're the one who called me 'ma'am'!"

Beside her, Dorothy gasped at an apparently grave offense. Nellie swiftly apologized.

"Are you all right?" Nellie asked.

"Oh, I'm fine," Marian said grandly. She took a sip of her pint and shrugged, like fainting on the street was all in a day's work. Apparently it was. She flashed a grin. "Just a little stunt for a story. That ambulance driver will be sorry he tried anything on me."

Harriet rolled her eyes. "If only men would be original for once."

Dorothy shook her head. "If you really wanted a stunt story, try taking the trolley while Black." And then she told Nellie briefly that she was simply trying to get from one place to another on the public transport when issue was taken with her presence, as it happened, and there was a scuffle.

"How *is* your arm, dear?" Harriet inquired.

Dorothy rubbed her shoulder. "It still hurts, but that hasn't stopped me from writing my stories, filing my columns, teaching my students or living my life."

"Success is the best revenge," Marian said.

"Happiness is the best revenge," Dorothy countered. "The

whole experience has made Raymond very protective of me. I think he might propose sooner rather than later."

Nellie wasn't much for romance, so she didn't quite follow the latest in Dorothy's ongoing courtship with Raymond, a fellow newspaperman and editor at the *American Freedman*. But her curiosity was piqued when Marian asked if Lucy had spoken yet. After listening in, Nellie gathered that Lucy had turned up after witnessing something terrible and couldn't yet speak of it. In the meantime, Dorothy and some friends were seeing to the girl's safety and comfort. "Very kind of you," Nellie remarked.

Dorothy shrugged slightly. "We take care of each other."

"Bet there's a story there," Marian murmured. "If you can get her to talk."

"In good time," Dorothy replied.

But Nellie was still stuck on mentions of stunts and stories and various newspapers and deadlines and the possibility that she had fallen in with some lady journalists. What luck! What an unexpected twist to her day. She wanted to laugh out loud but didn't want to seem crazy. Besides, it was likely that these women were her competition—and in competition with one another—yet they were all so friendly. If there was one thing Nellie had learned so far, there was little space on the masthead for women. Maybe just one. So it didn't quite make sense.

"Wait—are you all reporters?"

"Dorothy writes for the *New York Age*," Harriet said, and Nellie nodded. She knew the paper; she knew *all* the papers in New York. Their editors, their audiences, the numbers. The *Age* was a respected and popular Black newspaper. Harriet continued. "Marian here writes for the *Herald*."

"I do the usual society interviews and occasional stunt, if I can convince the editors, which isn't very often," Marian said. But then she heaved a wistful sigh. "I'm just a girl, standing in front of the world, asking for a decent job that pays well and doesn't bore me to tears."

To which Nellie raised her glass.

To which Marian raised her brow.

Their eyes met, and Marian's gaze was cool, calculating, evaluating. Nellie had the feeling they could be great friends but were more likely to be great rivals, each one chasing limited space on the masthead, competing for interviews and exciting stories. *Stunts!* She hadn't read many in the papers, so it was new, uncharted territory. Yet she'd seen Marian in action this morning and was already burning with curiosity to read the whole story.

Maybe she'd even try something like that herself, if she could get in to pitch it. A stunt was something she could do. Even better, it was also something a man couldn't pull off in quite the same way as a pretty young woman. Like Marian. Or Nellie.

Nellie took a sip of her drink, as Dorothy said, "Harriet here is the grand dame of the newsroom at the *World*." Nellie near spit out her drink. She'd known Harriet was Someone, but now she knew that she was The Someone she needed. She was about to gush about the *World* and her luck in meeting Harriet and how much she wanted to write. She was about to make a cake of herself.

Marian cut her off. "And who did you say you were?"

"Bly. Nellie Bly."

"Like the song. So it's not your real name, I assume."

Like the song, because a proper woman didn't put her own name in the newspaper, unless it was to report her marriage or death.

Nellie just said, "Of course not."

"Where are you from, Not Really Nellie?"

"Who says I'm not from here?"

"Oh, please." Marian laughed. "You have 'new girl' written all over you, with your wide-eyed wonder. So what's your story, Not Really Nellie?" She sat back in her seat and took a bite of her lunch in anticipation of some great tale.

"I wrote for the *Pittsburgh Dispatch* for six years. And I did six months in Mexico."

Those six months were a testament to her persuasive abilities. It was no small thing to get Erasmus to send a young girl reporter on assignment to a foreign country. Once there, Nellie filed reports on the people, the culture, the government. Did readers of a local newspaper in Pittsburgh need such reports? Probably not, but Nellie and her mother had needed to get away after the scandal of her mother's divorce, and Nellie wasn't going to waste a chance to further her career. So, Mexico. It was all fun and games until she upset members of the government and they hightailed it back to the States.

But Nellie didn't want to get into all that now.

So she did what she did best, which was start asking her own questions.

"I suppose you were born and raised here, then?" Nellie asked Marian.

"Uptown."

Dorothy grinned. "Society girl gone rogue! Jilted by her intended, the lovely Marian is cast from high society and must now make her way on her own—"

"Sounds like a dime novel," Nellie said.

"Sentimental rubbish," Marian said. "But maybe I'll write it. Earn a pretty penny for it."

"Maybe I should try my hand at novels instead of newspaper work. I'm trying to get hired at one of the papers, but none of them will give me the time of day," Nellie said. "Apparently women are too emotional."

All four women burst out laughing.

"It's one of the great myths of the age that women suffer from an excess of delicacy, nerves and feelings," Harriet said, with traces of laughter in her voice. "As if any one of us could afford to have a nervous condition or delicate sensibilities."

Marian and Dorothy raised their glasses.

"I am also told that women are too fragile to witness crime scenes, fires and other unsavory business," Nellie said, to eye rolls all around the table.

"The things I have seen and endured would make most grown men faint," Harriet said dryly.

And Dorothy murmured, "I as well."

"And yet," Marian began in a way that piqued Nellie's curiosity. "I'm having some luck getting hired to do stunts. Apparently nothing sells like a girl in danger."

"A certain kind of woman," Dorothy was quick to point out. They all knew what she meant: young, pretty, pale-skinned. *Respectable.* Like a princess in the fairy tales that all the girls imagined themselves being and that all the men imagined themselves charging in to rescue. Like Marian. *Like Nellie?*

"I'd do it," Nellie said quickly, to match the pace of her heartbeat at the very idea. Real stories, with danger and maybe even with purpose. "Anything other than typing up reports on charity luncheons and household hints. God save me from the ladies' pages."

Marian grinned. "Harriet runs the ladies' pages for the *World.*"

Nellie's stomach took a turn. Of all the women in the world to insult! Especially today, when Harriet had bought her lunch. Today, when Nellie would take any job at the *World,* even if it meant sweeping floors or fetching coffee.

Harriet, however, was not in the slightest bit ruffled. "Scoff all you want, ladies, but I don't have to risk my life for a story and no man will ever try to take my job. As long as I'm writing about beauty routines, slimming regimes, this season's fashions and household hints, I'll have a paycheck of my own."

There was something to be said for that.

On the sidewalk outside, after lunch had concluded, after Marian dashed off to the *Herald* to write up her report on the handsy ambulance driver, after Dorothy strode toward the office at the *Age,* Nellie fell in step with Harriet and began to apologize for being dismissive of the ladies' pages and to thank her profusely for the lunch. It had felt like more than just lunch, almost an initiation into something.

"This all feels too good to be true. What's the catch?" Nellie asked.

"There's no catch." Harriet must have caught Nellie's expression of disbelief. "Very well. One day you'll have an opportunity to help a fellow female reporter and you must take it. Even at an expense to yourself."

"Of course," Nellie said without thinking twice. Harriet waved her off and cut to the chase. "The man you want to speak with is Cockerill." Nellie nodded—she remembered meeting him already. "You need to remember that the only thing he cares about is winning the numbers game."

"Right. Of course." It was all one big pissing contest between the papers as to who sold the most copies.

"Nothing sells like a crusade," Harriet continued. That was one of the things Nellie loved about the paper. It didn't just report the facts of the day; it whipped up emotions to make people care about stories and issues. Pulitzer's campaign in the paper had raised funds from readers to pay for the base of the Statue of Liberty. They sent in pennies and now Lady Liberty stood proudly in New York Harbor.

"And a girl in danger," Nellie added.

"You're a quick study." Harriet smiled approvingly.

"If I can get an interview, I'll say so."

"I can get you in," Harriet said, and Nellie's heart fluttered. "But then it's up to you."

THE NEWSROOM OF THE *NEW YORK WORLD*

With Harriet, Nellie walked right past the doorman, showing no small amount of glee. He'd started to voice his objections when he caught sight of Nellie, but then Harriet said, "She's with me," and Nellie grinned so hard her cheeks hurt, and now they were in the thick of it.

The newsroom was an explosion of activity right before her eyes. There were men hunched over desks with sleeves rolled up and jackets flung over chair backs, while they wrote at a furious, feverish pace. In a bright corner, Nellie noted another man who sketched quickly—probably making the illustrations that would appear with stories of murder, mayhem, fires, crimes, making the news accessible even to those who couldn't read English. There were people talking, arguing, asking questions, shouting answers. It wasn't uncommon for the printing presses in the basement to churn out new editions of the paper throughout the day, as stories were updated and revised to include the very latest information.

On one wall was a sign that read TERSENESS! ACCURACY! TRUTH! And hanging high up on the wall was a large clock. The hour right now: five minutes before one o'clock. But the small hand was ticking forward, counting down the minutes until deadline, when another issue would be sent to print.

Hello, *World*.

Nellie breathed in deeply, getting a good lungful of smoke,

ink, paper and men. She had missed this. The rush, the urgency, the sense that there was no time to fret or waver, one just had to do the job and get the story done. There was no time to think or dwell on her own *stuff*. The newsroom was never boring, even if the actions were essentially the same—gather facts, write up the story, repeat. There were always new angles to explore, new people to interview, new questions to ask and combinations of words to put together. It was the opposite of laundry and folding sheets and feeding babies and all that drudgery that was expected of her as a woman in the world.

Then one got to revel in the feeling of having pulled it off another day.

Nellie turned to Harriet. "How can I ever thank you?"

She smiled. "Women have to look out for each other because no one else will. Remember that." And with a firm but affectionate squeeze of Nellie's arm, she melted off into the newsroom. To look that fabulous, to carry yourself like a queen and to have no one find it remarkable was the ideal. She belonged here, she was one of them and it was mutually accepted. Harriet's example was enough to make a girl feel hopeful for her prospects.

Prospects that began and ended with one Colonel John Cockerill, deputy editor. Mr. Pulitzer was the owner, the dreamer, the publisher. He was found on his yacht more often than not. So Cockerill got it all done, every day, on deadline. He'd come up to the city with Pulitzer from their days in St. Louis after that pesky murder business. His office was off to the right, behind a frosted-glass door with his name and credentials painted on in gold.

Nellie took a deep breath and went for it, no matter what little quakes of intimidation or anticipation might be zinging through her. She moved with a purpose through the newsroom, catching some curious glances but mostly being ignored. She strode toward that door like it was a sure thing, her destiny. She didn't rush, she just moved, as cool as you please toward her future. And then—

"No."

That's when she saw him. She hadn't taken notice of him at first because he was so calm in this room otherwise frantic with activity. He was a young, slender man, smartly dressed in a dark blue wool suit with sleekly combed hair laced with pomade. At present, he was deeply absorbed in the business on his desk, which seemed to involve account books and, alas, appointment books.

"I'm here to see Mr. Cockerill."

He didn't even look up. "Not without an appointment."

"I have an appointment at . . ." *Right now o'clock, this very minute, or whenever he'll see me as long as it's today.* Nellie caught a glance at that big clock hovering over the newsroom. "One o'clock. I have an appointment with Mr. Cockerill at one o'clock. Mrs. Ayer recommended me."

Her mother always said, *Energy rightly applied will accomplish anything.* To that, Nellie added, *Anything stated confidently enough will be taken as fact.* Write that down in *Nellie's Guide to Getting Ahead.*

But this sleek little man with an incredible air of his own authority and importance—who still had not looked up to see pretty little Nellie with her fetching new hairstyle and friendly smile—was not having it.

"Not according to Mr. Cockerill's calendar."

Only then did he deign to look at her. Their gazes locked. His eyes were hazel, fringed in dark lashes, shrewd. Hers were gray and determined. He didn't believe her, but there was no way on earth she was relinquishing an inch when she'd made it this far—the door was *right there!* So now she would have to die for this little lie or brazen it out until it was true fact.

This was to be a contest of wills, then.

Nellie had all day for a contest of wills.

She was *this close* to the deputy editor of the *World*. Which meant she was *this close* to the chance to charm and impress him and talk him into giving her a job doing stunts, and all her problems would be solved and her future—one with a career and without laundry—would be assured.

Nellie smiled serenely. She had all day. Literally. All. Day.

"I'll wait here until Colonel Cockerill has a moment."

"He won't have a moment."

"I'm not leaving until I see him." She was still smiling. Her cheeks hurt from it, but no matter.

"You can wait over there."

Triumph! Nellie turned to take a seat "over there," and that's when she saw him.

A man, waiting.

By all appearances he was just a man reading a newspaper. He was all long legs and broad shoulders and strong arms holding up that morning's issue of the *World* before his eyes like she wouldn't guess immediately that he was eavesdropping on her conversation and watching her too.

She went and sat in the chair beside him, helping herself to one full glance as she did so. Nellie noted the following about him: wheat-colored hair kept a little longer than was fashionable, blue-green eyes behind a pair of black-rimmed spectacles, a strong jaw, a full mouth.

She looked away. Quickly. Given the circumstances, it was likely that they were rivals, so there was really no point in taking a long look at him to learn the precise shade of blue-green of his eyes or the curve of his top lip.

His sleeve brushed against hers; a fleeting touch, but the sensation stayed with her nonetheless.

His fingers, she noted, were ink stained. A fellow writer. Definitely a rival.

A better use of her time and attention was reading the newspaper over his shoulder and quickly learning the morning's headlines: POLICEMAN FACES JURY FOR MURDER; RACING AT CLIFTON N.J.; WALL STREET WALLACE SET TO WED HEIRESS; DEMOCRATS WILL WIN. The usual mix of important political news and local scandal, the latest from the sporting world, important issues of the day and the gossip that riled everyone up.

An even better use of her time was watching the door to Cockerill's office. Through the frosted glass door, one could see the shadows of two men in the middle of a discussion. Any minute now that door would open. Nellie intended to be the first one through it.

CHAPTER FOUR

Colton

THE NEWSROOM OF THE *NEW YORK WORLD*

Sam Colton couldn't help but overhear the conversation between the girl and Roy, Mr. Cockerill's personal secretary, who doubled as his guardian at the gate. By "couldn't help but overhear" Colton meant that he deliberately and unapologetically eavesdropped on a conversation that may or may not have been material to his future. He was a reporter and always on the lookout for a story.

And what a story she was already. A pert young woman, a swish of skirts and petticoats, strolling through the newsroom like her heart beat to the same rhythm of everyone at work and like her hips swayed to the beat of reporters typing out stories at the frantic pace of a daily newspaper.

He looked. Of course he looked.

Being a gentleman, he looked discreetly over the top of today's paper.

He listened too. She was a brazen liar with that business about a one o'clock appointment. Roy knew it. Colton knew it. She knew it.

He knew it because *he* had an appointment with Mr. Cockerill at one o'clock. He had come all the way from Chicago for the meeting.

Colton had come to New York for two reasons. The first, selfishly, was for the stories. It was the same as anywhere, he supposed—the crimes, fires, society gossip, feuds with the mayor and corruption in the local government, business news—but at a breathtaking scale and intensity seen nowhere else. The city was teeming with tales wanting to be told, crushed up against tenements, flirting with one another on Fifth Avenue, boasting on Wall Street. The stories here knew how to put on a show, how to dazzle and impress. How to make you clutch a handkerchief to your breast as you swooned.

What really set Colton afire were facts. He liked the process of tracking down the evidence, conducting interviews and earning the trust of sources so that they'd talk. He lived to hit the pavement and follow the leads. He liked observing, collecting and fashioning facts into a narrative. He was diligent, methodical and thorough in all things.

But Colton was also new in town and had called in favors to get this interview. He was well established back in Chicago, but he'd been warned that he'd have to start at the bottom again in New York.

No matter; Colton possessed the quiet confidence and unshakable determination of a man who knew what he wanted and that he would attain it, all by his own work. He wasn't worried about some girl reporter getting in the way.

Oh, he knew a man was supposed to want to conquer the world, amass a fortune, wield power over as many minions as possible. He was expected to claim land, kisses, women, territory, and then fight to the death to possess them forever. He was expected to assert his dominance over all, especially women who dared to challenge him.

But Colton wanted to uncover stories and reveal them to the

world. Stories that mattered. Nothing was going to stop him from it.

He wanted to feel like his time on Earth wasn't wasted.

Speaking of one's time on Earth, there was also the matter of Minnie.

Coming to New York and staying in New York was a matter of life and death for his sister and her delicate constitution. For the longest time it had been just the two of them against the world, after illness took their parents, one right after the other. Being faced with the prospect of losing his sister, of being utterly alone in the world, meant that of course he would do anything to protect her. The doctors here were the best in the country, so they were told, but Minnie had her heart set on a *lady* doctor, and there were oh but a handful of them in the world; most of them—all six or so of them—were in New York.

He needed work, immediately, that would pay well.

He had bills, to say nothing of a woman's life to save.

So, Colton needed this position. He needed this interview to be a success. The stakes were life and death for Minnie and him. A nice constant sense of creeping anxiety had been with him, reminding him all morning, and now *she* swished in with her nonsense about her one o'clock appointment.

His competition was stealing glances and reading the paper over his shoulder like she was cramming for an assignment at the last minute. She had an energy about her that threatened to start fires. Her body was practically humming. He didn't believe in mesmerism and magnetism and all that, but this woman and her palpable energy made him reconsider.

"I couldn't help but hear that you have an appointment at one o'clock," he said. Someone had to state the obvious. Someone had to get to the bottom of this. Colton had to claim his territory before it was too late.

She peered up at him with those gray-blue eyes. "I do."

"That's funny."

"Is it?"

"I also have an appointment at one o'clock."

He wasn't calling her a liar to her face. He was simply stating facts. They might have been facts that contradicted the words that had come out of her little pink mouth—he should *not* be considering her mouth—but where was he? Facts. Journalism. The news.

"You're not calling me a liar, are you?" She smiled, and she was just so . . . pretty. Her whole face lit up. "You seem like too much of a gentleman for that."

In another time, place or universe he might have thought that she was flirting with him. He *was* too much of a gentleman to call a woman a liar to her face. But he was too much of a reporter to take her at face value. Instinct told him she was a walking, talking story.

One he was not going to chase. For a thousand reasons.

"There must be a mix-up," he said.

"Something like that," she murmured. She glanced at him and he felt it like a caress, soft, tender and intimate. She was trouble. She was a distraction. He could not afford it.

Case in point: Before he was even aware of it, Cockerill's previous meeting had concluded and the door was now open and this girl was a few steps ahead of him on the way to that open door, that office, that precious, coveted one o'clock appointment. But Sam had the advantage of long legs and a quick pace so that they both arrived at the doorway at the same moment. His determination and chivalry were no match for her ambition, and she strode into the office ahead of him.

CHAPTER FIVE

Girl Meets World

THE OFFICE OF COLONEL JOHN COCKERILL, DEPUTY EDITOR

Nellie had met Cockerill once before in the middle of the busy newsroom, when he'd told her the *World* already had a woman on staff and stalked off. She was back now with new ideas and renewed determination and a certain desperation. There had been a scuffle at the door with Mr. One o'Clock as to who would enter first. She won, and now Cockerill looked up, surprised and alarmed at the intrusion. His expression did not soften when he saw it was a young woman who demanded his attention.

This time, Cockerill was trapped behind his desk, and she stood between him and the door. The windows behind him provided a wealth of natural light and a breathtaking view of the city, but her attentions were fixed on him.

Cockerill seemed ancient to Nellie—though he was probably only in his forties—with salt-and-pepper hair and a very distinctive mustache. There was something roguish and rough about him, but that didn't scare her; she'd grown up around unpolished men. He sat behind his desk, which held enough piles of paper that it seemed as if a newsstand had collided with the archives of a very prolific writer. In short, a mess of paper. One particular pile was held down and protected from whatever breeze might make its way into the room by a pistol.

She hoped it wasn't loaded.

Hot on her heels was Mr. One o'Clock, as she'd already taken to calling him in her mind. Between the pistol on the desk and the handsome man with such devastating eyes and every right to be here, she didn't know which was more of a threat to her. But what option did she have other than to push through and get what she wanted? This was her moment and she wouldn't waste it.

"What the hell is this? How the devil did you get in here?" Cockerill demanded.

Nellie smiled. It was her secret weapon and greatest liability. "Mr. Cockerill, my name is Nellie Bly." There was a wonderfully embarrassing moment during which she clearly expected him to remember her from their brief interview the other day and during which he clearly did not. "We met once before."

"Clearly an encounter burned in my brain," he said dryly. "How did you get in here?"

"Mrs. Ayer—" she began and he cut her off.

"What do you want? Money? Help? Is this a charity call? Did I . . . ?" He gestured vaguely to her midsection, asking, not in so many words, if he'd gotten her with child and she was now here to demand he marry her or pay for her to take care of it.

Another woman might have gasped, or blushed or protested. Nellie changed the subject.

"I'm here because you need a stunt-girl reporter on staff."

It took him a moment to catch up with her, to catch her meaning. She was here for a job. He stopped shuffling around his desk looking for spare change to give her.

"I need a what?"

"A stunt-girl reporter." She hadn't put the words together before like that. But it sounded fun. It sounded like it would sell. It sounded like something she wanted to do.

"Do I?" Was that a bemused almost smile? She decided to believe that it was. Between him and Mr. One o'Clock, frozen in shock behind her, she had an audience, and Nellie warmed up to it. Confidence pulsed through her, washing away any sense of modesty or subtlety.

"If you want to sell more copies than the other papers, you do. I know the *Herald* has a girl doing stunts. I saw her in action today." Nellie paused for a beat. "She's good."

She let that sink in.

The *Herald* potentially beating the *World*, thanks to a girl reporter.

Cockerill leaned back in his chair, which suggested he was going to listen as Nellie told him, an editor of the best paper in the best city, how to better do his job. Excellent. She layered it on thick. "Nothing sells like a crusade and a girl in danger."

"Let me guess," Cockerill said dryly. "You're just the girl I need."

She smiled. "Yes." Obviously.

Cockerill's gaze flitted to the left of her, where Mr. One o'Clock Appointment stood, ready to claim his precious hour of Cockerill's precious attention.

"And what are you? Her husband, beau, brother—" Cockerill gestured with his hand, waving the blue pencil he used for edits.

"Oh no no no—" He was quick to disabuse him.

"We're not together," Nellie and Mr. One o'Clock said at once. She turned to scowl at him. And in that moment, in that gaze, she noticed something: the hard set of his jaw, a narrowing of his eyes. He otherwise seemed calm and at ease, but, ah, there were stormy seas beneath. Whoever he was, he wasn't happy with her or how this interview was proceeding.

"Sam Colton, sir." He stepped forward and extended his hand. They did the manly handshake thing. "It's a pleasure to meet you. I'm here about the reporter job at the city desk."

"Right. Colton."

"I had an appointment." His gaze shifted to Nellie for one pointed second. "At one o'clock."

The opportunity was slipping away, like a tide going back out to sea, sucking everything on the shore out with it.

"I have fantastic story ideas," Nellie said in a rush. "I could travel to England and back in steerage to report on what it's like for immigrants coming to New York."

"Our readers already know that," Cockerill said, bored.

"I could go undercover as a shopgirl. Or a showgirl."

The two men exchanged a look that was so very easy to read. *Can you believe this girl?* they asked each other. *Is she for real?* Nellie was no stranger to those looks. She wracked her brain for more of her ideas—she'd jotted down pages of them in her notebook, which had been stolen along with her purse. And she couldn't say that without sounding like the sort of nitwit country girl who got her purse stolen in the big city.

Colton cleared his throat in a very *I'm an adult man and going to converse man-to-man* sort of way. He might have to share his interview, but he wasn't going to let the opportunity go to waste. "Sir, I come from five years at the *Chicago Tribune,* where I made a name for myself for my investigative work."

Cockerill grunted his interest.

"I did six years at the *Pittsburgh Dispatch,*" Nellie said quickly.

"Let me guess, you wrote for the ladies' pages," Cockerill drawled.

"Not *just* the ladies' pages—I did an eight-part series on female factory workers."

"I led our coverage of the Haymarket riot," Colton cut in.

"That was you? Great work."

"Thank you, sir. And from such an esteemed editor like yourself—"

"I could get myself arrested! I could spend the night in jail. I'm sure conditions are terrible, which will make for a *great* story. And look at me—as a nice-looking young woman, they'll never suspect that I'm a reporter. I'll get details no one else can."

Cockerill's eyes flickered with interest, so of course Colton had to cut in with a trump card. "You were well acquainted with my father, Henry Colton. From your days in St. Louis."

"How *is* Henry? Still practicing law? I owe him everything for representing me in that pesky murder trial."

Oh God. The dreaded friend-of-a-father connection. Nellie might be young, but she already had an idea of how the world worked, with men trading favors and connections to give their sons a leg up in the world. She could have the exact same qualifications as Colton, but if his father was friends with Cockerill . . . she might as well just go work as a shopgirl or a showgirl.

They were chatting amiably now, man-to-man, about mutual connections, as if she wasn't even there. Any second, Colton would be asked to take a seat, they'd break out the whiskey and she'd be asked to leave. Unless . . .

Nellie had one more idea. One she was scared to even suggest. But she was more scared of the alternative.

"I could go in disguise to the insane asylum at Blackwell's Island."

Both men stopped talking at once. They had all seen the stories in the papers these past two months, alluding to wretched conditions. The blind items, the sources who remained unnamed out of fear. They'd heard of women who were here one day and gone the next. *Blackwell's.* No woman would go there willingly.

Which to Nellie meant a story waiting to be told; however, no reporter had yet gained access to the asylum. Her mad idea to go in disguise hung in the air like smoke, refusing to go away or be ignored. But she got him. Finally got him. Cockerill, in spite of himself, was intrigued. He leaned forward with a glint in his eye that made no secret of his interest.

"What, like as a nurse?"

"As a patient."

"Can you act insane?"

I have no idea, Nellie thought. Then she said, "Of course."

"You must be joking," Cockerill replied.

"Or already insane," Colton added. "A stunt like that is risky." Turning to Cockerill, Colton said, "You can't send a young woman into such a dangerous situation."

Nellie rolled her eyes. "Women get sent there all the time," she pointed out.

"She has a point," Cockerill said gruffly. "But so do you. It *is* dangerous. Worse than dangerous. Apparently, it's a fucking nightmare. Deplorable. A circle of hell where decency and humanity go to die a slow, horrible death. Or so the rumors say. They won't let us send a reporter, so I'm sure it's even worse."

"If you're too scared to run it, I could always take my story ideas to the *Herald*," Nellie remarked. Casually. Just a thought. "I could help them corner the market on stunt journalism. It's new. Exciting. Sensational."

She felt Cockerill turn his head toward her. She felt his gaze really appraising her now, considering if she would really do it, and what a sensation it would be if the *World* ran it.

"I'm sure you don't need me to tell you how much such stories will sell," Nellie continued. She finally had his attention with talk of sales and besting the competition and helping him win.

"Doing stunts isn't journalism," Mr. One o'Clock interrupted. "Journalism relies on the collection of facts, the testimony of experts and verification."

"That's what I'd be doing," Nellie said. "It just wouldn't be boring."

"Journalism is meant to inform, not entertain," Mr. One o'Clock retorted.

"Or it could inform and entertain at the same time," Nellie replied. "The *World* didn't get to be the biggest and best paper in New York by being a dry, dull recitation of facts."

Cockerill had been thinking this whole time, and bluntly appraising her, trying to evaluate if she was to be taken seriously or if she was seriously mad.

"You'll really get yourself committed to the insane asylum?" Cockerill asked. He lifted one brow. He was curious. Nellie's heart started racing because it seemed that she might just pull this off. She'd always believed in herself, but still the moment was heady.

She could feel their eyes on her, both of them, as they waited for her to say no, as any sensible female would do. There was danger and then there was . . . this. There were no facts, only rumors of ghastly suffering. Women went in but they never came out alive.

She met his gaze. She projected all the confidence she'd ever possessed (not an insignificant amount) and then a little bit more. "Yes. I can and I will."

Mr. One o'Clock, Mr. Sam Colton of Chicago, turned to her, shock plain on his handsome features. "You're willing to get yourself committed to an insane asylum for a story?"

Was he horrified or impressed? Nellie couldn't quite tell. The more important question was what Cockerill was thinking. She had approximately three seconds to convey that she would indeed do the story and she was a serious reporter.

Nellie squared her shoulders. "If it's as bad as they say, then it's an important story to investigate."

"It'll be risky," Cockerill said, pointing out the obvious.

"It's no place for a nice girl," Colton said.

She turned to him. Smiled sweetly. "Perhaps. But they couldn't possibly send you."

THE ELEVATOR

The elevator doors slid shut and closed with a *ping,* ensconcing Nellie and Mr. One o'Clock in this velvet-lined box that would take them down to the lobby. She could feel the heat of him seething and radiating in her general direction. And yet he remained a proper distance away, his eyes trained on the counting of the floors.

Blackwell's!

Her mind was racing. What had she been thinking? Her heart was pounding. It was impossibly dangerous to not only her body, but her mind and freedom too. Cockerill had offered an outrageous assignment. And she could not wait to sink her teeth into it. He wouldn't let her officially accept it on the spot—but he gave her twenty-five dollars not to go to the competition and told her to think about it overnight. She was due back tomorrow to discuss the details. Alone.

Without this other reporter standing by.

He was in a mood. Definitely. Certainly.

Nellie knew about men and their moods. She knew to get away quickly, and if that wasn't an option, to pretend to be invisible and to make herself small. Unfortunately, she wasn't very good at it. She knew that any giddiness she was feeling would injure his precious ego and she ought to keep it to herself.

Blackwell's! What a story! She bit back her grin.

He turned to her one floor down. "What," he began, "was that?"

She kept her eyes trained ahead. "That was me, seizing the opportunity."

"Do you always burst in, uninvited?"

Most definitely. "I do what I need to do."

Blackwell's Island Insane Asylum! What a story it would be. There was no way it wouldn't be an explosive piece. This would make her career in New York—if it didn't break her first. She'd scarcely been in New York City a week before she heard the place spoken of with fear. *Be careful or* . . . It was a constant threat to women and girls that they might end up there.

Beside her, Mr. One o'Clock took one of those full, deliberate deep breaths one took when trying to regain control of one's emotions. "That was my interview, and now—"

She wouldn't feel bad about what she'd done. She would not! "I bet it was no trouble for you to get an appointment."

"What does that have to do with anything?"

Everything. She turned to face him. "I have spent the past four months trying to get into the building, let alone in front of Mr. Cockerill himself. Any editor on Park Row will give you the time of day. That was my one shot."

All right, so taking his interview had hardly been polite, possibly even downright rude. But she only did it because of a complete lack of other options. The world made it damn hard for a woman to do anything other than swan about at home, sighing over marriage prospects and fretting over delicate nerves—and, oh, all the housework and taking care of men and their feelings.

She'd had the devil's own time getting in front of Cockerill. Besides, what kind of reporter would she be if she didn't chase every opportunity?

Apologies to Mr. One o'Clock, but she had a life to live.

The elevator pinged once more as it slowed to a stop on the ground floor. The doors opened to the lobby, where they were hit all at once with a burst of sound and activity.

Nellie set off—she had to get back uptown. She had to do her research. She had to prepare. She had to pay off her debts to Mrs. Parkhill, cab fare and all.

Colton was hot on her heels. So what if she felt a rush, a thrill?

"What if you're not the only one who wants to write for the *World*?" he asked. "What if you're not the only one who needs the gig?"

All right, she'd bite. She stopped and spun on her heel to face him. "Why do you *need* the gig more than me?"

He paused for a second. "I have family to support."

"Maybe I do too," she replied hotly. "I suppose next you're going to say that women are too emotional for newspaper work and can't be trusted to collect facts."

"No, I would not say that at all."

Well then. That caught her by surprise. That made her look at him with softer eyes. But Nellie couldn't afford to get swoony over the man. "The difference is that you can walk into another newspaper and get an interview. I bet you can stroll into the *Sun* right now and have an offer by suppertime. And I can't. I know, because I've tried."

She would not feel guilty or sorry or ashamed or any of the things he and the world wanted her to feel. She would not put her own needs and ambition on the shelf.

Women have to look out for each other. Because no one else will.

Well, sometimes they had to look out for their own selves too.

"I'm not sorry. So if you're hoping for an apology, you'll be disappointed."

And then he surprised her. They were out on the street now, the city rushing around them. He nodded courteously and said, "Good luck with the story." Nellie couldn't help but feel like she'd need it.

CHAPTER SIX

What Girls Are Good For

THE ORDINARY, NEW YORK CITY

That morning Nellie had breezed into the *World* for another meeting with Cockerill to plan the stunt. He had been gruffly surprised to see her; if he thought she'd be scared off by the assignment, he didn't know how hungry she was for a chance. Then they got down to the business of confirming the details. Nothing like this had really been done before. Many of the particulars would be left up to her.

They were firmly in agreement that she would, in fact, get herself committed (she had no idea how to do that but declined to say so). She would, in fact, remain in the asylum for seven days (how bad could it be?). He would then secure her release. Then she would write a compelling story about her time there.

It would be front-page stuff, surely.

Cockerill did try to scare her off with rumors of how bad the place was; he didn't know Nellie Bly if he thought he could scare her when the story of a lifetime was on the line. As Cockerill detailed the abuses he'd heard about, Nellie stopped thinking of her big story and started thinking of the women.

"If the rumors are true, then it's a story that needs to be told."

Then she went to lunch.

Nellie met up with Harriet in the newsroom and they went down to the Ordinary for lunch with Dorothy—Nellie's treat, now that she had advance funds from Cockerill. Yesterday Nellie had been on the verge of despair and today her stomach was all aflutter with nerves—not that she would ever admit as much in the vicinity of Newspaper Row, where someone would use it as an excuse not to hire female reporters. But the truth was, she could hardly touch her pint and trimmings. She told Harriet and Dorothy why—her big story, and what an important one it promised to be.

"Sure, but why do *you* have to do it?" Dorothy was so sweet with her concern.

"I'm lucky to get the assignment," Nellie said. There was no need to be nervous. None. She was *blessed*.

"Insane asylums or face creams. Those are a woman's options in journalism," Harriet remarked dryly. "But then again, at least we have options."

"Please don't tell Marian," Nellie said.

"Where is Marian anyway?"

"She's chasing an interview with the mayor," Harriet started.

And Dorothy finished, "The one who is young, single, handsome and rich."

"I know of him," Nellie replied. His name was Hugh Grant and he was already affectionately spoken of as the Bachelor Mayor by friend and foe alike. As one might imagine, the race was on among the high-society debutantes to win his heart and/or his hand in marriage. Or so Nellie had gathered from her cursory glance at the society pages. "I thought Marian didn't write gossip for the ladies' pages," Nellie quipped.

"We all do what needs to be done to pay the bills," Harriet said.

Dorothy shook her head. "Her assignment sounds much better than yours, Nellie. I don't think you'll have much competition for it, if that's what you're worried about."

"Other reporters have been trying to get the story," Nellie said. "They haven't been able to get access to the asylum, which is why I'm going to get myself committed."

Harriet shook her head. "Blackwell's Island. Dear God."

"I know."

Thus far, Nellie had learned that the Blackwell's Island insane asylum had been built in the 1830s with the loftiest ambitions to provide the highest, most noble care for those unsound of mind. She could find no account that it still did—and no solid definition of what constituted an unsound mind either. The threat of Blackwell's was often used to keep women in line. The steady disappearance of women to that place was enough to ensure that the threats were effective.

Dorothy shook her head. "Heaven help you. Are you certain you can't get an assignment to Bloomingdale's instead?" The Bloomingdale was the "nice" asylum for "nice" women. Far uptown, it was still on the island of Manhattan. Not like Blackwell's, which was on its own island along with a smallpox hospital, a penitentiary and a workhouse, all cut off from society and surrounded on all sides by the East River and whatever terrors lurked in its depths.

Nellie shook her head. "Blackwell's or bust."

"How will you get in?"

Dorothy scoffed at Harriet's question. "How will she get out?"

"I'll act insane, I guess." Nellie took a sip of her pint as if it were a trifling matter to act insane and get picked up and banished to the island of misfit Manhattanites. She would have to fool doctors—that made her nervous. Beyond that she didn't know what it would take. At this point, a person might admit that they were in over their head, assigned with an impossible task that was doomed to fail. Nellie hesitated. Then gave in. "I'm just not sure how."

Harriet laughed. "Make yourself inconvenient and you'll get there soon enough."

Nellie wrote this down in her little notebook, newly purchased, with blank pages and a crisp cover. *Inconvenient.* "What does that even mean?"

Harriet only smiled cryptically. Before Nellie could ask any other questions, Dorothy leaned forward. A smile played on her lips. "Did you know that Harriet was once committed to a sanitarium against her will?"

"Dorothy . . ." Harriet murmured in a way that warned off further questions. Nellie had further questions. It was impossible to imagine Harriet—fashionable, commanding Harriet—out of control of her wits or her life. "Like I said, make yourself inconvenient and you'll get there soon enough."

"Inconvenient I can do. Mad, I'm not so sure. I'll have to convince doctors and nurses and experts . . ."

"The bangs are a good start," Dorothy teased. Was she teasing?

"Hey!" Nellie fluffed them with her fingers. It had certainly been a *choice.* But they were both laughing.

"Well, you remember Lucy?" Dorothy asked, changing the subject. Nellie nodded, recalling her speaking of the young woman she was giving shelter and safety to after she'd apparently witnessed something terrible.

"How is she?"

"Improving. She is even speaking a little to say hello or ask for water. But she still won't say a word about what she witnessed or what happened to her. I have no doubt that she would be sent to Blackwell's or worse if my friends and I weren't helping her recover."

"So I could try not speaking. Or claiming amnesia," Nellie said thoughtfully. "She's lucky to have you."

Harriet finished her meal and set her knife and fork down across her plate. "Another word of advice, my dear. Try not to actually go insane. There is nothing worse than being told that you don't know your own mind or body. If you aren't mad when you go in, chances are you will be by the time you come out."

Of all the things to worry about, Nellie didn't worry about that. "I only have to last a week," she said confidently. "Cockerill said he would secure my release after that."

"Do you trust him?" Dorothy asked. "I wouldn't trust him."

That was a good question, one Nellie purposely refused to consider in any depth. She wanted that story so badly that she wouldn't let herself consider what was at risk if Cockerill went back on his word. She would potentially be looking at a lifetime of imprisonment—unless she could talk her way out of it, and Nellie had extraordinary faith in her abilities to talk herself into or out of situations. *But no one ever heard of women leaving Blackwell's alive.* Minor detail! Just imagine her byline on the front page! It was a risk worth taking!

And if she was making a stupid, foolish, idiotic mistake to trust him? Well, she wouldn't be the first girl to throw her life away on the word of a man.

Harriet was more matter-of-fact. "If he wants the story, he'll get her."

Of course he wanted the story. Because if she could prove the rumors were true, it would be explosive. It would dominate the newsstands for the day certainly, maybe even the week. It would handily best the numbers of the *Sun*, the *Mail and Express*, the *Herald* and all the other papers and was thus sure to please Pulitzer. Cockerill had something to win with a story like this, and all he had to do to get it was to risk the life and freedom of a fresh-faced girl, new to city life. Everyone knew girls were disposable. They came to the city in droves, with stars in their eyes and hope in their hearts.

If Nellie failed at this, she'd be dredged up as a cautionary tale. *Stay home, girls! Stay safe! Get a man to protect you!* This had to work. It just had to.

Nellie had an enormous amount of confidence in herself. But she also wasn't about to take foolish and unnecessary risks. Leaning forward to confide in her two new friends, she said, "Just in case, I'm telling you both."

MRS. PARKHILL'S BOARDINGHOUSE, NEW YORK CITY

Darkness had fallen. Night was in full swing. Nellie stood before a mirror with one lit candle for light and for dramatic effect. The shadows on her face as the single flame wavered were downright spooky. She had just one thought, which she voiced aloud: "I should have asked Marian about this."

Yes, she was talking to herself in the mirror. Because why not? She *was* trying to act insane. Which, if Harriet was right, meant making herself inconvenient or even difficult—definitely unladylike. She wouldn't need to avert her gaze or smile demurely, bite her tongue or swallow her opinions. Now she deliberately mussed her hair and stared wide-eyed at her reflection, trying to forget all the rules she'd been brought up with.

Harriet's guidance was all she had to work with. Her research hadn't turned up a clear definition of insanity. The supposed symptoms in women were so varied, she scarcely knew where to begin, and much of it seemed to stem from a woman's wandering uterus. She didn't know how to fake *that*. Nellie did know that it felt rather freeing to talk to herself in the mirror.

It was amusing to make faces, especially. Nellie widened her eyes. She smiled too hard, the way you do when a man on the street tells you to smile and you want to make a point, so you smile so hard it looks like a grimace.

She pretended she was Marian and winked.

She pretended she was Dorothy and smiled sweetly.

She pretended she was Harriet and tried to look like someone's fairy godmother, wise and all-knowing and straight from the pages of the fashion magazine *Demorest's Monthly*.

She pretended she was that Sam Colton fellow and did her best to look firm and mildly horrified at the impropriety of a woman waltzing into his job interview and stealing the show. Nellie had to hand it to the man; he did take it all in stride. He was clearly not happy with her or the situation, but he hadn't lashed out or punched a wall or given her reason to think how misguided it was that women were considered the overly emotional half of humanity.

Nellie knew about angry men, especially ones who lost control of their tempers and became violently *emotional*. Her mother's second marriage had been a disaster from the start; Mary Jane had been desperate for someone to protect and support the family. She couldn't have picked worse than Ford. They had suffered through his drunken outbursts together, and Nellie had learned to be wise to the men around her, adept at reading them and gauging how far she could push.

But while Mary Jane made apologies, Nellie made plans.

She would see to it that she—and her mother—never had to rely on a man again.

In her head, she apologized to Sam Colton for not being the slightest bit sorry that she had crashed his interview. A man with his credentials ought to be able to walk into any of the papers and walk out with a salary and some plum assignments, like all the good ones they never gave women—unions striking, corruption within the police force, or grisly murders.

If he worked for another paper, that would make them rivals. Which was something of a pity, she thought, as she remembered his blue-green eyes and his broad shoulders and, most appealing of all: the fact that he had not once said "but you're a girl" or made comments about her nerves, emotional state, or qualifications. What a rarity he was! A fellow reporter who hadn't made a single quip about women belonging in the home or on the ladies' pages.

Nellie smacked her cheeks a few times. She was getting drowsy, but sleep was Not Allowed. She had to act insane, not like a nitwit young woman mooning over a man, when she had the opportunity of a lifetime ahead of her.

She had only this one night to prepare.

The only preparation she had planned was staying up all night, reading ghost stories and letting her imagination run wild and hoping a lack of sleep put her out of her mind enough to be convincingly mad in the morning.

So that's what she did.

The sun was almost up when she thought of Mr. One o'Clock again. The flash of his eyes as he considered her a worthy rival. He hadn't belittled her or stormed at her. He had just walked out of the *World* . . .

. . . with a hot tip about their latest exposé in progress.

No.

With a lead like that, he could walk into any of the other newspapers and have a job and an assignment by suppertime. Why, she had practically dared him to do it!

Damn.

Nellie forgot about her reflection and started to pace—five steps before she hit the wall and had to turn around and walk another five steps before she hit the other wall. It was wholly unsatisfying and did nothing to relieve her spiraling agitation.

He knew what they were planning.

Colton didn't know the details. She and Cockerill hadn't ironed out the particulars in front of him—they weren't that careless—but he knew enough to ruin her story if he were so inclined.

Nellie had given him every reason to be so inclined.

It was unthinkable that Nellie would let a man best her at her own story. She would just have to move faster, work harder and be more daring than anyone could ever imagine.

CHAPTER SEVEN

Marian

CITY HALL, NEW YORK CITY

Usually the ladies' pages did not concern themselves with political men, because women couldn't vote and despite the efforts of the suffragists, far too many women weren't interested in the franchise. Besides, husbands tended to be terrified by women with political opinions, and what were the ladies' pages but ways to catch or keep a husband? Hugh Grant, the mayor of New York, was an exception because he was young, handsome, single and rich. All that *and* he was politically powerful and poised to be more so. Already, there were whispers of him running for the senate next. Already, legions of young single women were plotting for his attentions.

Marian Blake arrived for the interview determined to make the most of this scoop, the result of mutual connections. Both she and the mayor had been raised in the same circles, of Mrs. Astor's Four Hundred, summers at Newport, that sort of thing. While Hugh had done all the right things—the degree from Princeton, the right clubs, flirting with the right women at the opera—Marian had caused a scandal that resulted in her being cast out of society. But old friends and connections came in handy when she needed a favor, a source, an off-the-record quote or even an interview.

"Miss Blake, good to see you." Hugh greeted her warmly, like the politician he was, a little sparkle in his eyes revealing that he remembered her from before but was too much of a gentleman to comment on the circumstances that had brought them to this.

"Mr. Mayor, I am honored." Marian smiled back at him. She was going to have fun with this assignment. The mayor was handsome, if one liked the tall, distinguished sort with brushed-back hair, a strong jaw and a charming smile. Though she could have done without his senior adviser, a gray-haired man introduced only as Branson, sitting stonily in the corner, ready to interject if she asked the mayor anything untoward or compromising or flung herself at him in a fit of passion.

His office at city hall was large, spacious and impeccably appointed in a strong, masculine style. They both took seats on the upholstered chairs set before the fireplace, as if this were a friendly chat between old friends. Marian flashed another smile. "Congratulations on your first year in office, Mr. Mayor."

"Almost a full year. But thank you nonetheless."

"You seem to have been born to politics. Your father, may he rest in peace, was also once mayor of New York. How has coming from a political family helped you?"

"It has been an inspiration. Especially my father," Mr. Grant began with a faraway look in his eyes as he remembered the late Hugh Grant senior, who perfectly fit the definition of elder statesman. "His ambition was always that I should follow in his footsteps, and so from a very young age, he guided my education so that I would be prepared for a life of service."

Good answer, Marian thought. Of course he couldn't say that his wealth, connections and legacy made it all but inevitable. His famous devotion to his father meant no other path was even considered.

"I think of my father every day I step into this office. I ask myself if I am upholding our values and principles and if I am making him proud."

In the corner, Branson nodded approvingly. Marian jotted all this down, catching his quotes on the page. And also *father issues.*

They chatted more about his hobbies and interests (horses, yachts, the opera) and what it was like to be mayor (an honor, a privilege, and all-consuming), and then Marian turned to more serious questions, which he was not expecting from her.

She didn't miss the flash in his eyes as she asked him about the rise of immigration—people were arriving from Ireland, Germany and elsewhere in droves. Too many, according to some. Where did the mayor stand on the issue? Marian asked him about epidemics in the tenements and what he planned to do about them. And did he have sympathies with the growing reform movement?

"Those are some hard-hitting questions for the ladies' pages," the mayor remarked. Marian just smiled and asked him another question.

"Many of the city's papers are reporting on rumors of deplorable conditions at the insane asylum at Blackwell's Island, but the administrators at the island won't allow reporters to visit and see for themselves. Can you comment on that?"

Mr. Grant seemed to be taken by surprise—she couldn't help but wonder if he was shocked by the question or that a woman was asking it—but he recovered well. "I have every faith in the Department of Public Charities and Corrections to manage things well."

"But it sounds like they aren't. What do you and your administration intend to do about it?"

"I shall leave that to a commission to report on."

A bit like asking the fox to guard the henhouse, Marian thought, but Branson was glowering at her in the corner and she didn't want to get escorted out before she asked the rest of her questions. She glanced down at her notebook. Another gentle, ladies'-page sort of question.

"Will you be attending the Wallace wedding?"

In other words: Would he attend *the* social event of the calendar year? Would he participate in the high-society spectacle that it promised to be?

"Of course. Mr. Jay Wallace has been one of my father's biggest supporters, and I am proud to say he is one of mine as well. His guidance and support during my campaign was invaluable."

"Does your friendship with Wallace mean that you will give preferential treatment to the other Wall Street tycoons?" Marian smiled. She'd caught him by surprise again. He'd thought she was going to ask about his wedding gift for the couple, as if the Wallaces didn't already own half of New York.

"That's a bold question. I can't imagine it is of interest to your readers."

"Women have children to feed and families to support. They will want to know if the mayor will look out for their needs or those of his donors and friends."

"I will be a mayor for all New Yorkers."

"Now for a more traditional ladies'-page question," she said, and he chuckled. "Do you know what you'll be wearing to the wedding?"

"No one's ever asked me that before," Mr. Grant replied, laughing. In the corner, Branson scowled at the inanity of it all. Honestly, she had to agree with him. He was a man; he would wear a suit. Full stop.

"Well, this is your first interview for the ladies' pages," Marian replied.

"Is that what women want to know about?"

"It's what men think women want to know about."

"I will wear whatever my valet dresses me in," Mr. Grant replied. It was, at least, an honest answer. And while she was here, while she had the opportunity, Marian had to ask another question, one that had been on her mind ever since the story first broke.

"You knew the late Mrs. Wallace. In fact, you were reported to have socialized with them on their yacht. Were you present the night she died?"

"What—? Why—?" Mr. Grant's cheeks reddened. In the corner, Branson, furious, stood—this interview was clearly over. As for the mayor, he was flustered by the question, not expecting it from the likes of *her*. She knew that a phalanx of lawyers had instructed him not to utter a single word and never dreamed that she would get an answer on the record from him. But a wealthy woman dies from a fall off the family yacht and her husband's wedding to another woman is on the calendar mere months later. How does one not inquire? There was no world in which Marian Blake did not ask the question. But she was far from surprised when the mayor refused to answer her.

CHAPTER EIGHT

A Delicate Mission

I took it upon myself to enact the part of a poor, unfortunate crazy girl, and felt it my duty not to shirk any of the disagreeable results that should follow.

—Nellie Bly, *Ten Days in a Mad-House*

SECOND AVENUE, NEW YORK CITY

After staying up all night making faces in the mirror and quietly panicking about what Colton knew and what he would do with the information, after one last morning bath and a tender goodbye to such precious items of modern civilization as a toothbrush and soap, Nellie set out on her assignment.

Mrs. Parkhill, whom Nellie had repaid in full with her advance funds from Cockerill, eyed her warily as she came down the stairs dressed in what she had deemed her dullest old dress. She purposely did up the buttons wrong and had worn it all night to get that wrinkled look. She didn't dwell long on why she equated a lack of fashion sense with insanity; instinct and experience told her that people would treat her well if she looked smart and put together.

Her bags were left behind. Everyone knew women could not travel without an excess of luggage, so it seemed downright daring—or mad!—of her to travel without baggage.

"Are you all right, Miss Bly?" Mrs. Parkhill asked.

Nellie was starting to feel out of her mind. A lack of sleep will do that to a girl. Add to it a dose of nerves and an inappropriate giddiness and you had Nellie that morning. She was smiling. She couldn't stop, even though Cockerill had told her she was too smiley to pull this off. His exact words had been "You're too goddamn smiley to get away with this."

She was *on assignment.* She was living the dream. Yes, yes, she was in for a few dreadful days, but after she got out . . . visions of front-page bylines danced in her head.

"No, I don't think I am. But I'll be back, Mrs. Parkhill, see if I'm not!" Then Nellie gave an awkward laugh. She would be back—right? Her landlady told her to take care.

She set off downtown.

Nellie could have had some friends drop her off at Bellevue and wash their hands of her, but she and Mr. Cockerill wanted to know not just how bad the conditions at Blackwell's were, but how hard—or easy—it was to find oneself there. There would be doctors to deceive, and her stomach was in knots over the prospect of having to convince educated and authoritative medical men of her insanity.

But first, she needed to be dragged before a medical professional with her sanity already in question.

So Nellie set off alone, the better to make herself an inconvenience. If she started acting odd, unpleasant or unpredictable, she was more likely to be sent directly to the authorities if there was no man around to take responsibility for her. No husband, father or brother would be told to "get a handle on his woman" like she was an agitated horse.

She walked down Second Avenue, dazed and slightly unsteady from a lack of sleep. It definitely had her in a certain mood. When Nellie felt her features falling into a scowl, she pasted a blank expression on her face, the one the painters called "dreaming." It was beautiful on a canvas hung in a museum but a little disconcerting in real life.

But just imagine if she did start acting like a woman in a work of art—frolicking in groves of trees in Central Park, naked as the day she was born, save for a wisp of sheer fabric that provided neither warmth nor modesty. In a museum, critics lauded it and evaluated the shadows and light. In real life, she'd be locked up by lunchtime.

Maybe she ought to try that . . .

Nellie laughed at the thought, a full-throated laugh in the middle of a crowded street. A woman alone, laughing at nothing, turned no heads. This was New York City, after all, and everyone was too focused on their own business to spare a thought for hers. Maybe this would be harder than she thought.

Nellie kept walking down Second Avenue, where redbrick and stone tenement buildings rose four, five, six stories high on either side of the street. Laundry fluttered on lines overhead. There came a clatter of horse-drawn carriages, trolleys and people. So. Many. People. This wasn't the fancy part of the city; it was the part where all the foreigners arrived and set up shop. She heard a different language on each block, it seemed, and there were different food smells every block as well. Most were downright enticing. She remembered that she hadn't eaten since yesterday.

Eventually, she reached just the place. A modest town house kept in decent repair. A sign out front read TEMPORARY HOME FOR FEMALES. Nellie stood there for a second and took a deep breath.

No one was paying the slightest bit of attention to her, and yet she felt the eyes of the world on her as she prepared to embark on the performance of a lifetime.

There was no going back after this.

TEMPORARY HOME FOR FEMALES

The lodgings were a certain kind of home for a certain kind of woman. Those who came to the city on business, to start a new life, or to find work stayed in boardinghouses for a night or two, or maybe longer. Meals were included; rooms were sometimes shared. A temporary refuge, where women came and went, hopefully unbothered.

Nellie pushed open the door, which had a cowbell functioning as a doorbell, and stepped through the vestibule and into the foyer. It was trying, that foyer, to be neat, bright, respectable, *nice,* in spite of obviously having seen better days. The wallpaper was faded; the floorboards were worn and scuffed but free of dust. It seemed like a place that *cared* and all it had to recommend it was its care; there were few resources in reserve to deal with problems.

The same could be said for the proprietress herself. The woman who emerged to greet the new arrival was short, round and on the far side of fifty. She might have been pretty once, though no one would describe her thusly now. Nellie knew from her working days in Pittsburgh that the drudgery of housekeeping could really take it out of a woman. But, like the foyer in which she stood and the parlor that she could see just beyond the doorway, the proprietress was doing her very best to put on a good front. Neatness and respectability were all she had to work with, and so by God she did.

She introduced herself as Mrs. Stanard and asked how she might help Nellie.

"I'd like a room, please."

"All I've got is a shared one."

"That's fine. I don't sleep anyway."

Mrs. Stanard smiled politely and tilted her head slightly at Nellie—what an odd thing for someone to say. But no matter.

"We charge thirty cents a night."

"I have seventy cents."

Make yourself inconvenient also meant *make yourself poor.* Much bad behavior was tolerated if one had enough money, particularly if one was a man with money; it was practically a universal truth. Nellie was not here to be tolerated. She was here to make a terrifying nuisance of herself and to be sent off to the authorities as swiftly as possible. So, she had brought only seventy cents with her.

In the process of finding the money in her pocket, Nellie accidentally on purpose let her little notebook drop to the floor. The pages fluttered, revealing vile drawings of disturbed people and violent weapons, and utter nonsense she had written, in case anyone looked and used it to judge her private thoughts.

Mrs. Stanard looked at it now, with just a hurried, worried glance. She even paused, as if she *ought* to care or inquire further about why this young lady was drawing pictures of knives and scrawling wicked words, but she honestly didn't have the time, now, did she, managing this whole house when good help was so hard to find. And really, did anyone ever have the time to get to the bottom of a young girl's unusual and questionable behavior? No.

Besides, Nellie didn't *really* look like trouble, despite her efforts. Nellie held herself still while Mrs. Stanard gave her a frank appraisal and noted her pale skin, her wide eyes, her nice hair (bangs notwithstanding). Her dress was haphazardly buttoned and rumpled. But there was nothing wrong enough about Nellie to refuse her a room.

Thirty cents was thirty cents. Mrs. Stanard was here to make money.

"Your name, girl?"

"Nellie Brown." That was the name she and Cockerill had agreed on. So he could find her should he attempt to do so. Again, she felt chills race up and down her back at the worry that he would just leave her behind bars for the rest of her life.

"Any bags, dear?"

"I . . . um . . . Yes. Yes, my trunks." There were no trunks, other than the ones that suddenly existed in Nellie's mind.

Which is to say, there were absolutely no trunks in the world that belonged to Nellie Brown, who also did not exist. But that did not stop Nellie from putting on a performance in which the trunks were real to her, very vital.

Her eyes clouded with worry; her lip quivered.

Her trunks! She *must* have them.

Mrs. Stanard looked around for them. She even went as far as to peer out the front door—a girl might have had trouble with trunks on the steps. Nellie hid a smile behind her gloved hand. The trunks would turn up approximately never, but that would not stop her from inquiring about them. Repeatedly.

"I must have my trunks," Nellie insisted.

"I'm sure the trunks will turn up eventually," Mrs. Stanard said. "Where have you come from anyway?"

"I don't know," Nellie answered. "I can't remember. I can't remember anything. And my head hurts terribly." Mrs. Stanard looked at her curiously. But she had meal preparation to oversee and other matters to attend to. A wisp of gray hair escaped her coiffure and she anxiously tucked it back in place. She did not like things out of place and out of sorts.

"Well, come have a seat in the parlor and we shall see about your trunks later." Nellie followed Mrs. Stanard to the parlor, to see whom she might terrorize there.

Like most other girls, Nellie had been brought up to be mindful of the comfort of others, to always consider everybody else, to make herself small and inconspicuous so as not to bother anyone. Mary Jane had tried to instill those lessons in her daughter, especially after her marriage to Ford, who had one hell of a temper, and nothing set him off like the combination of alcohol and a mouthy woman. Nellie had learned to tiptoe around him and his moods, but she hadn't completely learned to shrink and silence herself into oblivion.

And thank goodness for that. Writing an outraged, opinionated letter to the editor had secured Nellie's start in the newspaper business. When the *Dispatch* had published a letter from a desperate father despairing over what to do with his five daughters, Nellie sat down and wrote her uncensored thoughts on just what girls are good for (*Anything! Let them work! Let them live!*). Upon reading her letter, old Erasmus had been impressed with her spirit and pluck. That was how she got her start at the newspaper in Pittsburgh.

Here she was now, ready to make more trouble.

The parlor was occupied by other temporary women. There was Woman Trying to Read a Novel while her young son made a nuisance of himself as he bounced a ball against the wall. Repeatedly. By some miracle, it did not disturb Sleeping Woman, who sat in a rickety rocking chair nearby, with her head thrown back and her mouth open to emit snores and catch flies. Across the room, a kind-looking woman with gray hair kept her hands busy with knitting a blanket in soft red yarn.

Nellie as herself wanted to ask them all a thousand questions:

Who are you, where did you come from, why are you temporary and where are you going? What about work, or family, or who would you have voted for in the last election if you had the franchise? But Nellie Brown didn't ask questions—unless they were about the state of her trunks—and so they were destined to remain unknown to her.

Within an hour she was dying of boredom. *Dying.* She had not planned to be bored, but nevertheless, she had sunk into that state and had taken to muttering songs under her breath to keep herself awake. Beside her, Woman Trying to Read a Novel was immersed in her story, emitting the occasional sigh as the flimsy pages turned. With the promise of more such hours of nothingness ahead of her, Nellie cracked and asked a question.

Sleeping Woman had since woken and was now passing the time with her nose buried in a newspaper. It was the *Herald*. Marian's paper. For one snap second Nellie felt like she oughtn't read it out of loyalty to the *World*. But the newspaper wars were real and it behooved her to keep abreast of the happenings of the city and her rivals.

Besides, the *World* hadn't published her yet.

Nellie leaned over Sleeping Woman's shoulder. Sleeping Woman appeared to be about sixty years of age, unless she'd had a hard life and then maybe she was only forty or fifty. Everything about her was tired—her hair, the lines in her face, the weary way she sank into the chair and sort of gave up there. Nellie was surprised she had the energy to keep abreast of the news.

"What are you reading?"

"The newspaper."

"What's the news? Any murders? I do love to read about a good murder." Nellie grinned in a way that she hoped was disconcerting. Women were supposed to be too delicately composed to take an interest in violent things like murder.

"A good murder!" Across the room, Mrs. Knitting was aghast.

Nellie nodded enthusiastically. "The more gruesome the better. You know, the police almost never catch the murderers. Especially in the city because there are so many."

There were shudders all around the room. Mrs. Knitting especially.

"They almost never catch the female murderers," Nellie remarked oh-so-casually. But she let her eyes widen and she didn't try to hide the mischievous sparkle. No longer sleeping and now wide awake, the woman next to Nellie tightened her grip on the newspaper, the soft pages crinkling in her hands.

"As it happens, I don't care to read about murder," she huffed. "I'm reading about the Wallace wedding."

"A wedding? Boring." Nellie rolled her eyes.

"It's a nice distraction. It says they'll have a million roses."

"A million!" Even Woman Trying to Read a Novel set down her book. "I can't even imagine what a million roses looks like."

"Well, you can go see on the day of the wedding. They're expecting crowds in the streets."

"When is it?" Mrs. Knitting asked.

"It's too soon, if you ask me. Mr. Wallace only lost his wife three months ago." Mrs. Knitting gave Nellie a Look, like she oughtn't to get any ideas, but really, how could one not?

"Murder?" Nellie asked with wide eyes.

"Apparently, she fell off their yacht while it was at sea."

"Was she pushed?" Nellie asked, genuinely intrigued.

"I'm sure it was an accident," Mrs. Knitting said. But that was a dull explanation and Nellie ignored her.

"What a way to go. Pushed off yacht. I can add that to my list." Nellie took out her notebook and pencil and flipped to a blank page and mumbled, "Ways to commit murder," as she wrote it down along with *push off yacht into shark-infested ocean waters.*

When she looked up, the other women were staring at her, aghast.

"Or did she drink too much champagne and take a tumble?" Mrs. Knitting asked. "One of the many evils of drink."

They all agreed that it was entirely plausible that one of those wealthy society wives drank too much champagne at lunch or dinner one day and stumbled overboard, with the weight of all her diamonds pulling her down to the dark, murky depths of the ocean. They all agreed that drinking was evil and thanked the Lord for the good work of the temperance movement and swore that they always abstained from spirits.

Nellie muttered again, "Murder, I tell you."

"You needn't look so keen about it," Woman Formerly Reading a Novel said, looking away warily.

Mrs. Knitting met her gaze. Nellie met it and held it and stretched out the moment until it grew unbearable and she looked away. There was something fun about acting ridiculous, but Nellie still felt a little uneasy about making decent women uncomfortable when they were just trying to pass the time in a temporary home for females.

But she had an assignment. With visions of the front page and a byline dancing in her head, Nellie proceeded to spend the next hour muttering to herself about murderers and being eaten by sharks. She found it amusing for the first five minutes but it really began to drag after an hour, and they were all greatly relieved when Mrs. Stanard emerged and informed them that dinner was ready.

Women should be seen and not heard. That ridiculous age-old maxim hardly applied when women were among other women, as they were at dinner that night in the Temporary Home for Females. All around the dinner table, the women made small chat over the meal, about everything from the suffrage conference one had attended and another woman's trials finding a lawyer who would risk his practice to help her divorce her husband to the latest dime novels and best places in the city to buy stockings.

Like all other girls, Nellie had been brought up with the saying *If you don't have anything nice to say, don't say anything at all.* Tonight, she would break the rule.

"This food is terrible," Nellie declared before she had even taken a bite. "Just look at it—I don't even have to taste it to know I won't find it satisfactory."

Of course it wasn't good. One did not go to Temporary Homes for Females for fine cuisine. Nevertheless, the other women ate what was offered to them with nary a complaint. Perhaps some were hungry enough or knew that gnawing feeling of endless hunger too well to turn up their noses at a slice of cold beef and potato. Perhaps they hated it as much as Nellie did but were just too polite to say so.

Mrs. Stanard pursed her lips. Her dismay was plain and Nellie felt badly for her atrociously rude behavior. She wanted to whisper her secret and explain and apologize. But . . . she had to get to Blackwell's. To do that, she had to conduct herself as no decent woman ought to and act downright rude. Even if it made her stomach turn to insult a workingwoman who was trying *so hard.* So Nellie held forth about how more salt would have gone a long way, and no one joined her conversation, and when that became tiresome she beckoned to Mrs. Stanard, who had already grown weary of Nellie.

"I think all these women are crazy," Nellie said. Loudly. Apropos of nothing. Because it seemed like a crazy thing to say. There were eye rolls all around the table as many of the women objected but would not actually say so out loud at the dinner table.

"These women? Oh, no. This is a respectable house!" Mrs. Stanard fluttered. Then she narrowed her gaze at Nellie. She managed to be both polite and threatening all at once. "I can assure you we don't keep crazy women here."

Nellie hid her smile behind her napkin. *Good.*

No one wished to share a room with "that insane girl," as they had already started calling her. They had all asked her questions—who she was, where she was from—and Nellie had feigned amnesia. She knew nothing about herself, but she was missing her trunks and very worried about some bad men after her. And oh, what a headache she suffered! Their amusement turned swiftly to concern—and outright fear among a few of them.

Nellie listened as they talked about her after dinner in one of the parlors. "I would rather spend the night on a park bench with rats and robbers—I'd feel safer" or "I'd rather take my chances with the sharks after being pushed off a yacht" or "I'd feel safer in prison with those murderers she keeps nattering on about." And "What was Mrs. Stanard thinking giving her a room?" They all agreed that Nellie looked nice enough but there was something *off* about her.

Nellie might have felt badly about making everyone feel so scared and uncomfortable, except for the fact that a few of the women had made a game of cruelly teasing her. On the one hand: Her ruse was working! If this reporter thing fell through, she could work on the stage. On the other hand: How dare they? As far as they knew, Nellie Brown was an innocent girl, lost and far away from home, her memory and trunks stolen from her. A little compassion might be nice.

But then again, Nellie was deliberately making a nuisance—and inconvenience—of herself. She embarked on another round of "Where are my trunks? I must have my trunks!" And then she began to sob uncontrollably about those bad men being after her.

Finally, she let herself be consoled by Mrs. Knitting, who was in fact a woman named Mrs. Ruth Caine, a professional proofreader on her way home to Boston. Ruth, as she told Nellie to call her, would share her room. Everyone else visibly expressed relief and commended her bravery.

Mrs. Caine shut the bedroom door and smiled at Nellie. They were alone in a small chamber with two narrow beds, one washstand and a window with a view of the avenue.

"If you don't have a brush, you may borrow mine," she offered. Nellie was tired, hungry and anxious, and the kindness nearly undid her. She agreed to let Ruth brush her hair.

As she did, Ruth spoke soothingly to her about how nice all the women here were, and there was nothing to be afraid of, and she saw a lovely hat in the shop window down the street that perhaps they could go look at tomorrow, and Mrs. Stanard makes a very good breakfast. She spoke about how Nellie would certainly find her trunks and her family and everything would be well, and Nellie's heart was nearly bursting with anguish. She felt such pride in her performance, but deceiving a good, kind woman like Ruth was making her feel wretched.

"Your bangs are quite the fashion statement," Ruth said with a kind smile that made Nellie genuinely scowl. "What happened that made you cut your hair thusly?"

Nellie wanted to tell her about being desperate for work—newspaper work only, please—and desperate to make her mark on the world. She wanted to show everyone just what girls were good for. She wanted to talk about how hard and lonely it had been, those first few months in the city, when she *had* felt insane for leaving her life behind—especially her beloved mother—on the mad dream of becoming a newspaper reporter in New York City. A few managed to do so and make a name for themselves—Fanny Fern and Jennie June came to mind. As Nellie had discovered, a few more managed to get work as journalists—but only one per newspaper, please. There were just enough female reporters to inspire a girl like Nellie, but only one per paper—so, not enough to make it an easy or likely job to get.

There were all kinds of madness, she supposed, and hers was daring to dream.

None of this could be confessed to Ruth, much as Nellie might wish to unburden herself, so she muttered some more about not being able to remember anything and refusing to sleep in case there might be murderers in the house. She made her eyes go wide, like she had seen things—terrible, unspeakable horrors—and she choked a little on her words, as if to suggest that they were stuck in her throat, refusing to come out. She let Ruth's imagination go from there. It was all too easy for women to imagine the horrors that might befall them.

"It's time to sleep now," Ruth said with a gentle pat on Nellie's arm. "Or try to."

"I won't sleep until my trunks arrive."

She didn't. Nellie stayed up all night keeping a watchful eye on Ruth, who slept fitfully, and on the mice that skittered along the perimeter. To keep herself awake she thought of every person she had ever known in her whole life. She started with her father, the judge, and tried to remember what he was like before he died. She remembered a kind, towering man who indulged her in everything—but that could have been just because she was six. He seemed to have everything sorted about life until it was revealed that he didn't.

She thought of her mother, dressing her all in pink and calling her Pink and doing her very best in very hard circumstances. She thought of all the men who had failed them: Mr. Jackson, who had mismanaged what little funds the judge had left for her, and Mr. Ford, possibly the worst husband in the world, and half the men in town who had failed to warn Mary Jane about any of them until it was too late and they had little legal recourse.

Just thinking of all these men, and all the disappointments they had wrought, did the job of firing up Nellie's resolve to never, ever rely on a man for her existence. Ruth's kindness might have nearly undone Nellie, but for a chance at security and independence for her and her mother, Nellie would deceive Ruth, say rude things about Mrs. Stanard's cooking (true as they might be!) and scare everyone with her nonsense about murderers.

Staying awake so long did things to one's brain. Any exhilaration for her scheme had long worn off, and now a fog was settling into her head. Memories tripped in and out, waving for her attention and vanishing as quickly as they'd come. Dreams fluttered in and fell over, passed out. Sleep. Oh, it called to her. It beckoned. Her bed was *right there.*

It'd been hours and days since she had last slept or eaten. Stars spun behind her eyes. Her head lolled forward, to the side, and back. Nearby, Ruth tossed and turned and occasionally cracked one eye open. She did not deserve this. No good deed goes unpunished.

In the battle of Nellie vs. Sleep, Nellie was winning. Barely, and at great expense. *Try not to actually go insane,* Harriet had told her. Nellie had laughed it off. But now a sort of delirium was setting in as dawn was breaking. And the day stretched ahead of her, an endless expanse of hours. With any luck she'd lay her head down at Blackwell's tonight.

THE PARLOR, TEMPORARY HOME FOR FEMALES

Nellie was starting to feel out of her mind, and the prospect of spending another day sitting around this parlor, with nothing to do, was certain to make her lose it. It was a commonly accepted medical fact that women's brains ought not to be overtaxed, but Nellie always suspected the opposite was true. Nothing made her feel like crawling out of her skin like staying at home all day with nothing to do. Challenge them, put them to work at occupations that involved their minds—anything but let them run on idle all day long.

When she came downstairs that morning, Ruth was already there in the parlor with the others, and she had Mrs. Stanard's attention for one of those ferociously hushed conversations.

Nellie lingered in the foyer and listened.

"She stayed awake *all night*," Ruth hissed. "I couldn't sleep a wink."

Mrs. Stanard wrung her hands anxiously. "Did you learn anything about her? Where is she from? Will someone claim her?"

"She says she can't remember anything. She spoke again about bad men being after her."

"Well, we can't have them coming here."

The woman who spent all afternoon sleeping huffed, "We were told this was a respectable house, Mrs. Stanard. If she doesn't go, I'm afraid we must all seek lodgings elsewhere."

The women seemed to be united in their opposition to Nellie's presence. Mrs. Stanard seemed genuinely torn; she did not want to cast some poor girl out onto the streets, mad and alone. But faced with revolt from a houseful of lodgers—and the damage to her reputation and livelihood that would ensue should they all leave at once—Mrs. Stanard reached for her hat.

The moment seemed as good as any to launch into another rendition of "Where are my trunks? I must have my trunks!" and if Nellie was a little unsteady on her feet from lack of sleep, all the better.

Mrs. Stanard jammed her hat on her head. "I'm going to handle this. I shall be back shortly." The front door slammed shut behind her. When she emerged an hour later, she was not alone.

When Mrs. Stanard returned with two police officers in tow, Nellie pretended not to notice. One, Officer P. T. Brockert, was a tall and unnervingly muscular fellow who seemed like the sort who joined the force for its proximity to the criminal element and not in a good and noble way. The other, Officer Fletcher, was unbelievably average and unremarkable; his uniform was the only thing that distinguished him and he probably knew it. The fact of it probably made him mean.

Mrs. Stanard spoke to them in a low voice. "I want you to take her quietly."

This is a respectable house. There are no insane women here.

Nellie pretended not to hear.

"If she doesn't come quietly, I'll drag her through the streets," the big officer said, with a little too much anticipation at the prospect. Nellie pretended not to hear him as well.

"Now, now, Officer. She's just a girl, no need for that," Mrs. Stanard fluttered. "I'm sure she belongs to someone who will care about her treatment."

"There are other ways to compel her," the unremarkable one said.

She didn't have to fake her eyes widening with fear. In this moment it occurred to Nellie just how much she was endangering herself. It was one thing to be a nuisance in a houseful of women; quite another to be a girl who doesn't even know where she's from and has no known protector, to be at the mercy of men in authority who operated on the firmly held belief that they were above women and above the law. Should anything happen to her at their hands, she'd have no legal recourse. The best she could do would be to make a fuss in the pages of a newspaper—if her story was deemed salacious and scandalous enough.

She could confess now. She could give up the ruse. This was probably her last chance to avoid some terribly violent and tragic fate. She could go back to Pittsburgh and get married and die a slow death of boredom.

Nellie lifted her eyes to meet theirs. "Have you found my trunks?"

"These men will help you find them, love." Mrs. Stanard's anxiety about throwing Nellie on the mercy of the world was plain on her face and in the way she was positively murdering the handkerchief she was twisting and pulling in undoubtably sweating palms. But what option did she have if she didn't want to lose all her lodgers? "If you'll just go with them, love . . ."

Because it suited her to do so, Nellie went with them willingly. She did not say goodbye to her fellow temporary residents, but she didn't miss their palpable relief as she left. Mrs. Stanard sweetly and briefly placed her palm on the small of Nellie's back as they set out—an apology for what would come next.

CHAPTER NINE

Colton

ESSEX MARKET COURTHOUSE, LOWER EAST SIDE

That girl had been right. Sam Colton could walk into any paper on Park Row and get an interview with the top editor. Not just because he was a man with impeccable credentials, but also because he was a reporter with a solid scoop that would give a newspaper a good chance to best the *World*. Sending a woman undercover to Blackwell's—the mere idea was insanity!

It was just the thing the *World* would do. And, thanks to Colton, it was just the story the *Sun* was going to get first. After that ill-fated interview that she crashed into like an avalanche, Colton took himself and his scoop next door to the *Sun*, to Charles Dana himself, and got the job along with the assignment to find that Nellie Bly and get her story before she got it herself. Colton did not feel the slightest bit guilty about this; all was fair in the newspaper wars. In fact, he had a feeling she would be disappointed in him if he didn't play hard.

Why it seemed to matter to Colton what she thought of him was not a thought that he cared to examine. So, with the particular skill of men when it came to uncomfortable emotional thoughts, Colton pushed it away and ignored it completely.

He focused on his new job instead.

There was just one problem: Colton hadn't been able to find her again. He had turned up at the *World* the next morning to see if he could catch her coming or going so he could follow her, but, predictably, the sidewalks had been too crowded, the streets too clogged with the stinking traffic of horses and carriages. His inquiries about a young woman with bangs and a too-big smile and a brisk, determined manner yielded him nothing but strange looks.

There was always the chance that Nellie had had second thoughts. Or that Cockerill had come to his senses and exhibited some sound judgment and called off the story (though given what one knew of Cockerill, that was unlikely to be the case).

While he was sweating promises he couldn't keep, Colton was sent down to cover the Lower East Side. The neighborhood had to be packed with stories, but he had a hard time understanding all the different languages, and the mass of humanity, seething and struggling, sometimes threatened to overwhelm him.

Somehow in all that, he was supposed to get eye-catching, heart-pounding stories. The bloodier the better. Bonus if there was a beautiful young woman involved, especially if tragedy had befallen her. He might have been an experienced investigative reporter in Chicago, covering bigger issues, but here in New York he was a new kid, a nobody. He'd have to take whatever assignments he could get.

Just like that girl.

But . . . Blackwell's was a thick, juicy assignment that was destined for the front page. The kind of important story that could make a career if she could make it in and out alive.

But at what cost?

Sam wasn't the sort of man to think that all women were

delicate flowers who could only survive in the most particular and favorable conditions. They were as resourceful and determined as any man. His sister had shown him that. Even so, according to the rumors that had been printed in the papers these past few months, that particular asylum for women was not for the faint of heart.

That girl Nellie didn't seem to be faint of heart.

And then, there she was.

The Essex Market Courthouse was a madhouse of its own. Located in a stately building, it was surrounded by a crush of hot, dark tenements and designed to intimidate. The court served the surrounding Lower East Side, which was a neighborhood with more people packed in one building than the number who resided in one of those Fifth Avenue mansions, both upstairs and downstairs. The tenements contained stories on top of stories, jammed in next to stories on either side.

Most of them, unfortunately for Sam, were in foreign languages. He walked down the streets—Orchard, Norfolk, Mulberry—hearing Yiddish, German and a host of other Eastern European languages as he dodged pushcarts and busy shopfronts and crowds. He learned what he could, though, and tried to make friends with police officers who could help translate. The courthouse was as good a place as any to get a lead.

"Well, I'll be damned," Colton swore under his breath.

"What? What is it?" Jedediah, a hotheaded young pushcart operator whom Colton had been interviewing about his role in a brawl with other vendors over some prime positioning on Orchard Street, swung his head around wildly to see what Colton was referring to without any idea what he was referring to. But then it was all too obvious.

"Oh," Jedediah said eventually, a hint of a grin under his bushy beard. "A girl."

Because Nellie caused something of a commotion when she was escorted in on the arm of one very large police officer, followed by one plain-looking one and one very anxious woman whose face was screwed up into a grimace. Her eyes darted around, taking in the crowds of confused, desperate and distressed people waiting for their turn with a judge.

It was Nellie he couldn't stop staring at. Her dress looked like she'd slept in it and like she'd buttoned it bleary-eyed and in a rush. A veil covered her face, but he could just make out those distinctive bangs underneath. It had to be her.

"Excuse me," Colton said to Jedediah, his interview abandoned, as he deftly moved through the crowd to follow her, keeping just enough distance so that her gaze wouldn't happen to land on him.

"Are all these people looking for their trunks?" Nellie asked loudly.

The large officer grunted. "Yeah, sweetheart. They're all here for lost luggage."

Nellie was not like the others here. For one thing, she spoke English. As much as she tried to make herself looked messy and unfashionable, he recognized what she was wearing as a "dress-down" gown. His sister, Minnie, had a dress like that—the one she wore for charity work or when she wanted to appear plainly attired, but was still nice enough that she wouldn't be embarrassed if she ran into anyone of her acquaintance. Despite what he recognized as her attempts to dress down, she still stuck out here.

Sam's gaze focused on her buttons—had they been deliberately done up wrong? His pulse quickened as it occurred to him that he might have stumbled on Nellie in the act of chasing her Blackwell's story. And so, he melted back into the crowd and watched as Nellie, being a pretty, pale-skinned woman without any discernible accent, was taken right up to Judge Duffy, past people who had been waiting for hours for their turn.

Judge Duffy had been on the bench long enough to be unfazed by nearly anything. He had salt-and-pepper hair and wore his black robes well. By some miracle, his heart hadn't been hardened by all the sob stories he heard day in and day out. If Nellie wanted a gentle judge, she was in luck. If she wanted a one-way ticket to Blackwell's, she'd want someone meaner. Sam pushed a little closer to the action—but not too close—so he wouldn't miss a thing.

"And who do we have here?" Judge Duffy peered over the box down at Nellie.

"Nellie Moreno."

"I thought you said your name was Nellie Brown!" the anxious older woman exclaimed. Now Colton was really intrigued. *Moreno,* he knew, was Spanish for "brown." But why did she switch? She must think fast on her feet, having observed the crowd here. The older woman said to everyone and no one in particular, "She said her name was Nellie Brown."

"Where are you from, young lady?" the judge asked Nellie Brown Moreno.

"I don't remember."

Sam's mouth quirked up into a smile at the flash in her eye. She was good at whatever she was pretending, but not good enough to hide a flash of annoyance at being called *young lady* by a patronizing older man. Judge Duffy tried again. "When did you come to New York?"

"I didn't come to New York."

"But you are in New York now."

She looked around her suddenly, making her eyes wide. Oh dear, was *this* New York? Sam ducked behind a large Italian man who was patiently waiting for his turn. Meanwhile, Judge Duffy and the anxious older woman tried to patiently explain to Nellie that she was in New York and they were trying to help her.

"I have lost my trunks and would like if you could find them," she said. Colton noticed she had started to affect an accent now. Slightly Spanish, perhaps? He couldn't quite place it, probably because she was faking it owing to some notion that it would help her case. It struck him as distasteful.

"She must be from the West," Judge Duffy said confidently. "I think I detect a western accent." A debate over the accent ensued. Officer Brockert swore she sounded just like she was from the South—give him a Bible, he'd swear on it. A clerk gave the opinion that she was from the East. Definitely from the East. Then someone got the idea that she was from Cuba and that seemed to stick. The older woman with her just groaned. Colton wracked his brain, trying to remember the newspaper she said she'd written for.

Meanwhile, Nellie let them all talk and Colton tried to see if she was smirking under that veil.

"A woman who doesn't know who she is or where she came from." Judge Duffy huffed. Stumped. This was a most unusual case. "Lift your veil, girl, so I can see you."

"No." Nellie refused.

"If the queen of England were here, she'd lift her veil."

Nellie considered this and acquiesced. "Fine."

Colton caught a glimpse; it was her all right. He'd recognize those bangs and that mouth anywhere.

Judge Duffy turned to the older woman with Nellie. "Madam, what do you know of this child?"

Colton moved closely to listen in. He flipped to a new page in his notebook and started jotting things down.

The older woman leaned in. "I'm Mrs. Stanard of 84 Second Avenue. I run a home for women—"

"What sort of home?" the judge asked suspiciously.

Mrs. Stanard was horrified by even the vaguest suggestion that she ran a brothel. "It's a respectable boardinghouse for working-women! This woman came in for a room, alone. She has been terrifying the house with talk of murder and her missing trunks. She hinted that bad men were after her. She would not go to bed; she stayed up all night!"

Nellie cut in. "Can you help me find my trunks? I *must* have my trunks."

"She keeps nattering about her trunks!" the woman cried, but the judge's attentions were elsewhere. On Nellie, to be exact. From where he stood, it looked to Colton like Nellie was pretending. Was Judge Duffy thinking the same thing or something else?

"A pretty young woman with no memory. Something bad must have befallen her. I would stake anything on her being a good girl," the judge remarked. "Why, she looks like somebody's darling!" Judge Duffy exclaimed, to some awkwardness all around.

All women belonged to someone; that was how the world worked, for better or for worse. In the eyes of the law, a married woman became subsumed into her husband. Any money she made belonged to him, along with her body. Before that, she was her father's property to do with as he wished (usually marry her off and make her some other man's responsibility). But to be Somebody's Darling was to be kept in the sort of way that wasn't mentioned in polite settings. Essex Market Courthouse was hardly Mrs. Astor's drawing room, but *still.*

The judge seemed to have realized what he said, and his face reddened appropriately while everyone in hearing distance shuffled uncomfortably and considered the proper course of action. Was she respectable—or not? Was she somebody's darling—or not? Who was this curious girl with the unidentifiable accent and ever-shifting surname, who was deeply concerned about the fate of her lost trunks? Who was she and what was she doing here?

The man Colton had been interviewing, Jedediah, had come to stand with Colton and watched the proceedings like it was a first-rate production of Shakespeare. "She's obviously been kidnapped and drugged and now has amnesia," he said confidently.

"Obviously," Colton agreed dryly.

"It happens all the time," Jedediah said forlornly, shaking his head.

"Does it really?"

"Indeed." Jedediah nodded gravely. Colton had his doubts but wasn't about to debate the question.

"You know what they say about women like that."

Colton knew what was said, though he wasn't necessarily sure it was true. It was said, and understood, and held to be gospel truth that loose women, fallen women, poor women, were a dangerous element because of their power to corrupt with sex and desire, which led to crime and danger. All because they didn't lock themselves up at home. *But look at her!* Colton wanted to shout. Look at any of them! How anyone could look at some of these girls or women and see *handmaidens of vice and decay* was beyond him. They were just people, trying to live their lives.

Judge Duffy, reddened, cleared his throat. "I mean, she must be some woman's darling! Somebody's sister. She looks, uh, like my sister. No, I mean my dead sister."

Colton winced.

Beside him, Jedediah cringed. Judge Duffy seemed aware that he was not helping himself. They all seemed to want the moment to just end already. Nellie wavered on her feet slightly and gave the impression that if the big strong officer wasn't holding her up, then she might just crumple over. Insanity, Sam thought, looked a lot like exhaustion.

What has she done to get here? He would have to retrace her steps—or follow her. Because obviously he would have to find out.

Something had to be done with the girl; they were all nodding, they all agreed. She could not just be left to fend for herself on the streets, or some truly terrible fate would befall her. No, a young lady needed to be protected, and if no man would step up for the job, then the state would have to do it. But that still didn't answer the question of what to do with a woman who appeared nice enough. In desperation, Judge Duffy looked around. "Any reporters here? Maybe they know something."

Colton held back. Nellie kept her head downcast too.

"I don't want to speak to any reporters," Nellie said, and Officer Brockert laughed and said, "Nothing insane about *that.*"

"You." Jedediah, next to him, poked him hard in the ribs. "You were just telling me you're a reporter."

"Shh."

Officer Brockert, who had his arm linked with Nellie's and seemed to be keeping her on her feet, said, "I thought I saw the new guy from the *Sun* around here."

Colton was witnessing Nellie Bly in the act and he was the only one who knew it. If he wanted payback for the way she stole his job interview, this was the perfect moment. He could announce that she was Nellie Bly, perfectly sane and undercover on assignment. He could claim her—the courts would probably release her into the custody of any man who was willing to take responsibility for a lone female. And just like that, her career in New York would be over before it had begun.

But so would his.

This was a lucky break and Colton knew it. He could dog her

steps, file reports every step of the way. It'd be a good story for him—much more interesting than brawling pushcart operators, apologies to Jedediah—and with the added sweetness of scooping her story. It was only fair, Colton told himself.

Officer Brockert was getting impatient now. "Oh, just send her to the island and be done with it," he huffed.

The older woman with Nellie burst into tears. "Oh no! Not the island! A girl like her will never survive it!"

Meanwhile, Nellie bit her lip and shifted her weight on her feet and glowered darkly at everyone. *Send me to the island already,* she seemed to say, but Colton was the only one who could read her.

The officer was exasperated now. His shift must soon be over and he must be keen for lunch. "What else are we going to do with her if no one claims her?"

Beside him, Jedediah murmured, "I'd claim her."

Sam held him back. "No, you will not."

Judge Duffy, now annoyed, glared down at her. "One last time, girl, who are you?"

"I don't remember."

"She is clearly a poor girl who has been drugged. Anyone can see that she is a good girl," Judge Duffy said. And with that, he gave his orders: "Take her to Bellevue."

Bellevue was not Blackwell's, but it took her one step closer to her goal.

Colton would catch up with Nellie later. But first, he set off through the crowds in search of the older woman who had accompanied Nellie to see if he could get a quote. "Mrs. Stanard! If I might have a word?"

CHAPTER TEN

Somebody's Darling

When I thought of what was to come, wintery chills ran races up and down my back in very mockery of the perspiration which was slowly but surely taking the curl out of my bangs.

—Nellie Bly, *Ten Days in a Mad-House*

EN ROUTE TO BELLEVUE

As Nellie was escorted out of the courthouse to a waiting ambulance, she thought of Marian and her stunt with the ambulance surgeon. *He'll be sorry he tried anything on me,* she had said over lunch. They had all nodded gravely, knowing what "anything" meant. Like most women, they structured their lives to avoid "anything," but now Nellie was walking right toward it, vulnerable and unprotected. She had fleeting second thoughts.

The ambulance surgeon was a lean, muscular sort with a roughed-up look about him—maybe it was the chipped tooth and the blood and other mysterious stains on the apron he wore.

He looked at Nellie with an expression that was a noxious mix of leer and sneer. Oh, *delightful.*

Because there had been no one to claim her, there was no one to rise to her defense, to prowl around her and mark her as territory that best not be infringed upon.

Fair game, she was.

Except she wasn't game. She steeled her spine and sharpened her gaze and willed him to understand that. She was also relieved when the judge himself came out to have a word with him. "Here is a poor girl who has been drugged. Anyone can see that she's a good girl. I am interested in the child and would do as much for her as if she were my own. I want you to be kind to her."

Nellie's heart ached for all the women who didn't look like the judge's dear sister.

For a moment she let herself imagine what it felt like to be a truly vulnerable woman, making this journey from uncertainty to uncertainty, body flooded with terror, all while this man leered at her and considered what *he* might like to do. Dear God, what he probably did.

"What kind of drugs have you been taking?" the ambulance surgeon wanted to know. Nellie was jerked back to the present moment, where a doctor held her fate in his hands. This was the moment she'd been dreading. Her acting versus a man's medical education.

"Drugs? I don't know about drugs," Nellie replied.

"Your pupils are large. I believe you have been taking belladonna," he said. He set about examining her tongue and taking her pulse. How could she match the pulse and tongue of an insane person? Nellie went on about her trunks again, the bad cooking at Mrs. Stanard's home, her refusal to return there. And she forced her eyes open wide and wouldn't allow herself to blink.

And with some rude nattering and a blank stare, she fooled the first doctor.

The tense drive felt endless, even though Bellevue was little more than a mile uptown. She couldn't even look at the city flashing by outside the narrow, barred window. She couldn't take a breath and take stock of herself, her situation, what next and where to. One had to be on guard, constantly vigilant.

And then she arrived. Unscathed.

Bellevue Hospital was a massive, intimidating stone structure that spanned the length and width of a city block and put one in mind of Gothic castles. The facade was cold, relentless, endless. Ivy crept up the walls and claimed it. Nellie looked upon it and felt the sinking realization that a girl could get lost in there and forgotten for all time. When the metal doors clanged shut behind Nellie, she thought there was a very good chance the world might not hear from her again.

BELLEVUE HOSPITAL

The iron doors closed behind Nellie in a way that would have been heartbreaking and soul crushing had she not worked very hard to get herself here. The whole place felt haunted by the ghosts of those who'd come and gone before. Just to be clear, by "gone" Nellie meant *dead* and not *discharged* because they had recovered after some tender care. There was no sign of tender care. Just ghosts and sickness and all the fear that went with it, all of it suffusing the air.

Nellie breathed it in. Her skin prickled with cold sweat.

She was escorted down a long, cold corridor painted in that particular shade of Institutional Gray. It might have been a fresh, sterile white once upon a time, but now years' worth of fear and despair had tinged the walls. Did she mention it was cold? Somewhere, windows were open so the frigid air from the East River whipped through the hall and settled in one's bones as soon as one entered. At the far end, women sat on decrepit willow furniture. She couldn't tell if they were coming or going or waiting to see a doctor or just *there.*

Nellie joined them.

Opposite Nellie sat an older, very unkempt woman who stared straight ahead. *Was she mad?* Her gaze was focused on something far away, perhaps in her imagination. But wouldn't anyone escape into their mind when left to sit here? There wasn't anything else to look at. Nellie noticed the woman's hands, reddened and swollen with arthritis. It must have made it hard to do things like brush her hair or button her clothes or make herself presentable. With such gnarled hands she probably couldn't do much of anything, so Nellie really didn't see the point of the leather restraints clasped around her wrists, keeping her in the chair.

As if there was even anywhere to go.

On her right sat a young woman close to Nellie's own age. She had short, thin brown hair and a slight frame, and her skin had that ashen tinge of someone who had been unwell. She trembled slightly. There didn't seem to be very much wrong with her that a cup of tea and a warm blanket couldn't fix, but what did Nellie know—she didn't possess a medical degree. Before she could introduce herself, a nurse interrupted.

"You there!" The nurse was a workhorse of a woman who moved like she had seen it all and was in no rush to see it again. She wore a black dress, white apron and cap and held a rope of keys. Her attentions were currently fixed on Nellie. "Take off your hat."

"I'd rather not. It's very cold."

"It *is* rather cold," the girl next to her said. "Perhaps I might obtain a blanket or a shawl?"

The nurse pretended not to hear; she only had eyes for Nellie's hat, which was hardly the most stylish thing. "If you don't take that hat off, I shall use force. I warn you, I will not be gentle."

Of this Nellie had no doubt. She took her hat off and handed it over. The nurse left in a huff. Thinking to get to work and get what stories she could, while she could—surely, the next doctor would see through her act and cast her out at once—Nellie turned to another woman next to her, one with black hair streaked with white and gray.

"I'm Nellie Brown."

The woman gave her a weak smile. "I'm Anne Neville."

"What brings you to Bellevue, Anne?"

She'd been sick from overwork, she explained to Nellie. First, she was sent to a Sisters Home, and when neither she nor her nephew could afford the fees, he had arranged for her transfer here.

"But is there anything wrong with you mentally?" Nellie asked.

"No," Anne said forlornly. "The doctors have been asking me many curious questions and confusing me as much as possible, but there is nothing wrong with my brain."

"But only insane people are sent to this pavilion, right?"

"Yes, I know. The doctors refuse to listen to me and it is useless to say anything to the nurses. You'll see."

Fooling the doctors was Nellie's primary concern. Although if they thought Anne here was insane . . . maybe there was nothing to it, for she was as sound of mind as Nellie. Just unlucky.

But just in case, and not wanting to return to the *World* empty-handed, Nellie began to converse with the woman on her other side. She introduced herself and asked the girl her name.

"Tillie," she sighed. "Tillie Mayard."

"How did you end up here, Tillie?"

"I was sick. I have since recovered, but now I have this nervous condition, so my friends brought me here."

"Your friends." Nellie had to wonder if Tillie's friends were foolish or heartless. But Tillie herself seemed too sweet to even pose the question to.

"Yes, just until I am a little better. It was too much of a burden for them to care for me. I hope with a little rest that I'll be back to them soon."

Inconvenient. Sweet Tillie—Nellie could already tell she was a girl who was too trusting, too obliging and too kind, and who had become a bother, and here she was. Tillie told her about her hopes for a recovery if she could just have some time and space to rest. Some warmth too. That would do wonders for her constant exhaustion and fatigue—why, she could scarcely hold a broom! But if she had time to rest, she could return and would no longer be a burden on the household.

"Are they taking good care of you here?" Nellie asked.

"I only arrived this morning. And I've been waiting here ever since," Tillie said. Not long at all to have much experience with the place. "What about you, Nellie Brown? What brings you here? You seem perfectly well to me."

Nellie was spared from answering by the arrival of a doctor. He didn't introduce himself, so Nellie didn't have a name to remember. He would just be A Handsome Doctor if she ever got to writing this piece. He seemed to be in his late thirties—young enough for a woman to still flirt with, but old enough to be thoroughly convinced of his own experience and expertise and unable to comprehend a word that challenged it.

Anxious with the task before her, she felt her stomach turn. She had to convince this doctor of her insanity; no one wanted to read a story with the headline ONE HOUR IN BELLEVUE. That story wouldn't even earn her enough for a one-way ticket back to Pittsburgh.

The doctor was accompanied by another nurse, this one with faded ginger hair and dull blue eyes. Nellie heard that her name was Nurse Scott. She seemed oh-so-bored by the patients, the work, everything. She stood favoring one leg, arms crossed, and with a jerk of her head toward Nellie said, "That's the one I told you about."

The doctor took a look at Nellie, from the top of her bare head, past her unfortunate bangs, to her face, where his gaze lingered, before dropping lower still. He was certainly evaluating her, but she had the distinct impression it was not her sanity that he was considering. If he told her to smile, she wouldn't be shocked.

"She *does* look like Somebody's Darling," he declared at last. This again? Please.

Nellie scowled at him. "Do you know me?"

"Sure, sweetheart. From home. Do you know where home is?"

"The hacienda," she said. Might as well keep up the Spanish bit to throw everyone off.

"And where is that?"

"I was hoping you'd tell me. I can't seem to recall."

Nellie made her face blank, as blank as her memory, which gave up no clues about her past, her home, who she was or where she'd been going. This seemed only to invite closer inspection. The doctor bent down to her level, his face uncomfortably close to hers. He spoke gently.

"Tell me what you remember, Nellie."

Dr. Bellevue put his hand on hers, which was resting on her lap. This could have been a friendly gesture. Perhaps it was established medical practice that simple human touch unlocked all sorts of secrets to the body. Maybe. More likely, this doctor thought she was Somebody's Darling and might be his and this was just a friendly test.

Beside her, Tillie sucked in her breath.

It occurred to Nellie once again, as the doctor's hand smothered her hand in her own lap, how vulnerable she'd made herself. How stupidly, dangerously vulnerable.

Nellie had no recourse for whatever might happen next. She glanced to Nurse Scott. No, there would be no help from her.

None of the things that might have protected her would now help her—like the existence of some man to rise to her defense, or some understanding that she was "a nice girl" and "proper" and "not that kind of girl." She was on her own, with nothing to protect her but some strange man's sense of decency. Good Lord.

She might as well embroider *no consequences* across her dress. If they would trust her with a needle and thread.

Anguish twisted in her chest as she thought of Cockerill and Colton exchanging glances when the topic of this assignment came up. They had thought of this, but she had not. *Cockerill, what have you asked me to do?* she thought. And *I'd better get the front page if I make it through this.*

If the doctor felt her stiffen under his touch, he didn't show it. Truth be told, he didn't seem to register any reaction on her part. He was staring at her intently, as if the mystery of her sanity would be revealed in the dilation of her pupils or the curve of her lips.

"Tell me what you remember, Nellie."

"Nothing. I remember nothing."

Beside her, Tillie was confused. "You don't remember *anything?*"

"If I take you out of here, will you stay with me?" the handsome doctor asked, and it was all Nellie could do not to let her eyebrows shoot up in shock. "You won't run away from me on the street, will you?"

He was handsome, but also the sort of man who preyed on insane, isolated girls. "I can't promise that I will not," she told him.

Next he asked her all sorts of questions about seeing faces on the wall and hearing voices at night. The easy path was to agree, because it was obvious which answers would get her diagnosed as insane. Oh yes, so much talking at night, she told him. Oh yes, faces followed her everywhere. In fact, did she see them now?

"Yes," Nellie said. "There is so much talking that I cannot sleep." That wasn't a lie. There was a lot of talking on city streets at night.

"I thought so. What do the voices say?"

"I cannot say, Doctor. It is not decent." That also wasn't a lie. The kind of talking on city streets at night was hardly the stuff of teatime conversations. He nodded thoughtfully, as if this was exactly as he'd expected. A textbook case.

"What do you do in New York?"

"I'm not in New York."

They did a few rounds debating where she was and then he asked again, "Tell me, girl, what do you do?"

She waited a beat. "Nothing."

The doctor dropped her hand and stood up to his full height. Nellie was glad to have her personal space back, but she didn't dare exhale. The doctor turned and spoke confidently to the nurse, who was still not the slightest bit interested. "What we're looking at is likely to be a case of hysteria."

"Apparently every problem with a woman is hysteria," the nurse remarked dryly. Almost as if she'd heard this before. Nellie wanted to laugh.

Headaches? It was probably hysteria. Sadness or rage? Also

hysteria. Ennui? Hysteria. Anything that ailed women was diagnosed as hysteria, a condition in which the womb wandered aimlessly around the body, causing trouble. It was also given as a reason that a woman should not overtax herself with thinking or studies or work or sexual desires. If one thought about it for a moment, really thought about it with logic and reason, the whole premise was ridiculous. Hysteria was supposed to indicate a problem with a woman, but one had to wonder if it wasn't a man's way of saying *I don't know what's wrong with her* or *I don't understand women.*

As long as it got her into Blackwell's . . .

The doctor had one more question. "Tell me, young lady, are you a woman of the town?"

Beside her Tillie gasped softly; what a rude question to pose so bluntly to such a nice girl. But "Somebody's Darling" meant more than one thing.

"I don't understand you," she said. The doctor turned to the nurse, who had yet to express the slightest inkling of interest in the whole proceeding. "Hysterics often have excessive sexual needs," he informed the nurse as if she were new, and she gave him a look as if she was certainly not on her first day here, thank you very much. "Which leads them to certain, shall we say, occupations, which have a corrupting influence upon society. They are very, very dangerous."

Nellie wanted to roll her eyes.

He addressed her again. "Tell me, have you allowed men to provide for you and keep you?"

"You mean, like a husband?"

Beside her, Tillie burst into laughter, which set her whole body off in a nervous trembling. Even Bored Nurse smirked. The doctor was not amused.

"I've seen enough," he said. "She's obviously demented. A hopeless case."

"Which one?" Nurse Scott asked.

The doctor looked around at Nellie and Tillie, who was trembling with cold, and the woman on the other side of Nellie, who sat just sat there, staring blankly at the wall. He looked at Anne, who had already given up hope of getting out. He started buttoning his jacket and picked up his satchel; one could see that he was thinking of his dinner already, perhaps a cigar, some other simple pleasure that they might never experience again.

"All of them. They'll go to Blackwell's in the morning."

The announcement sucked the air right out of the corridor. Tillie stopped laughing and her shaking increased. "Blackwell's!" she cried. "But I am not demented. I am perfectly sane!"

The doctor did a slow turn. He looked at Tillie, incredulous. "Have you only just found out that you are destined for an insane asylum?"

"My friends said they were sending me to a convalescent ward to be treated for my nervous debility, which I am suffering from since my recent illness. Oh, *please,* let me out."

Anyone could see that Tillie was sick in body but not mind.

And to think Nellie had been worried about fooling the doctors.

To think she had planned and enacted an elaborate two-day scheme of terrorizing the poor women of the Temporary Home for Females when she could have just had Marian or Harriet drop her off with a note, like an unwanted infant at a church door. *To whom it may concern: I do not want her.*

And the doctors would just take the word of an unsigned note or a "friend."

All because they didn't know any better or couldn't be bothered.

What a horrifying thought—one that sent chills straight to her heart—how easy it was to get rid of someone, and what little recourse that someone had. Protestations of sanity meant nothing; the doctor's tests seemed wanting. It was one person's word against another's, and what was the word of a woman?

Or women. Plural. No rumor about Bellevue or Blackwell's ever talked about the spacious accommodations or the empty halls in want of patients. Now Tillie was about to be sent off to Blackwell's Island, probably for life, when what she really needed was a warm bed.

"She is clearly sane," Nellie cut in, and the doctor took one look at her and burst out laughing. "You're not one to talk."

She opened her mouth to say something—but what? As long as they thought she was insane, it was pointless for her to defend or champion any of these women. She would only doom them all if she tried to advocate on their behalf. Nellie had mentally prepared herself for wretched, filthy conditions and terrible food. She had prepared herself for fear and discomfort. But she hadn't thought about the particular anguish of watching a perfectly sane girl be sentenced to Blackwell's—to death, most certainly—and she could do nothing to stop it. Nothing.

Unless . . .

Nellie could say something now. She could declare that she was Nellie Bly of the *Pittsburgh Dispatch* or the *New York World,* here on assignment, and that the public was going to hear all about this. But the doctor's laughter still rung in her ears and she recognized it would sound like the delusions of an insane girl—a female reporter?! Who'd ever heard of such a thing? A female reporter on assignment to an insane asylum?! Impossible! Lock her up and throw away the key!

Meanwhile, the nurse stood there, immune to Tillie's increasingly panicked cries, made all the worse by her desperate, exhausted attempt to control them. Finally, the doctor turned to leave, jaunty as you please, as if he hadn't just sentenced three young women to a living death. Bored Nurse followed. Three girls horrified at the turn their lives had taken was just not amusing enough for her.

Beside her Tillie wept and declared her sanity over and over, until she did start to sound insane. "It won't do any good," Anne Neville muttered with a jerk of her head at Tillie. "Best just accept it."

Nellie's own chest felt tight with panic. She felt sick at having given up control of her own life and heartsick for Tillie. At least someone was going to come and let Nellie out . . . right? Cockerill or Harriet. Although, truly, what did she know about Cockerill or Harriet?

"Oh my God," Nellie whispered softly. "What have I done?"

But then a commotion at the end of the corridor demanded her attention.

CHAPTER ELEVEN

Positively Demented

I heard someone at my door inquiring for Nellie Brown, and I began to tremble, fearing always that my sanity would be discovered. By listening to the conversation I found it was a reporter in search of me.

—Nellie Bly, *Ten Days in a Mad-House*

BELLEVUE HOSPITAL

There was a banging at the metal doors. Someone on the side of freedom wanted badly to get into this section of the hospital, which boggled the mind. Everyone in the place turned to see who was fixing to get in and dear God *why*. Even the woman with the gnarled fingers and blank stare turned to see what the commotion was all about.

Bored Nurse was mildly intrigued enough to go open the door.

From where Nellie sat, a good distance away, she couldn't get a good look at who stood there knocking. It was only when Bored Nurse shifted her weight and he craned his neck to see past her that Nellie caught a good glimpse of him. Oh, *damn*. She immediately ducked her head and slumped down in her seat before she could be ruined by locking eyes with her rival.

Beside her, Tillie was confused. "Are you all right?"

"I'm fine."

She wanted to look. She could not look. How the devil had Mr. One o'Clock found her already? In a low voice that sent shivers up and down her spine, and *not* in a good way, he said, "I'm here to see about Nellie Brown."

She could practically hear the quirk in his smile as he said "Brown" instead of "Bly." Oh, he was onto her, playing along. How long had he been following her? she wondered. How much did he know? How many facts of her story had he already collected? Nellie could feel her exposé sliding out of her grasp, over before it really began, only to be saved by the unlikely heroine of Bored Nurse.

"I don't know her," the nurse said with no attempt to hide her weariness. She was apparently immune to Mr. One o'Clock's good looks and keen interest or even the fact of his existence. But was he the sort to resort to charm, and if so, would she give Nellie up for a little light flirting from a handsome man?

Colton persisted. "She just arrived today. Young. Pretty. Looks like Somebody's Darling."

Nellie slunk down lower and lower and tried to pull the collar of her jacket up to obscure her face. She was *not* Somebody's Darling. Was she ever going to live that down? Even as she tried to hide, Nellie could feel Tillie's eyes on her.

"Why is this man asking about you?" Tillie whispered. Thank God she whispered. "He *is* asking about you, isn't he?"

"It's a long story."

"Apparently I have time. All the time in the world." This set Tillie off on another round of soft, kitten-like sobs. Nellie strained to ignore her and listen in to see if Bored Nurse was going to betray her identity or not.

"Who is asking?"

"Sam Colton, of the *New York Sun*."

The *Sun*! Nellie groaned. Well, she had been right. Look at him, already busy with an assignment and payback. How efficient. She had certainly handed him the keys to her own destruction.

"How interested are you?"

"What do you mean?" Colton asked, and Nellie thought it was all over. There was a beat of silence—Bored Nurse must have answered his question with just a look—and then he said, "I won't pay for access, if that's what you're suggesting."

Nellie could just imagine the color rising in his cheeks at the questioning of his integrity. She could just imagine because she would not look in his direction. She couldn't slide down any lower in her seat, but she wanted to.

"Then I don't know her or what you're talking about."

"I need to get in. I need to speak with her," he said, his voice now urgent, and it did something to her to hear him wanting to see her so desperately. Nellie felt it like a flip in the stomach. Like she was *attracted* to him or something, but she didn't even know him. They were rivals, and he had every reason to ruin this opportunity for her. And he had those blue-green eyes—they were probably gazing intently at the nurse, maybe even beseechingly. Had this place hardened her to the beseeching glances of a handsome man on a mission? Nellie's breath kept catching as she imagined all the ways this could go wrong already. It came down to Bored Nurse, who did not get paid enough and told him so, right to his face, before she shut the door.

THE DINING ROOM, BELLEVUE HOSPITAL

Just like that, Tillie and Nellie had fallen into some sort of friendship, based on nothing more than the fact that they were close in age and perfectly sane and sat next to each other on a bench at the hospital one day. Tillie really was the sweetest girl. Achingly sweet, the way your teeth hurt after eating too much candy (an experience that had happened to Nellie precisely once in her life). She was also cold, all the time, constantly trembling and forever on the verge of tears.

The nurses were unable (unwilling, more like it) to find her a shawl or an extra blanket, and so she shivered through dinner.

"Why didn't you want that man to know you?" Tillie asked later, over a plate of cold meat and cold potatoes and no salt. "Who is he?"

Nellie didn't want to eat the food at all. It was revolting. But she stuffed a bite into her mouth so she might avoid answering and have a moment to think up a perfectly plausible reason why she wouldn't want a handsome man to come to her rescue. "I'm sorry," Nellie said, choking a little on the food, and it wasn't entirely faked; the food tasted that bad.

"It's a very upsetting topic," Nellie confessed. "He and I . . . I am trying to get away from him." She finished in a whisper and let Tillie's imagination do the rest.

"Ohhh." Her eyes went wide and undoubtedly horrible visions danced through her head. She was painting Nellie as a tragic heroine, most likely. A foolish young girl who fell for the promises of a rogue. It couldn't be further from the truth, but that was right where Nellie wanted her to be, so . . . Tillie placed her hand on Nellie's and said, "I know that just because a man looks nice doesn't mean he is."

Breaking. Nellie's heart was breaking. Just cracking right here, at the dinner table, surrounded by women in various states of distress, both mental and physical. Her heart was breaking for Tillie and for her mother, Mary Jane, and for herself. Because Nellie knew it too.

But not about Sam Colton—he made her feel mad and jittery and insatiably curious and like she ought to keep her distance but she wanted to get close to him . . . all at once. She remembered how mad she'd made him in the elevator and how he was still a gentleman about it. Admirable, that. She might even call it attractive.

But he was also a journalist, which meant he would take her scoop and follow up with it—and expose it all before she could—because the public deserved to know or for some other noble motivation. She could tell he was the sort who prided himself on doing thoroughly excellent work. For some reason, that all bothered her.

She'd have to do a bigger and better story. That was the only thing to do. Thus, she consoled herself for the moment.

"I'm so sorry," Tillie whispered to Nellie, who was quite all right, all things considered. She made the mistake of looking into Tillie's eyes. Large, dark pools of feeling, care and concern. Pretending to be insane was one thing. Lying left and right, to perfectly kind girls, was another. This was the hard part. Nellie hadn't planned for it either, so she didn't know quite what to say.

Tillie, who hadn't touched her food because it was cold and she was cold, looked at Nellie curiously. "And also, if you are sane, why didn't you tell the doctor?"

"They don't seem to care much for our declarations of sanity."

"Isn't that the truth." Tillie sighed and Nellie was afraid that she would start weeping again. But no, she had more questions.

"But you told me your name was Nellie Brown and you told the doctor that you didn't know who you were or where you are from."

Damn and blast!

"I'm just wondering why."

Nellie hesitated. She probably could tell Tillie the truth, and should Tillie try to tell anyone, they would dismiss it as the rantings of a madwoman. But the fact was, if Nellie was going to reveal herself, it would have been earlier when she might have saved Tillie. She was too far into the investigation now; she had to stick to it. She had to finish. Especially with Colton out there, running around like he had a lead on a story. Her story!

Tillie was looking at Nellie with those eyes again, the dark ones aching with emotion. Her expression was the only thing warm and vivid about her. She trembled in the cold, rubbing her skinny arms, waiting for Nellie to confess to her. But she couldn't, she just couldn't! She wanted to be the girl with the exposé, the one who got into the madhouse, got the story and got back out (please God, let her get the story and get back out). So she just said, "I'm Nellie Moreno."

"But why didn't you tell the doctor—? And what—? Oh!" Tillie's whole face lit up. "I understand. Don't say a word, but I understand. Blink twice if what I whisper is true." She leaned in to whisper her idea that Nellie Brown Moreno was on the run from that handsome man and she had to fool the doctors into letting her stay here, where she would be safe from that Bad Man (even if he was good-looking) and it all made perfect sense and was darkly, tragically romantic. Not to worry, her secrets were safe with Tillie—no one would believe her anyway! Her soft laughter took on the tinge of a cackle when Tillie remembered again that she was here forever and no one would ever believe a word she said ever again. Then she promptly burst into tears.

EN ROUTE TO BLACKWELL'S ISLAND

The next morning they were fed some sad excuse for breakfast and offered no coffee or tea, which Nellie desperately wanted. She'd slept poorly last night, despite her exhaustion. The nurses had been talking at all hours and the other girls had been crying. It had also been so cold, and she'd only had one moth-eaten blanket to cover herself with. Thoughts of Colton crashed into her dreams, uninvited.

Dreams of him seated at a typewriter, his shirtsleeves rolled up and his elegant fingers dancing over the keyboard as he wrote a story about Somebody's Darling, a lost girl in New York City. In her dream, Nellie shouted at him to stop. "You're stealing my story!" But he only looked up at her with those vivid blue-green eyes and said calmly, "You stole my interview."

So, a nightmare really.

And then, Tillie.

"You didn't blink," Tillie said the next morning. "Last night. I said blink twice if my story about that man was true. You didn't blink."

"You started crying."

"I cried all night."

"I know." Another reason she hadn't slept.

"I'm sorry."

There was a heaviness in the air as they were prepared for departure. Another woman joined Nellie, Tillie and Anne. By eavesdropping on the nurses, they learned that her name was Mrs. Kisner, she was a German immigrant and she spoke no English. She kept asking questions that no one could or would answer. Though no one present spoke a word of German, they all seemed to understand what she was asking: Where are we going? What is happening?

Like Tillie, Anne and Nellie, Mrs. Kisner seemed perfectly sane.

No one in charge seemed to care.

So, the air was heavy as the sad, unfortunate group of women made their last-minute declarations of sanity and appeals for mercy, which were ignored by the harried nurses and the occasional doctor who passed through. The truth settled in heavy on their chests: They were being sent away to a horrid place, probably for the rest of their lives.

They did not want to go and yet they had to put their shoes on and walk down the corridor and sit there and wait for the ambulance and climb into it.

They did not want to do any of these things, and yet—

Should they break into a run during those precious few seconds between the door to Bellevue and being escorted into the ambulance? It was their last chance. Only where would they go? Tillie certainly couldn't go back to her "friends." Mrs. Kisner might manage, and in her heart, Nellie urged her on. But she seemed too polite and she seemed to have faith that if she could just find someone who spoke German they could sort out this whole misunderstanding. That was all this was, a misunderstanding.

And not, say, the tragic theft of a woman's freedom.

But Nellie felt . . . giddy. Was it wrong that she felt giddy? Oh, probably. Cockerill had practically dared her to do this and thought she couldn't pull it off—but she was about to. Her story was within her grasp and, with it, her dreams of making it as a reporter and showing the world just what she could do. Her ticket into Blackwell's was her ticket out of the narrow confines of the ladies' pages. Success meant more work, meant never relying on a man, meant that Mary Jane could come to the city, meant that mother and daughter could be together, safe and secure. That was all that mattered.

So Nellie climbed into the ambulance and took Tillie's hand and tried to ignore the gut-wrenching impact of the girl's sobs. She had glanced around for a glimpse of Colton and hadn't seen him. She doubted that he could reach her at Blackwell's—they weren't letting reporters in and it wasn't as if *he* could pose as a patient. Maybe her story would be hers and hers alone, after all.

After the ambulance ride, which stank of sweat, tears and fear, they arrived at the docks, where the most decrepit little boat waited. It might have seen better days as a cattle barge or trash hauler; now it hauled sad women across the East River. Two women presided over this floating contraption; they were coarse old broads who seemed to have little time, energy or motivation to put toward things like styling their hair or tending to their complexions or taking care with their dress. They clearly did not read *Demorest's Monthly* fashion magazine, Harriet's ladies' pages for the *World*, or even the ladies' pages for any paper. Then again, their work hardly wanted smart attire or the latest fashions or a dewy complexion. How freeing that must be, Nellie thought.

They were all shuffled inside the dingy little cabin, where Tillie was crying, Mrs. Kisner was consoling her in German, Anne sat stoically and the Lady Guards demonstrated a remarkable facility with spitting tobacco. Nellie looked out the dirty window, sneaking her last glimpse at Manhattan.

Sometimes you have to leave the ones you love, she thought, and in her mind remembered not just the city, but her mother back home. Nellie had not told her mother about this assignment.

She didn't want her to fret.

But now, as Manhattan grew smaller and farther away, and Pittsburgh even farther and smaller on the other side of it, Nellie wondered if maybe she should have sent her a note. *Dear Mama, By the time you read this I'll be typing up the story of a lifetime, but if something goes wrong, please come find me.*

She tried to focus on the city buildings, fading in the distance, but a wave of dirty East River water hit the window like a splash of cold water to the face.

And then they arrived. The distance across the water was not great, but the water was cold and the current was strong. One wouldn't want to swim it. One wouldn't even attempt it—unless one was desperate indeed.

Nellie stepped off the boat and took a quick glance around, looking for the landmarks she had learned about. The lighthouse at the far end, north. To the south were an assortment of stone buildings, which she knew to be a workhouse, a penitentiary, a smallpox hospital. This was indeed the island of misfit men and women, sent to spend their days until they expired, out of the way and gaze of everyone else in New York.

Rising ahead was the tall, bluestone Octagon Tower, connecting two three-story wings where the asylum inmates were housed. It was strange and unsettling, intimidating and imposing. The sad group instinctively made their way toward it.

Already she felt a crispness to the air—it was late September, after all. The leaves on the trees were starting to change color, magnificent shades of red, orange and yellow that made her think of fire.

Never mind about fire.

Ahead of her, a large, hairy man appeared at Tillie's side and grasped her tightly by the arm. He couldn't possibly expect that she would try to escape, because there was nowhere to go unless she wanted to take her chances in the East River. Nellie was forced to conclude that he took a little joy in the pain he could freely inflict on women who had no choice but to take it.

Tillie was crying. "What is this place?"

The rough man grunted and grinned. "It's Blackwell's Island. A place you'll never escape from."

Tillie stumbled and sobbed, and this rough man held on tight, dragged her to her feet and urged her on in no gentle terms toward that strange Octagon Tower and whatever lurked within. There were rumors, but no one really knew what went on inside. From the looks of the building, it couldn't be good. Of course a girl would drag her feet for that.

Would this be their last time in the sunshine and fresh air? Nellie tipped her face up to the sky, drinking in the feeling of sunshine on her cheeks and cool air whispering across her skin.

The building loomed. Closer, with each reluctant step. There was one small entrance at the base of the Octagon Tower, and they were jostled and pushed inside. The stench hit Nellie at once. She heard the sounds of footsteps echoing in empty corridors, cooks working in the kitchens, which must be nearby, and the murmur of conversations. It the middle of it all, a spiral staircase rose up and up and up to unimaginable heights.

Nellie let out the breath she didn't realize she'd been holding. She had done it. She had fooled judges, doctors, nurses and everyone she'd met. Now the story was hers, all hers, ripe for the picking.

She made a vow to herself: *Now that I am here, I shall act perfectly sane.*

CHAPTER TWELVE

Colton

WHO IS THIS INSANE GIRL?

The circumstances surrounding her were such as to indicate that possibly she might be the heroine of an interesting story.

—New York Sun

OUTSIDE BELLEVUE HOSPITAL

Colton was skulking around the creepy old hospital hoping to find someone willing to talk. Yesterday, he'd had great luck with Mrs. Irene Stanard of the Temporary Home for Females. She'd been a talker; so had the rest of the lodgers. They'd all gathered in the parlor and regaled him with stories of Nellie Brown, her obsession with murderers and mentions of bad men after her, her laments for her lost trunks and the way she'd stayed up all night terrorizing the woman kind enough to volunteer to room with her.

"And where is she now?" Colton had asked.

"Mrs. Craine left yesterday afternoon. She returned to Boston, where she is from." Colton raised an eyebrow and jotted that down, the soft lead of his pencil recording the memory for later. He circled her name and made a note to dig into whether she'd really gone home or if she'd moved to another boardinghouse.

It wasn't exactly high-stakes, heart-pounding stuff. Nevertheless he felt it: the thrill of the chase. The click of delight as one detail unlocked a door that revealed a new lead that might be the one to break the story wide open. He knew who and what. But he didn't know what next or, for God's sakes, why.

This wasn't the story Colton wanted—he'd rather be investigating working conditions in factories or uncovering corruption at city hall instead of chasing a woman around town. But if there was any woman worth following, it was Nellie Bly. If that was even her real name. He sincerely doubted it. Another note for later: *Find the real Nellie.*

But his first trip to Bellevue, last night, had not been a success.

Colton had pounded on the door and asked his questions but couldn't get a word on the existence (or not) of Nellie Brown. The nurse he'd spoken to didn't have the time of day for the likes of him, unless he paid up, which violated his sense of ethics. He knew Nellie had to be there—the judge had ordered her to go and he'd caught a glimpse of her with the ambulance surgeon looking a little bit afraid. Nurses, he decided, were not paid enough.

Still, he came back to try his luck in the morning. He spotted a sturdy-looking woman in a nurse's uniform emerging from the hospital, looking weary after a long overnight shift. She wore a hat that he recognized instantly, and so he approached and made his inquiries.

"She's gone. Left this morning." The nurse hardly slowed, and he fell in step beside her. Colton had hoped for a friendlier, chattier nurse, but he'd work with whomever.

"Do you know where she went?"

"Why do you want to know?"

"My name is Sam Colton. I'm with the *New York Sun.*"

She muttered something to the effect of "sounds like trouble" and kept walking.

"That's a fine hat you have there. Looks like the one Miss Brown was wearing when she arrived yesterday."

The nurse stopped and stared at him. Her weariness radiated from her. He wanted to ask her a million questions about how she became a nurse, what the conditions were like, what broke her heart or what gave her a sense of satisfaction about her work. He wanted to ask about her hopes, dreams, family. But everything about her said *I'm too tired.*

"She's off to Blackwell's with the lot of them," the nurse finally answered. *Good for Nellie,* he thought. Not so good for everyone else.

"Did she seem insane to you?"

"I'm not paid to think or to evaluate patients." But there was a sharpness in her eyes that told him she did indeed have thoughts and could evaluate patients as well as any doctor.

"What are you paid to do?"

"Keep them in order. Keep them manageable."

"Surely you must have opinions on the doctor's diagnosis. You have a lot of experience, even if it's not recognized."

That got a flash in her eyes, and something about her softened just enough. Then she flashed a wry smile that faded fast. "There's nothing to it, apparently. Just look at them and declare them hysterics."

"Is that what they diagnosed Nellie Brown with?"

"Hysterical mania."

"Is that a condition that could be faked?"

"Why would anyone do that? They'd end up at Blackwell's, and faking insanity would be the last thing they ever did."

Colton didn't have a good answer. He wasn't going to give up Nellie's reason, anyway. Not yet.

"What awaits her at Blackwell's?"

"Nothing good."

"Can you give me any details? Anything—how many other patients are there? What are they suffering from? Can you tell me about the food, the conditions, what do they do all day?"

She finally looked at him. "Trust me, you don't want to know."

But Colton *needed* to know. He had gotten hired on the basis of this one story—unmasking an exposé in progress—and Colton would be damned if he blew this chance to make a name for himself in the New York press. Or, to be honest, in his weaker moments, he would be damned if he missed this chance at payback for her stealing his interview.

He'd gone to press with the first part of the story—an "insane girl" going by the name of Nellie Brown or Nellie Moreno had been discovered with no memory of how she got to New York or where she'd come from. Colton carefully didn't mention that the whole thing was a sham. Not *yet*. The more column inches he got out of her story, the better.

He'd traced her as far as the haunting, haunted Bellevue Hospital. He learned she'd been transported to Blackwell's, where the asylum was considered the worst fate out of all the terrible options on the island: penitentiary, smallpox hospital, workhouse.

Then he met a dead end.

He could get on the island, but no farther. The asylum had proven difficult—no, impossible—to get into as himself, a reporter. Most of the doctors and nurses employed there also lived on the island, and when he caught up with them at the ferry on their nights out and days off, none were willing to talk. They gave him that same wary, terrified look and flattened their lips and quickened their pace.

At the same time, the story started to catch on in the city. People were curious about this nice, respectable girl who didn't know her name or home, who had been locked away. They were hungry for details and Colton was keen to provide them.

There was just one problem.

She wasn't getting out. He couldn't get in. And the clock was ticking on his deadline. Colton would have to try something else. Something that would tell him more about *her.*

CHAPTER THIRTEEN

Into the Madhouse

In spite of the knowledge of my sanity and the assurance that I would be released in a few days, my heart gave a sharp twinge.
—Nellie Bly, *Ten Days in a Mad-House*

THE INSANE ASYLUM AT BLACKWELL'S ISLAND

Upon arrival, the sad, unfortunate souls from Bellevue were shuffled into a small, dark room off the entrance chamber. The clothes Nellie had arrived in were unceremoniously stripped off in full view of the others (well, hello there) and taken away to God only knew where. They were given a different set of clothes to wear—well-worn and threadbare gowns, not fitted to anyone and so fit no one and offered little protection from the cold whipping in off the river.

Nellie wanted to laugh at how silly she must have looked in this asylum uniform, with an underskirt longer than the stained calico overskirt. But no one else was laughing.

In the midst of all this, her notebook and pencil were confiscated. "You'll have no need of this," an attendant said with a laugh. When Nellie demanded it be returned to her, the attendant insisted that she had hallucinated all of it. In fact, she insisted so thoroughly that Nellie almost wondered if she *had* hallucinated it. She thought of Harriet's warning: *Try not to actually go insane.*

Just like that, with her belongings taken and dressed in clothes that were not her own and didn't fit, she was no longer Nellie Bly or Brown or Moreno or any of her made-up names. She was just whatever real and true fragments of herself were buried too deep in her heart to be stripped away with her dress, stockings, underthings, gloves, notebook.

Next, they were lined up against a wall and made to wait. For what? And why did the mere act of waiting make Nellie feel eager to go on to the next thing, when the next thing was probably terrible?

It was a good time to steel her resolve and remember her first objective in being here: *survive.* Nothing else mattered if she didn't emerge with her wits intact and her memory full of things to write. Survive, in spite of whatever dire conditions she was faced with, whatever tortures she might endure, whatever pressures on her sanity might persist. She had to live and she had to stay true to herself. Surviving the madhouse already seemed daunting, and she was still stuck in the waiting room.

"How do I look?" Nellie tried to joke with Tillie but it fell flat. No one was in the mood to jest, and there was really no making light of the situation. With their clothing gone, their identities gone, separated from their homes and "friends," what were they now but just bodies in sack dresses, burdens upon the state, from now until death did they part?

Nellie decided to be quiet.

In the quiet, she listened. There was the occasional shout and some high-pitched chatter. There was some banging, the occasional shriek. Nellie heard footsteps marching up and down the hall and the *clink* and *jangle* of a rope full of keys as its bearer took brisk, purposeful steps. But for an asylum with hundreds and hundreds of women, it ought to be louder. Silence suggested they couldn't talk. Or wouldn't talk. Or had given up entirely.

Finally, a nurse in a uniform of striped dress and white apron arrived and gruffly indicated that they should follow her. Follow her they did, up the stairs curving around the interior of the Octagon Tower. Next, they shuffled down a long, dimly lit corridor. The smell got Nellie first: stale air, decay, the death of hope, the stink of despair. It was the sort of air that was unpleasant to inhale and made one's lungs feel tense and tight. They walked past a kitchen, and Nellie craned her neck to peek in but saw little activity. Then they were shuffled through a pair of doors that opened to a large room.

There, she faltered.

Nellie had always thought of herself as a girl with gumption. With more than her fair share of pluck, spark, grit, courage . . . all those qualities that made her a vexing girl who could not just fit in and be ladylike, no matter how many pink ruffly dresses her mother put her in.

But this made her stomach turn.

Made her heart sick.

Made her think, *Dear God, what have I done?*

This was where they all were: the madwomen of New York. This room, in the heart of the asylum. It had once been painted yellow in a likely attempt to be cheerful, but the color was now faded, stained and peeling. Good times gone awry. The room looked and smelled like piss.

Straight-backed benches lined the perimeter, and upon them sat the women. In normal times, Nellie would have given them a discreet glance and moved on or smiled politely. But these were not normal times and she allowed herself to really look.

One after another, the women wore the same ill-fitting dress of coarse muslin and calico that Nellie wore now. And they were just sitting there, one after another, staring blankly. Some were chattering to invisible people; one woman was laughing, though Nellie didn't see anything to provoke such a reaction. One or two were crying, but they obviously had reason for tears. Mostly they looked bored and depressed. They were all different ages, from tragically old to tragically young. Most seemed to dwell in some endless middle age where the bloom of youth was gone but they were not near death yet.

Though they all looked different, they had in common stringy hair and dull, ashen complexions that spoke of a lack of sunshine and sustenance. The look in their eyes—dead, dying, haunted—made Nellie shiver, and not just from the cold.

Why didn't they talk? Why didn't they move?

That's when Nellie saw her: an older woman in the corner mumbling to herself. Her voice was low, but she was very animated by what she was saying. She still had something to say. But a nurse strolled over and smacked her across the face and told her *enough.* She wasn't so mad that she wasn't stunned by it. Both Nellie and the woman.

Nearby a woman was rattling the bench. Nellie noticed that her wrists were bound to it with thick, worn leather. Was she violent? What would happen if the restraints were removed? Were they all in danger or was she just in trouble?

Nellie, Anne, Tillie and Mrs. Kisner were led into the room, walking past all these women, who gazed upon them, soaking in the sight of something new, something other than faded yellow walls and familiar insane faces. No one said hello. No one said anything at all. But they looked, long and hard.

Get their stories. She'd have to befriend them, get them to talk, to remember. She'd have to hold in her head all their sad stories and cautionary tales. If only they would talk. Why didn't they talk? They didn't so much as whisper to one another. Maybe there wasn't much to talk about anymore.

There was a window at least, with a view of the river and Manhattan in the distance. Something to dream of, she guessed. Or perhaps a certain kind of torture to be trapped here and to look out *there,* where people were living and breathing in freedom. That is, if you got a seat with a view of it.

In the center of the room there was a table with a white cloth, a heavy book and nurses seated around it, casually conversing quietly among themselves while sipping coffee. They all wore the same uniform of brown striped dresses, white aprons and white caps. They were also bundled in thick woolen sweaters as protection from the cold wind that came off the river and rattled the windowpanes. They seemed unconcerned with the madwomen around them.

A nurse indicated that Nellie, Anne, Tillie and Mrs. Kisner were to find seats on benches meant to seat three, though most had five female bodies squished onto them. Holding her breath, Nellie eased onto one with Tillie, and despite her attempts to adjust her position—not that she had many options—she couldn't seem to get comfortable. Beside her, Tillie trembled and sighed. Yesterday, they had been strangers, but now it was a familiar sound.

"I'm so cold," Tillie whispered.

"My back," Nellie muttered, as if she were an old woman and not just twenty-three.

Mrs. Kisner said something in German.

One of the nurses in the middle of the room turned toward them. She had blond hair and blue eyes and might have been pretty once, but it seemed some hard knocks had done away with her sense of warmth and kindness. "You'll learn soon enough, there's no talking here."

Nellie, being Nellie, thought to herself, *We'll see about that.* She had come here for stories—not just her own—and she was going to get them.

Mrs. Kisner, who still seemed concerned about this misunderstanding she had found herself in, did the rational thing and approached the person in authority. In this case, the Mean Nurse (Nellie thought the nickname fitting until she learned her real name). "You must stay in your seat," she said sharply. But either Mrs. Kisner didn't understand or she was undaunted. What *was* happening here, anyway? What were they waiting for?

Nellie watched avidly as Mean Nurse turned instead to a man who had just entered. He was boyishly handsome, with thick chestnut-colored hair and bright blue eyes. "Dr. Kinier, hello." She smiled. The doctor did not seem old enough to have graduated from medical school, let alone be practicing medicine. "We have some new patients for you to see."

"Kann mir bitte jemand sagen was hier los ist?" Mrs. Kisner asked politely, interrupting. "Das muss ein Missverständnis sein."

"What is she saying, Miss Grady?" Dr. Kinier asked with the barest glance at Mrs. Kisner. She was too old, too ill, too foreign, to be of interest to him. "Don't you speak German?"

"I have no idea, Doctor. You know I only speak English." Miss Grady was gazing at him intently, but for his part, the doctor avoided looking at all the women and instead concentrated on his clipboard of papers as if it were his salvation.

Mrs. Kisner persisted, and Mean Miss Grady waved her off again.

"Sit down," Miss Grady growled.

"These damned foreigners. Don't know why they have to send them all here," the doctor muttered. "Who is next for an examination?" He flipped through his pages with a huff of annoyance. "Tillie Mayard."

Tillie took a big deep breath. Squared her shoulders. Nellie could just feel the girl summoning all her courage and the very last of her strength. *This was her one and only and very last chance.* She would calmly tell them that there had been a mistake, that she was perfectly sane, just unwell. She would take any test to prove it. What she really needed was a warm bed and some rest and she would be back to herself in no time, ready to work and be good and helpful and everything a young woman ought to be.

The door closed behind Tillie and the doctor. As Nellie waited, a sickening feeling in her stomach gained hold because she was not optimistic for Tillie's prospects.

Mrs. Kisner tried again to approach Miss Grady. "Bitte, bitte. Das muss ein Missverständnis sein."

This time Miss Grady snapped at her, in flawless German: "Setz dich and sei still!"

EXAMINATION ROOM, THE INSANE ASYLUM AT BLACKWELL'S ISLAND

When it was her turn, Nellie sat on the examination table, cold and alone, with Tillie's cries that she was not insane ringing in her ears and aching in her heart. "Test me!" she had pleaded and sobbed. The doctor had brushed her off after a cursory examination that all new patients seemed to undergo. Really, the whole thing couldn't have taken more than five minutes. It made the poor girl hysterical with fear and rage, so much so that she did seem . . . crazy.

Though Nellie now hesitated over the word. *Crazy.*

What would the doctor say about *her*?

Dr. Kinier walked in just then, and didn't even spare a glance at Nellie, perched on the table. Instead, he went to a desk, where he started looking at his notes. Her hopes were not high for her experience with Dr. Kinier. Already, Blackwell's did not seem like a place that would attract first-rate medical talent.

Nellie watched him and wondered what this young boy doctor could possibly know about insanity, or what he could possibly have learned about the bodies, minds and lives of women. Then again, what did any medical professional know? They still thought a woman's organs wandered aimlessly around her body, like a woman who misplaced her purse and rushed around the house trying to find it before leaving the house. Nellie didn't have a medical degree herself, but it couldn't possibly be true.

A nurse, Miss Grupe, trailed in after him, all soft chestnut curls and giggles and a uniform that she must have tailored herself; it fit her very well. It was clear in her starry eyes and longing glances that she had hopes for the doctor; all her attentions were fixed on the doctor, and she had nothing to spare for the patient. She ought to have been pretty, with her dark hair and bow mouth, but something about the arrangement of her features made her just shy of lovely. Maybe it was the surroundings; doom and gloom were hardly flattering to anyone's complexion or spirit.

Maybe it was the giggling.

Lord save Nellie from girls who giggled.

What a luxury that was, to be silly. And to not be punished for it either.

"Nellie Brown," Dr. Kinier murmured as he looked at his papers. "Now, why does that sound familiar?"

The young nurse giggled, her curls shaking, her bow mouth quirked into a smile. "She's the one in the papers."

If the doctor had anything to say about that other than *hmmm*, Nellie missed it.

Because Nellie should not be in the papers.

Not yet.

She hadn't written a word. She had only just got here.

There was no story *yet.*

And yet.

"Colton." She hissed his name under her breath. It had to have been him. It could only have been him. Sam Colton, hot on her tail and chasing her story to make it his own. He must have had a late night writing up whatever facts he'd managed to gather about her. But how?! What he did, that thief, was claim the topic and the territory.

Just like that, she was a follower. Of her own story.

"It was in the *Sun,* I think?" the nurse said, her voice all airy-fairy, like the doctor would think less of her if she knew her stuff. The *Sun* definitely meant Colton. The *Sun* meant the *World* had been scooped. The *Sun* covering her and this stunt meant that her story was already less valuable.

Damn and *blast.* Nellie looked toward the door. Closed and locked, and even if she were to escape this little examination room, she'd never make it out of the asylum or off the island. It was an acutely agonizing experience to know that the world was going on without her and she was shut off from it with her hands tied.

Hell and damn and blast.

The doctor finally stood and peered at her, now that she was famous, because she was in the papers. "She does look nicer than most of the women we see here." He shined a light in her eyes and she squinted. "She's probably as cracked as the rest of them, though."

"I'm not cracked," Nellie said.

The doctor just smiled. "That's what they all say."

And then: "What is your age, Nellie Brown?"

"Um, I was nineteen last May." A lie. She was twenty-three. Either way, she was too young to be committed here for life.

Dr. Kinier proceeded to poke and prod at her. He checked her ears and tapped her knee and looked at her throat. How any of that determined her sanity she knew not. As he performed this cursory examination and moved on to listening to her heart, her lungs, he spoke to Miss Grupe.

"When do you get your next day off?" It took Nellie a second to realize the doctor was asking the nurse while listening to Nellie's lungs.

"Saturday," the nurse cooed. "And you, Doctor?"

"I as well. Will you go to the city?"

"I will if I'll see you there," she answered with a smile, while the doctor took Nellie's pulse and she wondered just what the nurse was here for and what the pulse of an insane person was like. Was it any different from that of a person who wasn't insane?

"I hope so. Will you measure her?"

The doctor moved back to his desk and began to write his notes. *Nellie Brown has a pulse, draws breath and is rumored to be written up in the papers.*

Nellie hopped onto the cold metal scale while the nurse made a show of fumbling with the various elements.

"Her height?"

"Five foot five," Nellie answered.

"You know I can't tell, Doctor." Miss Grupe giggled *again*, and Nellie thought she might actually go mad from listening to this. She wanted to shake the girl and tell her not to play stupid to get the attention of some man. But what was Nellie doing if not the same thing? What a world they lived in that made women pretend and still no one ever took them seriously.

In an instant the doctor was by her side, leaning in close to her (the nurse, not Nellie) and taking advantage of the opportunity to press up against her (again, the nurse and not Nellie, thank God).

The doctor adjusted the scales and murmured into the nurse's neck. "Her height is five feet, five inches. Do you see?"

"Hmmm."

"Seriously?" Nellie questioned.

"I'll need her weight next," the doctor said. "And when are you going to supper?"

"Six o'clock, and I'll need your help, Doctor."

The business repeated itself. With every excuse to brush up against each other taken. *At least it's not me,* Nellie thought. She just sat there while they flirted around her and took some occasional notes. She marveled at what a curious feeling it was to be here—to be alive and present and breathing the same air—but to be utterly ignored. It made the mind start asking pesky questions: Did she actually exist? Maybe she ought to pinch herself and see. Maybe she ought to say something.

"I'm not sick," Nellie declared in the strong voice of a woman who burst into newsrooms, demanding assignments and getting them. The doctor and nurse both just murmured *hmmm* but otherwise ignored her. "I do not wish to stay here. No one has a right to shut me up in this manner."

Dr. Kinier finished his notes and shuffling his papers and asked the nurse to see Nellie back to the others—she was just another crazy lady now—and when did her shift end for the day? As Nellie returned to the others, she thought, *Three. Three doctors she had been able to fool.* She wanted to claim it was a result of her tremendous acting skills, but it was obvious that the doctors simply didn't care enough to look closely or even listen when the women spoke. She'd come expecting evil, but indifference was proving to be just as dangerous.

CHAPTER FOURTEEN

Behind Asylum Bars

"You must force the food down . . . else you will be sick, and who knows but what, with these surroundings, you may go crazy. To have a good brain the stomach must be cared for."

—Nellie Bly, *Ten Days in a Mad-House*

With a shout instructing us to go into the hall, the women were thus invited to stand in line for supper. When she stood, Nellie's back already ached from sitting on the bench. She shuffled with the rest of the patients out of the room and into the hall, where they were all lined up.

A wait ensued.

It was an opportunity to stretch her limbs and she took advantage. Tillie, poor thing, was too tired to talk, so she just leaned against the dirty plaster wall with her eyes closed, singing softly to herself "to keep her wits about her."

So, Nellie talked to the other women in line.

She met Elsie, who was the same age as Nellie's real age. She spoke of a loving family and wonderful life, her studies, her charities. But she lost her intended suddenly, in a violent way. She suffered from a melancholy so thick and deep she could scarcely move or eat. She never smiled anymore. And the nightmares—oh, heaven help her, the nightmares. She apologized in advance for her screams. Her family had wanted to help her, Elsie told her. For years, they had tried. And here she was, hoping she might see a doctor, but it had been months or years and no one had spoken with her. She had come here for care, and it wasn't helping.

A white-haired woman with pink cheeks—Nellie was told she went by Mathilda, if anyone spoke to her at all—was engaged in a very passionate conversation with no one. Something about rents and bills and lawyers taking advantage. Lud, was this woman giving someone a piece of her mind and then some. Her tirade drew the ire of Miss Grady, who pretended to whisper something in her ear, but spat instead. Mathilda wiped her ear and said nothing. She stayed in line after that.

"Does she do this often?" Nellie asked Elsie, who said, "Yes. I envy Mathilda's spirit, to be honest. Mine is long gone."

"I meant Miss Grady. Is she always so violent?"

"Oh yes, they all are."

There was a mother of five who had been committed after "never quite recovering from her last baby" and just needing a moment's peace *or else,* and now she was here and sad and confused.

"I'm sorry," she said, and she started to cry.

Mrs. Kisner had found some other German-speaking women who were trying to gently break the news to her about where she was and when she would get back to her flat, her friends, her life (probably never), and Mrs. Kisner seemed a bit broken now, to have learned of it.

"How many times must I tell you to keep in line!" Miss Grady barked. She made her way along the line of women, pushing and shoving them into position. A gentle word would have done just as well, but she used the force of her body and temper instead.

All around Nellie were women in terrible states. Some were talking to themselves; others were laughing or weeping at nothing in particular, just everything. One ancient woman with a deeply lined face kept winking and nodding and uplifting her hands in a manner that Nellie could not seem to make sense of.

Most of them just seemed sad.

Behind Nellie stood a woman who somehow managed to seemed poised, even though she wore the same ill-fitting clothes and vacant stare as everyone else. It was the kind of poise that Nellie might have had, if the judge hadn't died without a will, leaving Mary Jane and her at the mercy of the wolves. The kind of poise she could have had if there had been money to stay in school, and perhaps take some lessons. Shoulders back, spine straight, head aloft as if a half dozen books were perched there.

When Miss Grady tromped by, she bumped against the poised woman, who said nothing.

Nellie touched the woman's shoulder and asked, "Are you all right?"

She was pretty. Or had been, once upon a time. Her skin was now sallow; her hair hung in a greasy braid. Her eyes were vacant. Haunted, maybe, if she wanted to romanticize it and spin ghost stories about her. Like she had seen things that she could not unsee. Like the candle inside her had been snuffed out. Now she was just this shell of a woman.

"I'm Nellie and this is Tillie."

Tillie was still leaning against the wall with her eyes closed.

"What's your name?"

At first, her reply was hard to hear. It was so faint, so mumbled. But Nellie leaned in close and listened. "Rose. Daisy. Violet. Rose. Daisy. Violet."

"Which is it?"

Beside her, Tillie confided in a low voice, "I heard them calling her Princess."

Which is to say no one knew her name. What had to happen that a woman forgot her own name?

The dining room at the asylum was like the Ladies' Ordinary back in the city, except terrible. A circle of hell, certainly. There was a roar as all the patients made a dash for spots and crowded around long tables, vying for a seat and for food in a desperate, uncivilized scramble for space and meager offerings. Some women were left standing, without a spot at a table or a dish in hand, and Nellie saw at least one start to weep from frustration. There was not enough to go around.

Fortunately, Nellie and Tillie found themselves squeezed in at a table; seated opposite was a woman with her head bowed in prayer. A waterfall of jet-black hair obscured her face. Her hands, chapped and skinny, were clasped together.

"Dear Lord," she intoned. Nellie and Tillie fell silent. Was that an Irish accent she detected? Yes, quite possibly. Wouldn't be the first she heard here today. "Thank you, I guess, for this disgusting excuse for a meal. I beg of you, Lord, please kill me before morning. I eat this vile sustenance in the hope that it is poisoned. Hopefully yours in Heaven soon. Amen."

She lifted her head, and when she caught Nellie and Tillie staring at her, she grinned. "Have to find my amusements where I can."

Nellie would guess her to be a little older than herself, and a lot more rough around the edges. When her hair fell into her face, she let it hang there, rather than tuck it behind her ears.

"You're new here," she said pointedly.

"I'm Nellie. This is Tillie."

She didn't introduce herself. Instead she said, with no small amount of sarcasm, "Welcome to dinner at Blackwell's. Please, enjoy."

Only then did Nellie look down at her plate—just her plate. No cutlery, tablecloth or napkin accompanied it. Her stomach sank while her throat closed.

"Tonight we have the finest prunes, and by finest I mean revolting," Prayer Girl began.

"Ew," Tillie whispered. Nellie's stomach turned to look at them.

"This mysterious pink liquid is presented as tea, but I can assure you it is not tea," Prayer Girl continued with her tour of their evening meal.

Nellie stared down at the last thing on her plate, a slice of bread with butter. It was unappetizing but still her stomach rumbled. It'd been ages since she had eaten. Just some crackers this morning, a bit of that cold and unsalted beef last night. Nellie took a bite and gagged as the taste of rancid butter hit her tongue, and the "tea" she sipped only made the hell in her mouth worse.

Only one week. She only had to survive one week.

"You can ask for a slice of bread without butter," Prayer Girl said. Too little, too late. She knew it too.

"But can you ask for a slice without worms?" Tillie held up her own slice of bread, and even in the dim light, you could see them. No longer squirming, but baked to death.

One week. Only one week.

"Rose. Daisy. Violet. Rose. Daisy. Violet."

"Don't mind her," Prayer Girl said, nodding in the direction of Princess, who was repeating those words over and over. She was picking at her food with a delicacy no others seemed to possess. When a nurse arrived with a drink for her, only her, she stared at it for a moment before she was forced to drink it. Every. Last. Drop.

"You don't want what she's having," Prayer Girl said. "Or maybe you do?"

Nellie asked what the cup contained, but Prayer Girl's only answer was another grin. She seemed like trouble, but she also seemed like she knew this place in and out, knew her way around and was willing to lend a hand or at least a word of advice. Even if it was too little, too late.

"So, New Girls, how did you end up here?"

Nellie dropped her truth. "A misunderstanding." Not technically a lie, even if it wasn't half the story of how Nellie had ended up behind asylum bars.

"Turns out my friends are not my friends," Tillie said. She was trying to be strong and perhaps even flippant, but her trembling chin gave her away. For the first time, Nellie wondered if the betrayal was hurting her as much as anything. *Women have to look out for each other,* Harriet had said.

"Your *friends* put you here?" Prayer Girl was incredulous.

"They brought me to Bellevue to recover from an illness . . ." She told her story. It was just as sad as the first time she recounted it. But now Nellie wondered who was supposed to care for those who cared for others. This was the place for those who had no one. *Inconvenient,* as Harriet had said.

"You need better friends," Prayer Girl remarked. Then, with a heartbreaking cackle, she said, "But I guess it's too late for that."

Tillie's shoulders sagged.

"What about you?" Nellie asked. "How long have you been here?"

"Too long."

"How did you come to be here?"

"Bad luck."

"Are you insane?"

"What do you think?" Prayer Girl retorted. "Wait—don't answer." She took a bite of bread—plain, without butter—and chewed and chewed like she didn't want to answer.

"What's her story?" Nellie asked, indicating Princess, to change the subject.

Prayer Girl shrugged. "I think she has amnesia. Or maybe it's the laudanum or maybe chloral. I'm convinced the nurses are dosing her with something to keep her . . . *agreeable.* I'd like to get my hands on some. A lot. A fatal dose, in fact."

"Do you really want to die?" Nellie asked.

"Look at me. Look at this place." Prayer Girl gave her a look. Like, *death, please.* "I don't even know how long I've been here. Time loses all meaning. And so does everything else." She fixed her green eyes on Nellie, and it was unnerving. Nellie didn't think she was insane—what was insanity anyway?—but there was something sharp and unpredictable about her. She had nothing to lose. Nellie was captivated, in spite of her better judgment.

Beside them, Princess was eating. She held her knife and fork and elegantly cut tiny pieces of prune and bread and chewed and swallowed and seemed oblivious to the taste and texture of the food in her mouth and the horrified looks of those around her.

"I guess she has something to live for," Tillie said. Given how the air was thick with despair and disgust, she was probably the only one. But still, Prayer Girl grinned like she had new toys. "Just wait until you see what comes after."

THE BATHS

After supper, the nurses shouted at the women to line up, which they did in a fumbling manner, and they were marched down the hall to a cold, wet bathing room. Nellie peeked ahead and glimpsed a row of tubs and naked women being forced in, scrubbed roughly, and unceremoniously doused with buckets of water. Rinse. Repeat.

There was no change of water.

One after another, the women were forced into the tubs, each soaking in the previous women's dirt. They didn't fight as much as Nellie anticipated—or planned to herself—and that was almost more unnerving. They must have given up.

"Everything you've heard is true, but worse," Prayer Girl said. Tillie started trying to sing to herself again—Nellie noticed it was how she soothed herself—but her voice cracked and the tears started falling. All the other women showed numb acceptance, as if they knew it was better to simply endure than to fight.

"Clothes off, ladies!" The nurses went down the line, forcing each woman to remove her clothes, pulling off overskirts and yanking at petticoats. They tugged at braids and wrenched arms out of sleeves. And then they got to Nellie.

"No, no, no—" Nellie protested. It had been a *day* already. She did not want to undress in front of all these women. She did not want to be exposed to the air and their eyes. She did not want to get in those cold, dirty tubs. She clung to her standard-issue garments, stained and ill-fitting as they were. She was not one of them; she would not be one of them. She tried to argue all these points; she tried to tell them that she'd only just arrived and was still clean.

"You can do it yourself or we'll do it by force," Miss Grady said. She bent her face close to Nellie's. "We won't be gentle."

They weren't gentle. Nellie's clothes were wrenched off and she was left standing there, naked and shivering and sick at the prospect of being seen, of getting into that revolting water, of being brutally scrubbed down by rough, uncaring hands.

And then before she knew it, she was plunged into the cold tub. Oh *f*— it was cold. Piped-in-from-the-river-in-October *cold*. A strong-armed, insensitive matron took a pad of soap and began to scrub Nellie all over her shivering, naked body. She couldn't look at the water she sat in. Didn't dare. She could only beg.

"Not my hair. *Please* not my hair."

They soaped up her hair. And then without warning one, two, three buckets of frigid, filthy water were unloaded on her head. It got in her eyes, her nose, oh God her mouth. Was she drowning? It felt like she was drowning. She couldn't catch her breath. She could only choke and try to spit out what she could.

And then Nellie was hauled out of the tub, shivering and goosefleshed and feeling near death. Someone handed her a towel after having just finished using it herself. The woman had violent eruptions all over her body, and there was simply no way that Nellie could bring herself to share it. Instead she shivered and gasped for air until she was handed nightclothes, which consisted of a short flannel slip emblazoned with large black letters that read LUNATIC ASYLUM B.I.H.6. BLACKWELL'S ISLAND. HALL 6. She wasn't a name or even a person anymore, just an occupant of a terrible place.

Wails in a familiar voice had Nellie turning around to look and see Tillie crying vehemently, begging desperately to avoid the bath and if she could not avoid the bath to please, please, please be gentle. "Shut up or you'll get it worse!" the nurse shouted at the poor girl.

Nellie would have gone through all of it again in a heartbeat so Tillie wouldn't have to endure it. But she did shut up and she did endure it, and that was the last Nellie saw of her for the night.

CHAPTER FIFTEEN

Marian

NEW YORK CITY

When Marian left the office of the *Herald* that night, she pulled a hat down low over her brazen hair, arranged the veil and pulled the collar of her jacket up. A plain dress discouraged second glances. She could not be seen, recognized or followed.

From the offices she went uptown to the Ladies Mile, where she spent an hour idling in one of the department stores. Browsing through all the jewelry, ready-made gowns, trinkets and art was an easy way to pass the time—and to lose anyone who might be following her. She could tell the end of the workday was near by the way the shopgirls were starting to wilt and shift their weight from one foot to the other.

When dusk had fallen, the city was darkening and the stores were closing, Marian slipped out and onto the streets. She made her way uptown, where the streets were lined with prestigious brownstones and the avenues were lined with stately mansions, each one with something to prove. Marian knew her way around. This was the neighborhood of her life *before,* when all that was expected of her was the right marriage, in the right dress, to the right man. What a bore.

When she got to a particular brownstone, she advanced toward the service entrance and knocked discreetly on the door. There was no answer for the longest time, and Marian was starting to fear that she wasn't going to get the story after all. The terror of column inches to fill and nothing to fill them with at that hour of the night almost had her breaking out in a cold sweat. Or it would have, if Marian was the sort of woman to sweat.

Finally, the door opened just a crack, enough for a familiar face to peer through. "Did anyone follow you?"

"Doubtful."

"Miss Blake, if anyone finds out that I let you in—"

"Don't worry, Jean. And the *Herald* is always keen to protect its sources. I am as well." A reporter was nothing without her sources. And besides, she and Jean had known each other for ages, as Jean had worked for the daughters of the Four Hundred, who had once been Marian's friends. She was part of the network of intelligence and informants Marian had assembled to do her job. It was comprised of wealthy old friends willing to talk and the servants and tradespeople who supported their lives, who had something to say.

"Follow me." Marian did just that, following Jean through dimly lit hallways. Louisa Newbold, the future Mrs. Wallace, was already out for the evening—perhaps an elegant dinner at Delmonico's, a velvet-lined box at the opera, or any number of glamorous parties. The household was quiet. Marian was careful not to make a sound as they went up and up and up the soft, carpeted stairs.

Finally, Jean stopped to unlock a door on the third floor and pulled out a key. Once inside, the lights were turned on enough to illuminate what Marian had come to see.

The wedding dress.

The Wallace wedding was the sort of society spectacle that was certain to sell papers. Nothing sold like the excesses of the upper classes—other rich people read about them to compare themselves and keep score, many more read about them with a sense of outrage and wonder. No detail was too small or insignificant to be shared widely and earnestly discussed. Everyone had an opinion on the menu, the quantity of champagne or the names on the guest list, even if they hadn't a prayer of being invited. Marian knew this, along with her editor on the ladies' pages, Elizabeth James. Because it was also understood that only a woman could write up the details of a wedding (fact: ask any man in the newsroom) and probably because she had ties to society (unconfirmed rumors, but true) and because there was no other woman to do it (allegedly), Marian went uptown to see about the wedding dress.

This scoop was a far cry from her ambulance story; no lives were at stake in her quest for the story; no person would potentially be saved by her reporting. But it would get her credit. Even if she didn't get a byline, she'd have a story that everyone in the city couldn't stop talking about. That had to count for something.

Even just a sneak peek of a dress. And oh what a dress it was. Pale gold silk with delicately shirred sleeves, puffed at the shoulders. The bodice was fitted, all the way up to the neck, while the skirt was a series of flounces and ruffles, all trimmed in a delicate lace.

"It's a Worth dress," Jean said.

"Of course," Marian murmured.

"It's made with silk and handmade lace in a pattern designed exclusively for Mrs. Newbold." Jean carried on with the details of the dress, including the exact number of genuine pearl buttons down the back, how many yards of fabric were required, the origins of the lace, the number of seamstresses working twelve-hour days. Marian wrote it all down. And then she paused to really have a look at the gown.

One could tell a lot about a woman by her taste in dress, and there were two ways to read this one. First, that Mrs. Newbold wanted to stand out and would do whatever it took to do so. There was no ruffle, pearl bead, flounce or lace detail that she would not employ to make her seem larger than life. This was a dress that gave everyone something to talk about.

Either that, or she was hiding something.

Let's talk about the two dozen pearl buttons on my gown instead of the short amount of time between the death of my husband's first wife and my own wedding. *Let me tell you about the origins of this lace veil* instead of when and how I met my second husband.

When Marian was done with her notes, done observing the dress from every angle, done reading into it, she turned to a fresh page in her notebook and began to do a sketch. She was as good as any society girl who'd spent hours practicing her sketches and studying art. Never once at Miss Porter's School did she imagine that she would use such skills for reporting.

A description of a dress was all well and good, but while she was this far uptown, she might as well fish around for more potential copy. Maybe she could parlay this into a few stories spread out through the week or—be still her beating heart—a Sunday feature.

"What about dresses for the daughters? They'll be at the wedding, of course."

"Of course. But I don't think they'll be happy about it," Jean replied, making a face.

"Still, they have to attend. Otherwise how will it look?" Marian asked dryly. Then she answered her own question. "It'll look like they're still mourning their mother when their father . . . isn't."

"Exactly," Jean said crisply, in a way that gave her opinion on the matter. The poor girls, who had so recently lost their mother, had to dress up and smile as their father married another woman, mere months after the funeral. Heart-wrenching.

"A few months isn't a long time to meet, fall in love and plan a lavish wedding," Marian mused.

"If you're asking whether they were acquainted before Mrs. Wallace's death, I can't say."

Marian nodded.

No one ever thought the first Wallace marriage had been a love match—Winnifred Crowly, as she'd been then, had a fortune, and young Jay Wallace had possessed charm and potential. They had one of those usual society marriages where he busied himself with business, she focused on the children and charity projects and together they went to parties. Wallace could have fallen in love with another woman. That was all too easy to believe. That he'd dallied outside of the marriage and the late Mrs. Wallace turned a blind eye was also believable because it was the way things were done among the Four Hundred.

That she died was a tragic accident.

Marian asked to see the daughters' dresses. She saw three beautiful satin gowns, cut simply in styles appropriate for young women. There were none of the ruffles and frills that would put them in competition with the bride, who of course wanted to be the center of attention on her big day. Just like any reporter wants to be on the front page.

Marian twirled her pencil, then gently bit the end of it. A wedding-dress reveal was all well and good for the Sunday ladies' pages. But if there was something more going on here, it would certainly land her the front page. She just had to ask a few more questions . . .

CHAPTER SIXTEEN

Poor Unfortunate Crazy Girl

People in the world can never imagine the length of days to those in asylums.

—Nellie Bly, *Ten Days in a Mad-House*

THE INSANE ASYLUM AT BLACKWELL'S ISLAND

On her first morning in the madhouse, Nellie woke up to find the woman she'd shared a room with awake and staring at her. Oh God. She wanted to roll over and go back to sleep and dream of being literally anywhere else on the planet, but the nurses were making their rounds, waking everyone and dragging them out to get dressed and get their hair combed with brutal, painful efficiency. Nellie lamented the state of her bangs.

After that it was on to breakfast, which was not worth getting out of bed for, not worth sitting at the table for, not worth spooning into one's mouth. They were all served cold, lumpy porridge with the faintest hint of molasses and tea that had Nellie wondering if maybe it wasn't tea at all, just very filthy water, and honestly it seemed possible. Afterward, the women were all lined up in the hall, shouted at, pushed into line and screamed at as they were ushered into that great faded yellow room, where they all found seats and then—

Nothing.

It had to have been at least an hour, perhaps two, and Nellie still could not find a comfortable position on these benches. They were so exquisitely uncomfortable, they had to have been designed deliberately to inflict torture. When she wasn't squirming in her seat, Nellie was watching the other women. They all watched one another; there was nothing else to do.

Some women mumbled to themselves, which didn't exactly strike Nellie as the hallmark of insanity. Who hasn't done so? Others had nervous tics or a habit of rocking back and forth, and one had to wonder if they were genuinely insane or if they were trying to find what amusement they could. Others wore such sad, hopeless and forlorn expressions that Nellie had half a mind to get up and try to comfort them. Not that there was any comfort to be found. Any movement on or from the bench led to a harsh reprimand from the nurses, who sat at the table in the center of the room as they ate fresh fruit and gossiped about the doctors.

It was a particular torture to watch, especially from where Nellie sat on a painfully hard bench, in a row with Princess, Prayer Girl, and Tillie.

Under her breath, Prayer Girl was muttering a gruesome list of ways to die (Lord hear her prayers). Tillie had run out of tears and was now staring around her in wide-eyed, mute horror. She had stopped singing to herself, and that had Nellie concerned. And Princess . . . her eyes stared blankly ahead and she mumbled about flowers. "Rose. Daisy. Violet. Rose. Daisy. Violet."

"Quiet down, Princess," one of the nurses barked from where she sat in the center of the room.

"Ah, Miss Grady," Prayer Girl said with a feigned fondness. "Not one you want to tangle with."

"So I gathered," Nellie said.

"She once left a woman deaf from hitting her so hard."

"Why? What did she do?" Tillie asked.

Prayer Girl had a one-word answer: "Existed."

"Ah." That answered Nellie's next question—how just two nurses managed to keep a room of at least one hundred women subdued. Some were restrained, she noticed now. Leather cuffs kept them tethered to the arms of chairs and benches. But most of them just sat there, soft heaps of sadness and despair. Fear of being hurt and an acceptance of defeat and the futility of trying anything kept them restrained as much as, or maybe more than, any cuffs—or anything else that might be in use.

Prayer Girl went on. "She's got fists and a key to the crib and she's not afraid to use either of 'em."

"The crib?"

"You don't want to know, New Girl. Not now. Not ever."

"I want to know," Nellie said.

"Imagine a crib—"

"Like for a baby?"

"Yes, but for an adult. And now imagine that crib with a lid that shuts and locks. And now imagine spending the night in that." Nellie shuddered just thinking about it. She had so many more questions: Had Prayer Girl been in it? Did they use it often? What got a person stuck in it? Prayer Girl answered with no, hard to say, and whatever infuriated the nurses that day.

"Do you get a blanket?" Tillie asked.

Prayer Girl rolled her eyes. "Of course not."

Miss Grady looked up at them from a book she was writing in to bark, "No talking!"

"And what's that book?" Nellie asked after a minute, when the nurse was no longer paying attention to them. There was a big, thick book in the center of the table. One nurse was confiding to another, who was writing notes. Prayer Girl explained.

"Oh, The Book. It's where they write up everything. Like, who has 'filthy habits' or who is getting doses of laudanum or worse. Who masturbates too much and who gets violent and needs to be restrained. Who was up all night torturing their cellmates. That sort of thing."

Obviously, Nellie would have to get her hands on The Book.

"Rose. Daisy. Violet." Princess's voice was a soft hum as she repeated those same flowers over and over. Nellie thought she, at least, might have something wrong with her. Nellie wondered what Dr. Kinier had diagnosed her with (if he had even actually examined her) or if there were any notes about her in that book.

"How would a princess end up here?"

"She's not actually a princess," Prayer Girl said with a roll of her eyes.

"But how did all these women come to be here?"

Prayer Girl shrugged. "Seems like bad luck for most of us."

"Bad luck. Bad friends." Tillie was still cold, but now she was getting angry at her friends and fellow servants who had left her to . . . this. There would be no care and no recovery for her unless a miracle happened.

"And now you have us!" Prayer Girl grinned, and her laugh was a cackle.

"No talking!" Miss Grady snapped. Nellie felt the nurse's eyes on her, noticing her, singling her out. That was bad; she did not want to be noticed or remembered. But she did want to know Miss Grady's story. How did one end up employed here? What made her so mean? What heartbreak or bad luck had hardened her? What millions of little indignities had worn away her kindness and consideration for others?

Time passed. It had been two hours or ten minutes, one of the two. "Are we supposed to sit here in silence all day?" Nellie asked.

"Yes."

"Does anyone ever play that piano?" There was a piano in the corner, gathering dust.

"No."

"Someone here must know how to play."

"Princess, probably. She seems like the kind to have had piano lessons, watercolor lessons, flower-arranging classes, but . . ." It went without saying that she was in no condition to do anything.

While the nurses were chatting about Dr. Kinier and their plans for an entertaining night in the city, Tillie heaved a mighty sigh. "I'm so bored that I am excited for dinner," Tillie said, and that was saying something.

They all paused for a moment to consider what cold, stale, rancid horror would be served to them tonight.

"When I get out of here, I'm going to eat a big steak," Nellie said. A big, juicy steak, salted and cooked rare with a heap of butter and a side of vegetables. She could just about taste it, she was so hungry.

Prayer Girl burst out laughing. "You think you're getting out of here."

Nellie forced herself to laugh. Ha ha! But Prayer Girl caught her eye, caught something in her stupid irrepressible smile, and her own smile sharpened as her eyes narrowed. Like she knew. *How could she know?* What did it matter if Prayer Girl knew the truth about her?

They were friends, right?

"No talking!" Miss Grady barked at them. And then shut up. For a moment. The longest moment that Nellie had ever lived. Time seemed to have slowed. Stopped. She felt the weight of it on her chest, and all of a sudden she couldn't breathe.

"So this is all there is until dinner?"

"This is it forever, New Girl."

"Oh God," Tillie moaned.

"Join me in prayer, ladies." They all clasped hands. Tillie's hands were so very cold and her skin felt papery. Yet the touch was comforting. Nellie realized it had been a while—since she had come to New York, in fact—since she'd touched another human, besides being stuck too close to them in a hot, crowded trolley. "Dear Lord. Please have mercy and kill us now. Fast. Slow. Doesn't matter. Though sooner would be better than later."

"Amen."

Nellie couldn't say it. She didn't want to die; she wanted to get out of here. She wanted to stretch her limbs and feel sunshine and eat a steak. She felt desperate to write this story and get it printed on the front page. Or any page. Even the ladies' pages. So the people of New York would know how much suffering happened here. She still had hope and something to live for, and it burned hot in her chest. She *would* get through this. She *would* write about it. And she *would* ensure everyone in New York—no, the world—would know about the terrible treatment. She hadn't been here a full twenty-four hours and already she knew she was in for it.

"That's it!" They were definitely in trouble now. Prayer Girl started grinning. Miss Grady shoved her chair out and stood, and in an instant she had Nellie and Prayer Girl in her grasp and was dragging them out the door. "I said *no talking*."

Miss Grady had Nellie by the hair with one hand and Prayer Girl in the other as she pulled them down the corridor toward the staircase in the Octagon Tower. Prayer Girl was laughing—Nellie hesitated to use the term "maniacally," but it did come to mind—as she called out, "Make it hurt, Miss Grady!" Nellie did not want it to hurt. And she hoped that on the other side of this, Cockerill and Pulitzer himself appreciated what she was going through so they could have some sensational copy to win a man's newspaper sales numbers pissing contest.

"Where are you taking us?" Nellie asked. She stumbled over her own feet trying to keep up as Miss Grady dragged them along. Fear of what came next was making Nellie's heart pound. She didn't want to be locked up in the crib that Prayer Girl had described, or restrained in any way.

"Are you going to give me a black eye like that old woman who came in last week?" Prayer Girl asked. Miss Grady's eyes said, *I want to.* Her lips, pressed in a firm line, said, *Maybe.*

And then, out of nowhere, a man's voice cut in. "Miss Grady, what are you doing?"

She stopped. Prayer Girl stopped. Nellie stopped. They all collided into one another. When Nellie had put herself to rights, she looked up into the warmest, kindest brown eyes she'd gazed into all week. They belonged to a man, fair-haired and mustached, dressed in a suit with a white doctor's coat. He was looking at their little scene with concern, as any decent person would. Under his appraisal, Miss Grady loosened her grip on Nellie's hair, easing the burning sensation on her scalp.

"Dr. Ingram, these two were talking out of turn—"

"Were they violent?"

"Couldn't risk these two inciting the rest of them, Doctor. It's just me and Miss Grupe trying to keep order with nothing to defend ourselves." Miss Grupe, of course, was prone to giggling, daydreaming and flirting with Dr. Kinier at any opportunity. She would be no help at all.

Nellie almost felt sorry for Miss Grady. Almost.

The doctor nodded. "Leave them with me."

And that was how Nellie found herself seated in a small, comfortable room (relatively speaking) with Dr. Frank Ingram, who seemed to possess more years, experience and attentiveness than Dr. Kinier, though that was really not saying much. He had fair hair that he pushed aside, the better for those dark eyes of his to observe and consider the woman before him. What really made her heartbeat quicken was the way he looked at her as if she were a person with thoughts and feelings. He seemed to be listening.

It was comforting and troubling in equal measure. A little kindness after the rough treatment she'd already endured would be nice. But she feared discovery. If this doctor should realize that she was sane and release her, she'd have little to share with the readers of the *World*. She wanted to expose every detail about the mistreatment occurring at this asylum.

Already, Nellie could tell that this doctor would be harder to fool. She knew it the instant she sat down and he put his pen and paper away and fixed her with his full attention. He was not going to fall for her "I don't knows" and "where are my trunks" and other nonsense. She debated resorting to her stock phrases but remembered her promise to act perfectly sane.

"You must be Nellie Brown," he said, his voice calm and pleasant. "I'm Dr. Ingram. I've heard about you."

Outside the room, Prayer Girl waited and prayed. Loudly. *Dear Lord . . . Please, in your infinite mercy, murder meeee . . .* The noises coming from elsewhere in the asylum weren't any more comforting.

And it was all ridiculous, so Nellie said, "What's a nice doctor like you doing in a place like this?"

He laughed. Of course he had a nice laugh.

"I could ask the same of you, Miss Brown."

"Call me Nellie." It would make her feel like less of a liar. She didn't want to lie to him. Which was a problem.

Even more of a problem: She caught herself trying to fix her bangs. Between the trauma of her hair washing last night and Miss Grady's fist today, they could *not* be looking fresh right now. But she was in an insane asylum, for God's sake—dressed in their standard-issue sad scraps of fabric basted together by the drunk and infirm—smelling like the worst of humanity and starving.

Her bangs were the least of it.

Dr. Ingram had to have seen worse.

Never mind that she was not trying to catch a man. She was on *assignment*. She was not here to flirt or make friends. But still she heard her mother in her head: *A doctor, Pink! A doctor!*

"I was talking. We were talking." She gestured to Prayer Girl, who had now moved on to singing rude sea shanties. Dr. Ingram quirked a smile. "There is little else for the women to do here. It is really impossible to expect that women just sit there, all day, with nothing to engage us, and not go mad."

Dr. Ingram stared at her for a second. She felt her skin prickle, like she'd said something wrong. "The women are already mad," he pointed out.

"Well, all this nothing hardly helps," Nellie replied.

"Dare I inquire as to the topic of your conversation?"

"What we would eat if we got out of here. What made Miss Grady so mean. How cold we all are."

Then Nellie noticed what made the room feel comfortable. It was warm, heated by a little stove in the corner. She had to get Tillie in here. Or she had to get the warmth in here out there.

"It is so cold here, Doctor. Many patients are freezing."

"You must not be used to the temperature, coming from Cuba. Tell me, Nellie, do you remember Cuba?"

Had she said she was from Cuba? Had the authorities all decided it? Was that where her trunks were?

"I don't remember anything. But I know that we are all so cold."

"The medical texts suggest that the insane do not feel temperature. I'm not certain that I agree, but the literature makes it difficult to . . ." He paused. She waited. ". . . enact changes."

"But has not anyone seen us? We are shivering in these wretchedly thin dresses while the nurses are bundled up in wool stockings and coats. It's not fair. Not with the chill coming from the river. And it's only October."

"You know the month? I thought you didn't remember anything."

She thought, *Damn it, Nellie.* She thought, *I know all kinds of things, Doctor.*

"Lucky guess. Tell me, Doctor: What happens in the dead of winter?" She made her eyes go wide with terror. "Does the asylum want us all to die?"

"I shall make some inquiries." He did in fact make a note. But he didn't answer her question.

"Ask them for warmer dresses. Shawls. Oh—blankets too! Some heat would be nice. Those unused fireplaces are mocking us."

"Do you mean they speak to you?"

Don't be ridiculous, she almost said. Instead she said nothing.

"The fireplaces had been in use, but we found they caused trouble among the patients," he explained. "On cold days, they would fight for space closest to the warmth. There were numerous injuries. To say nothing of the risk that someone might spread the fire."

The thought of fire in this place made Nellie stiffen. Just for a second before she caught herself and willed her body to relax, but her stricken reaction did not escape Dr. Ingram's notice. Nellie knew about fire, the heat of it. She knew how it felt close to the skin, warming her to an almost unbearable degree. She knew what a danger it could be.

Nellie knew how a little spark, with a little warm breath and encouragement, could become a full-blown fire. A little alcohol, a little kerosene from the lamp and candlelight to read by could become a raging inferno that could take down a house or a whole city block. She knew about how fires started and spread and how they were impossible to stop and control. She knew how fires hurt people.

"I see that you understand. In fact, Nellie, I see that you have some sort of reaction to the mention of fire."

"No, not at all. I don't—"

"I have observed you become still. Your gaze had a faraway look." He leaned forward, like they shared an intimacy, and she felt her skin tingle with awareness. "Like you were remembering something. What are you remembering, Nellie?"

She remembered what it was like to feel hot, bright and unstoppable. She wanted to feel that way again. So any memories or thoughts or feelings about fire were best not examined. Especially not in the presence of Dr. Ingram, of the brown eyes, handsome face and close, caring attention.

"Nothing. Nothing at all."

"It's all right if you wish to talk about something in your past. You can tell me."

"The nurses aren't fond of us talking."

"The nurses here . . ." Dr. Ingram stopped himself, but she caught it and wouldn't forget it: his instinct to confide in her in spite of his professional position and the duties that came with it. She might have one effect on him, which she wouldn't forget. But just when she thought she had an advantage, he spoke to her greatest vulnerability. "Never mind the nurses. Tell me, Nellie. What is it about fire that troubles you?"

Damn him for noticing. But she wasn't Nellie Bly if some man with kind eyes was going to tease out all her secrets and truths from her and turn her into a soft, sobbing female. What happened with the fire was between her and Mary Jane and firmly in the past and none of anybody's damn business. She came to New York to escape the fire and what had happened, so she wasn't going to breathe a word about it now.

But she did recognize that Dr. Ingram had the potential to solve some problems for her in the present. Shawls and heaters and better food were things he could possibly deliver to the patients, making her feel like she was making a difference in their lives right here, right now. All without revealing her true purpose.

CHAPTER SEVENTEEN

Colton

PITTSBURGH, PENNSYLVANIA

Colton had hardly stepped off the train when he confirmed that Pittsburgh had lived up to its reputation as the grimiest city in the country. Everything was sooty. He made his way from the station, straight toward the offices of the *Dispatch,* on the fourth floor of a building downtown. He didn't have time to stop and linger; he had a deadline. He didn't know how long Nellie planned to be in the asylum or how long she would take to write her story once she got out, so he was on a mad dash to gather as much as he could about Nellie and her story before she did.

The train journey to Pittsburgh had not been quick.

Colton thought of how stupid he'd feel if this trip yielded nothing. What a waste of time and effort persuading his editor that he should track the past life of a nobody reporter . . . even if she seemed destined to be a big-shot reporter. He'd mentioned the whole business of Nellie and the asylum to Minnie, and the way her eyes lit up and she begged for details made him reconsider everything he thought about journalism, the ladies' pages and what was considered newsworthy.

If Nellie pulled this off, it would be a huge story. If that happened, Colton intended to be so far ahead of it, no other papers could keep up. But that was a lot of big ifs to justify a long trip to Pittsburgh.

The *Dispatch* had its office on the main street in town, so it was easy to find and easy to talk his way into. The newsroom was full of men at work, typing up copy and rushing around drafts. He spied one woman at work at a desk. She was older, matronly, and was writing swiftly and efficiently.

"Excuse me, ma'am. I'm hoping I could ask you a few questions."

She paused from her writing to peer up at him from behind small spectacles. Her hair was styled elegantly and she had the softness and stoutness of body, and firmness of mouth, that spoke of motherhood.

"I'm curious about a woman who used to work here . . . Nellie Bly?"

If he was tentative, it was because Colton wouldn't put it past Nellie to lie, given the way she'd stormed into his interview and claimed it as her own. Her ease with adopting the persona of Nellie Brown or Nellie Moreno was remarkable. But then again, he believed her enough to take the train to Pittsburgh, of all places.

The woman before him narrowed her gaze and pursed her lips before she spoke sharply.

"Do you think that just because she's a woman and I'm a woman, both working at the same newspaper, that we must have been bosom friends? Or do you think that my deadlines are not as important as anyone else's?"

Colton backed away slowly. "I'm sorry for bothering you, ma'am."

"You'll want to talk to Erasmus," she said before turning back to her work.

Colton asked around and found himself at the desk of Erasmus Wilson, an older white-haired man with round spectacles perched upon his beak of a nose. Colton gave his name. "I'm a reporter with the *New York Sun*. I'd like to ask you a few questions about Nellie Bly."

At the mention of her name, the old man smiled and Colton felt the knot in his chest ease. He hadn't come to Pittsburgh on a fool's errand.

"New York, eh? She made it to the city, then?"

"Yes. Are you surprised?"

"I'm not surprised by anything that girl does. Not even when she fails to turn up for work and leaves me a note like this."

Erasmus pulled open the top drawer of his desk and rummaged around until he found the exact scrap of paper he was looking for, hidden among pencil stubs, old notebooks and paper-wrapped candies. He handed it over to Colton, who squinted to read the dashed-off note.

I'm off for New York. Look out for me. Bly.

To his eye, it looked like an impulsively written note about an impulsively made decision. But who just decided to quit their job and run off to the big city at a moment's notice? And for God's sake, *why*? Didn't she know how lucky she was to be working for a paper at all? Sure, he left Chicago for New York, but not without letters of reference and interviews lined up. He'd pursued his big-city dream in the same methodical, deliberate fashion he did everything.

Colton handed the note back, and it was tucked back into the drawer for safekeeping.

"So she did work for the *Dispatch*," he confirmed.

"Of course," Erasmus said, so proudly that Colton was ashamed for considering for a moment that she might have made the whole thing up. "She's a great reporter. We had her writing for the ladies' pages, of course. But she did good reporting on factory girls and other such stories."

"And how did she get her start here?"

"Why are you asking?"

Because I'm trying to ruin her big break. Because I suspected she was a fraud and I took the goddamn train to Pittsburgh on the hunch. But now I'm curious because I've never met a woman like her before.

"It's for a story I'm working on. We're doing profiles of courageous journalists."

It wasn't entirely a lie. It was just 95 percent a lie. After just a few minutes here it was abundantly clear to Colton that Nellie Bly was beloved and no one here was going to spill her secrets easily, especially if they knew he was a rival reporter who had come to ruin her big story. He was starting to feel like a creep. But he was also intently, embarrassingly, dangerously curious about her. All the more so now that he was here and seeing that she had a life, a job and respect from her peers. What made a woman leave that all behind?

"What's she working on now?" Erasmus asked. "She has an eye for a good story."

"A story about conditions at Blackwell's Island Insane Asylum."

"Terrible place, if the rumors are true."

"So terrible the rumors have made it all the way out to Pittsburgh," Colton remarked.

"We read all the New York papers here too," Erasmus said, and Colton was suitably chastened.

"Well, all right, then. Can you tell me how she got a start working here?"

At this question, Erasmus smiled and leaned back. Grandpa was ready to reminisce and tell a story. Colton had his pencil poised, notebook ready. But then he lowered them both and just listened.

"It started with a letter in the paper. A father had written in despairing what to do with his five daughters. Five! What were girls good for besides marriage and housekeeping, he wanted to know." Erasmus explained that he thought this might be a problem faced by other readers. Daughters. What to *do* with them? "That's when Nellie wrote in—she wasn't Nellie yet, she was just Elizabeth then—she wrote such a smart, lively and sharp reply. But she didn't sign her name! Just 'lonely orphan girl,' so we posted a notice and had her come in and write something up, and the rest, as they say, is history."

Colton felt something like a smile. He could just see a younger, irate Nellie outraged at what she'd read. He could just imagine her sitting at the kitchen table, determinedly composing her reply, completely unconcerned that the world was largely uninterested in the opinions of women and girls.

"Do you have a copy of the story?"

"Somewhere around here." Erasmus waved at the stacks of papers surrounding him. Old issues, drafts of new stories, books, source material, God only knew what else. "Nellie has her clips. Ask her; she'll show you."

He smiled, like Nellie carried her clips around with her at all times, just to whip them out and show them off should the occasion come up. Like Colton was friends with her and might meet her for a walk in the park or take her out to dinner. Once he imagined it, the idea stuck and didn't seem so terrible. Colton didn't even know what to do with that. Other than change the subject.

"You mentioned she wasn't Nellie yet."

"It's not her real name, of course."

"Right—the song." Erasmus started humming the tune. *Hi Nelly, Ho Nelly / Listen, love, to me*. And then said, "You know it's not done for a woman putting her real name in the newspaper. She needed another name."

"Only for the announcements of her marriage and death, right?" Colton asked, and Erasmus grunted. That was the unspoken rule about good girls and respectable women. "What is her real name, if you don't mind me asking?"

"Elizabeth Cochrane. Make sure you spell that Cochrane with an *e*. She likes it better that way. She thinks it's more impressive."

Of course she did. He was beginning to get a picture of this Miss Nellie Bly. A woman who burst onto the scene. A woman who spoke her mind. A woman who invented herself from scratch. A woman who claimed space on newspaper pages. A woman who was ambitious and wasn't shy about it.

She was really just a girl named Elizabeth. In this day and age you couldn't swing a cat without smacking a woman named Elizabeth. (It seemed all the others were named Mary. So of course she had to fashion herself into a *Nellie*.)

"Forward-thinking of you to hire a woman," Colton remarked. These days a paper might have one or two women on staff writing, mostly doing the ladies' pages. Or, even better, writing from home and submitting their copy by messenger. A few major columnists—Jennie June or Fanny Fern—had done it like that. For all his years in the newsroom, Colton had never seen one hire a young woman like Nellie and let her go off and do actual reporting.

"Not many editors are so welcoming of the fairer sex in the newsroom," Colton added.

"It's an editor's job to look for good copy that will keep readers interested. Nellie has a knack for finding just those stories. If you haven't noticed yet."

"It'd be good if more editors shared your perspective," Colton remarked. Truthfully. Honestly. Just not by the one editor he was trying to get hired by.

"Hopefully some in New York do," Erasmus said. Then, with a chuckle, he added, "But I don't worry about that one. I ought to, given what she gets up to. But she always lands on her feet."

"Why do you think she left for New York anyway?"

"Nellie . . . she's got big dreams. She's ambitious. She's—"

"Seems like she left suddenly," Colton said. And he gestured to the note. That little note, two lines of scrawl as if written in a rush (or did she always write in a rush?). Two little lines with no explanation of when or where or forwarding address. No preamble or reason. His own sister left longer, more detailed notes when she went out to the butcher to get chops for dinner. "Did she leave suddenly?"

"Maybe? Might have something to do with the fire, but—"

"What fire?"

Suddenly, Erasmus stilled. Even the sparkle in his eyes dimmed.

"You'll have to ask her mother, Mary Jane."

Tracking down Mary Jane proved to be more difficult. Erasmus had provided some direction, but finding his way there, through muddy streets clogged with carriages and workers, was something of a challenge. He persisted until he found her door. One among many in a working-class area where the street was packed with houses and neighbors eyed him suspiciously. Colton hoped he wouldn't get her in any sort of trouble or cause her to be the subject of gossip.

He was already thinking he shouldn't have come—why did he have to chase *this* story? He should be at the asylum, trying his damnedest to talk to doctors and nurses—when the door opened and he was looking at an older, wiser, more tired version of Nellie.

"Mary Jane Cochrane?"

"Who's asking?"

"Sam Colton, with the *New York Sun*. I'm hoping to ask you some questions about your daughter."

"Is she all right?"

How to answer that one?

"I'm reporting a story on her and her work in New York and—"

"So she got a job, then?" Mary Jane smiled with relief and Colton knew two things: that Nellie hadn't lied about having a hard time getting in front of editors and that she hadn't been in close touch with her mother about her madhouse story. Had Nellie just not wanted to worry her? Or was there another reason to keep her in the dark? God, he felt awkward now. "I knew she would."

"Yes," he said. "She's working on a story."

"And you're working on a story about her?"

"Something like that." What a cad he was, coming between mother and daughter. It was his job to be nosy and ask questions and get the damn story. But he didn't want to get Nellie in trouble. Correction: Elizabeth Cochrane with an *e*. Looking around the neighborhood, he could see why she wanted to fancy up her name, to match her bigger ambitions. She was running away from all this, and maybe more.

"Now, tell me, young man." She fixed him with that look that all mothers possess. The one that commanded the truth, pulled it smooth right out of your heart and soul and throat. How did they *do* that? "Would Nellie want me talking to you about her story?"

Colton paused. He could not lie. He couldn't. Not to that *look*. His own mother, may she rest in peace, would come back from the dead to smack him upside the head if he lied to someone's mother. "No, ma'am."

"Then I bid you good day." She smiled as she said it. No hard feelings! She started closing the door and then stopped. She had one more thing to say: "And tell Nellie not to forget her mother and to write to me more often."

Back on the train, Colton looked at his notes again. The opinions, the bursting in and out of nowhere, landing a job by just luck and grit. She seemed to check out. She seemed to be as she presented herself: Nellie Bly, daring girl reporter with ambitions to make it in New York. It might not have been the name on her birth certificate, but it seemed as real as anything else about her.

He smiled thinking about that extra *e* on her name. She really wanted to be somebody and she'd do anything to do it. Colton slouched down in his seat, with some idea of resting now before the train pulled back into the station in the city and he'd be off on his next round of interviews and gathering of facts. He let himself stare out the window at the passing Pennsylvania scenery. The trees were turning from green to deep, luxurious shades of red, orange and yellow. *Like fire.*

Colton startled. Straightened in his seat. Erasmus had said something about fire. He tore through his notes again, and there it was: *Ask Mary Jane about the fire*. But he'd forgotten to ask.

CHAPTER EIGHTEEN

The Horror of Fire

The eating was one of the most horrible things.

—Nellie Bly, *Ten Days in a Mad-House*

THE INSANE ASYLUM AT BLACKWELL'S ISLAND

At dinner that evening, Prayer Girl was sporting a bruise across her cheek.

Truth be told, she wasn't the only one who showed up at mealtimes with a bruise or menacing red marks around the neck. Nellie looked around and saw a handful of women bearing the handiwork of frustrated, angry nurses. Anne Neville, from Bellevue, among them.

"What happened to you?" Tillie asked when Prayer Girl took her seat at dinner with them. Another revolting meal. Nellie requested a plain slice of bread and picked out all the bugs before taking a bite. "Are you all right?"

"Nellie and her handsome doctor interrupted Miss Grady trying to kill me."

"You're welcome?" Nellie ventured, and Prayer Girl just kept up with her sullen expression. She was in a mood tonight. But honestly, who could blame her? The deep purple bruise blooming across her cheek looked painful.

"You don't really want to die, do you?" Tillie asked softly.

"Tell me, Tillie, what do we have to live for?"

"What about someone?" Nellie asked. It was just a question. But then Prayer Girl's eyes softened and Nellie knew it was the right one to ask.

"We were doing all right. Me and Jo," Prayer Girl said.

"Was Joe your sweetheart? Or your brother?" Tillie asked.

"Jo was my friend. She was my everything."

"I hope she didn't turn you in like my friends turned me in."

"No," she said wistfully. "No. She got away."

Nellie had more questions, and the story came out in bits and snaps that she was able to make sense of. Prayer Girl had come over from Ireland and had lost her parents here soon after arrival, likely caused by disease on the ship. It was an all-too-frequent occurrence. As she talked, Prayer Girl's hair fell into her face and she didn't push it away. She'd found a friend in Jo and they had gotten by, begging and living on scraps, doing their best to stay warm and fed and pick up the occasional job. When they could, they indulged in the occasional drink. But then the police had picked them up one night, on the pretense of public drunkenness, and now she was here. She was all very matter-of-fact and detached about it, but Nellie felt like Dr. Ingram, wanting to poke and prod, *But how are you really?* The truth was, she was perfectly sane in a madhouse and condemned here for life, and they all knew it.

She pushed her hair aside and looked at Nellie with a hard, unflinching gaze.

"Instead of asking everyone else questions, New Girl, why

don't you tell Tillie about your nice long chat with the good-looking doctor?"

"There's a good-looking doctor?" Tillie echoed.

"You should try to see him, Tillie. His office is heated."

"Be still my heart."

"That's what I said, and then Miss Grady—" Prayer Girl just pointed to her cheek, then sipped her tea. This was not the Prayer Girl Nellie had come to know. She seemed more subdued. And as Nellie looked around, she realized that was the word for it. Everyone on the outside talked about the shrieking and screaming of the insane, the din and clamor of the madhouse, but this—

This was just the soft din of people eating, some murmured conversations without any of the joy or laughter that accompanies meals with friends or loved ones. Nellie glanced down her table—a long, narrow, crowded table with women crammed in—and she saw Anne, from Bellevue, with a chunk of her hair missing, and shuddered to think what had caused that to happen. Nearby was Elsie, of the violently lost lover, staring morosely at her plate. The poor girl was wasting away. And she saw Princess, nibbling at a piece of bread when a nurse approached her and set down a cup. "Here's your wine, Princess."

Beside her, Tillie whispered, "She gets wine?" and Prayer Girl waved her off. "It's not actually wine."

Princess stared at the glass like it was an enemy she wanted to vanquish but couldn't quite manage to fight. "Drink up, now!" the nurse urged in a voice that sounded cheerful but wasn't really. It was plain to Nellie that she was laughing and mocking Princess. Even in her stupor, Princess seemed to realize it. She also seemed to know that not drinking it was not an option.

"Once I saw her drop the cup. Whatever was inside spilled everywhere," Prayer Girl said. "I think she did it on purpose."

"It's a drug, is it not?" Nellie asked, and Prayer Girl nodded yes. "But why?" Nellie asked.

"Keeps her subdued, which makes her easier to manage." Between Prayer Girl's bruised cheek, Nellie's own sore scalp and now Princess's wine, Nellie was beginning to see. Nurses walked up and down the aisles between the tables, supervising and on guard—against what? That all these desperate, hopeless women might rise up and demand a decent meal and a sweater? They might demand better care—or freedom. The patients greatly outnumbered the nurses—by ten or twenty to one. If they did manage to revolt, there would be no stopping them.

Nellie watched another woman as she slowly scraped rancid butter off a slice of bread with a look of resigned disgust on her face.

Others just sat there in silent protest, wasting away.

Princess drank the wine.

"It also helps her forget," Prayer Girl said, which made Nellie look hard and wonder what she was supposed to forget.

"Here's a question," Prayer Girl said, leaning in. "What would you rather suffer through: Being drugged into submission or the camisole?"

The camisole, she informed them, was not really a camisole. It was a shirt that wrapped the wearer's arms around them, as if they were hugging themselves, and tied in the back so they could not move their arms at all. The treatment was reserved for the violent, the flailing, those prone to outbursts. It was worse than leather wrist or leg restraints but better than the crib.

"But it has sleeves?" Tillie asked. "Is it warm?"

It didn't need to be said, but anyone could see that Tillie didn't have the strength for a violent outburst. She couldn't cause enough trouble to get the camisole, even if she tried.

Nellie had to get that girl in for a session with Dr. Ingram. He was sensitive, the only person in this whole place who seemed to care, and maybe he could see to it that Tillie had a chance to rest and warm up. Nellie might even be able to get him to enact certain other improvements. Sweaters, shawls, *heat!*

And she had to find out what Princess was drinking.

And maybe she had to lead a little rebellion.

NELLIE'S CELL, LATER THAT NIGHT

The first thing Nellie's brain noticed was the heat. It warmed her skin and seeped into her core. It had been an eternity since she had felt warm, and now she was verging on hot. Her body stretched and purred into it, like a cat in a patch of sunlight. *Warmth. Dear God, warmth.* It was the noise that caught her attention next: the *snap, crackle, pop* of flames and sparks licking their way through a building.

Nellie had heard that sound before.

There were screams too. Not the wails of women reliving whatever trauma had brought them here, or women tortured at night by their cellmates or women bored out of their minds, or women who screamed to see if their voices still worked.

Tonight, Nellie heard screams and cries for help. She heard the rattling of bars. She heard panic.

Somewhere nearby, Prayer Girl cackled, her voice rising to be heard over the flames. "Thank you, Lord, for this raging fire. I had only prayed for my own death. You don't have to take everyone down with me, but . . . God's will, blah, blah, blah . . ."

Nellie flung her blanket aside and rushed to the doorway of her cell and looked out. The heavy wooden door was firmly locked, with just a small window mostly blocked by iron bars. She peered out and saw nurses as they rushed down the hall. She heard the *clink* and *clank* of all the keys tied on ropes around their waists, all mixed up with the cries for help and the roar of fire.

On they ran, past the women screaming to be released, on their way to the one exit.

One. Way. Out.

They were taking the keys and they were leaving all these women to die hot, fiery, unnecessary deaths. Nellie among them. "But I don't belong here!" she shouted. "Take me with you!"

Miss Grady turned to look at her. Nellie said *please* and Miss Grady kept going. The nurse from Bellevue was here, wearing Nellie's hat, along with all the doctors and ambulance drivers she'd encountered. They all rushed out together.

Nellie was going to die for this story.

And the story was going to die with her. All the names and notes and tales of woe were trapped in her head and would never see the light of day.

Not like the last time she'd been caught in a fire. She'd been lucky then to find her way out, to emerge from the building unscathed—only to collapse in a heap while her body was wracked with coughs and her clothes were permanently singed.

The flames were coming here now—she could see them, hear them, feel the heat of them on her skin. The smoke was coming too, thick and black and about to choke them all to death. Her lungs were already starting to burn.

The women knew it too. You could hear it in their screams.

"Hey!" Nellie shouted to the nurses still streaming past her cell. "Let me out! I have a deadline!"

The nurses kept going and going. Prayer Girl kept laughing and laughing.

Nellie looked down at her hands.

She was holding matches. Like before, in Pittsburgh.

Why was she holding matches?

CHAPTER NINETEEN

The Evil of Enforced Idleness

> *I was never so tired as I grew sitting on those benches. Several of the patients would sit on one foot or sideways to make a change, but they were always reproved and told to sit up straight. . . . If they wanted to walk around in order to take the stiffness out of them, they were told to sit down and be still.*
>
> —Nellie Bly, *Ten Days in a Mad-House*

THE BENCHES OF UNBEARABLE AGONY

The next morning Nellie woke up cold, hungry, alone. She had only dreamt of the fire. The nurses walked slowly up and down the halls, letting the women out of their cells for another day of inedible food and eternal boredom. "Nurse" was a generous term for these women—"warden" was more like it, Nellie thought. Especially since she'd learned that many of them were inmates from the prison on the south part of the island, enlisted for work at the asylum against their will.

"If there was a fire we would all be dead," Nellie said. She couldn't stop thinking about how vulnerable they all were in here. She couldn't stop thinking about her nightmare.

"Fire? Yes, *please*." Prayer Girl was emphatically amenable to this plan. Maybe too much—one could practically see sparks and flames dancing in her eyes.

Beside her, Tillie shivered, as Tillie did. "Maybe then I could finally warm up."

"Dream a little dream . . ." Together they sighed, imagining this wretched place reduced to embers. They all turned to look at the stove, which sat empty, mocking them. They looked at the nurses, bundled in sweaters and gossiping about the doctors. Miss Grupe had an evening on the town planned with Dr. Kinier and could not decide what to wear. She wanted something that said *Marry me!* because she wanted to get out of here.

Didn't they all.

Nellie didn't want to think much about what awaited all these women should they make it back to the city. They'd be returned to families who couldn't bear them, who found them difficult and inconvenient, husbands fed up with their disobedience. They'd be left to make it on their own on the streets. But at least they would be free.

"We shouldn't get excited. It won't happen," Prayer Girl said glumly.

"Sometimes fires happen," Nellie said.

"Not here," Tillie pointed out. "I haven't seen so much as a candle."

The gas lamps were out of reach and rarely lit. Probably for precisely this reason.

"What do you know about starting fires, New Girl?"

Just like that, Nellie was back, back, back in Pittsburgh. Back in her memories. Ford had been in one of his rages, a frequent occurrence. And she wasn't going to *not defend herself*, was she? She was only human, with an insatiable will to live. One thing led to another. Heat. Sparks. Smoke. She could still hear her mother calling her name, her voice frantic with fear. *Pink! PINK!*

Nellie knew something about fires.

But this was one story that she didn't want to tell. Just in case Prayer Girl remembered it and got free and told someone. Nellie laughed softly, thinking how unlikely that was. Which made her stop laughing. No wonder people thought her crazy. Laughing then stopping for no reason that anyone could see.

"Well, do tell, New Girl. Make something up if you must. We have *all day*."

Nellie didn't want to talk about it.

"Fine. Don't tell me." Prayer Girl crossed her arms over her chest. She tried to slump into her seat, but these benches—good God, these benches were hideously uncomfortable. As if someone had calculated the precise angle for the back to meet the seat that would cause the most discomfort for a female of average size.

"But if you do want to talk about it . . ." Tillie ventured. She didn't say much these days, and when she spoke her voice was so faint it was hard to hear. Any unnecessary speaking or movement sapped too much strength from her, and so she sat very still and quiet and tried to stay warm and stay alive.

But for what?

Nellie sat very still and very quiet and tried to be a good friend.

For what?

"What else are we going to do, New Girl?"

"I have a better idea," Nellie said. With that, Nellie stood up. Prayer Girl hissed at her, "What the hell are you doing? Sit down!" Nellie was steps away from the piano before the nurses noticed what she was doing. The ripple of interest from the women gave her away. The hum of *something*, the sound of heads turning. The nurses called to her to stop, to sit down, to return to her seat. Miss Grady instructed Miss Grupe to run for help from one of the doctors. Then, with her mouth set in a grim line, she started toward Nellie, who sat with her fingers poised above the keyboard.

She dropped them to the keys and began to play. Dust fluttered up. The piano was woefully out of tune. But it was something in a room full of women who clamored for anything.

Because she had a sense of humor, she banged out the notes to "Nelly Bly," the song she'd named herself for. A mix-up with the typesetter had given Nellie her own distinct spelling. Either way, *Nellie Bly* wasn't just a pseudonym or a song. Nellie was turning her into a persona. She was daring. She defied expectations. And she certainly caused trouble.

Plucking out the melody to the song was her own little way of saying *I was here.*

"Stop that!" Miss Grady called sharply. Directed at Nellie, of course, and her brazen display of disobedience. It was directed at all the other women too, some of whom had stood up and started to sway in the awkward manner of those trying to see if their bodies still knew how to dance. When Nellie glanced over her shoulder, she saw the dancing; she saw Miss Grady and the fury in her eyes.

This was going to hurt.

She was going to pay for this impertinence.

But she couldn't regret it until—

"Stop!" A voice she knew cried out with a particular note of anguish that went straight to the heart. Prayer Girl. "Stop!"

For her, Nellie would stop. She let her fingers hover above the keys. She turned to see why. Her heart stopped in her throat as she saw Prayer Girl pushing others away from someone lying on the ground. The patients gathered and gawked at something—

some were still dancing; the music hadn't stopped for them yet—but many others were crowding around to see what had happened.

Nellie abandoned her song and pushed through the bodies. There, lying on the ground, was Tillie. She was in the throes of a fit. Her body convulsed and shook in a terrifying manner. Her eyes rolled back into her head. Prayer Girl was on the floor with her, trying to hold her still, and Nellie dropped to her knees to help. But poor Tillie's whole body was wracked with shakes and trembles and uncontrollable spasms.

Nellie turned to the nearest nurse, who stood frozen when confronted with an actual person in actual distress. "What are you waiting for? Go fetch Dr. Ingram!"

"Witchcraft," one of the women muttered. "The devil," gasped another. They jumbled in close for a better view. Nellie shouted at them. "Get back—she needs air!"

Her eyes met Prayer Girl's over Tillie's body, shaking between them. Was that an accusatory glance? Nellie wondered. Had she not started playing, had she not caused such excitement . . . Eventually Tillie's body went limp, still. She was alive, but whatever had happened had knocked her out.

"I'm sorry," Nellie whispered. "She's really sick."

"She's been telling anyone who will listen since she got here," Prayer Girl said, as if Nellie wasn't well aware. "It's not exactly breaking news."

For a second, Nellie stilled. What a curious choice of words. Breaking news. *Did she know?*

Their gazes held and around them the excitement faded and the women were ushered—shoved—back onto those torturous benches by nurses who heaved mighty sighs and vented their frustration with smacks and hisses.

And then footsteps, and then the friendly and concerned face of Dr. Ingram peered down at them.

"What happened?"

"She had some sort of fit."

"Did something trigger it?"

"Nellie started banging out a tune on the piano."

"Music can be very therapeutic; that is a relic from . . . kinder days at the asylum," he said. "But perhaps the suddenness of it was a shock to her system. Has she been ill?"

"Yes, since she arrived. As she's been trying to tell everyone, but no one will listen," Prayer Girl said sharply. She related everything to Dr. Ingram. As he listened, his gaze kept shifting to Nellie as if to seek confirmation that, yes, Tillie had terrible friends, yes, she was ill, all she needed was a blanket and a decent bed, yes, all true, et cetera, et cetera.

"I shall arrange for her to be brought to my office for examination."

"Start a fire first; she's always cold," Nellie said.

He smiled. "Ah, so this is your friend in want of a blanket."

Her friend in want of a blanket was stirring awake. "What happened?"

"You had a seizure," Dr. Ingram explained.

"Who are you?"

Nellie squeezed her hand. "He's a friend, Tillie."

"A handsome one . . ." She drifted off again. Dr. Ingram smiled.

"Take good care of her. But I don't think you could do any worse than . . ."

She gestured to the room, where one older woman was insisting on swaying and a nurse spat in her face to make her stop. It was revolting. And ineffectual. Dr. Ingram saw it—he winced, but that was the extent of his reaction. To think that as a precious male doctor, he could have had a word at the very least. But no. Nellie cooled to him and made no secret of her disappointment.

"Can't you say something?" Prayer Girl demanded. Her tone said, *You're a man, do something.*

"I do what I can, miss."

Nellie rolled her eyes in disgust.

"I'll go with you. And Tillie. Make sure she's all right." Prayer Girl was insistent. When Dr. Ingram declared she'd be fine in his care, she lowered her voice and spoke urgently. "We'll get in big trouble otherwise. You gotta get us out of here until their tempers cool."

"What about your prayers for death?" Nellie asked.

"Nellie, I pray for a swift and merciful death. I do not wish to be restrained in the camisole or spend a few nights in the crib. Or God forbid get sent to the Lodge."

"What's the Lodge?"

Prayer Girl and the doctor didn't miss a beat. "You don't want to know."

Just as Nellie was about to follow them to the doctor's office, another nurse rushed up, making a beeline for Nellie.

"Miss Brown?"

"Maybe?"

"Come with me." The words struck fear in her heart. A sudden pang of terror. Punishment certainly waited. Or not? "There's a visitor here for you."

THE RECEPTION ROOM, THE INSANE ASYLUM AT BLACKWELL'S ISLAND

The room where visitors waited was just inside the entrance of the Octagon Tower, so they saw little of the asylum itself. This was, of course, by design. Nellie followed one of the nurses there, though her heart and head were back with Tillie, Prayer Girl and the doctor. She couldn't imagine who might have come calling for her—except Cockerill, but it was too soon. Was it not? Nellie tried to make sense of the days and nights she'd spent here and struggled to come up with a number of days—was it three? Or four? She and Cockerill had agreed on one week. Already it felt like a lifetime.

In this little chamber, there was a small window with a view of Manhattan that Nellie just drank up, especially once she saw it wasn't Cockerill who had come to facilitate her escape. Nor was it anyone sent on his behalf. In fact, she didn't recognize them.

The couple was old enough to be her mother and father. They looked worn down by life, the world, everything. Their exhaustion and sadness were palpable. Nellie felt it like an ache in her own chest, even though she didn't know them.

The woman fixed her gaze on Nellie, hope shining in her red-rimmed eyes.

The father gripped her hand and said the wretched words. "It's not her, Maude."

No one had ever wanted anything the way this mother wanted Nellie to be her daughter. Not Tillie and a blanket, not Nellie and the front page. The mother looked and looked, her gaze searching for *something* she didn't quite see, but maybe if she looked hard enough she would find what she was looking for.

Her daughter.

Nellie had to stand there and break their hearts with the fact of her existence. What a torturous performance this was. Everyone's hopes dashed. The nurse, just leaning against the doorway, was bored by all of it. How could anyone be insensitive to all this heartache?

"Perhaps she has changed since we last saw her—"

"She wouldn't have shrunk and changed her eye color and—"

They wanted so badly for Nellie to be someone she wasn't.

Her instinct to try to help flared. "Who are you looking for? Tell me about her."

"Our daughter. Bessie is about your age. She has brown hair and brown eyes. She went missing one day, and when we read the newspaper story about the insane girl in the asylum, we thought . . ."

Nellie stilled at the mention of a newspaper story. Was this the same one Miss Grupe had giggled about or had there been more than one? The couple kept talking about their beloved long-lost daughter, whom they dearly missed, and Nellie only half listened. She hadn't met this long-lost Bessie. Or had she? Parents who desperately wanted a daughter seemed like the perfect opportunity to pass off another girl as their own . . . No one would be fooled, but everyone could pretend, at least until they were off the island. Too bad Tillie was so ill.

Or could *she* suddenly remember that she was Bessie and take this opportunity to get out of here and get her story published? It was one thing to hear that inane nurse giggle over something from the *Sun*, but for people to start showing up on Blackwell's godforsaken island meant that the story had struck a nerve. It had been widely read. Discussed. Considered. The more they spoke, the more they mentioned news reports and the *Sun*, the more it was painfully clear to Nellie that while she was frozen in time here, the world was still spinning, and someone was getting closer and closer to her story. Close enough even to make this all for nothing.

CHAPTER TWENTY

Marian

COOPER UNION, NEW YORK CITY

Her assignment was the sort that no man would ever want, and because of that, it was an assignment that women reporters had a chance at. It was a lecture by a woman; Marian could practically hear the men in the newsroom declaring to one another, *If I wanted to be lectured by a woman, it'll be by the wife, at home, over a steak dinner.* Even worse, a lecture by a woman about women, which would force them to consider the plight of the poor, widowed, orphaned and so on and so forth. There were a lot of that sort in the city—those alone, without a man, trying to get by on the scraps of work permitted them.

They were a problem, and one that everyone wished to pretend did not exist. It was hard to see all the suffering, of course. But it also forced one to consider that perhaps not every woman was a delicate middle- or upper-class wife and homemaker whose chief concerns in life were marriage and motherhood.

Just seeing these other women in the streets about their sad business of working at wretchedly paying jobs, or engaged in the even sadder business of begging, or forced into the tragic business of *vice*, meant that good, moral New Yorkers had to consider that, maybe, perhaps, not all was right in the world. Something had to be done.

Hence the lecture tonight.

Marian slipped into the hall at Cooper Union later than she'd have liked, just as the lecture was beginning, and she took a seat near the aisle and pulled out her notebook and pencil. A well-attired man with pale hair sat on the other side of the aisle and one row back; he caught her eye and smiled invitingly, but she ignored him.

Mrs. Shaw Lowell took the podium after being introduced as a Civil War widow—as if her age and relentlessly black attire didn't give it away. She wore her hair severely parted in the middle, with a little curl on each side. She had a full mouth and lovely eyes, along with the grim expression of one who was constantly consumed with the tragic plight of humanity.

She was also the recently appointed commissioner of the State Board of Charities.

Her lecture this evening was about the plight of these women in society, the dangers they posed and her proposed solutions to this terrible plague. In the no-nonsense way of these Reforming Women who had started popping up, she began her lecture.

"The poor among us are vicious and idle and must learn to enjoy work," she said. Marian wrote down, *does not like poor.* She'd grown up with a similar opinion, but it was hard to hold on to it when you were a reporter, surrounded by working poor . . . typesetters and factory girls and women who labored at whatever mean work they could get. No one enjoyed that kind of work, but they weren't vicious or idle—not like so many children of wealth and privilege she'd known. Marian saw a lot of things as a reporter that challenged how she'd been brought up to see the world.

"Such women lacking in moral restraint ought to be kept away from the rest of society. They ought to be kept separated until they are at least forty-five years of age so they can be prevented from multiplying their kind," Mrs. Shaw Lowell continued, voicing a popular concern that women prone to *vice* were a danger to them all. They had a way of increasing the burden on society.

Marian wrote, *lock up all the women.*

"This is why we require an asylum for troublesome women where they can be kept safely and separate from others. If they are in the workhouse or the almshouse, or if they are on the street, they are at risk for licentiousness. And procreation of their kind."

Marian wrote, *only the best babies. The best!*

Marian wanted to ask about women older than childbearing age—what was to be done with them? Mrs. Shaw Lowell was not taking questions at the moment. So Marian figured they'd probably knit themselves into oblivion.

Marian had other questions too, and they were the pesky sort that always had her mother saying "Hush, Marian," but that also made her a good reporter. Questions like, Why not give women a chance to work at a decent paying job? Why not give them access to care that will help with babies (or not having babies)? Such things were not spoken of in polite society, even though the newspapers happily printed euphemistic ads for them and cashed the checks and used the money to pay their salaries.

Mrs. Shaw Lowell carried on, detailing the dangers that poor, unattached women caused and the threats that their illegitimate babies were to society and decent people. Marian took notes but didn't believe a word of it. *Bad babies will outnumber good babies! Oh no!* She'd also kept her focus on her notebook and not the man across the aisle and back one row who kept looking at her. Ugh.

After the lecture had concluded and Marian had asked her questions and jotted down the responses, the man who'd been staring at her approached. Of course. He had the well-dressed air and confident demeanor of the wealthy—she recognized it from her days as One of Them. He was in his thirties but looked older, probably due to a life of dissipation—funny how it was all right when wealthy men acted thusly but not poor women.

She likely didn't have enough column inches to go into *that* topic.

He smiled at her. "Quite boring, isn't it?"

"Oh, I don't know. I found it all rather enraging," Marian replied sweetly.

"I suppose so," he said. But they both knew he did not suppose so at all. This sort of man was not in the habit of thinking deeply of the plight of the poor. Which begged the question of what he was doing here.

"What brings you here tonight?" Marian asked.

"I'm on the commission. Had to make an appearance. You know how it is."

"Indeed," Marian murmured. "And tell me how you became involved in the commission."

"My brother secured the appointment on my behalf." He grinned. "He wants to keep me busy. Give back to society." He chuckled. Marian feigned a smile. This was the sort of man who had no skills, talents or interests and would be eaten alive on the streets had he not possessed money and family connections. He bumbled through life with minimal competence. He was well-fed, smartly dressed, endlessly entertained (save for tonight). A woman might marry him and be rich and bored and spend all her days in department stores, purchasing whatever she wished.

"And who is your brother?" Marian asked.

"Jay Wallace. Maybe you've heard of him?" Of course she'd heard of him. Marian tilted her head, trying to decide if this was interesting or not. It wasn't remotely unusual for a rich man to keep his idle younger brother busy with the pretense of charity work. To look after women and children seemed like an odd choice, or maybe it was ironic. Maybe the purpose was to teach him a lesson about dallying with a certain class of women. Maybe. But also, why the devil might Wall Street Wallace need anything from the State Board of Charities?

"I am familiar with your brother. I've been reporting on his wedding."

"Ah, a much more pleasant story than all this," he said.

"You know, I didn't catch your name," Marian said.

"Vernon Wallace. And I don't suppose you fancy continuing this conversation elsewhere?"

Marian did not fancy it. Vernon Wallace was clearly the sort of man who would make a slobbery pass at her and get handsy in a carriage and call her rude names when she refused. But he seemed to be foolish and talkative and she had questions about his brother. She was about to agree when a woman Marian didn't know approached.

"Mr. Wallace," she said stonily by way of greeting.

"Mrs. Howard." He nodded curtly.

Marian waited through a wonderfully tense moment, while her mind ran wild with reasons these two people who clearly loathed each other were now face-to-face, with Marian in the middle.

After a moment Vernon Wallace took his leave, but not without handing his card to Marian.

Mrs. Howard muttered "Good riddance" to his backside and turned to Marian. "I know we are not acquainted, but I wanted to warn you away from him, if you are considering . . ."

"God no. I'd rather die a spinster," Marian said with a laugh, and the woman visibly relaxed. She smiled and her gaze softened. "I'm a reporter with the *Herald*. I was speaking with him for my article. I'm writing something up on Mrs. Shaw Lowell's lecture."

The woman nodded approvingly. "Not that it's any of my business," she began, "but his family doesn't tolerate women like us."

Which made it all the more curious that he was here. "How so?" Marian inquired.

"Women who are independent, opinionated, engaged with the world beyond parties and frivolities." Marian took a step closer, curious. There was a lot of feeling behind her words. She tilted her head to encourage this woman to go on. "I knew the late Mrs. Wallace. We worked together on suffrage. Oh, how he hated her involvement in the cause and the ideas it put in her head. It's not a popular cause within society right now, especially in the Wallace household."

Of course the woman was a suffragist. It was all the rage among a certain kind. And they had a certain point: It was outrageous that women paid taxes yet had no say in their representatives. Most suffragists didn't even stop there, and they railed against double standards of moral behavior and unequal pay, against a lack of education and professional opportunities for women. There was no shortage of injustices against women to protest.

Marian was more of a Marianist. She believed deeply and fervently in the cause of her own advancement. Her mother had instilled that lesson at least. They just had different ideas of how to do it. Marriage to a rich bore or literally anything else.

"It's terrible how she died. So young too," Marian said. The woman murmured her agreement and gave Marian a hard look before she handed over her card. She recognized the name as that of one of the wealthy society women who had started to get—gasp—political. They were always seeking signatures for suffrage petitions or writing editorials about the need for various reforms in all aspects of women's lives—a say in anything about their lives, really.

"Please call if you wish to speak more about it."

CHAPTER TWENTY-ONE

Among the Insane Patients

"Well, you don't need to expect any kindness here, for you won't get it."

—Nellie Bly, *Ten Days in a Mad-House*

THE INSANE ASYLUM AT BLACKWELL'S ISLAND

Another day at the asylum—Nellie was struggling to figure out if it was the fifth or the six or seven hundredth—and there was a ghastly occurrence. That morning while they were all pushed and jostled and smacked into a line for breakfast—"*Two by two!*" Miss Grady shrieked—something happened that had them all falling out of line and scrambling for a closer look. Not even the violence or threats from the nurses could contain the women.

Two terrifyingly large men carried out a body, covered in a sheet and laid on a stretcher. Nellie recognized one as the man who had escorted her off the boat when she arrived here. If she never saw him again it would be too soon.

But *a dead body*. Everyone wanted to know who it was and what had happened. From the chatter around her, Nellie was given to understand that the excitement wasn't because this was the first time a body had been carried out at breakfast—there was only one way in and one way out of the asylum—it wasn't even the second or third time that people could remember. It was just something novel and different among a group who was starved for novelty.

As the grunting men stalked past, the stretcher between them, someone reached out and flicked away the sheet covering the face. They all gasped; someone screamed. Elsie, the poor girl who had lost her beloved and never quite recovered. Her face and head bore the marks of a beating. *Who had done it? And with what?*

By the end of breakfast, they all knew that Elsie's cellmate—a woman prone to violence and filthy habits—had beaten her with the chamber pot for reasons that were not articulated. The night nurse had heard the screams but did not want to open the door to let Elsie out, lest her violent cellmate escape too. The night nurse, it had to be noted, was not a nurse at all but an inmate at the prison on Blackwell's Island, sent to the asylum to cover shifts that could not be filled in other ways, for obvious reasons.

The murderous woman, they were assured, had already been transferred to the Lodge.

"Makes you feel a bit sick, doesn't it?" Prayer Girl remarked.

"Elsie didn't belong here," Nellie said. "She was just sad. Grieving. The nurse should have opened the door."

"And risk a beating herself?" Prayer Girl laughed. "Have you *met* the nurses here yet, New Girl?"

She had, and Nellie wondered what had made them so cold and cruel to their charges. Did they not know any better? How exactly were they trained? Was it simply that they weren't paid enough to care, as that nurse at Bellevue had once said? Their hours were long and shifts were endless. Nellie supposed it was a difficult and thankless job, in a setting that was likely to make a sensible woman go mad if she wasn't on the verge already. Or maybe they were just born cruel, or life had made them so and it just happened to come out on the job and this was the job they could get.

Two nurses walked past, arm in arm, not even sparing a glance for all the patients who had just watched one of their own be carried out feetfirst to an unceremonious burial. They were deep in conversation about something. It could have been anything, from the situation with poor Elsie to whatever news came from the outside world.

Nellie was more curious about *where* they were going, as they walked off in a direction of the asylum she hadn't yet seen. There was no question about Nellie following them—she had a story to chase. She'd spent enough time sitting on those benches, collecting details of casual cruelty and heartbreaking incompetence.

"What are you doing?" Prayer Girl asked as Nellie started venturing away from the others. Nellie pressed her finger to her lips. *Shhhh.* She slipped out of the line and followed the nurses.

What a pair they were, in matching brown-striped gowns with fresh-pressed aprons and white caps. The rope belts of keys really completed the look and made it possible for someone to follow them by sound alone. Each one made a soft *clink* with every step. Nellie followed them down a corridor—as bland and indistinguishable as the rest—and around the corner.

First, she noticed the smell. A not unpleasant smell. A kitchen smell of melted butter and fresh-cooked eggs, of baking bread and oh dear God *coffee*. Nellie almost fell to her knees for want of it. A door open to the left revealed a kitchen, where cooks were busy at work making actually edible food. Eggs scrambled in butter, fresh-baked bread, potatoes sizzling as they fried.

It was all right there.

The dining room was across from the kitchen, and there doctors and nurses sat at a properly set table—a white tablecloth and everything—while they enjoyed eggs and conversation, while holding knives and forks. They were so leisurely about it too; no frantic rush to devour whatever one could before other patients got to it first. They also weren't starving. It was all so civilized.

Nellie spied Miss Grady, alone. She did not speak with the others, but her eyes were set upon Dr. Kinier, and Nellie had to wonder if she harbored affections for the doctor who was so cruelly dismissive of all foreign-born women. She calmly ate her breakfast—it was a particular torture to watch her bite into a fresh apple—a red one, with streaks of honey yellow in the skin that promised sweetness. The fruit was so fresh, so crisp, that Nellie could hear her crack into it from across the room. She might have moaned, imagining the fresh sweetness on her tongue.

Nellie caught Miss Grady's attention. She chose that moment to look in the direction of the insane moaning girl staring at her with hungry eyes. Nellie must have looked so utterly pathetic, between her wretchedly cut bangs and her hungry expression and ill-fitting dress.

Miss Grady only saw trouble.

She stood so suddenly that her chair clattered to the ground behind her, and she threw away the apple—unfinished!—and started toward Nellie.

The others just watched. No one helped Miss Grady, but no one helped Nellie either.

"You are not supposed to be here," she said sharply as she grabbed hold of Nellie. Again with the hair! She should have cut her hair, all of it, not just the bangs that made her look like she belonged here. If she'd cut her hair short, then Miss Grady wouldn't have as much to grip on to.

"Why are you so mean?" Nellie asked as she was dragged and

stumbled along after her. "Don't you think kindness would be more effective?"

Miss Grady gave her a strange look. This was not the usual sort of back talk she received from patients, apparently. Maybe that question did make her sound too much like a reporter.

"You ask too many questions."

True story.

If she'd been trying to escape, Nellie would have been devastated to find herself flung back onto those benches of agony in Hall 6. All eyes in the hall were on her, with a mixture of curiosity, pity and a consensus of *thank God that's not me*. Nellie felt panic storming through her veins as Miss Grady held her down and called for help. Nellie didn't fight her; she wasn't particularly keen to suffer one of the punishments reserved for "violent" prisoners. Or *difficult* ones. But her heart was thundering in fear at what would come next.

"Bring me the restraints," Miss Grady said sharply to one of the other nurses, who seemed as scared of her as everyone else was. Miss Grupe moved with alacrity. She didn't even giggle, for once. Nellie was led to a chair with arms instead of one of the usual dreadfully uncomfortable benches.

"You don't need to do this," Nellie said. "I'm not insane. Or violent."

"But you are trouble. And I do not get paid enough for trouble." Then, turning to another nurse, she said, "Tighten these while I write her up."

Nellie watched as Miss Grady marched toward the center of the room, where she picked up the book that was always on the table, flipped through the pages until she found the one she sought and started writing furiously. Nellie could just imagine the words: *Patient Nellie Brown found wandering the halls alone. Given restraints. Patient Nellie Brown found out of place. Reminded her of where she belongs.* Did she write the date? Nellie wondered. She had never wanted to know what day it was so badly in her life. She'd never *not* known. She ought to have remembered, but one hour blurred into the next here, and her grasp on the outside world was slipping.

"Please. Not too tight."

The nurse gave no indication that she'd heard—no sympathetic smile or nod. But the restraints were eased enough that the leather no longer dug into her skin. Still, they were tight. She would not be moving anytime soon. And she would suffer until then.

And then—that was it, then.

Tied up on this damned chair as she was, there was very little she could do to get comfortable. Nothing could be done about the way her feet barely skimmed the ground or her arms were held in place at perfect right angles or how the back of the chair was painfully upright.

There was nothing to do but look at her fellow patients. Watch them watching her. Nellie noticed the glazed eyes that had been open too long and seen too little the whole while. She saw the dead expressions of brains and bodies that had given up but couldn't manage to die. Some were very clearly unwell. An old woman in the corner was having a very heated conversation with nobody, and Mathilda was fighting with her lawyer again. Princess was there, her lips moving. While Nellie couldn't hear what she said, she didn't need to. The only words she uttered, over and over again, were "Rose, Daisy, Violet."

Nellie tried to imagine how they all might have looked *before.*

Before the world had broken them, stolen their freedom, condemned them to dirty baths and inedible food and a perpetual state of boredom. What had they looked like with freshly washed and styled hair, with a light in their eyes and a bloom in their cheeks?

She imagined all their first loves and first kisses, the hopes and dreams they had nurtured, the friends and families they had loved and lived with. And somehow all that went away and here they were.

The minutes and hours wore on, as they were wont to do. At some point, Nellie's nose began to itch. She tried wiggling her face muscles to make the itch go away, which must have made her look mad. Which made her think some of the women she'd seen in here twitching and contorting their faces might not have been insane; they were simply trying to scratch an itch in any way that they could.

But the itch did not go away. It consumed her. Nellie could think of nothing else. Oh, if she could just scratch it and be done with it!

"*Psst.*" Nellie tried to get the attention of the woman next to her, Mrs. Kisner. She turned and looked like she wanted to help, but she couldn't understand English and Nellie did not have the German words for "please scratch my nose." She maybe could have managed it in the fractured Spanish she'd learned while in Mexico, but that wasn't helpful here. There was rumored to be one Mexican patient, but Nellie hadn't encountered her yet. The woman on her other side did not seem to be altogether present.

It was just Nellie. And the itchy nose.

The most mundane thing. She had so little control over herself that she could not even scratch her own nose. Her fingers danced and her hands flexed, but the restraints around her wrists held firm.

She would not panic. She would not panic. She would not—

Okay, self, think of something else. She thought of Dr. Ingram. If he could just happen past, if he could just peek in and notice her here, he would see her and demand her release. She could tell he was kind and caring and not completely convinced of her insanity. She quite liked him, except that he seemed keen to probe her past and secrets, especially about the fire.

Fire.

Would have been nice to start one in the little stove over in the corner, that was just there, unlit, with some old ashes piled up inside. Warm the place up a bit. Make the place seem cozy. They could all gather round and tell stories and feel some camaraderie and comfort.

But . . .

What if a fire spread throughout the asylum while she was trapped in this chair? What about all the women who were restrained? Nellie might have been here only a few days, but already she knew no one was coming to untie her in the event of an emergency. Certainly no one came to her now. She was surrounded by women, all trapped by their own private torments. No one would dare risk the ire of the nurses and subsequent punishment to help her. She could not blame them for it, honestly.

So Nellie sat in her chair, in a quiet state of panic and worst-case-scenario planning, feeling quite alone in the world.

In the silence it was easy to hear the footsteps approaching. Nearly everyone's attention turned to the doorway, where a matron slunk in, annoyed by her errand. She gave a short huff and said to Miss Grady, "There is a visitor for Nellie Brown."

Oh thank God. She'd been in these restraints for likely an hour or two—the longest hours of her life—and the prospect of a visitor was like winning the lottery, Christmas morning, and landing the front page of the *World* all at once. She badly wanted the escape.

Miss Grady looked at Nellie and smiled. "She's busy."

"I'm not busy," Nellie said.

The nurse in the doorway looked at her warily. "Will she be violent?"

What if it was Cockerill? What if this was her chance to escape and she was going to miss it? Would Cockerill return twice for her and her story?

He was a busy man, busy with Important Things. And she was the girl who was crazy to think she could be a reporter, crazy to believe the word of a man, crazy to give up her freedom for a chance.

Nellie wanted to roar. She wanted to rip her hands free.

But no, she must remain calm. Polite. "Please."

IN LINE FOR SUPPER, THE INSANE ASYLUM AT BLACKWELL'S ISLAND

Nellie was gingerly touching her wrists, which had been rubbed raw after a whole day spent tied up. Nellie had not been excused to see her visitor. She told herself that it was probably a couple, unknown to her, in search of their own lost girl. Or it might have been a set of friends coming to gawk at her, the "insane girl from the papers," which annoyed Nellie for its casual cruelty—imagine visiting sick and insane people for entertainment! Either way, it reminded her that her story was already out there, getting away from her while she was stuck, tied up, silenced and helpless.

Worst of all to contemplate: It could have been Cockerill coming to secure her release.

An empty stomach didn't help.

Nor did the prospect of dismal, unsalted and rancid asylum fare. Especially since she now knew that down the hall and around the corner, the doctors and nurses were dining on delicious meals. She imagined roast chicken with the skin crisped, soft bread, fresh vegetables, sliced fruit for dessert, followed by actually hot and thoroughly steeped tea. Maybe even with sugar.

Instead, she leaned against the cold wall with peeling paint, waiting for a supper that surely wouldn't be worth waiting for.

What really hurt to think about was the chance that she had

missed Cockerill today. She knew Erasmus, her dear old editor from the *Dispatch*, would have stopped at nothing to ensure her safety (and her reporting). She did not know that about Cockerill. She barely knew the man, and definitely didn't suspect that he was in the business of second chances. He would not come for her twice.

Shit, *damn* and a dozen other swear words were going through her head when Prayer Girl slid up beside her in line. They had a way of finding each other in line for meals, in line to traverse the halls, in line to take their seat on those benches of unbearable agony. There was something about Prayer Girl that scared Nellie, but she knew her way around the place and was wonderfully unsentimental.

"Heard you tried to escape," Prayer Girl said in a low voice.

"Does anyone ever try it? The East River is right there."

Prayer Girl made a face like Nellie was daft. "Of course. Every few weeks they fish one out of the river. I think about it myself sometimes."

"Why haven't you?"

With anyone else, Nellie wouldn't have asked. But this was the woman who began each meal with a plea for imminent death, who was heard each night pleading with the Lord to deny her the morning, who could be heard in every spare moment murmuring her prayers for death in exceedingly gruesome and creative ways.

The river was *right there*. They could feel the cold wind whipping off it, stinging their cheeks and sinking into their bones. Getting out of the Octagon Tower would be a trick, but it was a relatively short sprint to the water. To something like freedom. So Nellie had to wonder if Prayer Girl was not really committed to her own cause. Maybe she didn't really want to die. Maybe she did have something to live for. Maybe all these women did.

"Because you need me, New Girl." She grinned. "And I know how to swim."

"How long do I have to be here before you stop calling me New Girl?"

"It'll be a sad day when I stop."

Unless she stopped because Cockerill came back, secured her release, sat her down with a hot steak and a typewriter so she could write a front-page story. Her mother always said she'd never lacked ambition. Even now, after all these days and nights in the asylum, her ambition hadn't left her. She needed something to keep her going.

"Where did you get off to, anyway?" Prayer Girl asked.

"I found the kitchens," Nellie answered, and Prayer Girl pulled a *not much to see there* sort of face. Nellie shook her head. "I found the kitchens for the staff. I saw fresh fruit and smelled freshly brewed coffee."

"Stop it."

"They were baking bread and cooking eggs in butter."

"Now you're just being cruel."

"There's a dining room for the nurses and doctors. With tablecloths and cutlery . . ."

"And you got caught and got the restraints." She paused. "Might be worth it to get a bite of decent food." Prayer Girl sighed dreamily at the idea. "What if I escaped here, dashed to the kitchens, gorged myself on actual food and then they beat me to death?" She smiled. "A girl can dream."

"I still don't know why you don't make a run for it."

Nellie did suspect the reason, though. Because this was a place designed to smother the spark in a woman, to make her small, to make her *manageable*. The rest of the world did what it could, by insisting women be seen and not heard, refusing them opportunities to use their brains or see the world or even know themselves. The world insisted that they do nothing but labor unpaid at the draining and thankless work of wives and mothers.

And if a woman was still uppity and unsatisfied after that? Any excuse could get her sent here, where the efforts to subdue her continued in earnest.

It started when they took away the clothes she'd arrived in. The ones she had chosen for herself that were made to fit her body. Fear of pain and punishment kept them all in line, most of the time. A lack of nourishment kept them perpetually starving and weak. And then the monotony sapped any remaining spirit left. Nellie could feel it happening to her already: She was sinking into the routine.

Nellie sighed. She was starting to sound like Tillie now. Where *was* Tillie, anyway? And the line toward supper started moving.

"Be careful tonight," Prayer Girl said.

"Why do you say that?"

"Because now they know you're trouble. And they don't like trouble."

THE MIDDLE OF THE NIGHT, THE INSANE ASYLUM AT BLACKWELL'S ISLAND

Nellie had managed to fall asleep on her hard bed, with her too-small blanket, with her jittery, anxious energy not dispelled from the nonevents of the day. Her wrists were sore from the restraints, and it had been hard to get comfortable. She imagined the doctors and nurses on comfortable beds after eating well-prepared meals of fresh food, and she seethed. But most of all, she tossed and turned and worried: *Had she missed Cockerill?* The visitor she hadn't gotten to visit with haunted her until she could keep her eyes open no longer.

She didn't know how long she'd been asleep when it happened.

She heard the sounds first: the key turning in the lock, the heavy *clicks* and *clinks,* and the door slid open. Nellie lay still in her bed, heart pounding, as she listened to the rustle of people slipping into her room. She so wanted to sleep. She did not want whatever this promised to be. The intruders, whoever they were, weren't exactly trying to be quiet about it. She didn't have a cellmate who might be awakened; because of her notoriety as "the insane girl from the papers" she'd been moved to her own tiny room. Or maybe it was luck, but she didn't feel lucky now.

"Hello?"

"Shhh."

A beam of light hit her eyes. Nellie sat up in bed, the sad excuse for a blanket falling around her waist, leaving her exposed in just her standard-issue nightdress, a flimsy little thing. She recognized the outline of a man but not the man himself. Her heart was thundering and she could feel her own fear pounding through every inch of her. She saw a female nurse with him—she recognized the apron and uniform in the faint light—and it gave her a sense of relief, which was undoubtedly misplaced.

"Nellie Brown?"

"What do you want?"

Nellie could feel her heart pounding. No one was ever woken in the dead of night for a good reason.

"We just need you to drink this."

The doctor held out a cup—she assumed it was a doctor and not some random man. But that was a generous assumption on her part. The room was too dark to tell what was in the cup, but Nellie had a hunch it was not unlike the "wine" they gave Princess at dinner. The wine that made her numb and dumb and unable to do anything but mutter the names of the same three flowers over and over. Nellie laughed and waved the cup away. "Oh no. No, thank you. I'm not thirsty."

"You must drink it."

Nellie stared at that dull metal cup. She wasn't foolish enough to believe that they had brought her a mere glass of water in the dead of night as some sort of kindness. There had to be something else in it—laudanum or whatever potent drug they used to make women senseless and pliable. Nellie looked at that cup and saw a test of what she was willing to do for her reporting, for the front page, for these women who deserved to have their stories told.

To take a sip, though, was to risk losing everything she had saved in her brain.

She didn't want to drink it. Whatever it was, she didn't want it inside her, stealing her thoughts or her movements or her sense of self. Maybe there were limits to her ambitions. The air was cool and tense as Nellie quietly, calmly refused to reach for the cup. First they had taken her hat, then her dress and notebook. They took her freedom and then proceeded to slowly rob her of her dignity. And now she was losing control over her own body.

The doctor was nearly growling now. She crept backward in her bed as much as she could, until she felt the cold cement wall at her back, seeping through the thin fabric of her nightdress. The blanket she pulled up to cover herself was a worthless scrap that offered no comfort or protection, especially from this man leaning menacingly toward her, letting her know with every movement that he was not the sort of man to take no for an answer. He thrust the cup into her face and a bit of it sloshed onto her cheek.

Beside him, the nurse sighed with impatience.

"You'll drink it or we'll come back with a syringe," he threatened.

Nellie, however, was not one to be threatened or intimidated by anyone. "I'm not sick. I'm not insane. I will not drink it."

"That's what all the women say. It's one of the first symptoms of insanity." The doctor thrust the cup in her face again. *Drink. Up.* That was what they always said: Insisting on sanity was the first sign of insanity. Convenient, that.

Nellie took the cup. Whatever was in it didn't have an odor, which did not console her in the slightest. Her hand trembled slightly as she fought the urge to toss it in his face. It would be funny—until she was punished severely for it.

"What is it?" Nellie asked.

"It's water. Drink it."

"You're waking me up in the middle of the night for water?"

He grunted. "They said you were trouble." Then, turning to the nurse, he said, "Prepare a syringe. We'll have to hold her down and inject it directly."

"Never mind, I'll drink it," Nellie said quickly. She caught a glimpse of smug approval on his shadowed face. Oh, how her temper flared at that, but she knew she had to stifle it. The cup was cool in her hand. She considered dropping it or flinging it aside. But that would only get her a shot in the arm, and this, at least, she could throw up as soon as they left. She took a sip and bitterness hit her tongue. This wasn't just water. It was control, and it was bitter to swallow.

It meant giving up her spark. Her fire. Herself. She had been causing trouble. She'd been uppity.

They were turning her into another forlorn woman, biddable because she was dead on the inside. She didn't want to become one of them.

"All of it." The doctor refused to take the cup back until it was empty. But it was hard to drink with a lump in her throat and sobs choked back. *For the story.* So she could never be at the mercy of a man again. *For the story.* So these women would have their voices heard. She had half a mind to throw the cup across the room when she was finished, but it didn't seem necessary to risk a double dose or worse.

Finally, the doctor and his silent attendant left, taking the empty cup with them and grumbling about difficult women. She rushed to the chamber pot and plunged her fingers down her throat, hoping to get rid of whatever she had just been forced to swallow.

CHAPTER TWENTY-TWO

Colton

THE FERRY AT TWENTY-SIXTH STREET

The asylum had swallowed her up. There had been no way to get to her, or get word of her. Colton had been trying.

From what he'd learned in Pittsburgh, one didn't have to worry about Nellie. Between her smarts, daring and charm, she would get the story she sought. Colton had tracked down her stories for the *Dispatch* and read up on the lives of factory girls and visiting opera singers, all composed in a lively, straightforward voice. Erasmus was right; she did have a knack for finding engaging, absorbing stories.

But from what he was learning about the asylum—nothing good—he worried anyway. What would happen to her courage, her pluck, her voice? Why did he care so much about her fate?

That morning, Colton's editor at the *Sun* had demanded to know where the latest installment of that "insane girl story" was and why Colton hadn't written it yet.

"Get out and don't come back until you have something we can print!" the editor had roared, and Colton had grabbed his hat and jacket and headed out before he even knew where he was going.

Somehow he ended up here, at the Ferry Station on Twenty-Sixth Street, where the boats went back and forth between Blackwell's Island and Manhattan. Colton had been on them several times, but never managed to breach the asylum walls. It was as hard as ever for reporters to get in.

Today he watched as a middle-aged couple clutched each other, hope in their eyes, as they boarded a boat. He was still there when they returned, looking, well, broken.

"Excuse me—" he called out. They stopped. "What took you to Blackwell's Island?"

The woman looked nervously at the man, her husband, probably. Colton noted that while their clothes were a touch faded and worn, they were clean and pressed. The woman had a lined face and white-streaked black hair. The gentleman had a cap and a bushy beard.

"Aye, we were there," the man said nervously, nodding. His eyes were as questioning as Colton felt.

"What brought you, may I ask?"

"Why do you want to know?"

"Sam Colton, with the *New York Sun*. I'm working on a story about Nellie Brown." He just had to say her name now.

"We just saw her."

Colton lowered his notebook and pencil. Might have had his jaw drop open too.

"You did?"

"We thought she might have been our daughter, who has gone missing. But . . ." They couldn't say it; they didn't need to. Nellie wasn't their girl. Colton could have told them that, didn't think they would have listened.

"How did she look?"

"Not well," the man answered. "Too skinny. Hungry. She'd done something funny with her hair." He motioned to his forehead.

"And can you tell me anything about the nurses or the doctors or the asylum itself?"

The woman burst into tears and turned her face into her husband's worn woolen coat. Her husband pulled her close. *Too much, Colton. Too much.* He didn't have the deft, sensitive touch required for an interview like this. He was too focused on getting facts and details; he didn't stop to think about their feelings. What a cad he was.

"I'm so sorry," he said softly. He tried again. "This must be very trying for you."

They nodded and went on their way, and his heart broke a little bit for them. Nearby, the coarse old woman who manned a dirty old ferry stood in a stained dress and expertly maneuvered a wad of tobacco in her cheek, then caught his eye. He'd been avoiding her—she was terrifying—but Colton had let his guard down. Now she smirked at him.

"I get a couple like that every day," she said, with a jerk of her head in their direction.

"That same couple?"

"Nah, they're always different. Sometimes it's just rich folks who want a lark and so go to gawk at that girl and other freaks in the asylum. You'd think there's better entertainment in a city like New York, but . . ." She finished with a shrug.

"That's abhorrent."

She shrugged. "Pays well to take them." She grinned. His stomach turned. Her teeth—what was left of them—were brown. "I'll tell you what they don't do," she said, and she let out a steady stream of spit. "They don't say they're a reporter."

"Yeah, I'm catching on to that," he said.

"Not just a pretty face, then," she quipped with a hungry look at him.

It was becoming plain what he would have to do: pretend to be someone he was not so he could get into the asylum, which was not his idea of how to conduct journalism. Not at all. He preferred on-the-record interviews, honest sources, verifiable facts, actual quotations. But that wasn't working. If he wanted a story about Nellie, he would have to become more like *her.*

CHAPTER TWENTY-THREE

Unspeakable Scenes in the Yard

Miss Grady said if I made it a practice of telling it would be a serious thing for me, she warned me in time.

—Nellie Bly, *Ten Days in a Mad-House*

A VISIT WITH THE DOCTOR

Nellie was singled out again, this time for a visit with Dr. Ingram. Prickles of concern danced up her neck. She had been identified as a problematic woman, a troublemaker, a cause for concern. It would get her drugged, or worse, and potentially out of reach of Cockerill.

Any day now. He had to come any damned day now. She was hungry. She felt filthy.

So it was with some trepidation that she walked toward Dr. Ingram's office, a rumble of desperate hunger in her belly and her eyes bleary from another night of unsatisfying sleep. A visit with the doctor, while fraught with risk, was a more appealing prospect than hours on the benches, imagining meals she couldn't eat.

Those benches had to have been the seating choice of Satan himself.

"I hear you've been causing trouble again," he said, and so began their little tango, where they danced around the fact that she was not insane. She didn't pretend with him, but she wasn't keen to blow her cover either. She didn't think the staff here would take too kindly to a reporter in their midst. They had too much sin to answer for to risk it being revealed in the pages of a New York newspaper. Maybe she was dangerous after all.

"You've been talking about me, Doctor?" Nellie smiled. She heard her mother's voice in her head (*A doctor, Pink!*). He smiled. "The nurses and I confer about the patients, yes."

"How is Tillie?"

"She is under observation. She is being taken care of. But you, Miss Brown . . ."

"Call me Nellie."

"I am not at liberty to discuss the particulars of Tillie's case. But we can talk about you, Miss Brown. I heard that you were wandering off."

The way he said it made it sound like she was a silly female who had simply gotten confused and wandered off, like a uterus wandering around the body, causing trouble. She didn't correct him. "Do they keep a list of vexing inmates? Or do the nurses and doctors chat over tea and fresh-baked bread?"

"You seem to have an interest in food. Mentioning the bread, sneaking off to the kitchens. Are you hungry, Nellie?"

"We are all starving."

She might honestly commit murder for fresh anything right about now. No wonder they had to drug and restrain all these women. Maybe they weren't insane, just hungry. Ravenous. The least she could do was plead their case. She, as soon as she got out of here, was going to have a big, juicy steak dinner. The rest wouldn't be so lucky.

"We do the best we can with our budgets." He sighed and looked uncomfortable discussing this with her. "The budgets don't allow much. We do the best we can for the number of patients we have."

"There's a lot of women here. Must be thousands."

"Sixteen hundred, I believe."

"The place hardly seems big enough," Nellie said. In some instances, they were crammed in, as many as six to a room meant for fewer. But that wasn't the worst of it. "They can't all be insane."

She did it; she held his gaze, daring him to see her and to see all these women as she did. They were poor, unfortunate souls who had gotten stuck in this place by a mixture of bad luck, bad friends, bad relatives. And they had no recourse. She wondered how he didn't see it—sanity, heartsickness, discomfort—in her or the other women and do something about it.

"The diagnosis of insanity is still a matter of some debate. We do know that women seem to suffer from it more than men," he said. Nellie frowned. That seemed like too convenient an explanation. More likely it seemed that men used insanity as a way to dismiss women who confounded their expectations, and as a way to excuse themselves from listening to and trying to understand them. The claim of insanity meant they could be locked away, out of sight and out of mind, so authorities wouldn't be reminded of what they didn't know or didn't understand.

But Dr. Ingram seemed so *nice*; it was a shame he should actually believe all that. He went on to say, "Women have more frequent complaints of phantom pain, nervousness, anxiety, depression and other feminine complaints."

"Those don't sound like symptoms of insanity to me. Sounds

like it might be a complaint of the body, not the mind," Nellie said. The doctor smiled kindly at her. One of those *silly female* smiles, and her warm feelings toward him hardened.

"I wonder, Miss Brown, what has given you cause to act out," he said gently.

"I just went exploring." She shrugged. And she thought, *I'm just doing my job as a reporter.* And then, to change the subject, she said, "You know, if there was a fire here, we would all die."

Nellie made her eyes a little round, a little wide, like *oh my God we all might die.*

Dr. Ingram's frown revealed his concern. "What makes you say that, Nellie?"

"I had a nightmare. There was a fire and all the nurses ran, taking the keys with them, while we were all left in our cells."

"Now, now, Nellie. The nurses would certainly ensure everyone's safety."

"Have you met the nurses here, Dr. Ingram?" Nellie didn't wait for him to answer. He was too much of a gentleman to speak ill of his colleagues. "Even if they try to free all the women, there wouldn't be time to unlock every door. At some prisons there are more modern systems that can lock and unlock a row full of cells with one turn of the key—"

"What do you know of locks in prisons, Nellie?"

She'd said too much. She hadn't been to prison, other than to report on a story, but she couldn't say that without revealing herself.

"I read about it somewhere," she lied. "Why don't you have it changed?"

He sighed. A mighty, weary sigh. "I offer suggestions until my brain is tired, but what good does it do?"

"You have to try. There is so much one could do here to make it better for the patients. Salt in the food. Or just some extra heaters for warmth. Many of the women here are freezing and underdressed while the nurses wear thick sweaters and drink hot tea."

"I'll see what I can do. But like I said, we just don't have the resources. Besides, no one else has expressed this concern."

"Maybe they feel like it's not worth it. Maybe they're afraid they'll be dismissed as lunatics."

"They are lunatics."

"Are you so sure, Dr. Ingram? Because from what I have seen, many of the women here are perfectly sane."

He cut her off, color rising in his cheeks. Lord save them all from men whose expertise is questioned. "Each patient here has been evaluated by multiple doctors, on multiple occasions. They have been diagnosed and certified as insane."

There was no convincing men that they might not know it all, so Nellie didn't even bother. What a thing to know by the age of twenty-three. What a reason for so many women's lives to be locked up and cut short.

THE INSANE ASYLUM AT BLACKWELL'S ISLAND

Was it her seventh day yet? Nellie had lost count, but she had a sneaking suspicion that a week had come and gone. Just when Nellie was starting to go mad with the monotony and cruelty of it all, something changed. Something happened. The nurses, who seemed to consider casual cruelty a part of their job, did something *nice*. They took all the women for a walk outside.

Fresh air.

Sunshine.

A tantalizing, torturous view of Manhattan, its buildings rising proud and glorious on the other side of the river.

There had been quite a skirmish for hats; Nellie had inadvertently taken an elbow to the nose as a large woman reached over her for a hat and yanked it back quickly. Nellie had grabbed two—one for herself and one for Tillie, who was in no condition to brave the scrum.

Once outside, Tillie closed her eyes and tipped her sweet face up to the sunshine and took a moment to just breathe it all in. After her episode, she had spent a few days convalescing and requesting tests of her sanity, all of which were denied. She was back with the rest of them now. And she wasn't quite right. She had long ago stopped singing to herself, and her voice, when she spoke, was little more than a whisper. Her movements were slight and slow, calculated to consume as little energy as possible, as if her spirit was trying to live but her body would like to give up now, thank you very much.

At least she got to enjoy this highly chaperoned, closely supervised walk around the grounds. They were nice enough—grass mostly, some trees. The budget barely provided enough for the women to eat, so there was nothing left for much by way of landscaping.

Nellie strolled slowly outside with Prayer Girl, Tillie and the others who were deemed "well enough." Up ahead Mrs. Kisner walked with Princess.

They saw a boat of new patients arrive. Some stood still and watched the new arrivals as they were escorted off the boat—some stoic, but some crying and fighting to the last. How long had it been since Nellie had arrived? How many boatloads of new newcomers had she witnessed? They had baths once a week and she'd only endured that torture once. She'd had a few visitors—all of them were there just to gawk at "the insane girl from the newspaper," which only made Nellie feel her captivity all the more. But how many? And when? She wracked her brain, trying to count, trying to remember which horrible thing happened on which day. But the days and numbers didn't add up to anything sensible in her brain.

Try not to actually go insane, Harriet had said, and Nellie had scoffed, but she was regretting it now. She didn't even know what day it was. Come to think of it, Nellie didn't know *anything* that was going on in the world. A war could have started, the president could have been assassinated, something important could have exploded. The patients here had no way of knowing anything of the outside world, unless they overheard the nurses gossiping about it.

For someone who lived and breathed hard, breaking news, this was a somewhat excruciating state to be in.

Beside her, Prayer Girl sighed. "Not you too, Nellie! What are you muttering about?"

"What if no one comes for me?"

"No one is coming for you," Prayer Girl said flatly. A worrying feeling was spreading inside Nellie. Worry that she had been duped. Like she wasn't Nellie Bly, Future Star Reporter of the *New York World,* but just idiot girl in over her head who realizes once it's too late. She could just see the headline now: AREA WOMAN BELIEVES MAN WILL RESCUE HER; ACCIDENTALLY SPENDS LIFE IN INSANE ASYLUM.

"That's right," Tillie said. "All those visitors she has been getting are for me."

Nellie and Prayer Girl turned to stare at her. The sweet, shivering girl was still cold and tightly wrapped up in her moth-eaten shawl. But her eyes were bright with anger or delirium or both. She couldn't honestly believe those visitors were for her, could she? Not once had she been summoned to meet with them. Not once had anyone asked for her.

"Tillie . . ."

"It's always 'Miss Brown, there is a visitor for you,' but I know those visitors are for me," Tillie insisted. "Someone is coming to take me away from all this."

Prayer Girl just shook her head. "Another one bites the dust."

"Tillie—" Nellie reached out to console her, but the girl jerked away.

"And I'm not just talking about *her,*" Prayer Girl said. She meant Nellie, too, was losing her mind. Nellie knew better than to protest it.

They walked on, along the river.

Princess had fallen behind—whatever she was on did not facilitate speedy movement—and she fell in line with them, muttering with every step. Prayer Girl grinned and nudged her shoulder. "Hey, Princess, should the gardener add some roses, daisies and violets?"

"Stop it," Nellie said.

"Rose. Daisy. Violet. Rose. Daisy. Violet."

"Yeah, yeah. We know." Prayer Girl rolled her eyes. "You've mentioned it a time. Or two. Thousand."

"Don't tease her," Nellie protested. "Don't let them make you mean."

Suitably chastened, Prayer Girl fell silent and kept walking. They were doing laps of the yard, kicking up dirt and wearing down the grass with every step, and looking longingly at Manhattan and evaluating whether or not they could swim the East River. Maybe it was possible, if you wanted it enough.

Maybe failure was a better alternative.

Cause of death: trying to live.

Prayer Girl poked Nellie in the ribs. "Look." She gestured to a group of women on the other side of the yard. They were a rough-looking bunch, wearing misfit dresses and the most comical straw hats. There were about fifty of them held together by a long rope affixed to leather belts around the waist. They were slowly marching around the yard. Some were shouting—the pace was too fast or too slow, or too disjointed or Lord only knew what else was on their minds. Others were pulling hair and flailing about. Others were just enduring, though a snap didn't seem far off. They were not a clean-looking bunch, and definitely not a sane-looking bunch.

"See that?" Prayer Girl was subdued now. "Those are the women from the Lodge. That's the only place worse than where we are."

"I wouldn't last the night," Tillie said.

"They seem actually insane . . . instead of just inconvenient," Nellie murmured. She'd heard about the Lodge and had some idea of getting herself sent there for additional material. But one look at these women had her revising her plans.

Prayer Girl stared at them thoughtfully. "Do you think that they were like that when they got here? Or did this place drive them to it? In other words, is that us in five years?"

"Oh God," Tillie moaned. "I'm never going to leave here, am I?"

The realization struck the girl at least once a day, and she felt it like it was the first time, every time. Nellie was finding it hard to watch. Tillie started to cry. Her shoulders shook but tears didn't come; her body didn't have enough left for it, Nellie supposed. Imagine a place that could make you run out of tears. It was sickening. But Nellie clung to hope. Cockerill would come. The *World* would save her, and she in turn would save them all. She couldn't explain, but—

"You will get out of here, Tillie, I promise."

Prayer Girl whipped her head around so fast her black hair snapped against Nellie's face. "Who are you to make promises like that? God isn't helping but *you* will? You, who are just some girl as hungry and powerless as the rest of us."

Maybe. But she was full to bursting with this story inside her, and if she could just get out of here, and get the story out of her and on paper . . . then she could keep the promises she made. But there was no point in saying any of that. A twenty-three-year-old woman declaring *I'm a newspaper reporter* was just as laughable as if she went around saying she was the queen of England.

Prayer Girl stepped closer, into Nellie's personal space. "You're stuck here, Nellie Brown. Just like the rest of us. And you're crazy if you think otherwise."

"Please don't fight," Tillie pleaded. "You're all I have."

"Maybe you're cursed to have bad friends," Prayer Girl snapped.

"She isn't," Nellie insisted.

"You make promises you'll never keep and I spend a majority of my days praying for death. Tell me more about her wonderful friends."

"Rose. Daisy. Violet. Rose. Daisy. Violet."

Prayer Girl spun around to face Princess. "Stop saying that!"

Princess stopped. Stared. Blinked. There was a vacantness to her blue-eyed stare and a deadness to all her movements that was profoundly disturbing. She was a shell of a woman who had seen better days. Her hair might have been pale gold but now it was just white, and it hung in limp strings around her face. Her cheeks might have been rosy; now they were ashen.

Her lips parted, but no sound emerged.

"Don't you have *anything* else to say? Literally anything?" Prayer Girl taunted. "Because I have some ideas for you. Lilac. Hyacinth. Geranium!" Prayer Girl was shouting now.

The worst part was that Nellie could have sworn she saw a spark in Princess's eyes, but that was all, just a spark. There was no movement of protest otherwise. It was almost as if the woman she used to be was still alive within her but just could not access her. So Prayer Girl could fight all she wanted with this living ghost, but she would get no retort, no other flowers.

"Lily! Magnolia! Daffodil!"

Even the women from the Lodge were looking over now. You could see them snickering. *Look at her!* What a *spectacle.*

"Oh, make it stop," Tillie moaned. "My head is throbbing."

"Please—" Nellie reached out for Prayer Girl's arm. "That's enough."

"You're not the boss of me."

Nellie gripped her arm, hard, and met her gaze head on. "No, I'm your friend."

The river was right there, slapping at the rocky island shore. The nurses were not keeping a watchful eye. No one would stop her if Prayer Girl made a run for it. Her eyes were stormy, like choppy waves at sea. Nellie wondered why she didn't. What—or *who*—did she have to live for? What was she holding out for? She prayed to God for death but didn't fling herself in the river or down the stairs or starve herself into an early exit.

"Prove it," Prayer Girl said, nearly spitting with rage. "Prove that you're my friend."

Of all the moments for one of the nurses to approach with a message that Nellie Brown had another visitor, that had to be one of the worst.

"If you're really my friend, stay with me," Prayer Girl dared. Nellie wanted to laugh—an inappropriate reaction to be sure. She thought about telling her the truth. That it might be Cockerill, that she could help her more from the outside, if she could just get *out.*

But then Tillie started shouting. "It's for me!" Tillie cried out. "It's my visitor!" She ran toward the asylum in a frenzy to get there first, but a nurse caught her easily and held her back as she sobbed and raged. Her cries and Prayer Girl's bitter laugh rang in Nellie's ears all the way back to the asylum.

Nellie's footsteps echoed in the empty corridor, following Miss Grady's. All the other women were still outside, drinking up the fresh air and sunshine and dreaming of escape. Her head was achingly full of sob stories, her heart was sick with them and her body was starting to tire.

So when Miss Grady indicated that Nellie should follow her, it was with high hopes that this was the moment she'd been desperate for, when Cockerill himself came to secure her release. Sweet merciful heavens, perhaps she could sleep in her own bed tonight. She had fantasies of hot baths and clean sheets and hours of sleep uninterrupted by people trying to force her to take drugs or the sounds of people crying and being beaten. The little things.

Mean Nurse was not exactly forthcoming about the who, what, where, why, of all this. She just marched forward, with a hand grasping Nellie's arm as if she might try to run.

"It's a nice day outside," Nellie said, apropos of nothing, just to get Miss Grady to talk.

"It's just weather. Like any other day."

"You sound like you've been here a long time. Too long."

"So?"

Nellie tried again. "Who has come to visit me?"

Miss Grady did not respond. Either she didn't know or she wasn't in the mood to chat. After all, chatting made them human to each other. Nellie imagined it would make it harder to watch the cruelty let alone participate in it, if one thought of the patients as living, breathing women and not merely lunatics.

So Nellie asked another question. "Do other patients receive this many visitors?" She already knew the answer was no. It was just her who got all the desperate parents, forlorn husbands and high-society gawkers. Just her, because Colton saw fit to write about her in the *Sun* and ruin her scoop.

"You ask too many questions."

To which Nellie smiled and thought, *You have no idea.*

Miss Grady marched along beside her, just daring her to try something. She would do nothing that might jeopardize her meeting with this mystery visitor. *Please let it be Cockerill. Please let it be Cockerill.* They marched along in silence. Footsteps slapping on the cold floors. Wind tunneling through cold, gray corridors.

Without any ceremony, Nellie was shown into that same small reception room where she met with the other visitors who had come to gawk at her and to have their hopes dashed that she wasn't their long-lost daughter/sister/wife. Miss Grady shut the door, leaving Nellie locked in with a strange man of uncertain intentions.

The man standing in the room—that small, hopeless room—had his back toward the door while he looked out the window at the view of Manhattan. He had the demeanor of a newspaperman, she decided. The shoulders, the jacket, the impatient stance because a deadline was looming. It had to be Cockerill. It had to be. Visions of typewriters and steak dinners danced in her head. Of hot baths and clean sheets. She didn't see what was right in front of her.

"It's about time you finally made it out here," Nellie said. "We said seven days, not ten. Or a thousand."

Slowly, he turned.

Swiftly, her heart sank.

His lips quirked up ever so slightly at the corners when he saw her. "I didn't realize you were waiting for me."

"You." She breathed the word like it was fire.

He nodded while she rattled off swear words in her head. "Sam Colton, with the *New York Sun*."

She smiled wryly. "Of course. Now I get to say I told you so."

"You were right. I could just walk across the street to get hired by the *Sun* immediately."

"And you came all the way to Blackwell's Island to tell me. What do you want, congratulations?"

"Not exactly." His expression focused. "I want your story."

Of course he did. This wasn't a surprise; it was to be expected. Pity he had come all this way and would only return empty-handed—she would make sure of it.

"Do you always crash in, uninvited?"

"You know, I wasn't sure that you would do it," he mused.

"And here we are," Nellie said. She spoke briskly, like she was important and had other matters to attend to, which was a complete lie. She was missing precisely nothing. Her friends were mad at her. She was starving and if she was lucky, the bugs in her bread tonight would be dead.

He pulled a notebook and pencil from his jacket pocket. "So you've been here about seven days," he began, and she was grateful for the information. But seven! "I'm not going to lie, Nellie, you look worse for wear."

"Not really anyone here worth getting pretty for." She fixed him with a look that said *you included* while she battled with the urge to touch up her bangs. Her hair had to be a wreck. "As far as you're concerned, Colton, I'm not here."

"I beg to differ. The story of Nellie Brown, *insane girl*, has captured the attention of the city. Let me clarify: *My* story. Everyone is talking about it."

So that explained all the visitors and those mentions from the giggling Miss Grupe and Miss Grupe's beloved Dr. Kinier. They all had Nellie sweating that her ruse had been discovered, putting her at greater risk than she was already. Just imagine if they discovered their cruelty was being observed by a reporter! She'd be dead by morning.

"How lucky for you to find a story that's attracting attention. Too bad it's not *your* story."

"Everyone wants to know all about you," he said. If she had hackles they would be up, at attention. He carried on, oblivious. "So tell me, Nellie Brown—or would you prefer Nellie Bly? Do you care to comment on your experience here at Blackwell's?"

Nellie wanted to stab him with his pencil. The very one he grasped with his elegant fingers, poised above his notebook like she might give him a quote for his blasted story. As if *her* words might appear in *his* story.

Someone get her in the camisole before she did the man an injury. Honestly.

"What do you want, Colton? Revenge or payback because I shared your interview?"

His gaze was intense. "Same as you. I want the story. And I want it on the front page with my name in the byline."

She laughed. "You're not even close."

"I'm here, aren't I? Told them I was your brother from Cuba and that I've come to take you home."

"How clever."

"You inspired me."

"I thought that kind of journalism was cheating."

"Well, they don't seem to take kindly to reporters around here, so I had to lie. Tell me, is it as bad as they say?"

"No comment."

"Doesn't look like they're treating you kindly." She caught him looking at her hair. She gripped her skirts to give her hands something to do other than fluff her bangs. As if that would do anything.

"You know, Colton, if you publish your story first, you'll only be promoting mine."

"Assuming you get out to write it," Colton replied, casually speaking to her darkest, most consuming fears. So she told him what she told herself. She scoffed and said, "Like Cockerill will pass on a story like this?"

He ignored her and murmured as he jotted notes in his stupid notebook. "She confirms she's here on assignment." She wanted to wrench that notebook out of his hands and throw it in the privy.

"You don't have a story, Colton. You're just chasing mine."

"I do have a story and it's already published. The city is buzzing about it. My editor wants more about the 'insane girl.' And I can't resist the chance to scoop the *World* after my interview."

Of course not. And all was fair in love, war and Newspaper Row. Didn't mean she liked it or had to hand over sensational details. But her stomach was in knots. She had the big story and it was getting away from her.

Worse, she was losing it to a man.

Well, Colton would never witness the full Blackwell's experience. No man ever could.

He would never hear the women's stories and would never be able to write about them with the knowledge that he was one bad day away from a lifetime of living death. He would never know the indignity and unfairness of being unable to declare one's own sanity and have it mocked. He would never know what it felt like to acquire a taste for rancid butter because one was so hungry, to feel as if he was going slowly mad, to cling to whatever friendships and comfort and moth-eaten shawls he could get . . .

He wouldn't get *that* story. But by publishing his version, he could distract attention from hers and position himself as the authority on her uniquely female experience. He could get the credit and all the opportunities that came with it.

She wouldn't be the first or the last woman to have her ideas stolen by a man. But it still burned. She would *not* add fuel to his fire.

"You have nothing, Colton. Nothing more than a local interest piece on a slow news day."

And then he surprised her.

"I could get you out," he offered.

She didn't want to give him a slow glance that said *do go on*. But something in her—her instinct to live, probably—leapt at his words.

He could tell he had her interested. He took a step closer. "Right now. Nellie Bly or Brown or whoever you are. You. Me. We could be back in Manhattan in time for a steak dinner at Delmonico's."

This morning Nellie had thought she might climb over dead bodies for a decent meal. She might commit unspeakable acts for a steak dinner. And Delmonico's! The haven of the wealthy, the Wall Street power brokers, the Four Hundred. All of which was to say, she'd be wined and dined and taken care of in proper style. It was not the regular haunt of girl reporters. Dear God, it would be delicious. A perfectly cooked steak with some fancy French sauce, preciously prepared vegetables and wine that had not been laced with poisons to make her docile. She could almost taste it. She had never known hunger like the one gnawing away at her insides.

Oh, hello, temptation.

God, she hated him for it.

He must have seen the hunger and the wanting plain on her face. He must have seen that she was willing to die for this exposé. His expression softened—she'd almost describe it as concerned and sympathetic—and it was a warm, dangerous feeling to be on the receiving end of Colton *caring*. When he spoke next, his voice was gentle and his gaze full of feeling, as if he truly cared and wasn't her rival at all.

"It's just a story, Nellie."

But it wasn't.

And the thing was, Nellie was hungry for more than just food. She and all these mad girls of Blackwell's were. They wanted freedom. They wanted to be seen and loved, cherished even. If not that, then understood and kept in care and comfort. Help getting well would be nice. Some nourishment for the brain and body and soul would go so far toward making them whole again. What Nellie was beginning to understand was that women arrived here with chips and cracks and little fixable injuries, but it was the asylum that broke them and made them utterly unsuitable for the outside world.

So here they stayed, starving and out of sight and waiting. For what?

Nellie, maybe. She was ambitious and arrogant enough to think so, even though the popular consensus was that ambition was an ugly color on a woman. But it didn't seem like anyone else was going to do anything about it—not even the well-meaning Dr. Ingram. Colton here was sniffing around the story, but the angle was all wrong. He thought it was about *her*.

So really, it was up to Nellie to get the real story. How do you give up on that, and the chance to help all those women, for just a steak dinner?

Even a Delmonico's steak dinner.

"It's more than the story you think it is, Colton. You're chasing me and my story for what—payback? I'm trying to change the world. So I'm not going to trade the story of a lifetime for a steak dinner. Especially if it means you'll get ideas about being my Prince Charming of Newspaper Row."

Colton shifted his weight and she caught his clean scent and she found herself leaning into it. Worse, she caught herself yearning. The look of pity and concern in his eyes put a stop to that feeling.

"You look like you're starving, Nellie. You look . . . unkempt." Which was a polite way of saying she looked filthy and smelled bad, all of which was true. "You are worse for wear, and for what? Did Cockerill promise you a job or just a one-off story? Are you even certain that he'll send someone for you?"

"If he wants my story, he will."

"What if the *World* doesn't want to be seen chasing a scoop by the *Sun*?" Colton lifted one brow, challenging her in the manner of heroes in novels, which just annoyed her.

"That's a chance I'm willing to take. Go back to Manhattan and get your steak dinner and stay out of my story."

"What are you trying to prove, Nellie?"

She gazed at him unflinchingly. "Women have to look out for each other, Colton. No one else will."

Colton's lips parted like he was going to say something, but then he thought the better of it. Nellie turned and banged on the door to alert the nurse that she was finished here, thank you very much.

But it was just Miss Grupe waiting.

"Take me back to the others, please," Nellie told her.

Miss Grupe looked at Nellie, then at Colton, then back at Nellie, with the expression of one trying to understand why four plus four was not totaling eight. Something wasn't right. Something didn't make sense.

"Are you sure?"

"Yes."

"But it's your brother from Cuba! He's come to take you home. Don't you want to go home?"

"Not with him, no."

Miss Grupe was so confused, she stopped giggling. "But this is your opportunity to leave. You might not get another."

"I'll take my chances."

"He says he's here to rescue you."

With one smart look over her shoulder, Nellie said, "He's mistaken. And he can quote me on that."

CHAPTER TWENTY-FOUR

Marian

WALL STREET, NEW YORK CITY

First thing that morning, Marian went to see a witch about Jay Wallace. She got the idea after her interview with Louisa Newbold, the future Mrs. Wallace, who was all too happy to talk about her dreams for the wedding and ambitions for her place in society. She was less forthcoming about the exact circumstances of their meeting—"our eyes met across the room at a dinner party in Saratoga sometime that summer." And in boasting about what a marvelous couple they were, she did utter one line that got Marian's brain whirring. *He brings the status, and I bring the fortune.*

What a curious thing to say about the famous "Wall Street Wallace."

Marian decided to investigate further. Which is to say, she went to Hetty Green. Marian found her under the stairs at the Seaboard National Bank. She had set up office there and the bank didn't dare say a word about it—not when Hetty was estimated to have a fortune of her own worth twenty-six million dollars.

It was almost enough to make Marian swoon.

Because Mrs. Green was a millionaire of her own making, all her eccentricities had to be tolerated. Like her office under the stairs, where she sat surrounded by trunks and papers and warmed-up oatmeal for lunch on the radiator. They still had to give her a name, though. One that put her in her place, or tried to. They called her cranky and insane and "the Witch of Wall Street."

If she was a witch, her fortune was by dark magic and not, say, a sharp understanding of financial markets and frugal living.

"Mrs. Green?"

"Who's asking?"

"I'm Marian Blake, a reporter with the *Herald*."

"So?" She was also famously rude. Marian found it refreshing. Mrs. Green didn't shoo her away, so Marian went ahead with her questions.

"I'm hoping I can ask you a few questions about Jay Wallace."

"Why? He's a crashing bore. An idiot. He is everything wrong with men, especially these fellows on Wall Street." Mrs. Green had yet to lift her gaze from a paper full of numbers in tiny eye-straining print. "They're all so damn sure of themselves but can't manage the fundamentals."

"But he seems to be doing well. He's got the Fifth Avenue mansion, the big yacht, and his wedding promises to be spectacular."

"He's all flash and no substance. I don't think he could even explain compound interest if you promised him a million dollars for it. If he took just a minute to do some due diligence, he might not be in the position he's in."

"And what position is that?"

"Up to his eyeballs in debt. Broke. And he'll take the coward's way out of it too."

"What's that?" Marian thought she was alluding to death. Suicide. Something dire.

Mrs. Green laughed and said, "Marriage."

Marian stepped out on the street and pulled her collar up around her chin. Not that there was any disguising the fact that she was a woman, frequenting a street that didn't usually host the female sex. There were a lot of stares until she got to Broadway and waved for a hack.

On second thought, she wanted to walk. To think. Something wasn't adding up. Maybe she was making something out of nothing. But maybe she was also on to a story that was bigger than a wedding, bigger than a woman's tragic death, bigger than all that.

Hetty had gone on to tell her that Wallace had been making a series of foolish bets and investments for the past year or "possibly forever." Mrs. Green was privy to this information because Wallace had told it to her, while he pleaded for some funds. He was willing to pay an outrageous amount of interest, which was tempting, but she didn't think he'd ever manage to pay it back. And now he was marrying a famously rich widow.

Actually, something was adding up. Marian gasped when it occurred to her. Murder, perhaps? Losing his wife and wedding a wealthy woman could be a way for him to save face and his reputation among society. It was ridiculous, like something straight out of a novel. It was just an outrageous idea—unless she could gather the facts to prove it. At that, Marian broke into a run.

Front page, here I come.

CHAPTER TWENTY-FIVE

Mad, Bad and Dangerous

> *What, excepting torture, would produce insanity quicker than this treatment? . . . Take a perfectly sane and healthy woman, shut her up and make her sit from 6 a.m. until 8 p.m. on straight-back benches, do not allow her to talk or move during these hours, give her no reading and let her know nothing of the world or its doings, give her bad food and harsh treatment, and see how long it will take to make her insane. Two months would make her a mental and physical wreck.*
>
> —Nellie Bly, *Ten Days in a Mad-House*

ANOTHER DAY IN THE INSANE ASYLUM AT BLACKWELL'S ISLAND

"I want you to know I'm not insane," Nellie told Miss Grady, who told her to shut up and take a seat with everybody else. Which she did. The memory of her day in the restraints and the doctor's late-night attempt to drug her into submission were still fresh in her mind. Her perfectly sane mind, thank you very much.

But she was having trouble keeping the days straight. When he'd visited, Colton had said she'd been in for seven days already. So today was at least her eighth or ninth day in the asylum—far longer than the seven she and Cockerill had agreed on. An hour on these benches felt like a lifetime, and they were, by her estimation, forced to sit here from six to eight each day. All damned day.

Meanwhile, Prayer Girl muttered ways to die and Tillie shivered and sighed. The moth-eaten shawl Dr. Ingram had managed to provide her with didn't do much. She had stopped singing softly to herself, as if she was fading away, right before their eyes.

So Nellie was ready for Cockerill to come secure her release, which was due to happen, oh, any day now. Nellie was itching to get out and start writing. She was desperate to feel like she was doing something other than just sitting here, working herself into a quiet state of anxiety as she imagined that Colton was scooping her story, or that Cockerill had forgotten about her, or that he had decided she wasn't worth the bother. The mere thought of Colton printing her story gave her such a rage fever, it warmed her up so much that even the wind from the East River didn't chill her.

But she wanted more for her story than just the bad food or the hygienic catastrophe that was bathing. She needed more than boredom and hideously uncomfortable furniture, the casual cruelty of nurses and the heartbreaking indifference and ineptitude of the doctors (Dr. Ingram excluded). She had all these women's stories—that was something Colton could never get. But she needed something else. Something to verify it all, something to prove it all wasn't just the rantings of a mad girl reporter.

Nellie's attentions landed on The Book.

That book held names and reports of drug doses and restraints so the nurses could know what was what at each shift change. It was a record of their care and cruelty, detailing arrivals and reasons for being committed, and listed who had "filthy habits" or other problems.

Nellie needed it.

She wanted to take in all the words and commit them to memory. She wanted the chance to rip out pages and hide them in the folds of this god-awful ill-fitting dress that barely clothed her and definitely did not keep her warm. She wanted paper-and-ink proof of what she witnessed.

But she could not just run up and take it.

She'd be slapped in restraints—or worse—faster than she could say *Nellie Bly, with the* New York World. A fact that probably wouldn't do her any favors anyway. She knew too much and had the power to get too many people in trouble. Knowledge that she was a reporter would get her hauled off to the Lodge, or "Retreat," and "forgotten" or "lost" if anyone came looking for her.

What Nellie needed was to create a distraction.

And she could not do it alone.

"I need your help with something," Nellie whispered to Prayer Girl, who, without missing a beat, drawled, "Well, I don't know, I'm really busy." Then she burst out into that cackle of hers that did make her sound mad.

"No talking," Miss Grady reminded them.

"I'm joking," she whispered.

"I know," Nellie said.

"Why do you need a distraction?" Tillie asked. "What are you going to do?"

"I want to know what's in the book at the nurses' table."

"Why? Who cares?"

"Why not?" Nellie shrugged. "What else are we going to do?"

"You have a point."

"We'll get in trouble," Tillie said. "We'll get sent to the Retreat. Or worse!"

"There's nothing worse than the Retreat, honey." Prayer Girl was probably right, but no one wanted to confirm. It sounded so nice: the *Retreat.* Like a woman could go off for a few days and rest when the social whirl and choosing what to wear became just *too much.* It sounded like a peaceful refuge where one bathed in warm waters and lounged around on soft chaise longues, and sipped delicate herbal teas, all made with fresh herbs picked from the kitchen garden. It sounded like a place where nurses spoke gently and doctors asked about symptoms and concerns and really listened. Maybe someone would play soothing music on the flute . . . and then after a few days, a woman could return to the world restored and refreshed, ready to conquer all.

The world did not want women to conquer all, which was probably one reason why the Retreat was a place to beat out whatever fighting spirit a woman had left in her after a stint behind asylum bars.

"It's just an idea," Nellie said. "I wouldn't ask you to risk the Retreat for anything."

"No talking!" Miss Grady, again.

They fell silent, not because they were ordered to, but because they were thinking. Was there another way Nellie could get her hands on that book? Perhaps she could sneak out of the dinner line. Starving as she was, she didn't mind missing a meal. But then Prayer Girl sighed.

"Maybe I'll do it. I'm bored. And I'm tired of waiting on a man." She looked heavenward and made an obscene gesture. "A girl has gotta help herself."

"God, I wish I had your bravery," Tillie said. "Then I might . . . I don't even know what I might do. I'm not even brave enough in my brain. Which is perfectly well, not that anyone asked."

No one mentioned her episode the other day. Or that she was constantly shivering and trembling.

In the corner, the nurses were taunting a new arrival, a girl named Urena. They'd all been given to understand that she had been born "silly," and it had quickly been discovered that she was very sensitive about her age. She was eighteen, she said, and grew furious if told anything to the contrary.

The nurses were amusing themselves by teasing her about it.

Miss Grady looked up from The Book. "It says here, Urena, that you are thirty-three."

"I am not! I'm eighteen."

"It is not good to lie about your age, Urena."

"I'm not lying."

"Such vanity," Miss Grupe said, which was a bit rich since Nellie would have guessed her to be the sort to shave a few years off her age. This went on for a bit, until poor Urena was in tears and shouting.

"We'll have to go fetch the doctor now," Miss Grady said. "She'll need help calming down."

What she needed was to stop being mocked and Nellie stood up to stay so. "Stop it!" All the women in the room turned to look at Nellie. They fell silent, and all one could hear were Urena's soft sobs. "Just . . . stop! It's hard enough being here without your abuse!"

"Abuse?" Miss Grady lifted one brow.

Beside Nellie, Prayer Girl muttered, "Now you're in for it, Nellie."

"That is the thanks we get for the care we provide you?"

"I don't know if 'care' is the word I'd use for it."

"And what does it matter what words you use, Nellie Brown? You are some confused girl who doesn't even know where she's from or who she is. And you are very difficult. Do you know what we do to difficult women?"

"Send them here," Nellie said. That was the moment a doctor arrived on the scene, armed with his syringes and camisoles. A pair of nurses held Urena in place for the injection and then bundled her up in the camisole, wrapping her arms around herself, confining her into a forced self-embrace. Then she was marched off to God only knew where.

After all that, Nellie didn't think Prayer Girl would be willing to create a distraction or do anything that would get them in trouble, so she dropped the subject for the rest of the day and spent her time trying to imagine other ways to get The Book. Despite Prayer Girl's pleas for death, she didn't really court danger or chances to escape—*Why?* Nellie wondered. So when they were lined up for bed that night, Nellie was surprised when Prayer Girl said, "I'm in. Tomorrow. Don't lose your nerve."

STILL IN THE DAMNED ASYLUM

Something was different today. Some of the women noticed it right away, some took longer, and others were totally oblivious to it.

"I don't like it," Miss Grady was saying to Miss Grupe. She shook her head and folded her arms over her enormous bosom. "It makes me nervous."

"Is that . . . is that . . . ?" Tillie, eyes wide with wonder, drifted over toward the source of everyone's fascination. The stove. A fire was burning, warming up the room. She was very pale and wan and Nellie gave a silent thanks to Dr. Ingram, who she was sure was the reason for this small kindness.

"Well, look at that," Prayer Girl said, pointing to the stove, which was all aglow with burning embers.

"Stay away from the stove!" Miss Grady barked. "It's only here on doctor's orders, and if one of you touches it, I won't light it up again."

So it *was* the work of Dr. Ingram. Nellie felt it like a valentine. It was maybe even better than Colton's offer of a Delmonico's steak because it came with no strings attached.

"Everybody sit down!" Miss Grady shouted and clapped her hands, while the other nurses pushed and smacked women who were taking just a tad too long. One really had to wonder what the rush was, since this was all they would do all day.

But not today.

Prayer Girl and Nellie exchanged a glance. Mischievous sparks danced in their eyes and smiles were barely contained. They were going to do something! It was the littlest thing, stealing the nurses' book and reading about her fellow inmates and all the ridiculous reasons they had been committed—novel reading, woman troubles, epilepsy, nervous conditions, vanity, disobeying their husbands. She was keen to read about all the treatments they were getting, the drugs, the restraints. And maybe she could find out some names. Who was Princess, anyway?

"When should we do it?" Prayer Girl asked. "I'm ready when you are."

"Not quite yet," Nellie whispered. "We should wait for the lull to set in."

"I hate the lull," Tillie moaned. "When you've been sitting so long and have to sit longer still. I get so tired and weary from just sitting. Isn't that something?"

"At least you're near the warmth today," Prayer Girl said.

"Thank God for small favors."

"I'm done asking God for anything," Prayer Girl said. This

had both Tillie and Nellie turning their heads. "If he were a man and I were a woman who fancied him, and I kept sending him letters and never getting a response, you would all tell me to move on. Any good friend would."

"But . . . but . . . it's God," Tillie whispered.

"I make it a point never to rely on a man," Nellie said. "Learned that one the hard way."

"Do tell, Nellie Brown."

Nellie shrugged. "It's all in the past." But then again, here she was, waiting for Cockerill to show up, whisk her away and hand her life back to her.

Maybe she should have been nervous that Prayer Girl had given up on prayer. Maybe she should have been concerned at how pale Tillie's cheeks seemed, even with this new heat. But Nellie was fixed on Miss Grady, who was reading a newspaper and sipping coffee like she was at home, at her breakfast table. Her ability to ignore the mass of unfortunate humanity was something else, truly. Miss Grupe, the giggling nurse, was sitting beside her with her head propped on her hand. She had that dreamy look in her eyes that suggested her thoughts were fixed on romantic fantasies with Dr. Kinier. To each her own.

They were slowly approaching the lull. The moment nearing midday when time slowed down and it felt as if all the air had been sucked out of the room. The moment when daydreams could not sustain you, and, in fact, your own thoughts were starting to make you sick and irritable. It was the time when one had to give up on searching for a comfortable position on the Benches of Pain and Suffering.

In a little while women would need to relieve themselves and wouldn't be able to hold it in any longer. Sometimes the nurses would escort a woman to the toilet, and sometimes . . . they did not.

"Are we there yet?" Prayer Girl whispered.

"Getting close," Nellie said. "But *damn* we are too far away from the piano."

"So?"

"I thought you would go play piano as the distraction."

Prayer Girl burst out laughing.

"I don't play, New Girl. When would I have learned to play the piano?"

"I said no laughing! No talking!"

Nellie's cheeks flamed. Of course. But also . . . damn. Nellie needed her to do something. She needed that book. She needed to see proof. Her plan was to run off with it, to slip into some empty cell or hide in the necessary and gorge herself on the words until they found her. It was, admittedly, a stupid plan riddled with flaws and chances to get caught, and for what—just what she could memorize under duress. But Nellie had this itchy, antsy feeling that she had to do something or she would actually in fact go mad. They would write down *Nellie Bly: admitted for ambition, trusting a man.*

"Don't worry, New Girl, you'll get your distraction," Prayer Girl murmured with a smirk that did things to Nellie's insides and made her stomach twist. Nerves. Something about Prayer Girl had her on edge. "What are you going to do?"

"You'll see."

"Why does that make me incredibly nervous?"

"But doesn't it feel good to feel *something*?"

Nellie didn't want to admit it, but, yes, it did feel good to feel something. Her nerves felt like they were dancing inside her, awake and ready to spring into action. Dear God, action! Nellie focused all her attentions and energy on Miss Grady, on the Giggling Miss Grupe, on The Book. So she was ready but not ready when Prayer Girl made a sudden move, in a direction that Nellie had not expected.

At first, it seemed Prayer Girl was just after some warmth. A few women cast their attention on the sight of Prayer Girl creeping up to the stove. It was a testament to how boring their lives were that *this* was interesting. For want of entertainment, no one said anything.

Miss Grady was reading a newspaper and sipping a mug of coffee; Miss Grupe was dozing.

Prayer Girl crept over to the stove and took off her shoe.

Her shoe?

Nellie tilted her head, curious. She didn't dare speak, but her eyes said, *What the hell are you doing?* But Prayer Girl wasn't looking for her approval.

She got her answer soon enough. Using her shoe, Prayer Girl scooped up some hot embers from the stove and flung them in the direction of the nurses. They skittered across the floor, hot little bombs of fear and danger.

"What the—?" Miss Grady looked at the embers, one of which had stopped just inches from her boots. She looked at Prayer Girl. So too did Miss Grupe, now wide-awake. "Oh my God!"

Prayer Girl just laughed. She continued scooping up the embers and flinging them around the room and across the floor, where they landed under benches and brushed up against feet and ankles.

Then they started a slow burn into the floor.

All at once the room exploded. Women leapt to their feet and onto the benches. Some screamed, some laughed. The nurses were shouting for order, but for once no one listened or cowered.

But Nellie—brave, daring Nellie, as she liked to think of herself—was frozen in place on the bench. This was not what they had planned. This was not what she had in mind. This was a catastrophe in the making—burning embers, in an old building with locks on the doors, full of women? This was going to make the front pages and *not* in a good way.

Nellie could see what terrible fate awaited—it was only logical. Her brain said, *Run!* Her brain said, *Go!* Nellie's brain shouted, *You idiot, this is your chance!* But Nellie was frozen in fear.

This was how fires started. Great, roaring fires that hotly consumed everything around them. Nellie knew how fires ended. She knew that they didn't always end well.

She knew that if one got angry and threw a lamp, the oil and flame and glass crossing together when they hit the wall was enough to start one. She knew that flames liked upholstered chairs and wooden dining tables and wallpaper. She knew that they could terrorize grown men, even the sort like Ford, who went around terrorizing everyone else. She knew a fire could make grown men cry for mercy.

But Nellie wasn't *there* anymore. She wasn't at that Pittsburgh fire that raised too many questions. She was *here,* frozen to this bench. More than once she thought she might die on these benches, but of boredom, not a raging inferno.

All around her, the madwomen of Blackwell's raged in panic. Some sprinted for the doors; some pushed at the windows, beating the glass until it shattered. One particular woman went for Miss Grady's coffee—to drink in big, desperate gulps. The nurses had fled, probably to get help.

Prayer Girl was succeeding with flying colors—it was the perfect distraction. And yet.

"What are you doing?" Nellie screamed at her.

"What does it look like I'm doing? Creating the distraction that you wanted. Now, go. *Go!*"

But Nellie was stuck, held in place by fear and memories. She could hear her mother calling for her: *Pink! Pink!* She remembered darting through the rooms, looking for a way out. She remembered looking back over her shoulder for Ford, hoping he wasn't following her and hoping, as wicked as it was, that he was stuck and that the flames were feasting on him. She wanted her mother's great mistake gone . . . but she didn't want to go with him.

She thought of Dr. Ingram's observation that she had become still at his mention of fire. Like she was remembering something.

Well, the good doctor wasn't wrong. Here was her big opportunity and she was stuck in the past. It was done—what should it matter? She had survived; it was time to move on! No one mourned Ford. Not even a little bit. Not even at all. And no one asked questions about what Nellie had been doing there—she left for New York before they could.

No one knew that Nellie didn't feel sorry either.

"Go!" Prayer Girl screamed. Her usually pale cheeks were flushed crimson from the heat and excitement. "This is your chance!"

The other patients were frantically pushing one another around, trying to get away from the embers. Some were trying to flee the room—maybe the island, maybe this life—but were finding the doors locked. Others were stuck in place as Nellie was. And still others were stuck, restrained at the wrists and ankles. Their screams would haunt her forever.

What do you do?

And then Tillie. Dear God, poor Tillie. She had started to shake uncontrollably; the commotion had triggered one of her episodes.

Who do you save?

Everywhere she looked was mayhem and lives in ruin. Panic and fear and desperation mingled with smoke and little flames. Nellie had to decide whom she felt like saving. Or if she wanted to be anyone's heroine at all.

Nellie would think about this later, the way she seemed to dance through the mayhem. Twisting, turning, arching her back like a ballet dancer to avoid crashing into others as they pushed and wailed. She kept her eyes on The Book, lying there, its pages splayed open and its secrets right there for the taking.

So she went to take it. Because so far, there was no story she didn't chase, risk she didn't take, room she didn't crash into, or lead she didn't pursue. The girl her mother called Pink might have been too scared to move. Elizabeth Cochran (without the *e*) might have been frozen in terror. But she wasn't those women anymore. She was Nellie Bly and Nellie Bly got the story.

She would never forgive herself for the way she left Tillie behind, as she writhed and vibrated while her brain protested *too much, all at once*. But she had to prove that lady reporters could get the facts. She had to prove that lady reporters could get the story.

Nellie grabbed The Book.

She looked over her shoulder and saw that Prayer Girl had, at last, thank God, stopped flinging fire and rushed to Tillie's side. They were together. They had each other.

The Book was dense with pages, and its leather cover was dried out. There was no time to run, no place to hide so she could read it. Instead, Nellie started tearing out pages and trying to secrete them away in her dress, in her undergarments, stuffed them in whatever cracks she could. What she would give for a pocket right about now!

As Nellie pulled at the pages, she read snatches of script:

Gretchen: arrival unknown. Became violent when denied extra food. Given restraints.
Sarah: turned in by husband, has lust for men. Must be kept in camisole at all times, to keep her from touching herself.
Edna: admitted for drunkenness. Must be kept away from spirits or becomes violent.

It was a heartbreaking read. Woman after woman admitted for nervous conditions, worries and anxieties. Women complained of mysterious pains in their abdomens and problems with their menstruation, headaches that wouldn't go away. Some used alcohol too much. Some were just drowning in grief from the loss of loved ones.

Nothing here would help with any of that.

Gertrude: filthy habits, must be kept in crib at night.
Louise: believes her dead parents are with her, refuses to obey doctors.

Maybe Nellie hadn't needed to pretend to be insane at all. Nellie could have gotten picked up for public drunkenness or raved about stomach pains and she would have ended up here all the same. And then, there it was:

"Princess": must be kept on laudanum, regularly dosed. By orders of Commissioner.

That was curious. Why would the commissioner care about a particular patient? Nellie slowly ripped out one page and then another, with some idea of getting out of here with written proof. Facts.

That was ridiculous, of course; these shapeless dresses didn't have pockets where a woman might hold something to read or a slice of bread or a weapon. God forbid a girl have a possession of her own and a place to keep it close. So she shoved them under her arms and in her unmentionables. Not her ideal, but really, what else was she going to do?

The commotion in the hall wasn't exactly quieting down. An army of nurses had answered the cries of "Mayday! Mayday! Insane patients acting insane!" Miss Grady led the charge—she directed an especially stout nurse to grab hold of Prayer Girl. It took three nurses to wrestle her into a camisole.

"The Lodge for this one, Miss Grady?"

Miss Grady barely gave her a second glance. She didn't see how Prayer Girl stilled, but the fire was still bright in her eyes. Miss Grady dropped her sentence. "Yes, the Lodge for this one. And restraints."

Prayer Girl erupted. She wrestled with herself, all tied up in that fabric, stained mysteriously from a previous occupant. She whipped her hair around and snarled, "*Hands off me.*"

She wasn't mad.

She was angry as all hell.

She had every right to be. Prayer Girl was just a woman named Maeve, picked up off the street for promiscuity because she was spotted late at night, drinking and dancing too close with another woman. It was just the daring thing she would do—living and loving out loud and in public—and she was paying dearly for it. She was back to praying.

"Dear God, please burn this whole place down! Don't mind if I'm in it. But don't burn that book before Nellie Brown gets to read it!" She started laughing, and it took three nurses to get her out of the room.

Miss Grady turned to Nellie. Her heart started pounding in

her chest. Her stomach heaved and all of a sudden felt like it wanted to be sick. There was a look in the nurse's eyes like she had been waiting for this moment and now she was going to savor it.

Dr. Kinier rushed in with his medicine bag. One could practically see syringes full of tranquilizing drugs spilling out of it. He tended to Tillie first. Then Mathilda, who, through it all, had not ceased her dressing down of the unscrupulous man who had cheated her out of her business and her money.

None of that distracted Miss Grady from her fixation on Nellie. She marched toward her, shoving other patients out of her way. "You. Come with me."

CHAPTER TWENTY-SIX

Colton

THE INSANE ASYLUM AT BLACKWELL'S ISLAND

Colton was back on Blackwell's Island, notebook in hand and succumbing to his bad habit of biting on a pencil out of nerves. The Octagon Tower looming in front of him just had an air of foreboding about it that made him anxious, even though he wasn't at risk. There was no danger for him here; only reward.

But he had seen and heard and smelled enough to imagine what those women were enduring. Having seen Nellie, a mess after only a week, he didn't even want to think of the state the other patients were in. They certainly didn't have her determination, grit, pluck and purpose to survive.

He shifted on his feet, waiting, thinking that it might sound like he admired her. What with her determination, grit, pluck and purpose. Dear God, *Blackwell's*. It'd been well over a week now, and as far as he knew, she hadn't gotten out yet, alive or . . . otherwise. He knew. He'd been watching and waiting around, trying to get someone to talk and to give him some facts that he could piece together with all the other details of her and her story that he had painstakingly tracked down.

And damn it, all of it made him admire her.

He still had to get the damn story before she did. His editor at the *Sun* was breathing down his neck about it, often ranting about the whole reason he had hired Sam was for this scoop, so he'd better file *this* story before the *World* did—or else.

So here he was, waiting outside the Octagon *again*, hoping to find someone willing to talk to him on the record. He straightened when he saw two people—a man and a woman—emerge walking side by side. They moved as if eager to be done with the place and to get somewhere more pleasant—home or literally anywhere else.

Colton pushed the pencil into his pocket and moved toward them.

"Excuse me, do you have a moment to talk—?"

The man stopped and brought himself up to his full height. Which, Colton noted, was still a good two inches shorter than him. He was wary, while the woman on his arm was staring at him. "Who are you?" he wanted to know. "If you are not a member of the staff you should not be here."

"Sam Colton, with the *New York Sun*. I'd just like to ask you a few questions about one of your patients." The man glanced questioningly at the woman by his side, who was standing a little closer than professionalism dictated. When they didn't brush him off right away, Sam went on. "She goes by Nellie Brown."

"Don't know her," the man said gruffly.

The woman, who had been staring at him, suddenly burst into a smile.

"I remember you! You're her brother. From Cuba."

Shit, damn and twenty other swear words. Being recognized for his previous attempts to penetrate the asylum walls was not something Colton had prepared for. But the other man came to his rescue.

"Look, I don't know what you're doing here, but you shouldn't be here," he said, looking around nervously. "We're just leaving and I suggest you do the same."

Another brush-off. Another dead end. Another blank page in his notebook that wanted scoops and quotes. Colton bit on the pencil again. He had one last card to play and he hesitated to do it because it would get Nellie in trouble. Or worse, it would put her in danger. But his sister's medical bills weren't getting paid or going away.

And Nellie had all that determination, grit, pluck and purpose.

He also didn't doubt that she might do the same, if the tables were turned.

"Wait—" Colton said. "There's a reporter in your midst." There was just enough light left in the day to watch the color drain out of their faces. He let them sit with the dawning horror for just a moment. "I'm wondering if you'd like a chance to tell your side of the story."

"Nellie Brown, you say?"

It turns out they had something to say after all. Colton had his pencil at the ready as they started talking. "I'll need your names," he said. They supplied them: Dr. Kinier and Miss Grupe. They had plenty to say, and Colton wrote it all down with his tooth-marked pencil.

CHAPTER TWENTY-SEVEN

She Is Cursed Before She Leaves

Miss Grady called me into the hall, and . . . calling me all the vile and profane names a woman could ever remember . . .

—Nellie Bly, *Ten Days in a Mad-House*

THE INSANE ASYLUM AT BLACKWELL'S ISLAND

This time when Miss Grady had Nellie by the arm, her anger was palpable. Nellie could feel it in the punishing way her fingers dug into the soft flesh of her arm, pushing for bruises to burst across her skin. Her rage was loud too, and she kept up a steady stream of curses and foul names, all directed at Nellie.

But even with bruises blooming under Miss Grady's fingertips, even with an outraged tirade full of mean words in two languages, even with fear pulsing through Nellie's veins, she had a question.

"Where are we going?"

"You'll find out soon enough. And then you won't cause me trouble anymore."

"Is it the Lodge?" *Please don't say the Lodge. Please don't say the Lodge.*

Miss Grady didn't answer. This was the way to the baths, was it not? Was that any consolation? The thought of that filthy, cold water made Nellie's stomach turn all over again. She glanced up at the nurse, taking in the hard set of her jaw and determined stride. She wasn't dreading this at all. Given the glint in her eye, Nellie would almost say that she was keen for whatever was to come next.

Nellie couldn't bite back her questions anymore. "Why are you so mean to the patients here?"

"I could ask why you are so disruptive," she retorted. "But I know. It's madness. Lunacy. Idiocy! You just need a firm hand like all the others."

"Maybe we don't need a firm hand but kindness."

Miss Grady laughed. "They just need to behave."

"Were you always like this? Or has the work here changed you?"

"I do the job I was hired to do."

"Why this job?" Nellie asked. Miss Grady scoffed. What jobs were there for women, and immigrant women at that? Hardly any, and all of them undesirable.

"What will you have me do, Nellie Brown? Sew shirts for pennies a day? Work in a factory under the lecherous gaze of some man? Empty chamber pots for the rich?"

At once, Nellie understood. The pay here could not be much better than what was given for sewing or gluing hatboxes in a factory. The setting might be a far cry worse than any uptown brownstone or Fifth Avenue mansion, but at least here, Miss Grady had power. Even if it was only power over the weakest, sickest and most helpless creatures in New York, she had authority to do as she wished without being questioned.

Just this moment, as the nurse hauled Nellie down the hall, obviously against her will, none of the doctors or asylum staff they passed so much as raised an eyebrow. After all, Nellie was just some madwoman and this was the least she deserved.

She still had questions.

"Were you like this before you got the job here or has the position changed you?"

"I said, *stop talking.*"

Miss Grady wouldn't look at her. Wouldn't dignify her with answers or even a glance. Or maybe she had to keep her distance from the patients in order to do this job.

"To be honest, I'd rather not. If I could just go back to the others—"

"And cause more trouble? And make my job harder? I don't think so." This time, Miss Grady laughed. The sound made Nellie slow her steps, which made her stumble and which would hopefully slow down her arrival at whichever torture Miss Grady was looking forward to inflicting. But Miss Grady just tightened her grip on Nellie's arm. This time, tears pricked Nellie's eyes. It was just a little pain! But it was also fear. She had been pushing Miss Grady's buttons for days now. Seven, at least.

"I'm going to teach you a lesson once and for all, Nellie Brown. You won't bother me again as long as you're in this asylum."

There was no point in talking.

But that didn't stop Nellie. She had to do something to stop this, to slow this, to change this.

"It's hard enough being a woman," Nellie said. "It must be harder still being a foreign woman here. I know how hard it is to come from so far and to start a new life. No one makes it easy." Miss Grady glanced at her but would not give any indication that Nellie's words meant something to her. She'd taken great pains to hide that fact, but they both knew that the world made things unnecessarily hard for her because of her German and Irish ancestry.

"Men are not the only ones who want to be powerful," Nellie continued. "Or just feel powerful. The world doesn't make it easy for a woman to feel powerful. I think most of us would be content with just feeling control over our destinies." Such were Nellie's thoughts, voiced aloud, as she was dragged down the hall on the way to something unpleasant, at the mercy of a woman who was considered insignificant at best once she left these asylum walls.

"Stop. Talking."

Finally, Miss Grady stopped and pushed a door open to the bathing room, a place Nellie had hoped she would never, ever see again. Miss Grady found some restraints and put them on Nellie's wrists so she could not open the door and escape while the nurse was busy filling up a large basin of water. Nellie thought of the papers she had stashed on her person. If she was stripped down to nothing, they would be discovered and she was certain to receive an even more severe punishment for having them. It would raise questions too. Questions she didn't want to answer.

Next, Miss Grady unceremoniously hauled Nellie over to the dirty basin, and she stared at her reflection in the water, with specks of dirt, scum and strands of someone else's hair floating in it. One hand was placed on her neck and her heart and lungs and blood started to panic inside of her. The other hand grabbed a fistful of her hair.

I should have cut my hair.

"Since you won't listen—" Miss Grady began, and it wasn't the first time Nellie had heard that, but that was her last thought before her head was plunged under the water. She wanted to fight. She wanted to scream. She wanted to ask more questions, like *Why?* and *How dare you?* But if she opened her mouth she would die.

Her lungs were on fire.

Her heart was pumping furiously.

Her fingers were twitching and gnawing helplessly in the restraints.

Just when she thought she was about to die, her head was pulled up and she sucked in the hugest gulp of cold air.

"When I say no talking, I mean no talking." Nellie sucked in great, heaving breaths. "No one cares about the stupid questions of an impertinent girl."

It was probably true. But Nellie refused to accept it. Or this. She squirmed, trying to escape, but Miss Grady held on tight.

Anger had to go somewhere. This, she knew. Sometimes it meant lashing out; sometimes a woman was far too adept at swallowing it down, where it festered inside and made one's stomach burn and heart ache. But sometimes it came out like this. Nellie almost couldn't blame Miss Grady. What were you supposed to do when the world made you enraged and you had no way to handle it?

Miss Grady was under the impression that her point had not yet been made, and so before Nellie could take another breath and hold it close, her head was once again thrust under. She was held under for one, two, three, Nellie wanted to scream, four, five, oh my God she was going to die like this, six, seven and—

It was believed that terror was stronger than mental confusion and a brush with death was *just the thing* to right a garbled brain. It was supposed to make her afraid and thus manageable.

Water was also just the thing to snuff out the fire in a woman.

Mercy came by way of a knock at the door. Miss Grady swore quietly while Nellie heaved great big breaths of air, trying to quiet the fire in her lungs and calm the pounding of her heart. Another nurse was at the door, bearing a message: Nellie Brown had another visitor. Miss Grady was needed to help quell the patients in Hall 6.

"She's busy," Miss Grady barked. "I'm busy."

"I'm not busy," Nellie said. "I insist that I be taken to see my visitor."

There was some debate between the nurses as to Nellie's availability. It took every ounce of control within her to calmly assert her need and right to see her visitor. Nellie knew in her bones—her cold, weary bones—that this was her last chance to get out of here. By some luck or miracle, Nellie, sopping wet, was given over to this other nurse.

Nellie followed her down the hall, to the receiving room in the Octagon Tower. She didn't dare hope it was Cockerill; if it wasn't, she vowed that she would claim to be the long-lost daughter/sister/mother/wife the person had come looking for. Honest to God, she would do it. She practiced in her head. *Yes, it's me, [insert name here]. Please take me home to [literally anywhere but here]!*

She would find her way back to the newspaper office from there, wherever *there* was, as long as it was not *here.*

She might even let Colton whisk her away, though the mere thought unsettled her stomach. Or maybe that was her pride. Miss Grady hadn't been able to drown that out of her.

There was a man in the room, a brown coat thrown over his suit, tapping his foot, anxiously waiting. A *time is money* sort, *no patience for fools* kind of anxious man. The smell of cigars and ink clung to him. He turned, Nellie gasped and he gave her a *shut up* look before telling the nurse to close the door and leave them.

It was Cockerill. "Well, you certainly smell like you've been in a madhouse for ten days."

"Ten! We agreed upon seven."

"Ten sounds better in the headline."

Nellie couldn't think of a reply. She was still dizzy and lightheaded from Miss Grady's punishment, and she thought there was a very good chance that she was hallucinating this whole encounter. She was also sopping wet. Which Cockerill noticed, and he eyed her warily. He started to ask but then seemed to decide that, no, he didn't want to know, not right now. She would save it for the story.

She nodded.

"You know, I didn't think you'd do it," he said. "And then I didn't think you'd pull it off."

"I said I could and I would. I did."

He nodded. Clearly. "A lawyer is finishing up the paperwork for your release. Then let's get out of here. This place is godawful. I've been here a half hour and already my skin is crawling. Barely made it in the door before I was swarmed by some lunatics."

"Half hour?" Nellie scoffed. "Try ten days."

"Save it for your story. You have a deadline. You have the front page on Sunday. Looks like it'll be a good one if you can get yourself together."

While a lawyer with Cockerill handled the paperwork of her release, Nellie was given back her clothes—her notebook and pencil were long gone. She managed to secrete a few of the pages from The Book into her dress, another miracle. Soon she was crossing the East River and nearing New York, where freedom and steak dinners and a clean bath awaited her. There was no small ache in her heart as she thought of the women she was leaving behind. But it was hard to be sad with this sunshine on her face and the city in her sights.

She was once again a free girl after ten days in the madhouse on Blackwell's Island.

CHAPTER TWENTY-EIGHT

Return to the World

I had looked forward so eagerly to leaving that horrible place, yet when my release came and I knew that God's sunlight was to be free for me again, there was a certain pain in leaving. For ten days I had been one of them. Foolishly enough, it seemed intensely selfish to leave them to their sufferings.

—Nellie Bly, *Ten Days in a Mad-House*

THE OFFICE OF THE *NEW YORK WORLD*

When Nellie returned to the office the morning following her release from the asylum, the newsroom fell silent. The other reporters, editors and staff stopped what they were doing to see if the rumors were true: Had she really survived ten days in the madhouse? Nellie was fairly confident they weren't looking at her bangs—the second thing she'd done, after eating the steak dinner of her dreams, was to wash and *gently* comb her hair—so Nellie knew she looked every inch the professional reporter.

But now she actually had to do the job and write up her investigation. Today was Thursday; she had just two days to do it.

Cockerill had already impressed upon her the need for a ridiculously fast turnaround of her story. He feared the *Sun* might scoop them, which according to him would be the worst thing in the world. They had already published a few articles that suggested they were onto the story; the city was starting to chatter. Nellie promised to write fast.

It wouldn't be hard; she was bursting at the seams with every mistreatment she had witnessed and all the stories of the women she'd met. She had so much inside her, pulsing and bursting and wanting to explode across the page. Her fingers were twitching with the urge to start writing, and so she ignored everyone looking at her and found a desk.

Any desk would do; she wasn't particular like that, especially on deadline. The one she slid into had a prime view of the large clock that now said nine o'clock, as well as the large sign that shouted TERSENESS! ACCURACY! TRUTH!

She pulled out paper and a pen, and when her fellow reporters saw she was just going to do her job, they went back to drinking coffee and doing their own work. Well, except for one fair-haired man who came within three feet of her desk before Nellie shook her head *no* and he melted back into the crowded room.

Then, with a stack of fresh sheets of paper before her, Nellie began to write.

> ***On the 22nd of September I was asked by THE WORLD if I could have myself committed to one of the Asylums for the Insane in New York, with a view to writing a plain and unvarnished narrative of the treatment of the patients therein and the methods of management, etc. Did I think I had the***

courage to go through such an ordeal as the mission would demand?

I said I could, I would and I did.

Nellie wrote all morning. Coffee appeared and she gratefully but absentmindedly drank it while the words poured out of her about all the people she had fooled—some reluctantly, like Mrs. Stanard and Mrs. Caine. With any luck, they would read it and forgive her. She wrote of her wish for any wayward girl to find a kind soul like Mrs. Caine. Nellie wrote about the doctors who took her pulse and looked in her eyes and declared with unshakable conviction that she was positively demented. They were about to be exposed as fools and frauds before the world; Nellie wasn't the slightest bit sorry about it. She wrote about Tillie.

How can a doctor judge a woman's sanity by merely bidding her good morning and refusing to hear her pleas for release? Even the sick ones know it is useless to say anything, for the answer will be that it is their imagination.

Nellie wrote about the wretched food she'd choked down and the slow starvation of body, mind and soul. The endless physical discomfort married with the suffocating sense of despair she'd experienced and the impossibility that the conditions at the asylum would make anyone well. She detailed the endless hours on hard benches, and how the tedium seemed to drain the soul and spirit out of a woman. She wrote about how they spoke of hot meals and fresh fruit before giving up and saying nothing because what was the point? They were going to die here, and they knew it.

One day an insane woman was brought in. She was noisy and Miss Grady gave her a beating and blacked her eye.

> ***When the doctors noticed it and asked was it done before she came there the nurses said it was.***

Nellie wrote about the giggling Miss Grupe and the cruel Miss Grady. She spared no detail of their cruelty, just calmly wrote down everything she had witnessed and experienced—the simpleminded girls they teased, the old women they hit. She detailed Prayer Girl's pleas for death. At some point, Nellie paused to shake out a cramp in her hand and glanced at the clock, declaring each minute closer to deadline. Then she had still more to write: about the baths, the spitting, the poor unwell women who were beaten and mocked until they cried.

> ***The Insane Asylum on Blackwell's Island is a human rat-trap. It is easy to get in, but once there it is impossible to get out.***

Nellie wrote all morning and through the lunch hour. The stack of papers on her desk grew thicker and thicker. Cockerill came over and helped himself to a handful of pages full to bursting with her scrawl. The urgency of her story didn't help her handwriting.

She scowled at the fair-haired man, who tried to approach again. She had apologetically waved off Harriet's invitation for lunch with one word—"deadline"—and Harriet nodded with understanding and returned a little later with something for Nellie to eat at her desk. Nellie looked up with a grateful smile. There was something about being so understood and so cared for, without any words needing to be exchanged. How opposite from that mad and bad place where she'd spent the last ten days.

They were all still there, locked behind asylum bars. Prayer Girl, Tillie, Anne, Princess, Mad Mathilda and the rest of them.

This time yesterday, she had been one of them, and now she was clean, fed, properly dressed and consumed with exciting work that challenged her brain, while they all suffered the monotonous horror of their life in the asylum.

Nellie paused, thinking of them. Her pen poised above the paper released one glob of ink, splattering across the paper, obscuring a line she'd just written about Dr. Ingram. He had meant well, but had he done all he could? Before she could rewrite it, Cockerill appeared before her in a huff.

"Your handwriting is atrocious. I'm going to get a damned stroke from just looking at it."

Nellie peered up at him, unblinking. "Do you want me to stop writing?"

He scowled at her. "No, damn it. Hurry up. I want this for the front page on Sunday, so it'll need to go to the girls in copy tonight and the typesetters tomorrow." He started to leave before he turned and gruffly said, "Also, I need to know what happens to Tillie."

"I won't nearly be done with the whole story by this evening," Nellie protested.

"I need something. My sources tell me the *Sun* is about to drop an exposé of their own. Could be as soon as tomorrow."

"Well that can't happen."

"We can't stop it."

"Then we'll have to top it. Run the story over two Sundays. I can have the first part ready soon," Nellie said. There was a beat of silence as Cockerill was affronted by her idea, her demands, her naked claim to *two* front pages. And then another moment where he considered it anyway and saw its merits. She sensed she could push a little more.

"With my byline, both times," Nellie said, with breathtaking audacity for a woman. Cockerill's eyes narrowed at her. She had asked for the unthinkable. Almost no one got bylines, not even the male reporters. But she had just survived ten days in the madhouse and so she was feeling brave. Cockerill didn't answer her—at least not with words. But he snatched another few pages from her desk and took them back to his office and shut the frosted-glass door.

Nellie kept writing.

She was just getting to the part about Princess and the laudanum, and more about the wretched unsalted and rancid food, and the mayhem that was mealtimes in the madhouse, when that fair-haired man approached once more. He was a tall, strapping gentleman who seemed like he ought to be out west logging or something of the sort. But his fingers were ink-stained, as were the cuffs peeking out of his black jacket. He ought to have been intimidating, given his size and bulk, but he wasn't.

"What do you want?" she asked without looking up.

"I'm Walt McDougal. I do the pictures."

Nellie set down her pen and rubbed her eyes. Her own handwriting was giving her a headache just to look at it. She thought about asking another reporter for a whiskey but decided she didn't feel like dealing with "But you're a woman!" or some other such nonsense.

"What did you have in mind, Walt McDougal?"

"I need to draw your likeness."

"You cannot draw my likeness."

"Boss says the story wants a picture of a girl in distress to go along with the story of girls in dire circumstances."

"He thinks he wants that, but he's wrong."

Walt raised a brow and she raised a brow right back at him. Yes, she did think she knew better than the famous Colonel

Cockerill of the famous *New York World*. With a huff, she explained. "If my likeness appears in the paper with this story, I'll never be able to do undercover work again."

"Are you on staff now?"

"No, but I'm about to be."

"Did Cockerill say so?"

"He will do."

"You're confident."

"I am," she said. And: "You can't draw me."

"I have to draw something. Illustrations sell papers. Especially if—"

"The story is about an insane girl. I know." One day she'd unpack the world's fascination with women in danger, but not today. She placed her palms on the desk and leaned forward.

"Draw a girl. Any girl. An everygirl, if you will. Draw her making mad faces in a mirror or having her hair brushed so hard it yanks her head back. Draw her crowded, starving and wretched. Draw her sitting on the most uncomfortable bench that has ever been invented, staring soullessly at a bleak future and eventually death. Draw it so every woman looking at this girl should feel like she is one bit of bad luck, one heartache, one annoyed relative away from a lifetime behind bars without a trial to certify her insanity and with no prospect of ever again being free."

She was breathing hard. Walt's eyes were wide with horror, his fingers grasping tightly onto his pencil and sketchbook.

"Jesus, Nellie. Can I just do your portrait?"

"No. And don't worry, I'll take it up with Cockerill myself."

Nellie pushed open the door to Cockerill's office without even a perfunctory knock and despite the protestations of his secretary, Roy: "You can't go in there without an appointment!" Eventually

Roy would learn that certain rules did not apply to Nellie Bly. Maybe today was his lucky day. Or maybe she should say "tonight." The window behind Cockerill's desk revealed that darkness had fallen; parts of the city sparkled from the newly installed electric lights.

Cockerill was at his desk, his eyes squinting at the papers in one hand as he tried to read them in the glow of a lamp. She recognized them as pages of her story. Beside him on the desk, a cigar smoldered in the ashtray, nearby a glass of whiskey. It was *that* time of day, apparently.

Nellie didn't bother with any preamble.

"You can't include my picture with the story."

Cockerill didn't even look up. "The story needs pictures."

"But it can't be *my* likeness. Not if I want to go undercover again."

Cockerill turned to look at her. His brown eyes evaluating her. His mouth firm beneath that statement mustache. It went without saying that she wanted to go back out there again. This may have been a lark to Cockerill, but for Nellie it was her future.

"Don't you want to be a famous reporter?" he drawled.

"I want them to know my name. My work. I don't need them to know my face."

Walt chose that moment to enter, after a gentle knock. His ink-stained fingers clasped a portfolio of empty pages, just waiting for direction. Cockerill looked from him to Nellie to the pages in his hand and back again at the girl. She gazed at him steadily, willing him to see that this story was sensational—she could feel it as she wrote it. The madhouse had been horrible, but this part—writing it all down with the promise of seeing the atrocities in print, made it feel worthwhile. When she thought of the public reading her words and knowing about the suffering that happened at Blackwell's, Nellie felt shivers. *Do stunts,* Marian had flippantly suggested. But Nellie had found her life's work.

So she stood still and firm and willed Cockerill to understand this. She couldn't be recognizable on sight. Not if he wanted more of the gold he held in his hand.

"Fine. Make it any girl. Do the moment she's making faces in the mirror. And that moment with the judge. And one of a doctor examining you. Damned quacks, more like it, according to you. Now get out and let me finish this."

"Yes, sir." Walt turned to go. Nellie too.

"Not you, Nellie Bly." Cockerill squinted at something on the page. "Tell me what the devil this says."

She looked at the page Cockerill held out, and the line in question that he pointed to with thick, ink-stained fingers. Nellie looked at the line and read it aloud for him. *"Poor girl, how my heart ached for her! I determined then and there that I would try by every means to make my mission of benefit to my suffering sisters."*

"Has anyone ever told you your handwriting is terrible?"

"Yes, every schoolteacher I've had, my mother and my editor back at the *Dispatch*. It didn't stop him from printing my stories, though."

"Well, good for him. We have to make some changes here, then it's ready to go. We'll do two installments. You'll have the Sunday front page for both."

The front pages! Two weeks running! Nellie's heart was nearly bursting with pride. There would be no ignoring her and the women at Blackwell's now. There was no way an editor could look at her, or any female reporter, and say they were too emotional and delicate to chase down a story. So Nellie smiled, a satisfied grin, and tried not to smile too much, all at once.

But: *The front page. For two weeks.*

"You smile too much," Cockerill said, but Nellie kept grinning. "We'll just need a few changes first," Cockerill said. She was still smiling when he picked up the pages and flashed them in

Nellie's direction. It was only then that she saw the blue lines streaked all over them from his editing pencil. She stopped smiling.

"There is too much about this girl Tillie," Cockerill began. "She's a bit weak as a character."

"She's a person who was ill, thus the weakness—" Nellie began.

"And this Prayer Girl character will have to be cut entirely," Cockerill said.

"She's not a character; she's a real person," Nellie replied hotly. "I couldn't have survived without her."

"She'll upset too many readers with her foul mouth and vile prayers. Didn't know women even talked like that." He chuckled. "She sounds like me."

"Some women do," Nellie retorted. "Some women don't have nice things to say. Especially when they are perfectly sane and locked against their will in an insane asylum. We shouldn't silence them for it."

Cockerill gave a short huff. "Look, someone like Prayer Girl is just going to get a certain sort of reader in an outraged froth. Prayers to God for death? The pope will come after us! We'll get angry letters—"

"Since when do you care about angry letters from readers or even what the pope thinks?"

"Good point. I don't give a damn about the pope, and nothing sells newspapers like angry readers. But I know this: She'll distract from the rest of the women in your story who are more sympathetic. You don't want to lose out on everyone's sympathy and attention. Think of the other women in the asylum."

"I think of little else besides the women in the asylum. Whether they are perfectly sane or truly mad, they deserve better care than they are getting. And they deserve to have their stories told."

"No one is going to hear it amid the uproar over Prayer Girl. C'mon, Nellie, you're young but you're wise to the ways of the world."

She was. The world only cared about a certain kind of woman—young, pleasing to the eye, respectable (or the appearance of it). Nellie knew she fit the bill, and if she walked the line, she'd be in a position to shine the light on Blackwell's Island and so many other women's stories.

But Prayer Girl deserved a place in her story. Nellie wouldn't have survived the whole experience without her dark sense of humor, her wicked guidance. She felt sick thinking of Prayer Girl in the Lodge with all those truly violent and insane women. She'd been removed from the official record, lost forever. Remembered privately, only by Nellie.

Cockerill drew a big, thick blue line through a section about Prayer Girl at mealtime.

"She's important," Nellie blurted out. "She should stay in the story."

"She'll lose you readers and she'll lose you support," Cockerill said. "And this Princess person. Does she really just say those three words over and over?"

"Yes."

"What do they mean?"

"I don't know." She'd never managed to know. She never would know.

"Then we'll have to cut it. It's boring. I said your story could have the front page, not the whole front section. We can't have every madwoman and her particular insanity taking away from the rest of the news."

Women could only ever take up so much space.

Cockerill carried on, brandishing that pencil like a filet knife, slicing and shredding Nellie's story to pieces. He wanted more on the bad food. "Make me taste it. Make me *gag* on it."

He wanted more gruesome details on the bathing, which had Nellie shuddering. She had treated herself to a long, hot, *clean* bath with a fresh bar of soap last night, and still . . . still . . . her skin crawled at the memory. But remembering it wasn't as bad as living it, and so she would put pen to paper with the worst of it.

Miss Grady he liked—"What a wicked woman; I had a schoolteacher like her once." And that explained a lot, in Nellie's opinion, which she told him. He scowled at her and went back to his critiques. More sob stories, more cruelties, make it *worse*.

Next Cockerill had a laugh at all the doctors she had fooled. "Exposed as frauds by a girl. Ha! They're going to be mad as all hell and I don't give a damn about it."

Nellie also didn't care about the pride and reputations of the doctors, who would be embarrassed and shamed in the press. *Good.* As they should be, sentencing innocent women to a living death because of their own incompetence, or their pride, or some foolish collective agreement that a man is probably right and a woman is probably hysterical.

All of it was an outrage. And if Nellie had to cut out Tillie and Princess and Prayer Girl so the truth could be revealed and the story told? She rocked on her boots. Hesitating. They deserved their spot in the story. They deserved to have their existence recorded and their lives recognized.

"And what if I don't agree to these changes?" Nellie asked. *Women have to look out for each other.* The least she could do was ensure that their names and their stories survived them. "Maybe another paper wants the story, just as I have written it."

"You can do that, but then I'll ensure that it's the last thing you ever write for a New York paper." Threats. How predictably boring. Cockerill didn't even need to make them. They both knew the market for girl reporters in the city was not large. In fact, this was it.

Even with *this* story.

"Let me ask you something," Cockerill said as he leaned back in his chair. "Do you want your name on the front page of the *World*?"

"Yes. But—"

"The story is good. Make the changes. It's for the best."

Nellie, for once, was not smiling. She recognized the truth of the situation: that she could accomplish what she wanted—attention for the plight of the asylum women—only if she made Cockerill's suggested edits. She would do it. He knew it; she knew it. But she would hate the way that women weren't allowed to be portrayed as they really were—rude or wicked, boring or weak—if she wanted to write a story about women's lives and generate sympathy or concern. She hated how even in the darkest, most dire hour of these women's lives, some were more "respectable" and "deserving" of attention than others. It was wrong. But not as wrong as not telling what she could. The women deserved to be heard.

"You were right, by the way," Cockerill said gruffly, eventually. "A man never could have gotten this story."

There was that, at least. Recognition. Something of a consolation.

She managed a half smile.

"Don't tell me you're all mopey because we made some cuts. If you want to be a real journalist, you'll have to get used to it."

"If I'm 'all mopey' it's because they are still stuck in there. They may not make it in the final printed story, but they are still locked in the asylum. We have to find a way to get them out."

Cockerill leaned forward, his gaze suddenly steely. "Are you a newspaperman or some crusader?"

"Yes," Nellie answered evenly. "You can't possibly suggest that we print this and that's the end of it. We can't just leave them in there."

Cockerill's lips twitched under his mustache as he decided how frank to be with her. "Listen, Nellie, here's how it works. We write the story. We publish the story. Everyone who reads it decides what happens next. It's not our job to save them."

Nellie scowled and started to gather her things.

"You did good, Nellie Bly."

"I hope you and Mr. Pulitzer remember that on payday," she replied with a cheeky smile, but she wasn't joking and he knew it.

Cockerill gave a bark of laughter. "Don't worry, Nellie. We will. In the meantime, quit thinking about how to save them and start thinking about how you're going to top this." He held up the sheets of paper. "If you're all right with these changes, we'll send it on to Helen to copyedit and proofread it." Nellie nodded and turned to go.

She was nearly out the door when she paused, her hand on the knob. Between recent events and the long day of writing, finished up with Cockerill's brutal edits, Nellie was suddenly exhausted. She was so exhausted that the thought of having to get herself from here to her bed in a room on Ninety-Sixth Street—practically Canada!—made her want to lie down under a desk somewhere. But there was one last question to ask: "Whose job is it, then?"

"What?" Cockerill had already poured another splash of whiskey and started working on another reporter's copy. This meeting was finished, as far as he was concerned. But Nellie had one more question.

"Whose job is it, then? To save them?"

"I don't know. The mayor's?"

CHAPTER TWENTY-NINE

Extra! Extra!

> *PLAYING MAD WOMAN: Nellie Bly too sharp for the Island Doctors*
>
> —*New York Sun*

THE ORDINARY

The next day, Nellie dropped into her seat with a huff and slammed a newspaper on the table. Marian raised an eyebrow, while Harriet and Dorothy gave her a sympathetic smile.

It was supposed to be a celebratory luncheon, in honor of her two-part series. The first installment of her story claimed Sunday's front page. The headline—BEHIND ASYLUM BARS—was emblazoned across the top, unapologetic all-capital letters. Her words filled up column after column, and they were interspersed with Walt's illustrations. There was Nellie making faces in the mirror, standing before the judge, and being examined by a doctor. He made her look like any woman. That was the point.

That Sunday, Nellie had taken a stroll around the city. Everywhere she looked, people were reading the story: on park benches and on stoops, while waiting for the train or riding it downtown. She could just imagine it being read at breakfast tables and hearthsides all around the city. By Sunday evening, no one could talk about anything else in Manhattan and her piece dominated the conversation in the city for the week.

Pulitzer himself had given her a cash bonus; Cockerill had officially welcomed her to the staff. She walked around, cheeks flushed with satisfaction and pride in her work. She bought a new hat. She wrote to her mother.

To say anticipation was high for the second installment—INSIDE THE MADHOUSE: NELLIE BLY'S EXPERIENCE IN THE BLACKWELL'S ISLAND ASYLUM—was a massive understatement of epic proportions. People in New York were outraged, horrified and desperate to know what truths she would reveal when the story dropped in the upcoming Sunday paper.

But then Colton had to go and ruin everything.

"Well, it was all for nothing," Nellie said with a huff. "The *Sun* has scooped my story."

Despite frantic writing, during every waking moment since she'd left the asylum, another paper had beaten her to press. She was already at work on the second installment. And now Colton had stolen her thunder with the piece in the *Sun* today, Friday, two days before the second installment of her own bombshell report.

"How bad is it?" Harriet asked. "I saw the headline but haven't had a chance to read it yet."

"Bad. Terrible. Horrendous," Nellie grumbled. Harriet smiled sympathetically. Dorothy winced on her behalf. Marian was unconcerned. Nellie wondered if they were all good enough friends that she could ask them to help her commit murder upon the person of Sam Colton, Mr. One o'Clock, Mr. Exclusive Story Stealer.

"In fact," Nellie continued. "Let's look at just how bad it is."

She snapped open the paper. Right there on the front page. Nellie read the headline out loud: "'The *Sun* Finishes Up Its Story of Insane Girl.'" She looked up, outraged. "They make it sound like it's their story. It's mine!"

It was all there: the names of the doctors who had examined her, the length of time in the asylum, commentary from the nurses, the sudden circumstances of her relief.

The writer—she presumed it was Colton, it had to be Colton—had even made an investigation of her, with details of her mother and her time in Pittsburgh. Admirably thorough. Or incredibly questionable.

"He does say some nice things," Dorothy said, reading over her shoulder. "I quote: 'She is intelligent, capable and self-reliant, and except for the matter of changing her name to Nellie Bly, has gone about the business of maintaining herself in journalism in a practical, business like way.'"

"At least he didn't print your real age," Marian quipped.

"There's nothing wrong with a woman's real age," Harriet said.

"He also says you're pretty," Dorothy said. She smiled and kept reading. "He says 'she was in good looks and comeliness of person.'"

"Yes, compared to, and I quote, the 'ranks of insane poor which the city affords institutional refuge,'" Nellie added. "Not that I care what he thinks of me in the slightest."

"Do you know who wrote this? I think he might fancy you," Dorothy said.

"Yes and no." Nellie explained to them about stealing his interview and they all agreed a girl reporter had to do what a girl reporter had to do. She mentioned his visit. "He must have been investigating me for days to get all this information. He has everything: interviews with the staff, details of mealtimes and the clothing we all wore."

He had even managed to get intelligence from The Book, the one Nellie had so desperately wanted. According to him, the doctors had written that she was "*Very much depressed; she said that she heard voices but soon refused to talk.*"

If he had gotten all of this information so quickly, what else had he learned? Bad enough that he should drop this story two days before her own. Worse was the sinking feeling that more might be to come.

"Think of it as a preview for your own story," Harriet said. "It shall only whet the appetite of readers for more."

One hoped. In fact, Nellie fervently hoped it would work like that, but she wasn't wildly optimistic about it because, well . . . the world. She had put so much into the story for it to be taken over by a man, and the thought of him getting credit for breaking it had her in a feverish rage. So typical. So unfair. So . . . argh. She punched the paper, trying to fold it back into something manageable that she could shove out of sight.

"You should eat something," Harriet said gently. This was probably true. Nellie stared down at her lunch—her hot, freshly prepared lunch—and thought about mealtimes at the asylum and how they all would have drowned in those disgusting bathtubs for just one bite of what was on her plate. Nellie took a bite of it—a hot stew, thick and well salted, with meat, potatoes and other vegetables. Harriet continued. "Think of the women in the asylum who are going to be helped by all this attention."

Right. She should stop thinking about her own ambitions. She should stop complaining about Colton and start to appreciate that she was at least playing the game. She should think of her next move. Maybe there were some changes she could make to the article she'd written, or maybe there was another way she could draw attention to *her* experience and her story.

Or she could think about the women.

"What he doesn't have is the women's stories," Nellie said, as it dawned on her what was missing from Colton's piece. His article was just the dry facts of Nellie's great scheme, along with some details about Nellie herself. He didn't have anything about Tillie or Anne or Elsie. "And oh, what sob stories they were," Nellie continued. "Cockerill wouldn't let me include all of them. Some were too rude, offensive or boring."

"Well, now I'm interested," Marian said. "Do tell. Especially the offensive ones."

"My best friend there always prayed for death before every meal and loudly at bedtime. It was always a *Dear Lord, please kill me before morning* sort of thing. Another woman was committed for being sad over the death of her lover, and so many were completely sane. There was this one woman who everyone called Princess, who only ever said three words. *Rose. Daisy. Violet.*"

Marian dropped her fork with a loud clatter on her plate. Nellie, Dorothy and Harriet all looked up to see Marian, looking pale and shocked.

"What did you say?" Marian asked fiercely. She was leaning in, nearly at risk of getting her jacket in her bowl of soup, and she had a glint in her eye like she was onto something.

Nellie hesitated. "Princess. She only ever muttered the same three flowers."

"What were they?"

"Rose. Daisy. Violet."

Marian just sat there, still, but breathing hard, like her corset had been laced too tightly and she'd just sprinted across town while an angry mob chased her. Her cheeks were flushed.

"What did she look like? This woman?" Marian asked urgently.

"Tired. Sad. They called her Princess because she was still so poised."

"Go on," Marian urged.

"Her hair was blond . . . once. Now it was greasy and white. She was probably forty or so?"

"Oh my God," Marian breathed. She knew something about Princess. Nellie felt something tighten in her chest. There was something in Nellie's story that she had missed, but Marian knew what it was.

"What is it?"

Marian's gaze glittered now. Some great secret had been unlocked to her and only her. "They're not *words*; they're *names*."

Harriet sucked in a breath, like it all suddenly made sense to her too. What was going on? Nellie watched, stunned, as Marian downed the rest of her drink and started gathering her things—affixing her hat, buttoning her jacket, reaching for her notebook and pencil. "I have to go."

Dorothy and Harriet carried on with their meal like it was a usual occurrence for one of them to dash up in the middle of lunch and run off to chase a lead. Nellie, however, was on tenterhooks. What the hell was she missing? If it was something about Princess, then it was definitely Nellie's business.

"What was that all about?" Nellie asked. Marian was rushing her way through the crush of tables full of working girls enjoying their lunch break. She was making a beeline for the door, the street, the office . . .

"You might have just inadvertently unlocked the story she's been working on," Harriet said smoothly.

"I thought she was working on some fluff piece about a society wedding," Nellie said.

"About a rich man remarrying very soon after his first wife's mysterious death," Dorothy said.

"They have three daughters," Harriet explained.

"Rose. Daisy. Violet." Nellie repeated the words like Princess did, feeling the weight and significance of them on her tongue and in her whole being. Oh my *God*. Oh my God.

NEWSPAPER ROW, NEW YORK CITY

Nellie chased after Marian, dodging pedestrians, street vendors and newsies shouting the day's headlines. It was an effort to catch up with her; Marian walked like she had places to be, people to see and news to break. But Nellie felt like she was losing another strand of her story, and so she hustled to catch up.

Finally, she got close enough to shout "Wait!" and close enough for Marian to turn and give her a look over her shoulder. Thankfully, there was a big tangle of horses and carriages that prevented traffic from flowing and sane people from attempting to cross the street, so Marian did actually pause and wait.

"What are you doing? Where are you going?" Nellie asked, somewhat breathlessly.

"It should be obvious. I'm chasing a story."

"But it sounds like you are going to use something I said, something I discovered—" It wasn't logical. But Nellie felt so damn possessive of her work, and of the women in the asylum.

Marian turned now, to face Nellie full on. She was taller by a good four or five inches, so Nellie really had to look up at her and try not to feel small compared to this towering woman with fiery hair and an expression to match.

"Listen, Nellie. You may not have noticed this yet, but it's hard out here for a girl reporter—"

"Oh, I noticed—"

"And if you haven't noticed, newspapers aren't exactly on a girl-reporter hiring spree. Maybe one girl makes staff, if at all."

"You don't have to tell me. I just spent—" Marian waved her off.

"Getting off the ladies' pages is harder than getting out of Blackwell's. I have a chance and I'm taking it. And there is nothing you can say or do to stop me." Nellie was speechless and Marian smirked and went off on her way. Over her shoulder, she called out, "Thanks for the hot tip, Nellie!"

Nellie watched her walk away, carefully threading her way through the muck of the street, in between stuck carriages and irritable horses. She walked briskly. Marian had a lead. Marian was going to take it and run with it. Nellie didn't even know quite what Marian *had,* just that it seemed important and connected to Princess, of whom Nellie felt protective. And, to be honest, she felt like she had let Princess down by allowing Cockerill to cut her from the story. And now? Nellie was a mess of feelings, not all of them pretty.

This must be the catch, Nellie thought. Harriet had gotten her into the newsroom and only asked that she one day repay the favor to another female journalist. *One day you'll have an opportunity to help a fellow female reporter and you must take it. Even at an expense to yourself.* She had made a promise. But her desire to claim her territory and to be the one to write up the story was strongly at odds with what she knew in her heart was the right thing to do.

So Nellie swore and even kicked a streetlight, which did not make her feel better in the slightest. She felt herself becoming—perish the thought—emotional. But there was no denying the mixture of anger, uncertainty and jealousy pulsing through her that wanted release. She wanted to kick another streetlight, but in sturdier boots. She wanted to throw something. She wanted to stomp her feet and then lie down on a park bench and scream.

But that would get her sent right back to Blackwell's.

Which only made her more mad.

Men could vent their frustrations—they could walk around punching holes in walls and picking fights—and it was manly. But should a woman emit one garbled scream of frustration on Broadway, then she'd be locked up for life.

Nellie was reminded of all the women who were in fact locked up for life, even though they were perfectly sane. Even the ones who were genuinely unwell deserved better than they got. Nellie took a deep breath and tried to get over herself, to stop thinking about losing her story and to start thinking about the whole damn point of any of it.

Women have to look out for each other because no one else will.

Nellie stopped and took a deep breath. When she looked up, she was facing city hall. The classically styled building stood surrounded by a leafy park in the middle of downtown Manhattan. Newspaper Row was right across the street, the better to keep an eye on the government. The courts were right there as well, stately and forbidding. But it was city hall that caught her attention. City hall, where the mayor worked. Nellie knew her next move.

CHAPTER THIRTY

City Hall

THE MAYOR'S OFFICE, CITY HALL

At first Nellie was refused an interview with the mayor. Apparently, one did not just walk in and get an audience—especially when one was a flush-cheeked, slightly-out-of-breath woman claiming to be a reporter. She was promptly sent away. But after her second installment dropped and she introduced herself as Nellie Bly, she promptly got her interview with the mayor.

His name was Hugh Grant, but shortly after his election, Marian had taken to calling him the Bachelor Mayor and the name had stuck. Not that Nellie cared in the slightest about the marital status or marriageability of the mayor or any other man. With her story burning up the newsstands, she could afford not to be romantic.

But she was interested in whoever would help her get Tillie, Prayer Girl and some of the others freed. And she was very keen on using the current outcry over her story to lobby for better conditions at Blackwell's.

Hence, the mayor.

His office was decorated in a style that Nellie would describe as

"Powerful Old Man Wants to Demonstrate How Powerful He Is," and she was suitably impressed for a moment. The ceilings were high; the windows commanded an impressive view of the newly erected Brooklyn Bridge and the offices of the *World*. All the furniture was slightly too large, especially for a female figure, the better to make her feel like a wayward child should she visit to lobby for her cause of suffrage, or temperance or charity.

The mayor was seated at his desk when Nellie stood at the doorway, escorted by a distinguished-looking older gentleman who she learned was called Branson. For a second, she caught a glimpse of the mayor at work and in deep concentration: lips parted slightly, his pen moving swiftly and determinedly across the page as he affixed his official signature to an important document. Then the mayor stood to greet his visitor and Nellie saw why he had all the women in the city swooning.

The Bachelor Mayor was handsome. If tall, dark hair, a strong jaw and a firm sensuous mouth was your thing, which it happened to be for so many women. With his dashing smile and an air of confidence and an attentive gaze, he was an eminently attractive man. Nellie wasn't entirely immune. In her head, she could hear her mother sighing. *A mayor, Pink! A mayor!*

She gave him a cheeky smile. Then he smiled, making his eyes crinkle deliciously, and he said, "So you must be the little reporter with the big story. It is an honor to meet you."

"I prefer to go by Nellie Bly." She strode smoothly into the room. Branson nodded and took a seat in the corner. "And, yes, I'm the journalist who has exposed the deplorable conditions in Blackwell's asylum."

"Please." The mayor gestured toward a seat opposite his big wooden desk and she settled into the large, overstuffed leather chair. The thought of well-fed old men sitting comfortably in chairs like these while the girls in the asylum starved and sat all day on those wretched benches of hideous discomfort renewed her determination for being here.

Mr. Grant sat behind his desk and fixed his attention on her, and Nellie felt that she might be the one with the power. Something about the spark in his dark brown eyes, and the way his gaze dropped to her mouth. Something about how she had the attention of the whole city and the front page of the *World* at her disposal.

"Congratulations on your work, Miss Bly. It was a powerful story."

"Thank you. I'm glad you're familiar with it."

"Who in New York isn't aware of the insane girl who fooled all the doctors and authorities in order to obtain the most gripping story of an age?"

Nellie tried to resist a blush, but she did smile. A little light flirtation with one of the most powerful men in New York wasn't the worst thing in the world. "The thing is, Mr. Mayor, my work is unfinished. As you know from my reporting, there are women who are perfectly sane, yet kept against their will in the most wretched conditions."

"It's a tragedy."

"I'm here to ask you to secure their release and to do everything in your power to improve conditions in the asylum for those who must remain. Everyone deserves proper care and compassion."

The mayor's expression said, *Who, me?* and asked, *All of them?* Just for a second, but she saw it and it made him a little less handsome, to be honest. She looked at him with her gray-blue eyes and challenged him to impress her.

"You want me to free them all?"

"I didn't think I'd need to talk a man into being a hero."

The mayor had the decency to blush slightly. He held her gaze. "I have already appointed a committee to investigate matters at Blackwell's. They will undoubtedly make some recommendations for improvements, which my administration will support. It will all be included in the budget."

Well, wouldn't Dr. Ingram be pleased with that! But it wasn't enough.

"A committee."

"Yes."

"I think that if you saw conditions there yourself you would agree that a committee isn't enough."

Committees, as far as she knew, tended to be staffed by the idle rich and people with too much to do, and all working for some vested interest or another. They seemed to exist for the appearance of work, not the actual doing of work.

"I'm a very busy man, Miss Bly. I shall try to make a visit to Blackwell's myself, but I'm not certain that my schedule will permit it—"

She cut in with one of her irresistible smiles. "You're not scared, are you?"

"I beg your pardon?"

"It's very gruesome. Those with delicate sensibilities or merely a sense of human decency will find it very upsetting. It may even make them *emotional*. I understand if you don't have the constitution for it—"

"I am perfectly able to handle it, Miss Bly. I just am not certain I have the time. Branson keeps my schedule—"

Nellie pulled out her reporter's notebook and a pencil. "Can you tell me what is more important than starving women who are tortured and imprisoned against their will?"

She looked at him, cool as you please, and waited. Her fingers clasped the pencil, poised above a blank page. Her heart was beating sure and steady in her chest. This was what she was meant to be doing—holding the powerful to account, on behalf of the mad girls of New York—and she felt the righteousness of purpose coursing through her body.

Nellie Bly had all damn day for this.

But the mayor did not, and he was probably going to smooth talk his way out of this, which he started to do, and so Nellie decided to play one last card. Marian had given her the idea for it. After chatting with Harriet and Dorothy and putting some pieces together this week, Nellie thought she might have something. Not enough for a story to publish, but enough to be used as leverage over the mayor, should she need it.

It seemed she needed it.

"There is one woman in the asylum who stands out in my mind. She had a certain elegance and manners about her that hadn't been lost to her dire circumstances, though she does seem to have lost her memory. Or maybe it's just the drugs that she's constantly forced to consume. We called her Princess."

"She wasn't in your story."

"Not yet," Nellie replied. And then: "What do you know of Mrs. Winnifred Wallace?"

It took the mayor a moment to catch up with Nellie. She was running on hunches here. She'd been chasing leads and trying to get sources to talk, but she was new in town and could only get so much. Hopefully, it was enough. Her heartbeat was picking up the pace accordingly, but outwardly she was calm, cool and collected. She was just asking questions.

"She died in a yachting accident a few months ago," the mayor said.

"I think I've met her recently."

"You must mean his fiancée, Louisa." The mayor smiled as he

gently corrected her. "She is a lovely woman. The wedding is on Sunday. I am looking forward to attending. Jay Wallace is a close friend and supporter of my campaign."

Nellie smiled gently as she corrected him. "I mean his first wife. The 'old' one. She isn't dead. She's living at Blackwell's Island."

CHAPTER THIRTY-ONE

Back to Blackwell's

THE INSANE ASYLUM AT BLACKWELL'S ISLAND

This time, when Nellie disembarked from the boat and stepped onto Blackwell's Island, she was not one lonely girl in a pack of lonely girls. Her story had sold out on every newsstand in the city; it was reported on endlessly. She was the most famous reporter—male or female—in New York City. She was on her way to being a legend.

This time, when she stepped foot on Blackwell's Island she had the mayor by her side and the whole city cheering her on. An impressive retinue of advisers and reporters from the other big papers followed Nellie and the mayor for their tour of the facilities.

So she had nothing to fear. And yet the island still had a way of creeping into one's bones, settling there with a sense of doom and unease. She glanced around and noticed others in the group seemed to feel it too.

The unspoken but understood sentiment was that they were all hoping to see the gruesome things Nellie had written about: the cruel and violent nurses, perfectly sane women being starved of decent food and mental stimulation, doctors who claimed authority, knew nothing and flirted shamelessly with nurses instead of caring for patients. They wanted to see the crib, the camisole, the restraints, the Lodge.

They wanted to know if Nellie had told the truth.

A lady reporter can't get the news. A woman is too prone to flights of fancy and exaggeration; she cannot get the facts. This crowd believed that. Some of the men present had told her as much to her face. Nellie recognized the editors from the *Times* and the *Herald* and the *Mail on Sunday* even if they didn't seem to recognize her. She was looking forward to the satisfaction of proving them wrong.

The asylum loomed ahead—that bluestone Octagon Tower flanked by two halls, each three stories tall and full to bursting with women—and it was as imposing as ever. The group walked slowly and somberly to the entrance.

"Is it wrong of me to admit how terrifying this is?" the mayor whispered to Nellie, who replied, "No. It is terrifying. But just think of the poor women who do it every day."

They entered the same worn door as Nellie had done just weeks ago. Then, she'd been assaulted by disturbing sounds and smells. There was something of an improvement today. The foul stench that had greeted her upon her first arrival was no longer. The halls were quieter too. She wracked her brain, trying to figure out what was different, but couldn't put her finger on it. A sense of unease crept up her spine.

The group stood at the base of the tower, staring up and up and up at the spiraling staircase that led to all the horrors she had written about, wondering what they might see. She caught Colton's eye—of course he was here. His stories in the *Sun* about her had been popular. But before they could scowl or speak to each other, a neatly dressed gentleman appeared to greet the assembled group.

"Good afternoon, I'm Dr. Ingram, a doctor here at Blackwell's. Thank you for your interest in our program. I will be showing you around the asylum today." Nellie felt her breath catch. Something about this seemed off. Dr. Ingram paused, his gaze searching the crowd until he saw Nellie. Something in his expression softened. "Hello, Miss Bly. I'm glad to see you are well."

She had not written him like a fool, as she had the other doctors. She had not forgotten his small acts of kindness—the shawl for Tillie, the warm stoves, interference on behalf of patients about to get walloped by a nurse. But he had been in charge while all the abuses Nellie detailed had occurred. He said he could not do more, for want of funds. Perhaps that would change today.

Their gazes held for a long moment, during which the group started to shuffle uneasily. Nellie swallowed the urge to apologize for deceiving him. It had been for a good cause. Dr. Ingram turned away and began the tour.

"The asylum here at Blackwell's Island was constructed in 1839 in accordance with Quaker principles. The intention was to provide gentle care to the unfortunates . . ."

"This is news to me," Nellie whispered to the mayor, a strong presence beside her. "I witnessed nothing that might be deemed gentle care."

Dr. Ingram led them on a tour past the kitchens, where a massive barrel labeled SALT sat prominently in view of the door. She had written of their unsalted food—the least of their culinary crimes—but it made a point, that barrel.

It called her a liar.

Beside Nellie, a reporter from the *Tribune* took note of it.

Fine, Nellie told herself. The important thing was that they were now taking better care with the food. But then she caught the faint sound of a perfectly tuned piano being played somewhere nearby. *Since when?!* Since the city was watching, that's when.

As the group passed through the corridors, Nellie noted that those cold institutional halls somehow seemed brighter. Freshly painted. When one glanced through open doors, one saw nice-and-clean-looking patients, calmly sitting while the nurses read aloud to them from the sort of improving conduct books foisted on young women as an antidote to the novel reading that supposedly drove them all mad. Not only that, but the stoves were lit and the air was warm.

The cold Nellie had written about had been banished from these asylum walls.

The more they walked, the more it became apparent that care had been taken to improve things in the few short days since her story was published. Either that, or there was enough evidence for some of these reporters to claim that Nellie had made it all up. Thus, women cannot get the story. They are too emotional and forget the facts. They are too often seduced by the sensational to be reliable sources for the news.

She felt hot under her dress. The heat of embarrassment and rage. Good God, she was feeling emotional, but she would be damned if she let them see it. However, this farce was not to be borne.

And then there was Colton, his eyes on her, as Dr. Ingram continued with the tour.

"They knew we were coming," Nellie said in a low voice to the mayor. She struggled to contain the fury rising within her and to keep her voice calm.

"Of course," said Mr. Grant. "My staff would have alerted them."

Her cheeks now burned with embarrassment. What did she think—that the mayor just *showed up* places? She should have known it would be a whole production for him to attend and that the asylum would be aware and prepare accordingly. One did not want to be humiliated in front of the mayor—and the press of Manhattan—as Nellie was now discovering.

"You can smell the fresh paint," she hissed. "They have done this on purpose. They are trying to make a liar out of me."

The mayor turned and looked into her eyes and spoke solemnly. "I believe you, Miss Bly. Don't worry, we will still move forward with the investigation, the committee and the budget recommendations."

It wasn't just that.

It was personal.

Dr. Ingram and the authorities were making a mockery of her reporting.

It was already common belief that women were unable to gather facts, that they could not tell truth from fiction. Any number of editors had told her that, to her face.

And it was an affront to all other female journalists.

Nellie was furious.

"Dr. Ingram," she called out. She had interrupted his denial about the use of force and restraints, and he seemed relieved but still nervous about what she might ask. *Good.* "We both know that this is not how the asylum is usually operated."

"Your story has already inspired some improvements, Miss Bly. You should be glad of that."

"I will be glad of it if I can be assured they are permanent improvements, as well as ones that apply to the whole asylum—not just this hall, which has been spiffed up."

"Yes, of course we intend them to be permanent and—"

"Dr. Ingram," she cut in. "During my time here, we spoke of the limited budget allowed for the asylum. There has been no change in the funding . . . yet. Women could not eat a decent meal or wear warm clothes. And yet these halls seem to be freshly painted."

Where is the money? What is happening? The questions hung heavy and unanswered in the air.

"I cannot comment on decisions made by the committee . . ." Dr. Ingram began. He stumbled, not wanting to lie. But her reputation as a journalist was on the line, about to be undone by fresh paint and a barrel of salt.

"She's not lying." The crowd of reporters turned to see who had spoken. He introduced himself. "Sam Colton, the *New York Sun*. I had the chance to visit Miss Bly while she was here. While I had not the opportunity to view the asylum as extensively as our fearless reporter," he said, while nodding toward her, "what I did witness confirms her report."

Ugh, to be saved by Colton! She was grateful and seething all at once.

He nodded again. She gave him a polite smile.

"Are you two acquainted?" the mayor asked. Nellie answered, "No," just as Colton answered, "Somewhat." Nellie scowled at him. He was coming to her rescue again and she hated it. If Mr. Sam Colton confirmed what she said, why, then it must be true!

"But you didn't see much of the asylum. Just Miss Bly," Dr. Ingram confirmed.

"Well, they wouldn't let reporters past the visitors' room, which ought to tell us something." And then, turning to the superintendent, Colton asked, "Why wouldn't you let reporters in before Miss Bly's exposé?"

"That is a policy of the commissioners, and I should defer you to them."

"Show us Hall 6," Nellie demanded. Hall 6, where she had been confined with Tillie, Prayer Girl, Princess and all the other women whose stories she had faithfully related. If she could just deliver Princess to the mayor, it would prove something. He'd use his power to help all these women. "Particularly the sitting room."

Dr. Ingram led the way and Nellie pushed forward to walk next to him.

"You seem well, Nellie."

"I'm as well as I ever was," she said. "Why are you participating in this cover-up?"

"I do what I can, Nellie. If the board is displeased with me, I'll be replaced with someone worse. Someone who won't advocate for the patients or try to help them, as you know I have done."

"You're compromising."

"I'm trying."

Nellie saw that he believed that he was doing the best thing, the right thing. Truly. That his half measures were helping, that his deference to the board was strategic and noble. Maybe he was right. Perhaps it was for the best. But Nellie wanted more from him, for all these women.

She pushed through the doors, and then she was back, back, back. This room had not been refreshed; the walls were still covered in peeling, piss-colored paint. The room stank of it too—piss, ripe with sadness. The benches were still there, lined up and full of tragic women. Nellie spied Mathilda in the corner—for once not in the throes of a tirade at some man who had done her wrong. She spied The Book on the table, probably detailing whatever Mathilda had been given to keep her quiet.

It was all so familiar. But something—someone—was missing.

"Where is Maeve?" Nellie had been anxiously worried about Prayer Girl. The last she'd seen, Prayer Girl had been hauled off to the Lodge. Nellie had been hoping it hadn't happened, hoping she would see her today.

"She has been transferred to another ward."

She noticed Colton write down *Maeve.*

"And Tillie?"

Dr. Ingram coughed. "She has not been well, Nellie. She has

been transferred to the infirmary. I am not hopeful for her prospects."

Nellie was too late to help either of her friends. She looked around, searching all the faces, looking for familiar ones—one in particular. Miss Grady had the day off or had been reassigned to another ward. And Princess—Nellie could not find her among the rows of bleak women, all wearing the same dress with their hair freshly washed and ruthlessly brushed as if, oh, they were always in this fine state, how nice for everyone to stop by for a visit . . .

Everyone was watching her—Colton, the mayor, Dr. Ingram, the crush of other reporters—as all the things she had written about were not verified. They were waiting to see what she might do—would she insist on the accuracy of her reporting? Would the girl reporter get upset and cry? Would she have a fit? Was she hysterical after all?

Nellie kept her composure. Because she was Nellie Bly and she stood by every word of her reporting. Those in the asylum knew that what she'd written was true, and she'd see to it that it was confirmed and made known and the women were taken better care of. Even if she had to team up with the likes of Sam Colton to do it.

But first, Nellie had to get out of this room. The weight of the despair was crushing. The faces of the patients stared blankly at her in a way that was still unnerving. The reporters were worse, nakedly eyeing her as they awaited her next move. She pushed open the doors and stepped out into the corridor, intent on leading them on a full tour—to the baths, perhaps, or the Lodge. They couldn't have painted *every* hall. Surely the Lodge was still terrible.

Nellie led the way.

They were slow to follow, in a shuffle of stares at the patients and questions for Dr. Ingram. While Nellie waited, she glanced down a corridor as she passed by. It was empty, save for a nurse escorting a patient in an unusually gentle manner—their arms were linked and the nurse was gently proceeding at a slow pace. There was none of the stomping, the huffs, the pinched ears and firmly grasped arms that Nellie remembered. Curious, that. More of a performance from the staff. Unless it was something else.

A flash of red caught Nellie's eye. Red hair, to be precise. *Marian.*

There was only one woman in New York with hair that red who would also be in disguise as a nurse at an insane asylum.

It was Marian, of course, and Nellie slipped away from the group and swiftly caught up with her at the end of a hall that was like the Blackwell's she remembered. Dingy, dark, hopeless.

Marian was dressed in the uniform of a nurse: the brown-and-white-striped gown paired with a white apron and cap. She had Princess with her, who was the same as ever: pale and vacant and sad and murmuring those three names over and over. Rose. Daisy. Violet.

"Marian, what are you doing here?" Nellie asked in a harsh whisper. She glanced down the hall. What did she care if they were discovered? Nellie wanted to present Princess—Mrs. Wallace!—to the mayor.

"Well, if it isn't the famous Miss Bly," Marian replied. "Are you enjoying your victory lap?"

"Not exactly. Don't tell me you have given up reporting and taken up nursing."

"I'm taking a page out of your book. Like my disguise? I think the hat suits me. This brown, though, is wretched. No wonder the nurses are so cruel, if they have to dress like this."

"Rose. Daisy. Violet."

"And this one?" Nellie asked. Princess just stood there. Helpless.

"It took me days to find her." Marian linked arms with Princess and smiled. "But now I'm taking her home."

"You can't just *take* her, Marian."

"I can. I will. And I'll do it today too. Before someone else puts the pieces together and figures out who she is and what's at stake."

Nellie didn't need to be told; she had figured it out too. Princess was Mrs. Winnifred Wallace. Her death had been faked so that her husband was free to marry Louisa Newbold—in what promised to be a massive, spectacular wedding this weekend. Nellie hadn't put together the whys and hows, but she suspected Marian had. It would be a huge story. It would rock the city and knock Nellie's own exposé from top of mind. All the poor women here who weren't mistreated society wives would be forgotten.

"How will you get her out?"

"My brother has agreed to sign for her release. I'm taking her now to finish the process. She'll be on a boat back to Manhattan within the hour."

Nellie huffed. If a lawyer for the newspaper—a man she'd never met—along with Cockerill, whom she barely knew, could secure Nellie's release, it wasn't implausible that Marian's brother could walk in and claim responsibility for Princess. It wasn't like she was in any state to contradict. So, she would be gone within the hour.

"But I need her here," Nellie said impatiently. "A dozen reporters are here, along with the mayor, taking a tour to see if the horrors are exactly as I have described."

"The mayor? How impressive."

"He's only here because I promised he would see *her*."

Marian gasped. "You did *what*?! The mayor knows? Damn it, Nellie! Are you trying to ruin everything?"

"I had to mention it; otherwise he wouldn't attend, and if he wouldn't attend, the press wouldn't—" Marian didn't let Nellie finish her speech about how important it was to effect change in the asylum. She just swore and started leading Princess away, toward the one exit, where Marian's brother presumably waited.

"Marian, wait. What's wrong with the mayor knowing?"

Marian stopped and huffed, utterly impatient and annoyed. "Because he is friends with Mr. Wallace. I'm certain he's the one who had his wife committed."

"While that sounds sadly predictable, it's quite a charge to make."

"Remember that runaway Dorothy was helping? The one who refused speak?"

"Yes," Nellie said, after wracking her brain to remember. Dorothy had spoken of her at lunch on Nellie's first day, and how their community was taking care of her until she was well and recovered her voice. "Her name is Lucy. I suppose she's talking now?"

"Oh, yes indeed. She was Mrs. Wallace's lady's maid. She saw everything."

"Oh." It was all Nellie could say. Oh. My. God. How traumatizing. And how she must have feared for her own safety! No wonder she didn't speak.

"So if the mayor tells Wallace, who finds out that someone knows his secret—especially someone vulnerable like Lucy—then who knows what else he's capable of?" Marian raised one brow and let Nellie fill in the blank.

Damn. Marian had a point.

Beside her, Princess murmured her three words. Names, actually. "Rose. Daisy. Violet."

"Those are her daughters, Nellie. Three girls who miss their mother."

Something twinged in Nellie's heart. She missed her own mother. For so long it had been just the two of them against the world. She hated having to leave her behind in Pittsburgh and couldn't wait until she'd join her in the city.

"Everyone thinks I'm a liar. The asylum has taken pains to hide evidence of what I described. They have repainted and cleaned up and now I'm afraid it will only confirm these reporters' worst suspicions about female journalists: that we can't do the job."

For a second, Nellie thought she might have convinced Marian. For a second, her rival seemed swayed by this idea that they succeeded or failed together and had to work as one. *Sisterhood.* But then they both heard someone calling for Nellie.

"Miss Bly? Are you all right?" It was Colton. Once again, interrupting and ruining her story. The sound of his voice spooked Marian. "Touching story, Nellie. Truly. But we have to go." They started off briskly down the hall, and Nellie swore under her breath. But then Marian called out. "Try Hall 5—it has not been fixed up."

CHAPTER THIRTY-TWO

The Mayor

RETURN TO MANHATTAN

Nellie stood on deck of the boat as it ferried her and the others away from that terrible place. She stood alone, at the bow, gripping tight and staring at the city ahead, looming closer and closer. Her mind was churning over the events of the day—the duplicity of the asylum administration, the pathetic attempts of Dr. Ingram to protect both the patients and the commissioners and thus *no one,* Colton's defense of her reporting, and then Marian sneaking off Princess . . .

Nellie was vaguely aware of a man approaching her. She hoped it wasn't Colton. She wasn't in the mood for sparring.

It wasn't Colton.

It was the mayor himself.

For a moment, he just stood beside her and admired the same view of Manhattan's buildings rising to touch the sky. Slowly she became aware of him, the fine, soft wool of his coat, the warmth of his body, the proud way he stood as if impervious to the cold wind whipping off the river.

Finally, he spoke. "Not many women could get me to spend the afternoon in the madhouse, Miss Bly."

"I'm glad you came. I wish you hadn't come just for Mrs. Wallace, but nevertheless."

"It wasn't just for Mrs. Wallace."

"Whom we didn't see. Even though she was there," Nellie said evenly, though her grip tightened on the rail. "And it will come out that her husband had her committed against her will."

"I hope not," he said softly. "Marital problems ought to be resolved privately."

"It would complicate things for you if the public learned about Mrs. Wallace," Nellie said, and he didn't disagree. "Mr. Wallace is your supporter and close friend. He'll expect favors, but the public outcry will surely be against him."

"We didn't see her," the mayor said gently. "There is nothing more to say about it."

What else could he say? Marian had published an interview with him weeks ago stating his intention to attend the wedding. Everyone knew those sorts of men traded favors, enabling them to build fortunes and get away with murder. Nellie decided not to mention that Marian had snuck Mrs. Wallace out of the asylum. Yet.

Finally, the mayor said, "Let us hope it will be resolved quietly."

"Let us hope we remember all the other women there who are not as well-connected," Nellie said pointedly. What had become of Prayer Girl and Tillie? What else could she do to find them and free them?

"Ah, but they have you." The mayor turned to her with a smile that brought out the delicate lines at the corners of his eyes. "Their fearless defender who refuses to forget about them. What greater champion could those women want?"

"Having the law on their side would be nice," Nellie said dryly. "Having the men in power listen to them and make changes on their behalf would be good. I can't save them; I can just ensure their voices and stories are heard. But today . . ." She allowed herself something like a sigh while she willed her pulse to steady. "Today has made a mockery of my work. They have made every effort to cover their tracks and make it look like I was delusional when they are just cruel."

"After seeing Hall 5, it was clear they had attempted to cover things up. There will be an official inquiry, Miss Bly. A commission will look into everything. You have my word."

"Thank you. There is nothing worse than not being believed." She couldn't help but think of Tillie, who seemed to have gone mad protesting her own sanity.

"I believe you." He pressed his hand on her arm, strong and warm, letting her know that she had the mayor on her side. Between him and the front page of the *World* and her own daring, she felt powerful. It lifted her mood.

"Look at you, being the hero," she said, giving him a smile.

"Part of the job," he quipped.

"So beautiful," Nellie said, turning her attention back to the city, to the staggered mass of buildings. Each one on its own was interesting, and together they made up something that might have never been seen before in the world. "Yes," the mayor agreed. But out of the corner of her eye, she could see and sense that he wasn't looking at the city. He was looking at *her*.

CHAPTER THIRTY-THREE

Once Again I Was a Free Girl

THE ORDINARY

After the asylum visit, Marian had gotten word to Nellie that Princess was faring well. Winnifred was recuperating in the home of a good friend—and she was slowly being weaned off the drugs she'd been forced to take. A private nurse and one of the city's female doctors oversaw her care.

Nellie had discovered her, but Marian had saved her.

"Hopefully in exchange for one exclusive interview," Marian said with a somewhat apologetic shrug as she finished relating the story to Nellie, Dorothy and Harriet over lunch. "And, you know, sisterhood or something like that," Marian mumbled, in the manner of one who didn't wish to appear too emotional.

Harriet smiled. "I'm glad she is safe. And that Lucy is doing well too."

"Their reunion was so sweet to watch," Dorothy said. "As soon as Mrs. Wallace is a bit stronger, she'll go see her daughters."

They all took a moment to appreciate this turn of events. Not only were Mrs. Wallace and Lucy on the mend, but the press was still going after Blackwell's, the commission had issued a scathing report and changes were on the way for the women in the asylum. But their work was not yet done.

Marian took a sip and set down her pint and said, "What would you do if, say, hypothetically speaking, you let someone commit a massive crime just by holding back publication of a story?"

"It depends who. And the crime," Harriet replied.

"I definitely need to know more," Dorothy said.

Marian explained what her reporting had uncovered: Jay Wallace was up to his necktie in debt, and he'd already blown through his wife's fortune. He was also beginning to tire of her involvement with the suffragists and constant chatter about equality, the vote, the abhorrent idea of women's rights. So, he hatched a plan with his wealthy mistress, Louisa, who had ambitions to conquer society. They would get rid of his wife, marry and all live happily ever after in wealth and splendor on Fifth Avenue.

"Too bad divorce is so taboo," Dorothy said. "It seems like a much neater solution than faking someone's death and committing them against their will."

"She would never have agreed to it," Harriet said. "And not because of the scandal of divorce. It would have cost her custody and access to her daughters."

"What a hateful law," Marian said. "But it does work to trap women in awful marriages."

"My mother risked it," Nellie said. "But my stepfather was so abhorrent the town supported her."

"I'm so sorry, Nellie."

Nellie shrugged. The divorce hadn't quite been the end of it. Her six months in Mexico had been a reporting trip—and also a much-needed escape from her mother's angry ex-husband and the pitying stares of their neighbors. It was only after that fire, in which Ford had perished, that Nellie felt like she could leave Mary Jane in Pittsburgh and pursue her dream in New York.

Meanwhile, Mr. Wallace was still walking around Wall Street, sipping whiskey with the mayor and planning his wedding. Nellie felt a sense of foreboding.

"How did you uncover everything about Mrs. Wallace?" Dorothy asked. Marian laughed. "What I had thought were puff pieces and frivolous interviews actually led me to the pieces to put the story together."

"Taking the ladies' pages to the front page. I like it." Harriet smiled approvingly.

"Not quite yet, though," Marian said. "I am wondering if I should alert the police before the story runs."

Harriet laughed. Bitterly. "There's no point in doing that. He didn't do anything illegal."

"He faked his wife's death, had her drugged and committed to an insane asylum against her will. And yet it's not illegal," Nellie said with disgust.

"It's terrible," Harriet agreed. "But she's his wife to do with as he wishes."

"I have a newfound appreciation for the suffragists," Marian said gruffly.

"I would too, if they advocated for all women," Dorothy added. "Not just the ones who look like them."

It was all true and they all knew it. Honestly speaking, none of them were even surprised by the events they were discussing. A wife was her husband's property and had no say over her body or her money or even her children. There was a reason they all had chosen this hard and difficult course of being professional women in a world that didn't know what to do with them. There was a reason they worked so hard to blaze their own paths and risk their lives for stories. Because the alternative was handing over their autonomy and living helpless and dependent on the mercy of a man.

Nellie had seen how badly that could go. So badly, she'd endured ten days in the madhouse with the possibility of no escape just for a story that would be her ticket to freedom.

"You have to hold the story until after the wedding," Nellie blurted out. "And you can't let them know that you have it. Blindside him the morning after."

"Yes, but if I do that I run the risk of someone else scooping me," Marian said pointedly. "Or telling the mayor, who will tattle to his friend." It was clear she saw Nellie as a rival, nothing more. An enemy, to be kept close.

"You have to take the risk and hold on to the story," Harriet said. "They must go through with the wedding. Because bigamy, on the other hand, is a crime." Harriet smiled and dabbed her lips with a napkin. Nellie saw the faintest hint of color. Lip paint—how daring.

"It's all written up," Marian said. "The wedding is two days away."

"Let's just hope the mayor hasn't said anything to Wallace," Nellie replied. Marian was quiet for a moment, then raised her glass. "To the wedding."

FIFTH AVENUE, NEW YORK CITY

The Wallace wedding was all anyone could talk about—it made the front page of all the papers, and one would be hard-pressed to find anyone in the city who was unaware that Jay Wallace had pledged to love and cherish Louisa Newbold until death did they part, in a ceremony before Mrs. Astor's Four Hundred, in a cathedral on Fifth Avenue, followed by a reception with endless quantities of champagne.

That is, until Marian's story dropped the morning after.

The headline of the *Herald* screamed, SOCIETY WIFE PRESUMED DEAD, FOUND ALIVE AT BLACKWELL'S ASYLUM.

Thanks to an exclusive interview with Winnifred, Marian was able to provide the whole sordid tale. A marriage where two people had grown apart, especially due to her increasing participation in the suffrage movement, which threatened and enraged her husband. There were the details of his debt and desperation to maintain appearances. Readers finally learned what really happened that night on the yacht—Winnifred had been drugged and snuck off the boat, rowed ashore and bundled off to Blackwell's. Lucy had shared her story too.

Wallace had been arrested.

It was Marian's exclusive, but at Cockerill's direction, Nellie wrote a summary of it to appear in the pages of the *World*. She pointed out to Cockerill that he had deemed Princess "too boring" to appear in her own article. He had shouted at her to get out and find another exposé—as soon as she turned her copy in. As she wrote up the story, published without a byline, she thought of Colton, doing quite the same thing. She thought maybe he hadn't stolen her story—he had amplified it and ensured it saw the light of day. They were not in this business to keep secrets, after all.

Not that she would *say* that to him. They were still rivals and she couldn't imagine that would ever change.

Now, on a very quiet early morning, Marian and Nellie met to go watch Princess return to her castle. Calling the Wallace mansion a castle was not an exaggeration. The residence took up the better portion of an uptown block. It was done in the Italianate style (or overdone, depending on one's taste) and had clearly been designed to assert their importance and lord it over everyone else.

Nellie and Marian stood side by side, staring at the house, waiting for Winnifred's carriage to roll up. They were lucky that no other reporters had sniffed out this moment, when a wronged wife returned triumphantly to her home and daughters. They were all downtown, trying to get to Mr. Wallace in jail. But still, Nellie half expected Colton or another writer to show up, and she kept an eye out for it.

"Who knew becoming a suffragist would get you almost killed?" Marian remarked.

"Yes, who knew men were willing to go such lengths to get rid of difficult women?" Nellie replied. She thought again of all the women in Blackwell's. "Hysterical mania" was just another term for "complicated," "difficult," "confounding," and the asylum was just a place to keep them out of sight and out of mind.

"Then again, men do have a lot to lose," Marian pointed out. And wasn't that the truth. "Nuts?" Marian offered a small bag of fresh roasted nuts she'd bought off a street vendor. Nellie remembered that she'd run off without breakfast. "Thank you."

"I heard Wallace is pleading with the mayor for a favor," Marian said.

"Seems likely, but I'll confirm it," Nellie said with a confidence that had Marian turning her head.

"Oh, will you? And what disguise or scheme will you adopt to get that intelligence?"

"None," Nellie said, which was saying a lot. The mayor, she had discovered, had taken an interest in her. It was not an unwelcome discovery and it had happened thusly: She had dashed over to city hall to get a quote from him and to follow up on the inquiry and commission, and somehow they had ended up on the same side of the desk, standing a little too close together, their gazes a little too heated. Nellie had asked him to pull some strings to get Prayer Girl and Tillie freed and he promised he would. She might have also dropped her notebook and their hands might have brushed as they both bent down to retrieve it. Their mouths might have come perilously close to touching.

She might have felt *something*.

Very well, she most certainly did. The hot, feverish flush of desire. Not just because of the favors he could bestow, either. She had heard her mother's voice in her head (*A mayor, Pink! A mayor!*) and smiled. So Nellie didn't rush the moment. She let her lips part and her eyes meet his. Nothing happened, but she knew that wasn't the end of things between her and the mayor.

"Oh—look!"

Nellie and Marian hushed as a shiny black carriage rolled to a stop before the house. Was this the moment? Was it her? The front door of the mansion slowly opened, and out stepped Louisa Newbold, dressed, for once, like she didn't want to be noticed. The other day she had worn a wedding dress; today she donned a plain dark traveling ensemble and had pulled a veil over her face. She stepped out, like she couldn't wait to be free of the house and all it represented. She took a few steps toward the carriage, where the driver waited, ready to open the door. She paused and looked around.

"Where are my trunks? I must have my trunks!"

An army of footmen emerged, their hands and arms full of Louis Vuitton luggage. She was clearly making a run for it. Her plans to conquer New York society had come so close to success, but now she wouldn't be able to show her face here again. She'd probably resurface in Europe or San Francisco after a few years of lying low.

"Duped by a man," Nellie said. "Poor girl."

"I don't know that she was duped," Marian mused. "She

wanted the same as us: More than anything, she wanted to see her name on the front page. She just thought she had to marry a rich and powerful man to do it."

"We'll just have to show her and everyone else another way."

It wasn't long after that that Princess finally did arrive. The moment called for quiet. Mrs. Wallace was hardly recognizable as the broken woman Nellie had known in the asylum. She was not quite herself yet—would she ever be again?—but the drugs had worn off significantly and the tender care of her friends had brought her back from the brink. Now she stood as tall and elegant as ever and moved with a slow but steady grace toward the house.

She hadn't gotten far when the door burst open and three young girls tumbled out in an explosion of ruffles, lace and shrieks of "Mama!" Winnifred knelt down to gather them all in her arms. All of them, all at once.

Nellie saw her eyes close. Her lips moved. "Rose. Daisy. Violet."

"Say, Nellie, you're not crying, are you?" Marian peered closely at Nellie. Yes, her eyes were hot and maybe there was a lump in her throat as she thought of her own mother and how much she missed her. It had been hard coming home to an empty room after the asylum, hard not having a mother there to embrace her and stroke her hair and say, "You're home now," and promise everything was all right.

"A touching scene. Mother and daughters reunited at last," Marian said.

"It'll make good copy," Nellie said, with a mischievous glint in her eye.

"May the best reporter win," Marian said. And then they were off, walking as fast as decently possible without breaking into a full-on run. They were so far uptown they were near the park. It would be a trek downtown. They'd have to endure the hot crush of the trolley, the thick swarm of pedestrians on the sidewalks.

"We could split a cab," Nellie said. They would always be rivals in the papers. But maybe, otherwise, they could be friends.

Marian grinned. "I'd like that."

CHAPTER THIRTY-FOUR

Nellie in the City

NEWSPAPER ROW

Just like that, Nellie had made her way into the *World* and found a place for herself. She had a desk, a byline and a reputation as the city's most daring reporter. Her days had been busy, chasing stories, writing copy and living the dream.

It was any old Tuesday, and the sun was blazing a path over the horizon, letting Nellie know it was time to call it a day. The doorman—she'd since learned his name was Bertram—had doffed his hat as she stepped out of the elevator and into the lobby. She strode briskly onto the sidewalk, where the city was still alive and busy and seething with anticipation for after-dark activities.

She paused when someone called her name. "Miss Bly!" She turned and then she saw him, cutting quite the figure in his dark suit. Sam Colton, of the *New York Sun.*

"Well, look who it is, crashing in unexpectedly," she said, a smile playing on her lips.

He flashed a grin and said, "I think you'll be glad of it once you hear why I've come. It's about Maeve."

News of Prayer Girl? This Nellie had time for. "How is she?"

"She's just fine," he said. "I tracked her down in the Lodge and arranged for her release."

Nellie let out a breath—the kind one didn't know one had been holding—and suddenly she felt tension in her chest ease. She'd been worried and wracked with guilt, and now she had word that Maeve was all right. Rescued by none other than Mr. One o'Clock. Lucky girl.

"Thank you, Colton. Is she settled somewhere?"

"She has a job making hatboxes." Nellie smiled at that, imagining her complaining about the tedium of the work and grateful all the same. Hopefully she was reunited with Jo too.

"How did you find her?"

"Crashed in uninvited. Asked questions. Kept being persistent."

"You put your reporter skills to good use," she replied. "For a good cause."

There was just one question she didn't dare to ask: *Why?* This wasn't information that would make the papers. Given the way he was looking at her with those blue-green eyes, Nellie was afraid she knew the answer.

"I did it for you, Nellie. I didn't want you to think you had to save *all* the girls in New York." She managed a smile. It was a lovely gesture, and the right thing to do, but she didn't want to think about what it *meant* as to his feelings for her. Not here on the street, with carriages crashing past. Not while they still wrote for rival papers. Not when she was the darling of the New York press and didn't want anything—or anyone—to jeopardize it.

Instead, she asked about Tillie.

Colten paused and in the silence she knew. But he was no coward, so he said it anyway. "She didn't make it, Nellie. I'm sorry."

"Damn." Nellie swore and looked away, and Colton did too; she clearly didn't want to cry in front of him.

"She was sick and passed away in the infirmary."

He explained that the asylum, no surprise, didn't keep very good records, so there were few other details that he could offer her. He didn't know if Tillie ever got enough blankets or warm soup or actual medical care. There was no way of knowing if she could have been saved. All he could report was that she was no longer stuck at Blackwell's.

"At least she won't be forgotten, because of your story."

Her story, which had outraged the city and made a difference. "Thank you, Colton. You didn't have to look into them and come over to tell me. I really do appreciate it."

"After what you wrote, I was curious too. And I had another reason for coming to tell you in person."

"Oh?" In spite of herself, Nellie was intrigued. He was her professional rival, but this was starting to feel . . . friendly. Maybe even . . . something more?

"I did once offer you a steak dinner at Delmonico's, and if you want to, Nellie, we could go sometime . . ."

She eyed him cautiously. He was easy on the eyes and had proven himself to be a decent and honorable man. She could do worse for a dinner companion. He was also a smart reporter—and a ruthless one. "Colton, are you trying to get a scoop on my next big story?"

"Maybe. Or maybe I just want to get to know the girl who stole my job at the *World*."

"I'm not telling you anything, but I will take you up on the offer for dinner." She decided instantly. Because she was a young, single woman earning her way in the big city and she could, if she wanted to. And suddenly, she very much wanted to.

They set off into the sunset, toward Delmonico's and an expensive dinner that would break the bank but already felt like a night to remember. They hadn't gone more than a block when she stopped and made one thing clear. "Colton—*this* is completely off the record."

Author's Note

Nellie Bly is a real historical figure and this novel is based in truth. In 1887, she was a reporter for the *Pittsburgh Dispatch* when she left for New York City and never looked back. She struggled to find work until she landed the gig to go undercover as an insane person at the women's asylum on Blackwell's Island. The two-part story she published was explosive; it kick-started her career in New York and pioneered investigative journalism.

Nellie's real name was Elizabeth Cochran (she later added the *e*), and she was born in Pennsylvania in 1864. Her father, a judge, died while she was young and left her and her mother impoverished, and her mother's second marriage made things worse. Nellie got her start in journalism after writing an outraged letter to the editor in response to a father's letter despairing about what to do with his five daughters. She did a few years at the *Dispatch*, then six months in Mexico; then she was off to New York, where her asylum story was just the beginning.

There is very little about her story that a fiction writer needs to make up.

While the beats of her story and many details of her personality as I have written it are based in fact and truth, I have taken some liberties with Nellie's time in the asylum. For example, I invented the characters of Prayer Girl (inspired by one line in Nellie's madhouse story about a woman who prayed loudly for death) and Princess (inspired by the real-life case of Elizabeth Packard, who was committed against her will by her husband). The dire conditions and the ill treatment of the women are based in fact. Nellie's reporting is still available today; *Ten Days in a Mad-House* is a captivating read, along with her other work.

While Nellie is most well-known for her madhouse exposé and, later, her famous trip around the world in seventy-two days, she spent the intervening years pursuing dozens of fascinating stories—some stunts, some interviews, nearly all with a focus on the lives of women. There is very little written about Nellie's personal life, so I have had fun taking liberties imagining the experience of a young, independent single woman in Manhattan in the 1880s and 1890s.

The characters of Marian Blake and Sam Colton are fictional, though they are inspired by real-life reporters. Marian's character is drawn from another pioneering female journalist, Winifred Black, who wrote for Hearst's *Morning Journal*. One of her first big stories was fainting on the street and writing about her experiences with the ambulance and hospital system. For Colton, I had in mind journalists like Jacob Riis, who blended photojournalism with reform in his book *How the Other Half Lives* and sought to improve the living conditions of the poor. The reporting "Sam Colton" publishes for the *Sun*—and quoted in this novel—is real.

Harriet and Dorothy have real-life counterparts as well. Harriet Hubbard Ayer was a society wife who divorced her drunk husband and found work selling antiques before launching one of the first cosmetics companies. It made her a millionaire, but a scheming business partner had her committed to an asylum against her will—and it was a year before she could escape. For her next act, she oversaw the ladies' pages for the *World*. Harriet didn't start until 1896 and I haven't found any record of her and Nellie crossing paths, but I wanted to imagine what it would be like for those two dynamic women to be at the same paper at the same time.

There were many Black female journalists in this era, and Dorothy is a fictional example. This is the time when Ida B. Wells did her powerful reporting on lynching in America, when Victoria Earle Matthews was writing for a variety of Black papers. Ditto Mary Church Terrell and countless others. There was a vibrant Black press at the time, and many Black women who made a living writing for it.

I do want to make a note about the nurses: What I have written here is based on what Nellie reported. While she didn't seek to understand their cruelty, I tried to consider it. I would like to explicitly say that nursing and caretaking are two of the most important, hard, noble professions, and both attract many good, kind people to its ranks. These folks are woefully underappreciated and undercompensated, and I hope that as a society we can recognize the value and dignity of care work.

Another character to highlight: Mrs. Parkhill is inspired by Mrs. Elizabeth Gloucester, who was the richest Black woman at the time of her death in 1883. She was born Elizabeth Amelia Parkhill and she built her fortune by operating a network of boardinghouses. I discovered her fascinating life story in the *New York Times* Overlooked obituaries. Though she predated Nellie by a few years, I wanted to take the opportunity show a wealthy and successful woman of color in the Gilded Age.

There was in fact a bachelor mayor of New York City named Hugh Grant. While his term was a few years later, I had to take the liberty to include him because how does one not include a bachelor mayor named Hugh Grant? I have also taken liberties with details of his life and character. He has father issues because my husband always wants more about heroes and their relationships with their fathers.

I am always more interested in the stories of women, their work and their friendships, so I was drawn to Nellie Bly and her life story. She was a true pioneer for women and a tremendous journalist who did incredible, groundbreaking work. She also wrote in a charming, personable voice—she was always ready to go undercover, but she was never afraid to be unapologetically herself in print. Nellie used her platform to shine light on women's lives, and she blazed a path for other female journalists to follow. As of this writing, women run the newsrooms at the *Washington Post,* CBS News, ABC News, NPR, MSNBC, Reuters, the *Financial Times, The Guardian* and the *Economist*—thanks, in part, to the hard work of Nellie Bly and other female journalists who claimed space in newsrooms and on front pages throughout history.

For more on Nellie Bly and her fellow stunt-girl reporters, I recommend the following books:

Around the World in Seventy-Two Days and Other Writings, by Nellie Bly, with a foreword by Maureen Corrigan

Nellie Bly: Daredevil, Reporter, Feminist, by Brooke Kroeger

Sensational: The Hidden History of America's "Girl Stunt Reporters," by Kim Todd

Front-Page Girls: Women Journalists in American Culture and Fiction 1880–1930, by Jean Marie Lutes

For more about *The Mad Girls of New York,* please visit: MayaRodale.com.

Acknowledgments

It was the middle of the pandemic in 2021 when I finally got around to reading a book that had been languishing on my TBR pile for years: *Charmers and Cranks,* by Ishbel Ross. This old, out-of-print book, published in 1965, contained short biographical sketches of "famous American women who defied the conventions," including Nellie Bly. I had always vaguely known about Nellie Bly—she's the subject of many *historical women who dared!* books for young readers. But I was charmed and captivated by this sketch and delighted to discover there was more to her than just one or two big stories.

Now intensely curious about her, I went in search of her biography *Nellie Bly: Daredevil, Reporter, Feminist,* by Brooke Kroeger, and discovered I already owned it, had read it and highlighted it. I read it again. Halfway through, I had the idea for my next novel. My work as a historical novelist would not have been possible without the biographers (often women) who took the time to research and record the lives of notable women in history. These women exist and their stories are riveting, important and too often overlooked. Those who do this important work have my everlasting gratitude.

I am also incredibly grateful to my agent, Stephanie Cabot, for her enthusiasm and support of this project, and my editor, Kerry Donovan, for getting excited about Nellie as a feminist heroine and giving insightful direction on how to make her story better. Many, many, many thanks to friends who read early versions of the story and offered feedback: Molly Bidlack, Caroline Linden, Katharine Ashe, Jayashree Kamble, Courtney Wetzel, Robin French, Shelbi Stoneback, Maria Rodale, and Tony Haile.

Author photo by Paul Brissman

Maya Rodale is the bestselling and award-winning author of funny, feminist historical fiction and romance. A champion of the romance genre and its readers, she is also the author of *Dangerous Books for Girls: The Bad Reputation of Romance Novels Explained*. Maya has reviewed romance for NPR Books and has appeared in Bustle, *Glamour*, Shondaland, Buzzfeed, The Huffington Post, and PBS. She lives in New York City.

CONNECT ONLINE

MayaRodale.com
facebook.com/MayaRodaleWriter
twitter.com/MayaRodale
instagram.com/MayaRodale